Queenie's Teapot

CAROLYN STEELE

Copyright © 2017 Carolyn Steele

All rights reserved. This book or any portion thereof may not be reproduced or used in any manner whatsoever without the express written permission of the publisher except for the use of brief quotations in a book review.

All characters appearing in this work are fictitious. Any resemblance to real persons, living or dead, is purely coincidental.

ISBN-13: 978-1540853721
ISBN-10: 1540853721

Cover by Rebecca Poole of Dreams2Media.com

CONTENTS

Chapter One	1
Chapter Two	11
Chapter Three	23
Chapter Four	31
Chapter Five	43
Chapter Six	53
Chapter Seven	63
Chapter Eight	71
Chapter Nine	79
Chapter Ten	89
Chapter Eleven	97
Chapter Twelve	107
Chapter Thirteen	119
Chapter Fourteen	129
Chapter Fifteen	139
Chapter Sixteen	153
Chapter Seventeen	163
Chapter Eighteen	173
Chapter Nineteen	185
Chapter Twenty	193
Chapter Twenty-One	203
Chapter Twenty-Two	213

Chapter Twenty-Three	223
Chapter Twenty-Four	231
Chapter Twenty-Five	245
Chapter Twenty-Six	255
Chapter Twenty-Seven	261
Chapter Twenty-Eight	271
Chapter Twenty-Nine	279
Chapter Thirty	291
Chapter Thirty-One	299
Chapter Thirty-Two	309
Chapter Thirty-Three	323
Chapter Thirty-Four	333
Chapter Thirty-Five	345
Chapter Thirty-Six	355
Chapter Thirty-Seven	367
Chapter Thirty-Eight	375
Chapter Thirty-Nine	383
Chapter Forty	387
Chapter Forty-One	395
Epilogue	409
Coming Soon	413
About the Author	415

ACKNOWLEDGEMENTS

Queenie popped into my head while I was bickering with Ken Chadwick in the queue at Tesco about the iniquity of self-service checkouts. Without his irritating insistence on contributing to job losses, this book would never have come about. To be fair, without his unwavering support and enthusiasm for a book that was written for him to hate, it would not have come about either.

When it was a rougher than rough first draft, several kind souls helped me batter it into shape: Amy Vansant, Jo Allardice and Ben Steele, you are all worth your weight in gold.

Then, it went to a couple of technical advisers: Caroline Mersey and Holly Freiburger, I am forever in your debt. Thanks to my longsuffering editor, David Antrobus, of BeWriteThere.com, there are fewer comma splices, even though they weren't a thing when I went to school. Any that remain are my fault for digging my heels in, not his for missing them.

And finally, a huge thank you to cover designer Rebecca Poole, of Dreams2Media.com, who always knows what I want, even when I don't.

Queenie Mason
129 Peabody Buildings
Whitechapel Road
London E1 1BY

Citizen Representative Summons

Your Representative Number
442358961

- You have been selected for Representative Service
- Your name was randomly selected from the electoral register

If selected you must attend for Representative Service at: Palace of Westminster
Westminster, London SW1A 0AA

On: Tuesday 6 January, 2032 **At:** 09:00 AM
For a period of: Not less than three (3) years

WHAT THE REPRESENTATIVE SUMMONS MEANS
Representative Service is an important public duty. You will be asked to oversee the governing of your country. You will be among many people chosen each term to form the administration of your nation and will represent the supremacy of the populace over wealth, influence and power, as set out in the British Republic's Constitution.*

- Pages 1 and 2 of this form are your **Representative Summons**. This tells you when and where to attend if selected.

- Pages 3-8 are your **Reply to the Summons**. The information you provide will assist the Representative Selection Committee in placing you where you will be able to make the most appropriate contribution, taking into account your education, skills and experience.

WHAT TO DO NOW
- It is important to read the enclosed leaflet **Guide to Representative Service**. It will inform you of the practical assistance available to Representatives who may encounter difficulties with moving/work/childcare etc. It also lists the circumstances in which you may be allowed to opt out of Representative Service and the conditions which might render you ineligible to serve.

- You must **complete, detach and return pages 2-8** to the Representative Selection Committee by referring to the section **How to reply to Your Summons** on page 2 of the Guide. You must return your reply within 28 days of receipt of this summons.

WARNING
You may be committing a **criminal offence**, punishable by a **fine of up to £5000** if:
- You **fail to return** your reply within 28 days
- You **fail to answer all questions** truthfully and/or
- You **omit any of the required information** with intent to influencing the committee's decision as to your suitability or otherwise for Representative Service.

This form and other Representative Service literature is available in large print and Braille formats, and also in Welsh, on request from the Representative Selection Committee (details on page 2.)

CHAPTER ONE

The ball of kingfisher-blue mohair dropped from Queenie's lap and rolled across the parquet, coming to a stop at the feet of the Chief Secretary to the Cabinet. Every gaze in the room followed it. Gerald Lambert sighed, fully aware his words would have to be repeated, his wisdom no match for the yarn, which was now reflecting so fetchingly in the high shine on his bespoke business shoes.

Caroline observed, not for the first time, that Gerald was the only man she knew who could look down his nose without moving his head. Ostensibly, she was taking notes on the day's proceedings, but her main task comprised committing to memory as many quirks and character flaws as were immediately obvious in the new intake.

The knitting might be an issue. She jotted *knitting* at the back of her notebook as she considered the current, woolly conundrum. Gerald would not alter his stance; he would rely on military bearing to re-establish lines of communication when the novelty wore off. The room was, however, full of people who had no reason to comprehend the significance of Gerald's posture. Yet. They were all still transfixed by the yarn. Some were even stifling giggles.

Caroline slipped from her chair, executed a parabolic trajectory towards Queenie which took in Gerald's temporarily fascinating brogues, scooped up the ball of yarn and deposited it back in Queenie's capacious tote bag. Knitted, she noticed.

'Thank you, dearie.' Queenie broke the silence with a toothy grin and a mighty glottal stop. 'I'm always doing that, drives hubby mad it does, the wool starts bouncin' around all over the floor when he's trying to watch the football, he reckons I do it on purpose every time there's goin' ta be a goal...' The hoarse guffaw morphed into a chesty cough. The silence in the rest of the room managed to deepen.

'You're very welcome.' Caroline modelled the hushed tone she hoped would prevail around the House once the intake had completed their orientation. She resumed her seat and turned her attention back to Gerald. 'You were saying, Chief Secretary?'

Gerald offered her an almost imperceptible sniff by way of acknowledgement, and readdressed the room.

'Your skills have been assessed on the basis of information provided on your personal profile forms. After lunch you will be assigned to a ministerial department and apprised of your duties by that department's chief secretary. At that point you should inform your *chief* of any reason why you might not be able to fulfil our expectations, as outlined in your summons, of a member of this government, for the full term of three years. Are there any questions?'

For the first time since this session's new motley shower had shuffled their way into the largest committee room of the House of Commons—and made a mess with their newspapers and smartphones and cups of coffee and bottles of water and ungainly coats—Gerald scanned the faces.

He wasn't really rude, Caroline mused, although she'd been shocked at his attitude back with her first intake. The theatricality wasn't just about intimidation or snobbery as she'd first thought; just boundary-setting. As Gerald allowed his focus to waft over the assembly, Caroline watched. And added to her notes. The ones who met his gaze, the ones who looked away, the fidgeters, the sniffers, the paper shufflers...

It was always an eye-contact-maker who asked the first question, determined not to be browbeaten by a mere civil servant. 'What happens if you've assessed our skills wrong?' Big guy at the back, Lancashire accent and a drinker's nose. Caroline wrote, *Predictable mind: Treasury?* as she tried not to mouth along to the reply this inevitable question generated every time.

'If you've been unable to express yourself adequately on your profile, we'll find you something less significant to do.'

'Where's the bar?' Small chap. Whimsical tie. Doing a terrible Groucho Marx impression. A couple of people near him tittered. Caroline wrote, *Comedian: Foreign Office?*

Queenie's hands were still now, the knitting in her lap—*what is that, some sort of tea cosy?*—and her face a picture of misery. 'Can I ask a question?'

She received a courtly bow. 'Please do, ma'am.'

'I can't do anyfing...I dunno why I'm here. I mean hubby said we all got to do it and all but the thing said, the bit of paper said, that if you wasn't good at stuff you'd, you know, go be one of the ordinary reps, just sit in a office and pass messages and such...' Caroline added *waffle* to the line that had begun with *knitting*.

'I mean I don't mind doing my bit. I said to hubby, I said it's nice and excitin' to go and be the thing, especially after Tesco's closed the tills and all but you talkin' about skills, well it ain't really right—'

Gerald raised his hand as though stopping traffic.

'Fear not, dear lady, we have considered your case most carefully. Now, just before I send you all off for lunch, I should probably introduce Caroline Grant. She is your babysitter. And please know that all of you'—he nodded to the early questioners in particular—'are currently babies. It's her job to hold your hands while you learn, God help us, to run this country.'

'Oi, Queens, this letter's for you.'

Queenie wondered for the umpteenth time why Bert always yelled from the front door. The far end of the hall was draughty and cold. He could just bring the letter through, couldn't he? And say something quietly for once.

She opened the door of the parlour, kicking the multicoloured, knitted-snake draught excluder out of the way.

'Bring it here then, is it a bill?'

'Don't think so, it's got that seal on, like when they wrote to me about the repping.'

'Oooh.'

Bert gave her one of his looks. 'Don't you go thinking they want you for a rep. What can you do for the bloody nation?' He gave the snake an unnecessarily vicious kick as he wedged it back under the parlour door, and threw the mail onto an already cluttered coffee table. 'Unless they want everyone to learn to knit.' He turned his smirk towards her, so she could see it was okay to laugh.

'They don't know that yet, though, do they?' Queenie was in no mood to pretend Bert's jokes were funny. And she wasn't through wondering, again for the umpteenth time, why he always had to chuck stuff about, as if *putting things down carefully* was something you had to learn at school and it was possible to have been off that day. 'You know as well as I do it's all, wossname, you know...random. They'll decide they don't want me when I send the form back. Like they did with you,' she added, as she picked up the letter and inspected the envelope.

'That was a misunderstanding.' Bert bristled. 'I didn't tell them enough about my committee stuff, I just said I'd been "active" in the working men's club. I should have told them about bein' sub-vice-president and all that. Still, it's just as well.' He smirked. 'How would you have managed for three years on your own?'

'I'd have been fine.' It was Queenie's turn to bristle. 'I can manage without you just perfect. Anyway, you'd only have been gone part of the time, I'd just have 'ad the chance to get used to the peace and quiet without you yellin' all day, and you'd have been back. Yellin' again.'

'Don't talk daft, woman.' Bert's voice softened; so he knew he was beaten. 'Is there any tea left in the pot?' He lifted the woollen tea cosy off the pot on the table and peered inside. 'It's a bit stewed. Make us another pot, eh, Queens, I'm gasping.'

'Make your own. I've got a letter to read.' Queenie settled into her armchair and ripped at the envelope.

By the time Bert returned with a full pot of tea, Queenie was chewing the top of a pencil.

'What's a *curriculum vitae*? Have I got one?'

'Nah.' Bert put the pot in front of her and nudged his cup towards it. 'You goin' to be mother, Mother?' He showed his teeth in what she knew was supposed to be a smile. Queenie wondered, as she often did, whether he really thought this was his best joke.

'Pour your own, I've got this to do.'

'I'll help you better with a cup of tea inside me.' His tone turned a bit wheedling. Queenie hated that even more than the yelling.

'I don't need no help from you, Bert Mason, I can read. What makes you think you can help anyway?'

'You just asked me what that thing was!' Bert nudged his cup a bit closer. 'Go on, Queens, you do the milk better than me.'

'If you can't even do a cup of tea for yourself, you'll starve when I go and be the government. You might as well get some practice in for when I'm swannin' about living it up in bloomin' Westminster and you're here all on your own. Now be quiet, I've got a form to fill in.'

Bert sighed, did the eyeroll that meant he'd lost but wasn't going to admit it, and poured some milk into his cup.

'By the way, that curricula thing is for when you've had

education and fancy jobs. It says on the form you don't need to have one, just send it in if you have. The form is, like, instead.'

'I can see that, now I've read a bit further on, thank you. I'll manage better if you just shut up and let me get on with it.'

Bert picked up the newspaper, made his way past the snake, and left the room. Queenie watched him go. His morning appointment with 'his bit of peace and quiet' in the bathroom was as much a ritual as the teapot battle. Did it all annoy her more these days? Back when she'd worked the tills at Tesco's, she'd quite liked coming home to it. Walking into the tiny flat, filled to bursting with Bert and his ways, it was like putting on a comfy old pair of slippers. But now? Now she never went anywhere, it was a bit...a bit what? There was likely a word for it. If she was the sort of person who had a curriculum thing, she'd probably know what it was. She settled for *samey*.

Why shouldn't she be a rep? Just because they hadn't wanted Bert didn't mean they wouldn't take her. Everyone in the country had the same chance of being picked; it was like a raffle. Just, be a citizen and you might get the letter. Some people messed up their forms deliberately. Not everyone wanted to go and 'run the country' for three years, or even do stuff on the local council, though that was part-time. She'd heard rumours that sometimes they took you if you messed up your form enough because it meant you were clever. And that manager at Tesco's, the one they'd sacked for having his fingers in the till, he'd wanted to be a rep so much he pretended to have done loads of fancy stuff. They'd turned him down just like they hadn't wanted Bert.

Queenie decided to do her best. She wouldn't mind a bit of a change. If they took her, she'd get out of the flat, there could be days without Bert's bathroom habits. She'd do it in pencil first, read it back, maybe even get Bert to look at it if he was in a good mood. Then she'd ink it in and send it off.

It was times like this she missed Angie. Angie would have known what to write…she was the clever one. They'd worked the tills together for years. Everyone who shopped at the Whitechapel Road Tesco's had known the pair of them. Queenie and Angie: they'd joked and chatted and questioned and comforted their way through the days until all the customers called them by name. Angie was the one who knew about the news—'current affairs', she called it. You couldn't rely on admiring everyone's earrings all the time to get a chat started because it only worked once and only if they wore them. Angie'd use a headline to get chatting to the quieter ones, then Queenie would make a joke about it, pretending to be stupid, and they'd all laugh. Well, sometimes she wasn't really pretending: Bert didn't approve of news—it interrupted the football.

Some people had even chosen their tills especially, for a chat, even if there was a queue. Mostly the lonely ones, the old people who never went anywhere unless it was shopping. Queenie realised with a sigh that she was one of those now too. But, just like everyone else, she couldn't go have a joke at Tesco's any more. People did their shopping in silence these days.

First it had been the automatic checkouts. But they'd been sort of okay because most people hated them. If you couldn't think of something nice or funny to say, you could roll your eyes and copy the computer voice—'no unexpected items in the bagging area for you today?'—and people laughed and you made more friends.

But then the gun things came in and that was that. Checkouts were finished. People cost too much. Angie got a job delivering pizzas—apparently you still needed people for that—but Queenie, well, she'd worked the tills since school. What else can you do when the only thing you know is admiring people's earrings or asking if they feel a bit peaky? Remembering someone's kiddie had been sick or asking about exam results, getting excited about the recipe for something that Jamie made on the telly and everyone wanted the ingredients for, that was all stuff nobody needed now. Of course she didn't have a curriculum thingy—*chatting* wasn't a job, was it? She decided to give Angie a call. It had been ages, be nice to talk, and maybe she'd have some ideas about what to write.

Bert handed the form back to Queenie.

'What do you think?'

'It's fine.'

'Fine? Is that all?'

'What do you want me to say? All you've ever done is knitting and talking. Unless they want the Chancellor of the Exchequer to start knitting money, you got nothin' useful to contribute. So, a form full of "not applicable" ticks is about the best you can do.'

'Yes, but I put a lot in the bit about "What else can you tell us?"'

'I can see that. What's all this pattern nonsense?'

'That was Angie's idea. She said following a knitting pattern was clever, because it means you can, um, *apply written directions to practical outcomes.* She's been doin' a course at the library for getting a better job.'

Bert snorted. 'It doesn't make any difference what you put. They want barristers and accountants and teachers, not silly old women who can't do nothin'.'

'Don't you be so nasty. If I can't do anything you can cook your own bloomin' tea. In fact, you might as well, because I'm going to do this over in pen and take it to the post office.'

'Get some fish and chips on the way back, will you, Queens?'

He turned to the telly, put the football on, upped the volume, and farted.

Queenie sighed.

CHAPTER TWO

The bedroom door slammed in Andy Carswell's face. The placard that read 'One does not simply walk into my room' fell to the floor. Again. Andy picked it up and tried again.

'Rules are rules. If you want a lift to Francesca's, help your mother clean up the kitchen first. And before you tell me it's not fair, let's please remember that life isn't fair!'

Music blasted through the door before he got as far as the first 'fair'.

He hung the sign back on the door and headed downstairs. He could smell coffee.

'Sounds like that went well.' Beth raised an eyebrow as she pushed the plunger down on the cafetière.

'I wanted to do that.' Andy pouted as he mimed pressing the coffee grounds.

'You could have been here pushing the coffee around, but you chose to push Sophie around instead.' Beth appeared pleased with her little joke. 'I suppose you told her that life isn't fair?'

'Of course I did, I know you laugh but it's true. It's about time they taught it in schools. In fact they should make them all work for exams and then allot the results by ballot, just so they know not to expect anything to turn out the way they want.'

'Ouch, grumpy, what's happened?'

'Nothing, I'm just sick of having doors slammed in my face when I'm being reasonable.'

'Hmm, reasonable can be really annoying when you're fourteen. Especially when it's not fair.' Beth winked.

'But I told her last night, "Help clean up and I'll take you." Then what happens? She spends all night on that blasted computer, makes more mess with midnight snacks and tells me there's no time to clean now because she has homework to do.'

'Yes, but in her world she'll clean up another time and she wants to go out right now.'

'You're too soft, Beth, that's one reason she's so spoilt.'

'I'm too soft? Who bought her the computer in the first place? There were going to be rules, remember? The Wi-Fi going off at midnight, etcetera. How come that never happened? Because it interrupted your online socialising. What would you do if you didn't have a new gag from Google to be life and soul of the water cooler with? Maybe recycle an old one? That would be terrible. Oh wait, no it wouldn't, you do that anyway.'

Andy opened his mouth to reply. And closed it again. The right riposte would come to him shortly.

'I'm not saying she's right.' Beth put her hands on her hips. 'I'm just saying she thinks she is just now, and the only way to get through to her is to understand that.'

'She needs to learn you don't always get what you want. Nobody ever did exactly what I wanted all the time. I had to—'

'Roll with the punches, yes we know. Any minute now you'll be saying it's all part of life's rich tapestry and doing the Groucho thing.'

Andy waggled his eyebrows and tweaked an imaginary cigar. 'If you've heard this story before, don't stop me, because I'd like to hear it again.'

He watched as Beth turned towards the sound of a snort from the doorway.

'Francesca's coming here,' Sophie announced. 'Then her dad's taking us to the shops.' She looked pointedly at Andy.

'That's nice, dear,' said Beth. 'Any chance you could give me a hand with the dishes while you're waiting?'

'Okay, Mum, I've got a few minutes.'

Andy's coffee went down the wrong way. As he took himself to the bathroom to splutter into the basin, he felt sure he heard someone laugh.

'Oh, by the way,' Beth called after him, 'a letter arrived for you.'

'Why do they want to know what your parents did for a living?' Beth was perusing the questions on the form, reading them out one by one.

'Dunno. Seems a bit weird, but I suppose they know what they're doing.' Andy poured Merlot into the last two wine glasses to survive from the set Beth's parents had given them as a wedding present.

'Always use the good stuff when making a big

decision?' She caught Andy's eye as she quoted his father at him.

He sniffed. 'It's not a decision really. I've got to send it, and if they want me I'll have to go.'

Beth picked up the envelope with the British Republic seal on it. 'They send out thousands of these things each time and only about ten per cent get taken. A bloke at work reckons he got out of it by sounding nuts.'

'They're probably wise to that one. They won't be as green as they're cabbage-looking.'

Beth rolled her eyes.

Andy took the envelope from her and fanned his face with it. He reckoned it probably gave him a thoughtful air; he'd try it at work sometime when the comedian act wasn't cutting it. 'I'll do it straight, there's nothing to lose. You said it says our income won't be affected?'

Beth nodded. 'Looks like there's expenses for extra costs like travelling too.'

'Well, then. And if this morning's little show was anything to go by, you don't need me around to handle Sophie.'

'You're hardly here anyway,' Beth muttered into her glass.

'Somebody's got to keep the lights on...' He began before spotting the elephant trap.

'And I don't?'

'That's not what I meant.'

'Yes, it is. Just because you swan up and down the M1 spouting a scripted sales pitch and old jokes at people doesn't make your income any more worthy than mine.'

'I know that.' Andy wished he could learn to recognise shaky ground a half-sentence earlier; it was always the same. He put a hand over hers and searched for the voice he used on stubborn clients. 'I'm sorry, I didn't think.'

'You never do. And you're going to have to live with Sophie spotting when you open mouth before engaging brain, just like everyone else does.'

Andy shrugged. He was warming to the idea of living in London for three years.

He returned his attention to the blurb folded in with the forms. There was a lot of it. He put it down by Beth's glass. He knew she'd read it sooner or later and tell him what it said, so he stretched out, put his hands behind his head and wiggled his toes.

'Could be fun though. Interesting. Make a change from the sales team. And as Dad used to say, all part of—'

'Life's rich tapestry?' Beth enquired.

The Red Lion in Parliament Street boasted a fine cellar, decent lunch menu and a private room upstairs dedicated mostly to the convenience of civil servants. The House of Commons cafe was all very well most of the time; rubbing shoulders with the people's reps was laudable and useful and, well, egalitarian, but occasionally, especially at the start of a new administration, discussions needed to appear less formal than they were. And for this, lunch at the Lion was perfect.

Minnow had ordered Diet Coke (no ice or lemon) for himself, espresso for Gerald and sparkling mineral water (with slices of lemon *and* lime, but no ice) for Caroline. The order never varied. Alcohol never featured. The days of gentlemen's clubs, a parliament full of drink, and drunks, snoozing on the benches of an afternoon were part of the old system. All washed away in the tide of righteous indignation that had wiped election-based oligarchy from the face of the earth. Well, almost. A few pockets of popularity culture still existed, mostly on small Pacific islands with 'elected' leaders who thought they were important, but mostly nations were content to see their engine rooms as a job of work. It had been touch and go with America for a while, but even they decided there had to be a better way after the first couple of Trumps.

Minnow thought back to his induction.

'Any task which can be conducted competently after an alcoholic drink is not work,' Gerald had thundered. 'It is a hobby, and we, ladies and gentlemen, are here to work.' A few faces had dropped but you got used to it. The Red Lion's cellar was still there of an evening.

When Minnow had first been drafted into Gerald's department he'd quaked. Nobody could quite tell him what the Cabinet Support Team actually did, and Gerald didn't seem like the kind of chap who'd tolerate people not knowing what they were for. He'd wondered briefly if he was part of some unwritten quota scheme for mongrels with a touch of the tar brush about them, but that was just fallout from the sort of playground nastiness that had turned him into a geek in the first place. Gerald only had time for competence. And now, on his third new government intake, Minnow reckoned he was up to the challenge. Apparently, a combination of psychology and computer science hadn't been as pointless a degree as he'd feared.

People and patterns. Thousands of experience forms besieged the office every three years, and Minnow's analysis of the information contained therein decided who went where. Who should be rejected for dangerous signs of enjoying importance, power or control. Who would make a good constituency rep: telling ministries what the people wanted. Who would give better service in a ministry, overseeing the civil servants who got things done. On paper, a person could look ideal, but the data might contain one minuscule red flag, easily missed. Minnow was looking forward to seeing how the tweaks he'd made to this year's analysis played out, even if some of the tick boxes he'd asked to have included on the latest forms had raised an eyebrow or two. He reckoned his new program would be the best yet at weighting outlying details according to their likelihood of representing trouble.

And trouble, the avoiding thereof, was what the Cabinet Support Team did. Gerald frightened everyone, Caroline befriended everyone and Minnow crunched the numbers.

'You're looking very pensive.' Caroline slipped into the seat behind her mineral water and picked up a menu. 'Everything okay?'

'Yeah. I was just thinking back to my first new intake.' Minnow smiled as he took in today's whimsical shoes. He didn't generally notice what women wore, and Caroline didn't dress to be noticed as such, but the footwear drew your attention after a while. There were shoes to match everything, more colours than he had ever understood there to be colours.

'Oh yes, this is, what, your third?' Did she remember everything about everyone? Or maybe she just always knew what to look up about a person by what day it was. Gerald strode into the pub as Minnow nodded, and they both turned to acknowledge his arrival. He placed his jacket carefully on the coat hook by their table, sat at the chair behind his coffee and folded his scarf across his lap. He then placed his document case on the table and removed a pile of papers.

'Coffee, good, let's get started. Here are the ministry selections. I'll let you peruse them while we order. Usual routine, anything Caroline spotted that indicates a change, then final decisions ready for this afternoon. We have a few spares, so anyone you foresee trouble with can get shoved in with the reps or moved to local government.'

Minnow knew the decisions were mostly made, and mostly made by his system. The nation's new overseers weren't really decided over a bacon butty in the pub, it was just a bit of last-minute fine-tuning. Caroline's eye for a character trait his code might have missed was unerring. And, since she would have the task of keeping the new regime on the rails, it was common courtesy to allow her some input at this stage.

Gerald waved a menu at the girl behind the bar. 'Usual?' He nodded at Caroline and Minnow and they nodded back. The barmaid gave a thumbs up and disappeared to order two BLTs and chips and a veggie quiche and salad. Minnow liked to eat light at lunchtime.

'Home Office is pretty sound.' Gerald wiped his mouth with a napkin and waved at the barmaid for his vital second espresso. The first rarely touched the sides; this was the one he would linger over. 'Good spread of skills, some nice communicators. Got a secondary school teacher in the top spot, also trains mediators, might come in handy if the "bring back hanging" lot get vocal again.'

'What, treat them like naughty bullies?' Caroline mimicked shock before sniggering.

'Don't see why not.' Minnow chased a recalcitrant leaf of something trendy round his plate with his fork. 'It's all about communicating consequences. There's always one rep who thinks he's there to make a difference.'

'True.' Caroline nibbled on her final chip as though it might regenerate if she took long enough to finish it. 'Do we have any rumours of unsettled constituencies?'

'No reports from the outgoing cohort,' said Gerald. 'But you never know. Caroline, I'd like you to try and spot the irritable ones early again this year. It saved us a lot of time and trouble last time, and the cost of a bottle of wine per troublemaker is a lot less out of the taxpayer's pocket than the alternative.'

Minnow thought back to the riots of his university years. It was entirely right for the people to tell the government what they wanted; that was the whole point of random representation. No popularity contests or party politics, no rival gangs coming up with exciting ideas to get themselves a bit of power. The nation ticked over and the people got what they wanted...so long as it worked. But what happens when the people decide they want something inhumane? Or bonkers?

The solution, an *off limits* list, had been brought in to try and save time, money and the nation's reputation. Some issues were not to be revisited and that was that, but still, most cohorts would try and flex their muscles eventually, and you only needed one sleeper from a democracy gang in the House for the fires to get well and truly stoked. If Caroline spotted who it was likely to be before the something-must-be-done brigade got vocal over a dreadful headline of some sort, life in the House ran a lot more smoothly.

'Health is looking good.' Gerald continued after spending a few moments communing with his fresh *crema*. 'A doctor, a herbalist and a cancer survivor, patient in the top slot.'

'Hmm.' Caroline wrinkled her nose. 'Could be explosive.'

'The program recommended it.' Minnow tried not to sound defensive.

'Sounds fine,' said Gerald. 'Just keep a check on how the doc takes it, okay?'

'Sure.' Caroline took out her notebook and added a heading.

'Now, Treasury, I've got a couple of accountants and a couple of small business owners. Decent turnover, been trading a good few years, but I'm not sure about either of them for the top spot. They both seem to have trouble delegating, all that "I'm proud to work round the clock" stuff in their additional notes.'

'No women?' Caroline turned to Minnow. 'You normally manage to find me a thrifty housewife to cut through the jargon.'

'Not this time; the system pointed most of the women towards Health and Education...and before you roll your eyes, you looked over my shoulder last time we changed the weightings.' Minnow knew not to let too much frustration show in front of Gerald, but honestly, some people had no idea what 'random' really meant.

'What about the accountants then?' Caroline referred to her morning's notes. 'Is Doug Sideworth one of them?'

'Yes.' Gerald nodded. 'One on the way up, one on the way down.'

'And Sideworth is on the way down? Drink?'

Gerald nodded again. 'Yes, but that could work in our favour.'

'I'm not so sure.' Minnow pulled out a tablet and began swiping the screen. 'Drinking to the detriment of your job weights quite heavily against responsibility.'

'Indeed.' Gerald usually acquiesced graciously enough when he was about to disagree with you. 'But it's quite recent; family trouble. Might appreciate a new start, his mind's solid enough. Sometimes a recent disgrace can stop the power complex before it starts.'

'I'd prefer to see him somewhere safer. What about Employment?' She giggled. 'He can tell us what it's like to be losing your job.'

'I'll think it over. Are we agreed on all the others?' Gerald looked at his watch.

'Just one more.' Caroline referred to her notes again. 'Foreign office; please no more language students, they're impossible.'

Minnow laughed, caught Gerald's eyebrows in his peripheral vision, and switched the sound to a cough.

'We have a couple of business types who deal overseas. One knows a bit of German, the other's learning Japanese.'

Caroline sighed. 'We do have translators, you know. It causes nothing but trouble when they start trying to use that stuff.'

'I know, I know, but they seem to cope with cross-border trade, so they can't be that bad.'

'Put them in Trade and Industry then. Give me people

who don't think they're God's gift to Johnny Foreigner.'

'Got a bit of a find for the top job. I think you're going to like him.'

'Whimsical tie, old jokes?'

'That's him.'

'I spotted him this morning, seems jovial enough, but what's his background? Minnow, please tell me he has no language skills.'

Minnow swiped his screen again, more to remove the balsamic vinegar he'd applied looking up the boozer than to read anything. He'd been expecting this challenge. 'Um, outside sales of some sort of electronics, golf club, tennis club, teenage daughter, gregarious but no committees.'

'Father's a doctor and he's not,' Gerald added. 'So he'll either be a clown, a defeatist or a closet humanitarian. My money's on clown after this morning's performance. Whichever, he's unlikely to accidentally start any wars.'

'He'll do.' Caroline closed her notebook with a snap. 'Now. What about Queenie?'

CHAPTER THREE

Doug Sideworth sat at his kitchen table and turned the letter over in his hands. He looked out of the window, through the mad frou-frou curtains Katie had insisted on.

'If I tie them up like this'—she had balanced on the window sill with one foot in the sink, scrunching the curtains just so—'they frame the top of Musbury Tor, look!'

Doug had looked. She was right.

'Now we can remember that crazy, muddy walk when you proposed to me, every time we wash up.'

It had been Katie's idea to move to the old farmhouse on Grane Road in the twentieth year of their marriage. A sort of anniversary present to themselves; a renovation project within view of their special place. They'd met through the university hiking club and hiked through life, Lancashire and career ladders.

He'd be able to commute just fine, she'd added, when

they first viewed the house. They weren't far from Manchester and the walking would be on the doorstep. Both points were true: they weren't far from the office as the crow flew, but the single lane road from their house to the motorway, way up on the moors, wasn't always an easy commute. Fog, breakdowns, roadworks, there was always something to delay him getting home. And that, he reasoned to himself on this oddly portentous morning, was probably how the drinking began.

There was a difference between a swift one in the pub after work, waiting for the traffic to die down, and a large one waiting for him as soon as he fought his way home of an evening. The tradition had begun the first time fog delayed him for an hour as he tried to drive 'over the top'. Katie had poured the Scotch as she'd heard the car scrunch onto the gravel, adding an ice cube and opening the front door to hand it to him as he entered. He'd laughed and kissed her, she'd begged humble forgiveness for his terrible drive home, and somehow the Scotch on the doorstep became a regular thing.

When he'd pushed the kitchen table aside to make room for the hospital bed, placed (he explained to the Macmillan nurse) especially for Katie to see Musbury Tor through the window, he'd taken to having his doorstep drink at Katie's side, while he told her about his day.

Now, the kitchen table was back in its traditional spot. He sat there with the bottle most evenings, telling Musbury Tor about his day.

He looked around at the chaos. Katie had always kept the house perfect, as far as he could see. Occasionally she'd say, 'Oh, look at the mess!' although Doug had never seen it. But then the nurses had arrived and the kitchen had turned into a hospital. 'Mess' knew better than to dare. So, a clean and tidy kitchen no longer reminded him of fussy, funny Katie; it looked like those never-ending but over-too-soon twilight months of watching her dwindle before his eyes. Was that another excuse? Probably.

He considered his options, scribbling them on the back of an envelope as he thought them through.

1) Send a letter back exercising his right to ask to be excused people's rep duty. The notice said extenuating circumstances would be taken into consideration, and his circumstances were pretty bloody extenuating. 'Dear Government. Please excuse me from serving the country as a randomly selected rep because I went to pieces when my wife died and now I'm a useless drunk who's just been told by my employers to buck up or bugger off.'

2) Fill in the form and make a mess of it. Tell them all sorts of things they didn't want to hear and hope for the best. He'd heard that people who showed dodgy signs of enjoying power were removed from the system forever. He could claim to hanker after being a stage hypnotist because he loved having control over the helpless. Or that he pretended to be a gynaecologist in his spare time. Hmm, maybe nothing that might get him arrested.

3) Give it a proper go and see what happened. There was no guarantee they'd take him but if they did, maybe a new start would help. Some weeks he'd be in London, not looking out of his stupid frou-frou kitchen window. He could go to Human Resources and tell them he'd come back sorted out. They'd have to hold his job open for him anyway; no company was allowed to sack a rep. It could be the perfect solution.

The decision was all but made already, he realised, but

he was a charter and a box filler, and things should be complete. He popped two crosses and a tick next to his options.

'Okay, Katie,' he said to the curtains, 'look at the mess. When I've cleaned up we'll fill this form in.'

'Josh, Joe, get down here and start making your lunches, we're going to be late.'

Sally Farnham lined up baggies of carrots and raisins on the counter, next to two Transformers lunchboxes. She put the peanut butter and banana sandwich in front of one box and the cheese and Marmite in front of the other.

The twins weren't really old enough to *make* their lunches yet, but she insisted on a spot in the morning routine for putting stuff in the boxes. If they didn't bother, they got the wrong sandwich. She was determined to bring her boys up a sight more self-sufficient than their father had ever been.

'Come on, hurry up,' she yelled up the stairs. 'Joe's going to get the Marmite!' And the thundering of feet began. Sally wondered, not for the first time, what size four feet had to grow to before they came through the ceiling. At age nine, the boys' shoes already filled the hall behind the front door so that visitors had to climb over them. She'd need a spare room for them soon.

'Can we have chocolate today, Mum?' Josh eyed the carrots mournfully.

'There will be chocolate when you get home if you've eaten all your carrots.' She watched them catch each other's eyes and added, 'And don't go thinking you can tip them in the bin at school and pretend. I've got spies everywhere.'

'Awww, Muuum...' The chorus followed her out the front door while she struggled with her car keys and smiled a hello to the postman. As the kids struggled into coats and shoes, she took the proffered mail and riffled through it. A letter from the hospital, check-up presumably. She'd been cancer-free for a year, it would be about time. Couple of bills and something from the government. Another bloody survey, probably. Honestly, did they think single parents of twin Tasmanian Devils had the time to decide what they thought of everything under the sun? The last one had been about roads, for goodness' sake; like she cared. So long as they were flat and relatively uncongested so she could get the twins to school...she looked at her watch...

'Boys! Get out here this minute! And I'll be counting the carrots in the fridge when I get home!' The post would have to wait.

Sally sat with her coffee and contemplated the form. She could plead extenuating circumstances: the kids, the cancer, single parenthood. She was sure they'd see her predicament; there were ads on the telly about how genuine hardship meant you didn't have to do it. But why shouldn't she do it? She had things to say. She had opinions, so long as it wasn't about roads. If people like Sally always ducked out of repping, how would anything get better for, well, people like Sally?

The boys would be the main issue. She could ask Martin to have them to stay during the one week in four the reps were expected to be in Westminster, but he'd probably say no, and then what? They'd have to move; Hemel Hempstead was one hell of a commute. Even if he agreed, would she want the boys living with Martin off and on for three whole years? She laughed. They'd all be sitting waiting for someone to fill their lunch boxes when she got home.

There was an alternative, though. She had a read through the enclosed leaflet about optional provisions for accommodation and schooling. Citizens who lived too far from London to commute easily had the offer of a flat in Portcullis House for the duration of their service. There was a crèche and a school; the twins might quite like that. One kid might not want to be uprooted from familiar surroundings but her two had each other. If the system wanted to enable single parents to go and take part, why not?

Martin would scoff. 'What on earth have you got to offer the nation?' But then, she didn't have to tell him unless she chose to. Anyway, she was just sending the form off and it might not happen. She decided to keep it to herself for now, except maybe take the boys to London one weekend. Show them around a bit, see if they liked it.

She Googled Portcullis House. Apparently it was supposed to look like a ship from the inside; Josh and Joe would love that. Well, they'd say it was sick, which allegedly amounted to the same thing.

She poured another cup of coffee and began ticking boxes.

> *And finally, is there any aspect of government to which you feel particularly drawn? Please outline your specific qualifications or experience to aid t he committee in placing you where you can make the most relevant contribution.*

Sally wondered whether to sleep on it. She'd heard about the idiots. The 'I'd like to be Chancellor because I'm good at maths' brigade. There were also rumours that this whole bit was a catch. If you put anything in, you were automatically rejected for fancying being important. But they did seem to put people into spots that worked more often than not, didn't they? That teacher who'd finally sorted out the exam mess, two decades after the end of democracy. Maybe she'd originally put on her form, 'Yes, I know how to sort out the exam mess. Here's my flow chart of how to do it. You're welcome.'

Or maybe someone else did, and they decided that one was too big for his or her boots but nicked the plan anyway. Or maybe she didn't do anything much and they just gave her the credit.

You never knew quite how they did anything. Whenever anyone said, 'Hey, you, people who sort it out, how do you do it?' they just replied, 'We are overseen by a constantly changing representation of the people.' And then they'd say, 'Besides, it works. Would you prefer we spent your tax money on elections?' And the spectre of old democracy did the rest.

Sally giggled. And wrote: *Yes. I want to improve the social aspects of cancer treatment. I'd like to integrate traditional, medical, surgical and alternative treatments so that there are no rivalries between different disciplines, and I want to make hospitals more child-friendly for visitors.*

They could put that in their collective pipes and smoke it.

She sealed the envelope and put it in her handbag. She'd send it off on the way to pick the twins up from school. Before she lost her nerve.

CHAPTER FOUR

'Thank you for returning promptly, ladies and gentlemen, we have a lot to get through this afternoon. I trust you had a good lunch?'

Gerald scanned the ties during the rumbles of polite acquiescence. He'd have the faces memorised in a day or two, but for now, Caroline's *whimsical tie* note would help him home in on the bar-seeking comedian.

'And you, sir. Mr Carswell, isn't it? Yes, did you find the bar?'

Caroline flipped to the page she'd started on the new Foreign Secretary, and jotted *not easily embarrassed: stupid?* next to the doodle of the pattern on his tie as the man attempted a joke. She didn't usually sketch people's clothing choices, and this little drawing of the smiley stars and moons wasn't particularly a character note, although she guessed the ties, like the bad jokes, served as ice-breakers when cold calling. Both could possibly come in handy dealing with nations less versed in small talk than the good old BR, but Andy Carswell would be briefed on those soon enough—talked through his tie choices and told when and where to tone it down. For now, Caroline quite liked the design. She might have a go at incorporating it into her next guild project.

As she partially tuned out Gerald's 'there are no bars here because you are here to serve the people, not yourselves,' patter, knowing that the 'any job that you can do after a drink...' line was on its way, she returned her attention to Queenie.

Still knitting. There was no specific edict against knitting in meetings; Caroline did it herself occasionally when there was a time crunch to get a new guild project out. Knitting could be a useful prop and nobody knew this better. It served myriad purposes: it could be an ice-breaker, a make-busy cover for awkward silences, a passive-aggressive spot of attention-seeking, a reason to appear not to be listening, a cure for nerves, or, in some countries, a deceptively compliant nod to the role of women. Caroline had used it as all of these at some time or another during her career (although she only did the compliant lower-status woman thing ironically) but mostly it helped her think, and that was her job. Watching, thinking, solving personality clashes and ego trips before they caused a war, a riot or a financial meltdown.

Her job had been created after the riots. The permanent civil service finally realised that human nature, which had been the only real problem with old democracy, still existed. You could design ego out of the system all you liked; enable office cleaners to have as much oversight over policy and implementation as CEOs; ensure that representation actually meant representation instead of some mad popularity contest—you could try and weed out the sociopaths in the initial analyses—but someone always got a messiah complex halfway through their term. Of the fifty or so ministers, a few would begin to relish their bit of illusory power a tad too much and start trying to change things. Maybe they wanted to say they'd made a difference when they got back to civvy street, grandstand in the pub a bit, or maybe they actually thought they were 'doing good', but for the most part change was trouble. In Caroline's view, and in those of her bosses, the ship of state sailed most serenely when alterations of course were minimal.

The removal of popularity from government had freed up so much pointless expenditure on party politics that the nation had been able to afford the finest of minds in every department. The experts did their thing and the reps oversaw that none of them went rogue. Nobody was elected, but everyone was consulted. Ideas came from the people and were faithfully analysed and tested, sometimes tried, occasionally implemented. (But usually rejected, very politely, with a fistful of incontrovertible reasons.)

Things could get a bit rocky if a big groundswell grew for an unworkable plan, but the only time the civil service really lost control was when an ego exploded. Human nature created wars, poverty and financial crashes. Human nature was rapacious, but without old democracy there was nobody to bribe and nothing to gain. Caroline had absorbed the mantras at university, and nothing she had seen since had caused her confidence in the system to waver. And confidence was calming.

As was knitting. Even watching it put one into a state of meditation. She wondered what the knitting did for Queenie. Nerves? Probably right now, yes, but you didn't get that efficient by only knitting when stressed. Passive-aggressive? Possibly. Caroline turned to her page on Queenie and wrote: *ask about home life*. Once she knew what purpose it served it would be easier to corral.

Then she tuned back in to Gerald.

'The next two weeks will be an induction period. You will get to know your ministry, your government colleagues, your civil servants. Use the time to ask questions, ask everyone what they do and why. Your most important question is "why?" Practise asking it on all occasions. When the reps in the House demand a change of policy because the people have spoken, and it is within your sphere of control, your civil servant may possibly tell you it can't be done. Ask them why. If you are not happy with the reason, you can vote, back in this cabinet, for change. If the reason makes sense, you may encourage your cabinet colleagues to vote against change…*either way, you will have to be able to explain yourself.*

'Challenge everything. Why does a cup of tea cost eighty pence in the House cafe?'

'Market forces, obviously.' Doug Sideworth. Nice little show of confidence; Gerald didn't appear to be looking in his direction.

'That's jargon.' A woman spoke up from the other side of the room. 'Typical man. What does "market forces" even mean? It's nonsense. The cup of tea costs the price of tea, a teapot and water. At least it does in my house. And at'—she pursed her lips—'one pound twenty-five for a pack of tea bags, a cup of tea costs approximately, um, fifteen pence to make. Add a bit for the equipment in the cafe and the wages of the person pouring it and it should cost about twenty pence. The rest is just profiteering.' She looked squarely at Gerald. 'And why would you be making a profit out of us? We're *public servants*.'

Sideworth bristled. 'Market forces is the explanation for the difference you've just outlined, miss.'

Caroline winced. She was starting a page for the woman, who she'd identified as Sally Farnham. She couldn't wait to note down whether the 'miss' would elicit a reaction.

Sideworth continued, oblivious. 'We would think there was something wrong with an underpriced cup of tea, cheap bags or whatever. Eighty pence is a bit cheaper than a fancy chain might sell it at but enough to make it feel like a decent cuppa. It's what you and I are prepared to pay.'

'Thank you kindly for the lecture. But I still disagree with you. Market forces is a catch-all that might cover some prices, but now you've put it into words of one syllable for us, surely even you can see that it's not appropriate here. Our food should be subsidised, surely? Or even free? This whole set-up is paid for by taxes, we're away from home serving our country, so why should we pay 'market forces' prices? Oh, and it's Ms Farnham.'

Caroline tried not to let the smirk show as she scribbled her approval and flipped back to her page for Doug, the Employment Minister-not-Chancellor, and put a tick next to *predictable mind*. She could cope with that. The last thing the workforce needed was a free thinker.

Gerald coughed. 'Thank you, Ms Farnham, Mr Sideworth, you have ably illustrated what it is that we would like you to do. Are you satisfied yet with the explanation?' He addressed the question to the assembled company.

The usual mumbles echoed around the committee

room until Queenie put her knitting down in her lap and raised her hand. Gerald offered her a raised eyebrow.

'I'm probably wrong, hubby says I usually am, but when I worked in Tesco's they used to charge us for biscuits in our break, even though they were broken ones off the shelves what couldn't be sold and they didn't cost nuffing.'

Gerald raised his hand to stem the tide of giggles. 'Everyone's opinion has merit. The earlier you learn this, the less stressful your service will be. Please continue, ma'am.'

'The union rep went and asked about it and they said if you gave people free stuff they took more than they needed and it was a waste. So they charged us and then they put the money towards stuff for the kiddies at Christmas.'

'Precisely. We could supply endless refreshments at taxpayers' expense; however, we have a fiduciary duty to spend wisely. The money you spend here will be returned to you at the end of your service, or donated to a charity of your choice, if you wish.'

Sally Farnham and Doug Sideworth glared at each other before turning scornful faces to Queenie, who winked happily at the pair of them.

'Now, you all have, in your welcome packs, a note of the room to attend to meet with your ministry, plus a map of the buildings. You will spend the next few days in attendance there. You may find myself and Ms Grant dropping in from time to time to see how you are getting on, and we will meet again here at the end of your induction.'

For the first time that day, Gerald smiled.

QUEENIE'S TEAPOT

Queenie packed away her knitting and consulted the sheaf of papers in her folder. She turned each sheet over and looked on the back. She touched the arm of the person next to her, a timid-looking girl of twenty or so. She'd tried chatting and smiling earlier, but the girl hadn't met her eye. *Poor thing,* Queenie thought, *she still looks terrified.*

'I'm sorry, dearie,' she began, 'can you help me for a moment? I can't find that bit of paper he was talkin' about…the minister thing.'

The girl lifted her eyes from her papers, and Queenie thought she saw a little dampness.

'I'm sorry, what did you say?'

'Are you all right, luv? You don't look very well. Shall I call someone?'

'No.' The girl was whispering now. 'I'm fine, I just get a bit, you know, sort of anxious in new places. Especially when I don't know anyone.'

'We're all scared, luvvie.' Queenie took hold of her hand and stroked it, like she would a toddler's. 'And you know me now. Nobody knows what to do, and look at me, I can't even find me own bloomin' minister thing. You've got younger eyes than me, so you can help me, eh? Then that'll be you off to a flyin' start, helping. You're pratikkly runnin' the country already!'

The girl fished a tissue out of her sleeve and dabbed the corner of her eye.

'I suppose so.' She sniffled, and mopped her nose. 'I wanted to say I couldn't do it…on that form, you know?'

Queenie nodded.

'But my dad said it would be the making of me. Stop

me moping, sort me out.'

'Oh dear.' Queenie ferretted about in her knitting bag. She was sure she'd packed some tissues. You never knew when they might come in handy, and the kid looked like she could use a fresh one. 'And maybe you ain't quite ready to get sorted out?'

The girl sniffed her agreement.

'Perhaps your dad and my hubby should get together. At least your dad thinks you'll be doin' some good. Do you know what my hubby said to me when they wrote and told me to come?'

Was that a spark of curiosity on the poor little scrap's face?

'He said, "Blimey, they must be desperate, what the hell do you know about anythin' important?"' Queenie broke into her chesty laugh, which turned into a coughing fit again, and the girl giggled. 'I said to him, "well, hhhusband," I said, "hif I don't know nothin' about important stuff hai'll 'ave to learn, so that football can go off the telly for a start and we'll 'ave some bloomin' news."'

'Oh my, what happened?'

'I watched the news and 'e went to the pub.'

'I think he and my dad might get on!' She was laughing properly now.

'So, how about you be my first friend here and I'll be yours?' Queenie picked up the girl's hand again. 'What's your name, dearie? I'm Queenie.'

'Samantha, Sammy, but my dad calls me—'

'Never mind your dad, he ain't here, what do you like best?'

'Sammy is fine.'

'Okay, Sammy, let's make a plan. Every time we get a break I'm going to get two of those eighty pence cups of tea. One's for you. So you know someone and you've always got somewhere to go. If you ever don't come and get your tea I'll know you're all right and too busy to look after a stupid old woman. Deal?'

'Deal.' There it was, the real, proper smile.

'Come along, you two, let's get you to your next appointments.' It was the woman who'd picked up the wool. Lovely shoes, sort of pinkish colour.

'Samantha? Samantha Cho? We've put you in Education.' The girl's face flashed a moment of panic, and Queenie squeezed her hand. The wool woman—*Caroline?*—dropped her voice a bit. 'We know you had a tough time at university, but we think you can help us. Your experience might help us prevent someone else dropping out. That's why we need you.'

'There you are, Sammy! You know better stuff than I do. See you for tea.'

Queenie waved her knitting bag as Sammy left for the maze of corridors, papers in one hand and soggy tissues in the other. She looked at Caroline.

'She's not well.'

'I know.'

'I was going to ask her what my minister thing was but we got talking.'

'I know.'

'I can't find my bit of paper.'

'I know.'

'Is there anyfing you don't know?'

Caroline smiled. 'You don't have a ministry as such. Pop into Gerald's office with me, and we'll explain your role in detail.'

'He said I'd been considered...'

'Yes, that's right. And what I've just seen confirms that we made the right decision.'

'Do you people ever stop talking in riddles?'

'No.' Caroline held the door open for Queenie to walk through. 'But eventually you get to understand the riddles.'

The office was huge. It had panelling and a desk bigger than anything Queenie had seen at Tesco's. Gerald stood as they walked in and gestured to some comfy chairs by the window.

'Come and sit down,' he said. 'This could be quite a long conversation and we may as well be comfortable.' He lowered himself into one of the armchairs, tweaking the creases of his trousers as he sat. Caroline perched on the edge of one of the others, tucking her legs neatly to one side. Queenie put her knitting bag on the floor next to the third chair and sank into it, grateful for the softness. The seats of the chairs in the conference room had been getting a little hard, if she was honest.

'Oof!' Queenie kept sinking. 'Blimey. These chairs ain't easy to sit in, I'm gettin' eaten alive!' Gerald and Caroline looked politely out of the window as Queenie tried to rearrange her legs and her clothing. She wondered which knickers she'd put on this morning and whether they were on show as she struggled with the lining of the only decent skirt she owned. It had been half price at Tesco's, and Bert had laughed at her for buying it. She'd told him when she put it on this morning, 'You ain't laughin' now, are you? I've got a place to wear this to...' but if he could see the pickle she'd just got in he'd laugh himself into a bloomin' heart attack.

'Now I know why you sat on the edge like that.' She nodded at Caroline's sleek and dignified posture. 'I won't be able to get out of this now without looking like that thing on the telly, you know that bloke who dresses like a woman with his legs in the air?'

'Kenny Everett?' enquired Caroline, with a sidelong glance at Gerald.

'Nah, not him.'

'Monty Python?' Caroline was grinning now, but Gerald looked a bit cross.

'Nope, hang on, I'll get it in a minute, Irish bloke...*Mrs Brown*!'

A puzzled look crossed Caroline's face. 'I don't know that one. Is it recent?'

'Not really, been on a while. I don't like it much, but Hubby says I've got no sense of humour. It's a bit, what's the word, undignified, if you take my meaning.'

Gerald ahem'd.

'If I could just interrupt a moment, Ms Mason. Oh, do you prefer Ms or Mrs, by the way?'

'Oh, I'm a missus, too old for all that mzz nonsense, Hubby wouldn't have it any other way.'

'Quite so, thank you. Mrs Mason, I'm sure you're curious as to the role we'd like you to fill in the new administration.'

'Oh yes! I don't have much education, you know, I left school when I had our Deborah and I've only ever worked in Tesco's, not that I do that anymore either. Hubby said you prob'ly need a cleaner for the offices.'

'Not quite.' Gerald cleared his throat. 'Mrs Mason,

Queenie, we have looked into your skills, taken up your references, and you appear to have one specific talent that could be invaluable for us.'

'Well, I'll be buggered...oh!' Queenie's hand flew to her mouth. 'I'm sorry, oh dear, I was just surprised, I didn't mean to swear at you.'

Caroline raised her hand. She was still smiling. 'I'm sure you'll swear at us again before your time here is over. However, what Gerald is trying to say'—she looked at him like he was a naughty kid—'is that you've been chatting to people all your life, passing the time of day, cheering them up, making friends. I saw you do it just now with Samantha.'

'She likes to be called Sammy,' Queenie said. 'Even if her dad doesn't approve.'

'There you are, you see,' Caroline continued. 'Your ability to put people at their ease, get to *know* them, is your talent, and we have one post that requires nothing else.'

'No exams?'

'No.'

'No NVQs.'

'No.'

'Just chattin'?'

'Indeed.' Gerald leaned forward and placed his elbows on his knees. He steepled his fingers under his chin and raised his eyes to Queenie's. 'Mrs Mason, we would like you to spend the next three years as the British Republic's head of state.'

CHAPTER FIVE

'Now I know why you put me in that chair! Did you put it in after people fell over when you told them stuff?'

'Yes and no.' Gerald's eyes almost crinkled. 'But now you mention it, perhaps we could judge when you're ready for public duties by your ability to sit down and get up again without resembling...who was that again?'

Caroline referred to her notes. 'A Mrs Brown, I believe.' She looked at Queenie for confirmation.

'Interesting.' Gerald's hands were still under his chin. 'I've not seen the lady in question. Perhaps I will continue to imagine Kenny Everett.'

Queenie caught the wistful moment in his eyes. *Blimey, they're just like us. They even make jokes, this is easier than Tesco's.* She realised Gerald was still talking.

'There will be all manner of strange places to sit during your service. Perhaps Caroline could provide a few pointers?'

'Queenie and I will spend most of this week together,' said Caroline. 'By the time we re-enter your office next Monday morning there will be no trace of any female impersonators, I can assure you.'

'What, not even Dick Emery?' Queenie knew her guffaw would turn to coughing—it always did, but she couldn't help it. 'Sounds like I get to spend three years prancin' round with a book on my head sitting in chairs. I thought it was more like opening fetes and stuff.' She rummaged in her knitting bag for a Fisherman's Friend and popped it in to try and smother the noise she liked to call 'chestiness'. Bert said it was like warthogs farting, but then he would.

'Under the British Republic's constitution'—Gerald's hand moved to his nose, as a blast of Fisherman's Friend fumes headed his way—'the head of state is mostly non-executive, since parliament is seen as sovereign. However, as the ultimate representative of the people, you will have some ceremonial duties regarding the oversight of legislation.'

Queenie's hands began to squirm in her lap. She wished she'd taken the knitting out when this whole interview began but it was too late now. 'If part of the job is understandin' what you just said, you'd better send me back to Whitechapel right now.'

'What he means to say,' said Caroline, putting a hand over Queenie's to still the phantom stitch counting, 'is that it's mostly opening fetes and things, but sometimes you have to sign things.'

'Oh, that's all right then.' Queenie sighed with relief. 'I thought for a minute there I had to learn all that jargon.'

'Well, we would like you to familiarise yourself with the

constitutionality of your role,'

'He's at it again!'

'Don't worry, I'll be explaining it all to you soon.'

'In real words?'

'In real words.'

Gerald sighed.

'Do you have any questions at this stage?'

'Um, yeah, there is one, well, I expect there's loads but I got one right now is all I can think of...'

They both did that thing where you put your head on one side, like there's a thought bubble you can see that says 'go on...'

'It's about where we live. The letter said if you live in London you don't 'ave to move in here, because you can compute, and Bert, that's my hubby, he said good because 'e didn't want to uproot and go somewhere fancy, he likes his old armchair you see, has it just so, so he can see the telly and that. He said he wasn't about to move to some fancy-schmancy place with uncomfortable furniture like you see on the adverts. Anyway, that was all fine but if I'm goin' to have to use one of them big cars with the flags on, well the one that came for me this morning 'ad trouble gettin' into the Peabody Buildings...I suppose I could always wait out on the Whitechapel Road...'

'I think that might be a bit of a security risk, ma'am,' said Gerald. 'As you may know, Buckingham Palace was turned into offices and renamed when we replaced old democracy, but one wing remains for ceremonial functions; receiving other heads of state, banquets, conferring of medals, etcetera. There is also an apartment set aside in the Mews for the current incumbent...'

Queenie looked at Caroline.

'That's you.'

'Thank you.'

'...where you will reside for the duration of your term. I cannot vouch for the distance of the furniture from the television, but we have had no complaints to date.'

'I'm sure we could move Bert's special chair in, if you like,' added Caroline. 'You could have one of these too, for practising with.'

Was that a wink?

Gerald heaved a book the size of a breeze block onto the desk. 'This is an annotated copy of the Constitution. I'm sure you'll find it useful while you are learning your duties.'

'Useful for what? Is there a wonky table leg in my posh new flat?'

Caroline laughed. 'Don't worry, there are only a couple of bits you need to know about.' She rose from the chair like someone who weighed nothing and whose legs worked properly and offered Queenie her hand. 'Let's go and get a cup of tea. I'm going to be by your side for as long as it takes to get familiar with what happens. We'll visit some of the ministries and spend some time looking at things you need to know over the next few days. Then you'll be ready for everyone's swearing in on Friday, and we'll start moving you in to Buck Place afterwards. You and Bert can have the weekend to settle in. We'll see Gerald back here on Monday morning and chat about when you'll be ready for those fetes.'

Queenie took hold of Caroline's hand. The two of them pulled and pushed a bit, and succeeded in turning Queenie round in the chair until she got stuck in it sideways. They both giggled and tried again. The more they laughed the less they achieved. Queenie wasn't sure it was possible for legs to get that tangled. And she finally remembered which knickers she had on.

Gerald stood and strode round the desk, taking her other hand.

'Are we going to count to three?' Queenie couldn't help it.

'Do you think we should?' Gerald's voice was grave.

'It can't hurt.' Caroline was helpless with laughter now.

'I seem to remember you and Minnow telling me that Mrs Mason was a perfect choice for head of state.' Gerald's tone was getting a bit chilly. 'I sincerely hope that by next week you will present me with someone of whom our country can be proud.'

'Oh, don't be so pompous. Queenie's perfect. Can you imagine any of the nasty little popularity-contest sociopaths we have to deal with around the world being able to resist her?'

'Oi, you two, I'm still 'ere you know.'

'My apologies, ma'am, that was uncalled for. It's been a long day.'

'And not just for you, mate. It looks like I could be stuck in this chair half the bloomin' night an' all.'

'Right then, here we go.' Caroline regained her composure. 'One, two three, hup!'

'Thank you.' Queenie had been lifted clear of the head-of-state-eating chair and deposited onto her feet. 'I could really do with that cup of tea now.'

Caroline collected the Constitution while Queenie retrieved her knitting bag, and the two women, in whose hands the fates of nations appeared to now lie, headed for the door.

Queenie turned. 'I've thought of another question.'

Gerald produced a new sort of sigh. Queenie wondered how many different sighs he had. Bert had the two: the 'don't talk while the football's on' sigh and the 'don't talk nonsense' sigh.

'Yes?'

'Yes, what?' *Was that another different sigh?*

'Your question?'

'Oh right! Can I bring my teapot?'

'There was no need to be quite so fierce.' Queenie stirred sugar into her tea with deliberation, as if it might help her think.

'I'm sorry, he's usually a little more placid, but sometimes he thinks it helps to establish who's who at the start of a new term if he acts a bit more bad-tempered than he is.' Caroline had opted for the coffee. Ninety pence. A tiny bit more for the guild at the end of the year, not that ten pence would buy much yarn, but she didn't much like the House cafe tea.

'He should learn about bein' polite to people he's only just met. That's what he wants me to do, isn't it?'

'Yes, but—'

'And anyway, he'd said "any questions" before, like he meant it, like I could really ask questions if I wanted.'

'Yes, but—'

'And it wasn't my fault, the chair thing, you tricked me into it to make me look stupid and that's not nice.'

'That's not really what we—'

'If I'm going to do the state thing I don't want to go

around lookin' stupid, do I?'

'No, but—'

'So I don't want no more tricks—'

'Queenie!'

'What?'

'Tell me why you need your teapot.'

Queenie met her eyes, direct, defiant. 'You don't really want to know, do you?'

Caroline didn't. Not really. But she knew it mattered. The displacement worry, there had to be one. Overwhelm people and they focus on a tiny detail. Deal with each detail and you strip away the layers of stress. Then people can function. They'd had a paramedic come and explain it at uni: people can't deal with going to hospital, so they worry about who's going to feed the cat; the cycle courier cares more about delivering the package than he does about his shattered leg. 'Embrace the displacement.' It was a rule. She'd ended up spending a lot of time with that paramedic. (Tiny, they called him. Because he wasn't.) Of all the things he'd taught her, this was one of her favourites.

'If it's important to you, it's important to the nation now, Queenie. Tell me, is it a thing Bert insists on?'

'Oh no, luv, it's me that's fussy about me tea. Now take this stuff for example.' She indicated the cup in front of her. 'They've put a tea bag in the cup and put hot water on. Then they take the bag out and put the milk in. It's not proper tea, not like you get in a pot.'

'Oh, I see, so you want a teapot in the kitchen when you move. I'm sure there will be one and if not we can easily get one.'

'No, that won't do. New ones ain't no good for years,

and even if there's one there, they'll have washed it, won't they?'

'I'm not sure I follow?'

'My teapot was my mum's before me and her mum's before her. They knew the best tea came from a pot that never got itself washed...you need the build-up of all that brown stuff, what do they call it?'

'Tannin?'

'Yes! Tanning. Anyway, when you get loads of tanning inside your pot it makes better tea. See?'

'Right, so you want to bring your teapot from home when you move into Buck Place.'

'Yes, but there's another thing. Can I bring it here?'

'To the House?'

'Can I bring it with me every day and ask them back there'—she nodded at the cafe counter—'to make my tea in it. Then anyone else who wants a proper cup of tea could have theirs made in it too.'

'You want to bring a teapot with you every time you come here and then take it home with you at night?'

'Yes.' Queenie nodded until all her chins wobbled.

'I'm not sure—'

'I can knit a bag for it, make a sort of waterproof lining?'

'I'm sure that won't be—'

'Way I see it is, while I'm bein' the state thing, I might as well improve the tea. It's a start, innit?'

Caroline caved. *Embrace the Displacement*—she should embroider it into a motto for her office wall.

'I don't see any reason why not, but I'm sure we can find a suitable container. There will be no need to knit it a special bag.'

Caroline kicked off her shoes. The coral, with kitten heels and pearl buttons. She dumped her briefcase on the table in the hall, pulled on a pair of fleecy slippers and headed for the kitchen. She poured a glass of Cab Sav, tipped some biscuits into Josie's bowl, refreshed the water next to it and sat with her wine at the breakfast bar.

Her third intake. Did it get easier? Not really. The rush to learn everything about everyone before they got comfortable enough to dissemble. You only had so long to watch people under stress. And she and Minnow had railroaded one or two past Gerald this time. She hoped nothing 'changey' would crop up too soon. The last few remaining pockets of old democracy round the world quite liked to sabre-rattle at times of change and you never knew what they'd latch on to.

'Now then, Jojo, what do we think of the new lot?' She watched the impossibly regal lilac-point Himalayan pad past her biscuit bowl and set up camp outside the cupboard with tins of tuna in it. *Did she just stamp her paw?*

'You can wait a minute.' Caroline wagged a finger at the cat. 'I have to do something important.'

She opened the cupboard above the kettle and retrieved a teapot. Caroline removed the lid and looked inside. *Yep, clean as a whistle.*

'Well, Lady Josephine Fitzwhiskers, head of state around here, I suppose if you can have your tuna, Queenie can have her teapot.'

Caroline opened the tin, tipped the biscuits away and forked tuna into the bowl. She washed her hands, picked up the glass of wine and settled herself into a huge armchair, deceptively similar to the ones in Gerald's office. She picked up her knitting.

Justin Walker stared at the ad. He'd been checking the iSawYou website off and on for a few weeks, feeling like an idiot. His dad had probably been hallucinating, talking nonsense, but then he'd promised. And you took deathbed promises seriously, didn't you? He'd always reckoned those tall tales about the glory days were mostly tosh; wishful thinking. *Yeah, Dad, you were a leading light of the Provisional Democrats, the Provos. They really did plot mayhem and murder back in the day, of course they did, that's why nobody has heard of them.* His daft old dad the terrorist; it was laughable. All the democrats had ever done, it seemed to him, was sit in church halls and reminisce pointlessly about the old days. But he'd promised to watch for an ad, a sign the Provos were back in business.

And it looked like here it was. From *Provisionally Yours, let's wake up together.* Most likely a genuinely sad old bastard hopelessly propositioning someone out of his league, in which case he'd make a prize pillock of himself, shake his fist at the ashes in the spare room (what the hell was he supposed to do with them?) and forget all about it. But all he'd undertaken to do was get in touch and tell them where he worked...

He downed the rest of his Scotch and hit 'connect'.

CHAPTER SIX

Meeting up in the cafe again seemed like a good idea to Caroline. Queenie appeared less anxious than in the offices and conference rooms. And with a cup of tea in her hands, she lost the need to knit. Carefully early, since nobody liked to be unaccompanied in their first few days, she consulted her plan for the week. People laughed at her for using an old-fashioned notebook and pen, especially Minnow. 'When are you going to embrace the century?' he'd say. 'There's these things called computers now, they're jolly handy, you can use them to do everything, and it's not just the young whippersnappers, my mum's got one!'

Caroline would wince and pretend to hate the very idea but it wasn't that she eschewed the technology. Outside office hours she was something of an early adopter; her phone did everything except feed Lady Jo. It was the nature of her notes. Not only was there a reason for the pen and paper, there was a reason for the tear-off pages...and the real fireplace at home. Some things just shouldn't be findable by the sort of hackers who could retrieve information from anything. Like Minnow.

She reviewed the plan.
Moving Bert
Knitting
Source a teapot conveyance
Visit ministries.
- Tue: Foreign, Education
- Wed: Treasury, Home
- Thu: Employment, Defence

Then Friday, as always, would be everyone's introduction to the House. Things would get easier for everyone next week, but especially for her and Queenie. Once the move was over they could meet more privately, relax into the role a little, maybe do a spot of clothes shopping. The days of people expecting their head of state to be a fashion plate had long gone; the public expected judicious use of their taxes, so ridiculous hats and the like were frowned upon. But a little advice on the best colours to wear for the inevitable photographs wouldn't go amiss.

The commotion in the kitchens roused Caroline from her planning. Several people seemed to be speaking at once. Then the clattering started. Crockery on metal? Caroline looked at her watch: ten to nine. She'd have time to nip through and see what was going on before Queenie arrived. As she closed her notepad one voice rose above the others.

'These can go 'ere for now, look I've made a space. Now who knows 'ow to make a proper pot of tea?'

'Nobody told me I wasn't allowed in the kitchen! I only wanted to put the teapot away, why can't I do that?'

'It's not that you're not allowed—you can go anywhere you like—but we need to know about it and make arrangements first.'

'I don't see why I can't put a teapot where I want to.'

'You can, Queenie, but someone needs to come with you. Suppose you hurt yourself and had to go to hospital, then we'd have to send someone with you, and—'

'So I can't go anywhere on my own?'

'Well, yes, you can sometimes, so long as we know; it's a security thing. There are people about who don't like the way we do things.'

Queenie's eyes grew as big as Jojo's. 'You mean...?'

'It's never personal, just that you represent a system. We try hard to keep tabs on old democracy sympathisers and monarchists and the like, but you never know. And anyway, it's about politeness too. Suppose you were working on your till at Tesco and someone you'd never seen before came and moved everything about, told you to put stuff in different places after you were used to how it was. You'd not like it, would you? And then if they said, "I can do it because I'm the new boss," you'd be entitled to say, "You could have said that first and told me you were coming." Wouldn't you?'

'I s'pose so.' Queenie looked crestfallen. 'I'm sorry, I just wanted to, you know.'

'Yes, I know.'

'Should I go and say sorry?'

'It's okay, they understand.'

'I've only been the state thing a day and I've messed it up already. Hubby was right, I'm goin' to be useless.'

'You'll be fine. It's a big adjustment, that's all. I was going to ask you how Bert took the news that you'll be moving.'

'He laughed. He said you was all mad and they should 'ave taken him, not me. He says 'e don't mind moving so long as he gets his chair and will there be a bigger telly and does he get his beer paid for by the taxes?'

Caroline watched Queenie's face and decided a conspiratorial giggle would be safe now they were laughing at Bert. 'Well, you'll get the same national average wage as everyone else, and so will he. Normally we don't pay spouses but in his case, because he'll have to move with you, he'll receive a stipend. He can spend it on whatever he likes.'

'He also wanted to know if 'e gets to go along on the jollies, you know, goin' to meet foreigners and that.'

'We'll chat about that all together sometime. Your trips will mostly be short. If a trade delegation thinks a visit from you will help secure a deal, or if the Foreign Office reckon your influence would be useful, person-to-person with another head of state, then we get you out and back as fast as we can. So Bert won't be on his own for long if he stays behind. The public have said they don't want taxes paying for holidays, and the civil service view is that being accompanied by a partner for show is somewhat old-fashioned, but I'm sure we can negotiate a reasonable level of contribution if he wants to come along sometimes.'

'I don't s'pose you could tell him it's not allowed? I quite like bein' able to get a word in edgeways without him tellin' me not to be stupid.'

'I'll have a think about that.'

'He'll be all right about it if he can still go to the pub

and keep up with the dominoes league after we move, can he do that?'

'I'm sure that won't be a problem. We can arrange transport.'

'Oh he'll like that, he always moans about 'avin' to walk back from darts and doms, especially when they've lost a match. You'd not believe how competitive it is, I mean, bloomin' dominoes, we used to play that in infant school. It's stupid if you ask me, but it gets him out of the way for an evening.'

'I'm sure it does, I'll make a note, look...' Caroline wrote *dominoes* on a page in her notebook and showed it to Queenie. 'Now, today we're going to start a guided tour of everything that goes on. Don't worry, there's nothing to learn; it's just that when you sit in on cabinet meetings, it's helpful to know who does what.'

'Do I have to go to everything all the time?'

'No, in fact you won't be able to—there are fetes to open, after all.' *Good, she returned the wink.* 'But the established principle of your constitutional role is that of observer. You are the embodiment of the People and as such, when you watch decisions being made, so does the public.'

'So, I don't do any of the decidin'?'

'No, but when new legislation is proposed, you will have the job of approving it.' *There go the stitch-counting fingers.* 'But we'll help you with that. In practice, anything that isn't both the people's choice and in their interests won't get that far, so if and when you okay something, it's just like a rubber stamp.'

'Phew, I fought maybe I 'ad to learn laws and stuff.'

'Not at all, but in a couple of weeks you'll understand it

better. Now, tell me about your knitting...'

The Foreign Ministry's Committee Room One was full. It always was on the first day, people appeared from all manner of dark corners to meet and be met by the new arrivals. A couple of youngsters were sitting on windowsills, and two more scurried off their chairs to lean against the wall when Caroline and Queenie arrived. They'd tried to be quiet, not to interrupt Shirley and Brian's presentation, but the whispered apologies each time knitting needles met ribs had caused a frisson of distraction around the room.

Shirley stopped speaking, Brian lowered the laser pointer from the display of mugshots of most of people in the room, and they both gave the newcomers a smile.

'Hello there!' Shirley Thompson's eyes followed the knitting needles as they progressed from person to person. 'We have two free seats just over there if you'd like to stay a while?'

Caroline nodded her thanks and settled Queenie into one of the chairs, managing—quite deftly, she thought—to take charge of the knitting bag in the process. She'd established, over one more cup of tea, that the knitting 'helped'. She'd tried to delve a little deeper but the lexicons of anxiety, body language and other pop-psychology terms had got her nowhere.

Now she had control of the bag, she could maybe see whether just having it around would 'help'. She turned her attention back to Shirley, who was speaking again.

'Caroline, you all met yesterday, but you may not know Queenie yet. She is this administration's head of state, so you will be seeing quite a lot more of her over the next three years.'

Heads turned, people murmured hello, and one or two of the younger ones waved.

'Blimey, 'ello.' Queenie beamed at the assembly. 'I'm goin' to 'ave to get used to bein' famous, aren't I?' She giggled and waggled her right hand in the air. It looked as though she was trying to screw an imaginary light bulb into her ear.

'We're just making introductions.' Shirley attempted to get the room's attention back on track by addressing Queenie directly. 'The new ministers here on this part of the chart'—Brian resumed his pointing activities—'will each take one of three areas of responsibility: people's republics, democracies and monarchies.' As Brian pointed to each face on the screen the corresponding face in the room nodded. 'And Andy, here, will take overall charge as Foreign Minister.'

Caroline's eyes went straight to the tie. *Was that a map of the world? Oh dear.*

'Here we have all your civil service specialists.' Brian pointed to the series of younger faces. 'Each has expert knowledge of somewhere, and will be watching events there carefully. If anywhere is likely to cause a problem we want to hear about it early.'

'There's loads of them; how will we know who does what?' One of the new ministers was gazing around the room, open-mouthed.

'They are all listed in your manual.' Brian's tone was impatient. There was a reason he usually kept his mouth shut and pointed at things. Clever man, brilliant strategist, but an unfortunate manner.

Shirley hastened to retake the lead. 'And each of you will be spending time with the specialists within your remit. That is what the rest of this week and most of next week is for. By then you'll be calling them your *specials*. And they will be. Listen to them: they will keep you out of trouble and make your life easier. For you, more than the other ministries, issues will arise from their work rather than from the reps in the house. And you are likely to get to know Queenie too—she'll probably accompany you overseas occasionally.' She nodded to Queenie as Caroline beckoned her out of the chair to leave the room and move on.

Queenie did the light bulb thing again, as Caroline offered her arm for a moment to ease her disengagement from the chair.

'Knit one, purl one,' Andy Carswell muttered, rolling his eyes as Queenie made her way back across the room. A few sniggers rippled here and there.

Caroline, following Queenie through the door, took a moment to open her notepad. She jotted *Carswell, Attitude?* as she heard Shirley, voice as soothing as shea butter, add, 'We do find here at the Foreign Ministry that sarcasm is a relatively ineffective tool. Generally there are subtler ways.'

'What I always say is...'

She closed the door. It looked like she'd found her first problem.

'Where are we going next?' Queenie seemed to have accepted Caroline carrying the knitting bag. Her eyes had gone to it as soon as the door had closed but, having seen it, she appeared content.

'I thought we'd pop into Education and see how your friend is getting on.'

'My little Sammy, oh yes, then maybe she could come and have a cuppa with us.'

Caroline checked her watch. 'I don't see why not, they'll be having a break soon.'

Queenie beamed. 'Which way, then?'

'This way, second floor. Are you okay to take the stairs?'

'Are heads of state allowed to use stairs? Might be a security risk.'

Caroline laughed. 'You're getting good at this.'

'Bits of it are fun. What did you think of the wave? I practised with some old videos of before, when we had the proper Queen.'

'Not bad.' Caroline tried to remove the image of a light bulb in Queenie's ear from her mind. 'It could maybe use a little work.'

'Bert said I was mad.'

'We'll work on Bert. And on the wave. Anyway, here we are, let's try to be quiet again.' Caroline opened another door into another committee room and all the faces turned to see who'd entered. Queenie waved again, a proper wave this time, and Sammy's face lit up.

'Ah, hello.' The speaker in this room was flying solo: no screen, no pointer, no pointer person. There were fewer people here, some empty chairs and space to move around. A chart stood on a stand at one end of the conference table. It had some boxes labelled Pre-School, Primary, Secondary, University, Trade College. Names had been scrawled into each with a marker pen. Caroline pondered, not for the first time, whether the world really did need laser pointers.

'Welcome to Education, we were just making some introductions…'

CHAPTER SEVEN

Minnow shouldered his laptop bag as he ambled into the cafe. He'd have a tea before heading home, let the traffic die down. He smiled at the girl behind the counter as she asked if he'd like the usual. His order never varied: Earl Grey with one slice of lemon, half a sugar and a saucer to put the tea bag on after precisely ninety seconds.

'We've got proper tea today,' she added.

'What do you mean?' Minnow's mind wandered down a little cul-de-sac where the House of Commons cafe had opened some sort of lost and found corner—umbrellas, reading glasses and the like.

'Queenie says tea has to be made in a dirty pot and mashed, so now we've put it on the menu. Same price as ordinary tea.' She announced this new bombshell with the sort of pride that makes you look half an inch taller.

'Wow, thanks, but I think I'll stick to my usual if that's okay.' Minnow wasn't a fan of change. 'But you might want to call it something else—otherwise you'll get bored with everyone asking if it's stolen.'

A cloud crossed the face on the other side of the counter.

'The old joke? Proudhon? Marx? Proper tea, property?' He was now regretting his pathetic attempt at small talk. Now he was going to have to explain.

'Oh, yeah.' The girl was clearly none the wiser. Maybe she hated chatter too.

Minnow moved along the counter, paid for his tea and thanked the cashier.

'Not having proper tea today, then?' The cashier beamed at him.

Don't, just don't, you'll regret it.

'Ah, no, thank you, I like this one. Uh, thanks for the saucer.'

He scanned the available tables and spotted a group by the window. He could see Caroline, an older woman and a really cute youngster. They were all laughing at something the older woman was saying. He carried his tea over and caught Caroline's eye.

'Hello! Come and sit down, I'll introduce you.' Caroline took a bag of what appeared to be knitting off the chair beside her. 'This is Minnow, everyone. He's my irreplaceable techie.'

They all smiled at him as he sat down.

'Minnow is our computer programmer in the Cabinet Support Group. His programs are what placed you in your jobs. Well, with a bit of input from Gerald and myself. Minnow, meet Queenie Mason, she's—'

'Head of state, yes, I remember. Hello.' Minnow offered a nod.

'And this is Sammy; Samantha Cho. We placed her in the university steering committee.'

'Oh yes.' Minnow riffled through the names filed away in his head. 'Flunked out of psyche...' *Shit*. 'I mean, you know, we thought your experience would—'

'It's okay.' Minnow decided she had a nice smile, but maybe that was just relief. 'It's the truth. I flunked out. My dad says it's because I spent too much time playing games, but he doesn't really get that programming is mostly about games these days.'

'Yeah, everything else has pretty much been invented, eh?' Minnow laughed, off the hook. 'Do you play?'

'Some. Didn't have a lot of time at uni and then, well, things got rough, but I might start again, pick up where I left off...'

'Where was that?'

'*Starcraft 2*, mostly.'

'Cool, what league?'

'Just got into Platinum when I stopped...my thesis was on player psychology in real-time strategy gaming.'

'Blimey, you look like you're catching flies.' Minnow shut his mouth as Queenie's signature chest rattle echoed around the cafe. A few people looked round. 'I dunno what any of that means but it sounds fancy. My daughter says we should get a computer but Bert says we managed fine without one all these years and I should be anti them anyway 'cos of losing my job to one.'

'You'll be learning to use one soon, you know,' said Caroline.

It was Queenie's turn to catch flies. 'No, really? Why? I'm not clever you know.'

'I'll show you when you've moved in. All your

appointments will be on a computer. We'll put them in for you, but you'll need to be able to check your diary. It's pretty easy really, and we can take our time.'

'And,' added Sammy, 'I can come and help! You've been so nice to me.'

'Oh I'd love that. We can tell Bert, "Bugger off and watch the telly, the women have *computering* to do."' Minnow joined in as the laughter spread. A few more people glanced their way. He wasn't used to being on the jolly table, the one people wanted to join.

'Now then, young fellow-me-lad'—Queenie addressed herself to Minnow—'why do they call you Minnow?'

'It started at school and then it stuck,' he mumbled, embarrassed to be the centre of attention again.

'Some say it's because he looks harmless but can catch very big fish,' Caroline added with a wink. 'But we think maybe it's just been so long, nobody knows how to call him anything else.'

Minnow nodded. And regarded his tea. He'd forgotten to check the time and retrieve the tea bag. He did it now, trying to decide whether it would require less of a squashing than usual with the teaspoon. He opted for a mini-squash, just enough to stop it dripping, instead of the usual squeeze to get every last drop before arranging it carefully in his saucer. He then stirred his tea three times clockwise, removed the lemon, placed it carefully next to the tea bag and lifted his cup to drink.

'You've got a saucer!' Queenie seemed delighted.

'Yes, you can ask for one if you want.'

'I never thought. I will next time. Can I borrow yours now, though?' She had up-ended the lemon and tea bag onto the table before he had a chance to object. He resisted the urge to straighten them.

'Here we go, luvvie, hand us your cup.' Queenie picked up Sammy's mug, swirled the dregs around and smacked it upside down onto the saucer. 'Now then, what have we got?'

'Dear God,' muttered Caroline.

'What was that, luv?'

'Nothing really, it's just probably the first time the House of Commons has seen tasseography.'

'Seen what?'

'Tea leaves. This.' Caroline gestured towards the mess.

'In that case it's about bloomin' time. The place has been here for centuries. We was told that on the guided tour.' Queenie sniffed. 'Let's 'ave a look.'

She turned the cup this way and that. 'Oooh.'

'Well?' Sammy put her elbows on the table and her chin in her hands and smiled up at her new friend. 'Am I going to meet a tall, dark stranger?'

'That's for me to know and for you to find out, missy.'

'How was your day then?' Caroline asked, after Minnow and Sammy had left. Minnow had reintroduced the subject of computer games while he helped Sammy into her coat. Caroline hoped that by the time they left the building he'd find the words to suggest they pursue them together. She made a note to check tomorrow.

'It was all right, really. Sort of fun. Meetin' people, learnin' things. It made a change from listenin' to Bert drone on.' Queenie turned her attention from the empty mug in front of her and looked around, suddenly anxious.

'I've not done any knitting all day. Where is it?'

'It's here.' Caroline produced the bag from under the chair recently vacated by Minnow. 'I've had it with us all the time, in case you wanted it, but you seem to have been all right.'

'I suppose I have. It's all been so busy, and people have been nice to me, sayin' hello and wavin' and listening when I said stuff.'

'What are you making, anyway?' Caroline investigated the contents of the bag.

'Proper tea cosies.' Queenie's voice quivered with pride. 'My daughter's husband sells them to Americans on an interweb site thing. They can't get enough of them.'

'Really? Goodness. I didn't know that.' Caroline began to examine the work. 'I see, it's all in the tension when you change colours.'

'Ooh, do you knit, dearie?'

'Actually, yes I do, but I don't often bring it to work these days. I make, um, art works mainly.' She wasn't sure what Queenie would make of her knitting guild's more nefarious exploits. 'When we start meeting in Buck Place next week, I might bring a piece along, then we can knit together while we're thinking and talking, and maybe leave it behind when we come here? What do you think about that?'

'That would be nice...well, the both knitting bit. But I'm not sure about leavin' it behind. I'd need it to keep me sane when we're in some of those big offices with the people using fancy words all day.'

'Give it time, you'll get used to it. You don't have to say anything in meetings if you don't want to. But if you do say something, they've got to listen to you.'

'They have, haven't they? It's not like Bert and his cronies, they just say, "Shut up, you stupid old bag, you don't know what you're talkin' about", but half the time it's them that's wrong and it takes me half an hour to explain why and then they say I'm goin' on. I tell 'em, I wouldn't have to go on if you'd only bloody listen.' Caroline glanced furtively at her watch. 'Am I goin' on?'

'Only a little.'

'Do you 'ave to go? I got one more question.'

'Certainly, I have a few minutes, what is it?'

'The sittin' thing. How you got out of that chair. I want to practise it when I'm at home...when Bert isn't looking.' Queenie added the final clause through gritted teeth.

Caroline began to wonder how the infamous Bert would adapt to his new surroundings. She'd add a page for him to her notebook this evening. 'The trick is not to get too comfy,' she began, as Queenie's face fell. 'I don't mean you can't be comfortable ever,' she added, 'but if you want to command people's attention, you perch on the edge and sit forwards a bit.'

'Like this?' Queenie shuffled to the edge of her cafeteria chair.

'Not as much as that. You can sit as far back as your knees allow you to, with your feet still on the floor.' Queenie shuffled back a bit. 'That's it, now keep your legs and backside where they are and lean your shoulders up and forward a bit, as though that chap over there'—she indicated the next table—'was talking very quietly, and you wanted to hear him.'

'How's this?' Queenie's back straightened. Her chin lifted. She looked, what? Interested? Alert? A bit of each? It was a promising start.

'Perfect.'

Queenie deflated. 'Oof, it's a bit 'ard on the old back, ain't it?'

'You'll get used to it. Watch what they do on the television, it's the same trick. You'll see it with people getting interviewed and on the news, etcetera. Watch the ones who have their conversations on sofas. They look comfortable enough, but actually they're sitting just like you did. Sounds stupid, but it makes them look more interesting...and they fill the camera better.'

'Do they? Blimey, I never knew there was right and wrong ways to sit on a perishin' settee. I'll 'ave to tell Bert.'

'Or you could not tell him.' Caroline was whispering now, in mock conspiratorial mode, as she got up to leave. 'You could just alter your posture and see if he listens any better.'

She was starting to get used to Queenie's laugh, she decided, although someone should probably look into that cough.

'Oh, one more thing before we go, wait there a minute.' Caroline crossed the cafe, disappeared behind the counter and emerged a moment or two later with a smiling young lad in tow. He held aloft a sort of box thing.

'This is Eugene. He works at your new flat, and it's going to be his job to make sure your teapot follows you about.'

'Oh bless you, luvvie, that's nice.' Queenie turned her beaming smile on the skinny lad.

'I've found you a box for now, ma'am. Just haven't made it waterproof on the inside yet.'

Queenie looked from Eugene to Caroline and back.

'I think I'm goin' to enjoy this after all.'

CHAPTER EIGHT

Queenie sat in yet another committee room, looking at yet another screen on the wall. Caroline had suggested she spend a bit of time on her own today; apparently she'd find the discussion interesting. Queenie found that a bit hard to believe, but she was determined to at least try and follow it. Caroline had other things to do: getting all the rest of the new people ready for the Opening of Parliament thing tomorrow and the first big debate on Monday.

Queenie had been through all the introductions now. Some of the faces she'd seen on Monday—how long ago that seemed—were here in Employment and Industry. She now knew that *Industry* had three ministers, or secretaries, or undersecretaries, whatever they were...it had been a bit confusing. Then *Employment* had two, and one of them was the chap who'd been a bit snarky with Gerald that first day. She'd missed the names, of course—they'd just done a quick hello for her when she arrived, and there'd been some nodding. Caroline had told her to save the wave for being out in cars, so she'd nodded too.

It wasn't so crowded now most of the people were back in their offices, doing whatever they did all day. Just the new ministers and their special civil service people. It seemed like every ministry had its own version of Caroline to look after them and tell them the rules. This bit of the week was for getting people up to speed with their actual jobs. Which seemed to be mostly about nodding, come to think of it. Queenie's job, from what she'd gathered so far, was to listen a lot and be friendly. She didn't have to decide anything, just 'follow proceedings on behalf of the people'. Mostly, she had to nod.

That nice young man she'd had a cup of tea with was there as well, the one with the funny name. Just one word. Something to do with fish. *Mackerel? Mussel? Minnow, that was it.* She wondered if he'd seen her Sammy again. She decided to have a chat with him as soon as possible; he seemed a decent sort, if a bit quiet, but she felt quite fierce about her new friend. She'd had her troubles and nobody was going to add to them while Queenie was around. She'd felt that way once about her Deborah, but these days she didn't need no looking after. Her and Colin had made it very clear they no longer needed Queenie and Bert in their lives. They had 'moved up in the world, Mother'. Who said 'Mother' anyway? Maybe Colin did. Deborah was 'in advertising' and he was 'in computers'. He was happy to sell Queenie's tea cosies to gullible Americans, but they didn't socialise. Queenie wondered what they'd say when she told them she was now 'in government', and giggled. How long before they'd decide socialising was all right once they'd moved to Buck Place? She might have a little bet with Bert.

She realised her mind had wandered. Caroline had asked her to try and listen without knitting today. She had the bag just in case and was doing her best, but some of it was boring. About companies and taxes and suchlike. But now Minnow had something to say, so she tried a bit harder to follow it.

'I'd like to introduce you all to Minnow,' the woman with the pointer said. 'We've covered all the areas of specialism you are likely to have to deal with from day to day, and I know you've mostly picked up the issues that are currently in the wind, but we do have a potential problem, inherited from the previous government, which could become urgent any day. Minnow is here to explain it to you.'

Minnow looked uncomfortable. Maybe he just didn't like talking.

'Yes, uh, thank you.' He spoke down into the screen of his laptop. Then he moved something, and what he could see on his computer was up on the screen on the wall. There was some kind of graph.

'Normally we ask outgoing reps to let us know of anything coming from their constituencies that they'd have brought up at the next House debate. Then we put a team on anything big that's coming from several places at once, so we can have some suggestions ready for the next intake.

'We also have an, uh, algorithm, that's like a...well, a *thing* that tells us how prevalent an issue is by the number and spread of the constituencies it's coming from. As you can see from the bars here, and here, and here'—he moved a little arrow round the graph—'we have over twenty per cent of reps reporting the same issue from several disparate regions. My national influence forecast analysis weights the spread as highly signific—'

'Spit it out, man, what's the problem?' The northerner, what was his name? Queenie flipped through the sheet of photos she'd been given: Doug Sideworth, that was it. Minister for Employment. She wondered if he was always this impatient and rude.

'Yes, well, what we're hearing from the outgoing reps is pockets of jobs being lost to, uh, computers.'

'What is that supposed to mean?' The Sideworth man was tapping his pen on the table now.

'It means...' Minnow looked up from his screen at the faces round the table. Queenie gave him a smile and a sneaky thumbs up. Minnow took a deep breath. 'It means that too many companies are saving money by replacing people with machines, and more people are now out of work than there are new jobs for...and local economies are suffering...and unions are talking about a general strike.' The sentence came out in a rush and Minnow looked glad it was over. The picture on the screen changed to another set of graphs.

'The top chart represents job losses per constituency, and the lower one is the average percentage income loss to local businesses, again per constituency.'

'Thank you, Minnow, very clear.' The woman with the pointer took over again. Minnow's face disappeared back into his laptop. She turned some switch or other and the screen went blank. 'Now, we've had notification that the unions will be voting on strike action this week, so we need to plan a response as a matter of urgency. Obviously Employment will be taking the lead on this one.' She nodded at Doug. 'Mr Sideworth, you and I, with the assistance of your chief secretary'—she nodded at a mousy-looking woman who Queenie seemed to recall might be called Deirdre, or something else like that from Corrie—'and the Employment team of specialists will formulate a plan to take to the House next week. We do, however, need some input from Industry here'—she nodded at more people—'since we may have to include some quotas or job creation plans.'

'Quotas?' One of the other ministers was talking now. 'Do you mean that companies will have to keep jobs that computers could do cheaper?'

'Precisely that.'

'Our stakeholders won't like that. It would eat into profits. Stupid idea.'

'I don't see the problem,' Doug added. 'If jobs are redundant, we retrain people. If they're too stupid to learn, we give them benefits. Nobody goes hungry.'

'It's a problem if the people decide it's a problem.' The woman put down her pointer and sat at the table facing Doug. 'That's what we're here for. The solution you just proposed would probably have worked back in old democracy. So long as the number of voters earning profits outweighed the number of redundancies, broadly speaking, the government would survive. But these days, if the groundswell is on the side of jobs, we have to listen. And try to be a bit creative.'

'And anyway.' Queenie realised why Caroline had said she'd be interested. 'People need to feel useful.' All eyes turned to her and she covered her mouth. 'Sorry.'

'Not at all.' The woman in charge smiled at her. 'Do go on, ma'am.'

'It's like when I was at Tesco's. They got machines to

do my job and people go there and shop just like always, but when they left before, after I'd had a laugh and a joke and a chat, they was smilin'. Now, they goes and shops and does it faster probally but they ain't smilin'. So whose job is it to perk up their day? I don't see computers doin' that.' She'd had a go at the leaning forward thing but it made her back hurt a bit, so she hunched back down into her chair. 'Maybe there should be chatting-to-each-other jobs in all the companies where the computers took over.'

'Maybe.' The woman looked serious, like Queenie had said something important. She turned to the blokes who were rolling their eyes at each other. 'You may hear it in different words from the unions but this is likely to form part of their argument, so you might want to give it some thought.' Somebody snorted, but then Minnow looked up at Queenie and returned the thumbs up.

'Now we've outlined the issue, let's take a coffee break. When we come back I'll take input from you all. Minnow here will start putting your suggestions into some modelling software, and we'll come up with a workable set of suggestions for the House.'

Doug Sideworth cradled his coffee. He looked out of the cafe window, taking in the iconic view of the Thames—County Hall and the London Eye, Westminster Bridge. He should be patting himself on the back and counting his blessings. He was here in the heart of things. They'd taken him, they'd given him a decent job. Employment, huh, that was a bit of a laugh, really, since he'd been on the verge of losing his job. So what the hell was wrong with him? He wanted to sound efficient and knowledgeable, to contribute sound common sense, but he was behaving like a total bastard. Every time he opened his mouth something rude came out. The comments were constructive in his head—professional and incisive. But even he could hear them mangling into arseholery as they entered the atmosphere.

He wondered if stopping drinking was the problem. Would the odd snifter make him nicer? Or had he always been prone to this sort of stuff? No, surely not, Katie would have told him. Wouldn't she?

He had to sort himself out. It looked like his ministry had a crisis brewing, the first of the new government, and he wanted to make a decent showing. He didn't think much of the whole paying-people-to-be-inefficient idea, but then he was a bean counter. His expertise was the bottom line. They should have put him in the Treasury. He'd have been good with the economy; it didn't smile and chat.

He took out his photo of Musbury Tor. He'd tucked it in his wallet for luck.

'Hi, Katie. You'll never guess what I'm looking out of the window at right now.'

Now he was being stupid. He looked up to see if anyone had heard him. The Queenie woman caught his eye and waved. She was with the computer chap. They were coming over. Doug groaned silently. *That's not the way to stop being an arse,* Katie whispered in his ear. *Be nice, learn to like people again.* Was that it? Had he stopped liking people since he'd lost the only one who mattered? *It's not their fault they're not me.* Doug supposed it probably wasn't.

He gestured to the seats at his table and attempted a

smile.

'Hello there, ducky, you look deep in thought. Working out how to save us all from the machines?' Queenie popped her mug and saucer down on the table and Minnow followed suit. 'I don't envy you, ducks. Fancy 'aving a real proper crisis in your first week. Me, I just 'ave to listen to stuff and learn to sit proper, while you've got some real governin' to do.'

The lad, Minnow, nodded. He seemed more at ease now. Maybe he didn't like people any more than Doug did. *See, you can care...*

'I've developed some software that should help us,' Minnow said into his tea as he removed the bag and placed it on his saucer. 'Quite looking forward to testing it, really.'

Say something real, Katie advised. *Don't try to be clever.*

'How does it work?' asked Doug. 'Can you explain it to an old-fashioned accountant like me?'

Minnow smiled and made eye contact. 'Well, it's like this...'

CHAPTER NINE

'All set?'

Queenie looked from Gerald to Caroline and then surveyed her surroundings. She'd been told about the paintings and carvings, the significance of everything, but it had all gone out of her head. She was sitting on an ornate but uncomfortable chair, with a bright pink pouffe for her feet, on a sort of dais thing with three even brighter pink steps.

'I think so,' she answered Caroline. 'I'm not sure about gettin' back down those steps wiv the thing on, not bein' watched by all those people.'

'Don't worry, we'll be with you every step of the way. Literally. You don't have to do anything at all except walk, until Gerald asks you to repeat the oath in the House. Then you'll have it written on a little screen in front of you as well as having him read it to you in sections. It's no harder than getting married.'

'In fact it's a lot easier,' Gerald murmured. 'This oath

only lasts for three years.' Queenie and Caroline tittered.

'What about all the people who are comin' in? Do I have to do any wavin'?'

'Nothing at all,' said Caroline. 'You don't even have to smile. Any sense that you're having fun might be viewed amiss by the papers; they love to get a shot of a stray smirk. Better to pretend nobody's there. That way you keep a serious look on your face, which the State infers as you taking the task of representing it really seriously.'

Gerald nodded. 'Quite so. You might want to see this as an opportunity to get used to crowds. Every citizen is entitled to come and see for themselves that you are promising to faithfully represent them against any attempt by government to subvert their wishes. Obviously we only have so much room, so the guests have been chosen by lottery from those who applied. Once this room fills up, there'll be crowds all the way to the Commons, and there all the galleries will be full. There's a live video feed to the old Lords Chamber, which will also be full. Your personal guests will be sitting in the Commons VIP gallery, so they'll have a good view of you taking your oath.'

Queenie chuckled. Caroline had asked her to work on the chesty guffaw a bit, and she'd been practising her posh chuckle with Bert of an evening. 'What is that noise?' he'd said the first time she tried it. 'Sounds like someone's shoved a feather up your tochus.' But she'd persuaded him to play along and tell her when it sounded better. He was starting to come around. Maybe it was because she did the sitting up thing while she asked. *That Caroline knows a thing or two.*

'My Deborah and her Colin thought I was takin' the piss when I invited them. But they're coming along…and

QUEENIE'S TEAPOT

Bert's had an 'aircut special!'

'I'm sure they'll be very proud of you. Now, Gerald will stay with you all the way but I have to go and check on some of the others. The new ministers will be taking their oaths after you and then the reps. It'll be a long afternoon. Oh, did you want to visit the loo before we start?'

'No, that's all right, luvvie, I got the feeling it might be ages when you started sayin' about all the reps askin' the same question, so I 'aven't 'ad so much tea today.'

'And remember, you don't have to say, "I will" to them all, you can just nod if you like.' *Again with the nodding.*

'I know, dear, they think it's about me promisin' to represent their constituencies, but it's mostly so they can get used to the sound of their own voice in the Chamber. I was listening.'

'Good girl.'

Caroline slipped away through some door round the back of the throney thing Queenie was sitting on.

Gerald stood to attention and nodded to some flunkey or other who'd slipped silently into the Robing Room when Queenie wasn't looking. How did these people move about so quietly? Maybe back when it was the old royalty you could be killed for making a racket. Or maybe the carpet helped. Fancy stuff this, none of your nylon pile makin' people staticky all over the place. Queenie imagined the flunkies all wearing plastic Crocs and getting shocks off everything they touched, and grinned. Maybe she'd imagine that every time she got scared of them.

The door opened and the room filled with people.

Gerald was particularly fond of this ceremony. It appealed to his sense of dignity; the symbolism was just right. A seamless melding of tradition and change, solemnity and popular enthusiasm.

Caroline had done an excellent job in the time. Queenie was, if not brimming with confidence, a little less anxious. She liked people, that was the main thing. And she appeared to be quick on the uptake. He stifled a sigh; he saw it all the time, and it was one of the reasons he persevered with the never-ending task of grooming governments. People mistook lack of education for lack of intelligence. It was the biggest problem with old democracy, in his view. People were too easily impressed by the wrong things.

There had been rows in the early days about exactly how to modify the pomp. Some of the noisier revolutionaries had wanted every trace of the old ways razed, to have the palaces and chambers made into hospitals and children's homes. Put the reps on plastic chairs in church halls, stick the instruments of state in a museum and run the country via Skype. But repurposing the traditions had won the argument, for both financial and sociological reasons. Some things just had to be *seen*. The reps, the ministers, Queenie, they'd all do their best— or not—depending on their personalities, their abilities and their values. But if the people could come and see the new intake swear to uphold the power of representation over oligarchy, well, they felt good about it.

There was no specific administrative need for two people to drape Queenie in a heavy red velvet robe of state, or in Queenie's case swamp her in it. There was then no particular governmental requirement for her to drag the thing down the pink steps, all the way through the Palace of Westminster to the Commons Chamber only to drag it up some green steps. The symbolism was there all right: the donning of a burden, the bypassing of the Lords—we're all equal now—the sober, ceremonial promises. But the main purpose was merely to be seen.

And around the world the fabulous settings, the art and carvings, the costumery, the sheer history of it all made for market confidence. Internationally, Britain could still do it; the soft revolution, along with the Robe of State, was made of the finest red velvet. Tourism was up, trade was buoyant, the pound stable. Pomp was an important export.

The room was full now. The robe ready.

'Queenie Mason.' He met her eyes. 'Do you willingly adopt the burden of the State of the British Republic for as long as the State requires your service?'

'Yes, luv.' Queenie's hand went to her mouth. 'I mean, yes.' She nodded vigorously.

The crowd who had been allowed into the Robing Room began to clap. The couple of flunkies manoeuvred themselves to her elbows and gently helped her to her feet. They stayed each side of her, supporting her as she stepped down to floor level. Their hands stayed at her elbows, as Gerald led the way down the roped-off path towards the door.

The clapping spread through the door and intensified as the onlookers in the Royal Gallery beyond realised she was coming their way. There were some cheers and a few whistles. Somebody at the back yelled, 'Good on yer, Queenie, luv,' and Gerald proceeded, content. This administration had won its first battle.

Deborah Chandler sat bolt upright, clutching her handbag in her lap and fuming. This was becoming one of the most embarrassing days of her acutely embarrassing life. Not only had they had to go through the same security screening as everyone else to get in, despite having VIP invitations, but Bert had set the bloody thing off.

'Unfortunately, sir,' the guard had said, 'we can't allow you to carry this into the House.' He'd held aloft a battered Swiss army knife and beckoned a colleague over with a basket to put it in. 'Please feel free to call for it at the gatehouse when you leave.'

'Dad!' Deborah had been mortified. 'What on earth made you bring that old thing along?'

He'd winked at her and the guard. 'Never know when you might need a bottle opener, eh, son?'

She'd known she was blushing when she took her turn through the airport-type scanner, but when it went off for her as well she'd begun to shake. She'd emptied her metal objects out of the Hermès crocodile bag but had been unwilling to let it go as she walked through. It had been a recent gift from Colin and was her pride and joy.

'May I examine the bag, ma'am?' The guard had been polite but she could feel him smirking. 'Ah yes, a little metal in the mountings of the, um, *diamonds*.' The guard must have known, as she now did, that genuine Hermès bags didn't do that. Her gift was a fake. And Colin knew she knew. He was still failing to meet her eye.

And now she was going to have to watch her mother make a fool of herself on national television. What they'd think of it all at work next week she couldn't bear to wonder. Maybe she could avoid them finding out; her name wasn't the same and even if it was, Mason was pretty common. Nobody knew where she came from, and she vowed to try and keep it that way. If they ever found out they'd be polite of course—ad agencies were like that: lovely to your face while they bitched about you behind your back.

'Never mind, luvvie,' Bert had said that morning. 'It's a day out.' She had observed his version of smartening up with disdain. The only good thing to be said about today was that the cameras didn't appear to care who was in the VIP Gallery. Yet. If she'd had any sense she'd have asked to go in with everyone else, just in case. She'd been a bit blinded by the whole VIP thing and not thought the day through. That was going to have to stop.

'Something's happening.' It was the first time Colin had spoken since they'd arrived. He turned to the door at the back of the chamber down below the gallery. Deborah followed his gaze. People were standing and clapping. A tall chap marched slowly in, followed by—*good God, just look at her!*—her daft old mum. She tottered along with two lads in knickerbockers holding her up. They all seemed to be dragging some sort of moth-eaten carpet behind them.

They plodded their way to the big throne arrangement at the front. The lads helped Queenie up the steps and bundled her and the carpet into the chair. She looked so tiny. Then the tall bloke turned and lifted his hand. The crowd went quiet.

'I bet 'e was a sergeant major once,' hissed Bert to Colin.

'Shh.' Deborah saw Queenie's eyes lift towards their spot. Bert waved; Queenie wrinkled her nose at him.

Deborah clutched her handbag a little tighter.

The man nodded to the chamber, acknowledging the silence.

'Ladies and gentlemen, citizens of the British Republic, ministers, people's representatives and public servants: I present your head of state for this parliament, duly selected by random ballot and tasked with serving your interests without fear or favour.'

Queenie sat forward a little in the massive chair.

He turned to face her.

'Will you solemnly promise and swear to serve the people of the British Republic according to their established laws and customs?'

Queenie's chin jutted forward slightly as she lifted her eyes to Gerald's and wrinkled her nose again. 'I will!' She shut her mouth with a snap. Deborah decided she looked like a Pekinese dog.

'Will you further, without fear or favour, represent equally the rights, needs and well-being of the citizens represented here individually and severally?'

Queenie said 'I will' again, a little less barkily this time.

People began to stand up in the front benches below.

'Is that it? What now?' Colin whispered to Bert.

'What are you asking him for? He won't know.' Colin wasn't talking to her but he could ask Bert stuff? Deborah wasn't having that.

'Actually, I do know,' Bert hissed back. 'It's in this leaflet she brought home.' He handed it to Colin.

'Goodness, this could take a while.' He whistled under his breath. 'She's got to promise to *represent equally* the requirements of every ministry and the constituents of every rep. So presumably she's got to "I will" at everyone down there.' He indicated the chamber.

'Oh look, some of them are getting up and gettin' out the way, there's loads more crowded at the door!' Bert's hiss managed to be at the same time quiet and piercing.

'It's like graduation without certificates,' said Colin.

'Shhh!' Deborah looked round at the other people in the galleries to see if they were annoyed with Bert and Colin yet, but they all seemed to be looking at leaflets and whispering to each other about what was happening too. Her grip on the bag loosened slightly.

The voices droned on. A few cameras flashed.

'Will you faithfully and fairly represent the people of my constituency, Stockport?'

'Will you faithfully and fairly represent the people of my constituency, Sunningdale?'

'How long do you think it'll be before we get a beer?' Bert was grinning at Colin now.

'Looks like a good half an hour at least. I hope she's got some liniment for her neck, that's a lot of nodding.'

Deborah scowled at the pair of them as they threw their heads back, laughing as uproariously as you can while trying to be quiet.

A camera flashed straight at them.

CHAPTER TEN

'Hello there, you look comfy, how did the move go?' Caroline grinned as she popped her head round the door of the small flat in the Royal Mews, set aside for the head of state's family.

The rooms Queenie and Bert had moved into over the weekend were comfortable to the point of luxury for many of their occupants, but far from lavish. They were fitted to last. No expense had been spared on actual quality; some incumbents had small children and precious little at home to take good care of. Caroline took in the current arrangement of the reception room: several chairs of the type Queenie had encountered so spectacularly just a week ago gathered around a coffee table covered with brightly coloured tea cosies. By the chair Queenie had tucked herself into sat a large basket of yarn. Caroline noted an absence of elderly recliner chairs and TV screens.

'We're all settled in, luv.' Queenie rearranged the cosies to one side, and Caroline realised that one of them actually covered a teapot. 'Would you like a cup of tea? I'll get another cup.' She moved to get up.

'No, that's fine, I know where the kitchen is, you stay there.'

'It's all right, you know, I've learned how to get out of these things.' There it was again, the gentle giggle. Slightly chesty maybe, but less likely to frighten the horses stabled below.

Caroline smiled and sat. 'Okay then, thank you.' She watched Queenie turn herself sideways and shuffle to the edge of the chair before putting her feet on the carpet and popping upright.

'I can't wait to see Deborah manage one of those.' Queenie threw the conspiratorial whisper over her shoulder as she pottered back with a cup and saucer. 'She's got some airs and graces since she married Colin and moved up west and started at the advertising agency. Then we was too common to be doin' with at the Peabodys. Bert used to have to drop these off at their house because she wouldn't visit.' She indicated the pile of knitted items.

'But now we're here she's taken a day off work special to come and collect them. I reckon she just wants to see if we're posh enough for her yet.' There it was, the guffaw-cum-coughing fit. Caroline found herself glad it hadn't gone for good. 'Oh, you might meet her while you're here, that would be nice.'

Caroline agreed that it would indeed be nice, took her tea and asked how Bert was settling in.

'Guess what? He's happy now he's here.' Was that a trace of over-emphasis on those aitches? 'He's got a room to himself through there. They put his chair in front of that dirty great telly on the wall and now he can watch whatever he likes without any nonsense from me.'

Caroline nodded her approval. 'So we can have our morning meetings in here without upsetting him?'

'Yes luv, I told him we was both goin' to be knittin' and he said he'd be keepin' well clear.'

'We might as well get started then, eh?' Caroline retrieved her own knitting from the briefcase dedicated to knitting-at-work days.

'Ooh, what's that?' Queenie peered at the dark square, which appeared to have a silvery white star and moon pattern knitted into it.

'It's a swatch I'm working on, trying to get the pattern right, eventually it'll be, um...' Caroline didn't really want to go any further just yet.

'I've seen something like it before, haven't I?'

Caroline grinned. 'Yes, the Foreign Minister's tie, the one he wore last week. I think he might be a good source of ideas.'

Queenie burst out laughing again. 'Blimey, girlie, you ain't as stuffy as you look, are you?'

'I'll take that as a compliment. Now, has anyone explained the pattern of your days to you yet?'

'Yes, the girl who comes and goes and sorts out what we need, she had a chat over the weekend. Most mornings there'll be people to talk to here till lunchtime, then I can go listen to the debates on weeks when the house sits and go listen to committees and such when the reps are away.'

'That's right. It's pretty much up to you where you go and what you involve yourself in. You are the eyes and ears of the people. But so are the ministers and the reps; they watch us, and you watch them.'

'And the people who come and talk to me in the

mornings?'

'Sometimes it will be someone like me or Gerald, letting you know what's going on, sometimes it'll be a minister or a rep, advising you something important is coming up. Most of the time it'll be people bitching about each other though, and telling you about their lives.'

'Just like Tesco's!'

'Precisely.'

'Then each morning you'll have a list of everything happening that day: which chamber is debating what, which committees are where. All you have to do is tell Eugene where you plan to go before midday and he'll arrange security.'

'And the teapot?'

Caroline coughed. 'We're hoping to use more than one teapot eventually. Then you can keep yours here and another at the House cafe. We're just having a spot of trouble finding one with the requisite, uh, deposits inside. Eugene spent the weekend scouring second-hand shops but all the teapots appear to be, um, *clean*. Therefore, just for a little while longer, yes—and the teapot.'

'Where are we goin' this afternoon?'

'The first sitting of the full House, it'll be in the Commons Chamber, with all the reps whose constituencies it affects. The rest of the reps will be watching by video link in the Lords Chamber. Sometimes there'll be two debates going on at once; we can get more work done each week the reps are in London that way, but when something big comes up we use the video feed.'

'Isn't there enough room in one of them for everyone? It seemed pretty huge to me.'

'Unfortunately no, you may not have noticed people

moving on to make way for others on Friday. It's a bit overwhelming to start with.'

Queenie nodded. 'No shit, Sherlock.' Her hand flew to her mouth. 'Oh, I'm sorry, I got to start watchin' my language.'

Caroline looked up from counting the stitches in a section of star. 'It's fine to be yourself to a certain extent...'

'I ought to be able to stop swearin' if I try, I'm sorry about that, you bein' a young lady and all.'

Caroline's eyes returned to her work. 'Not to worry, you should hear me when I get going. We just need to be a bit more careful for formal occasions.'

'I know, my Bert said that, he said, "You can't go turnin' the air blue in front of fancy foreign princesses and that," and I told him he was right for once.'

'Indeed.'

'But then he actually got a bit helpful.'

'Oh?'

'Yes, he told Colin I was a bit worried about the way I talk when he saw him on Friday, at the thing. Colin gave him a note wiv a website on that teaches elomecution, so I've started havin' a go. Eugene showed me how to get it on the computer!'

'Oh, that's splendid! Although you do know that you represent the people, not the establishment, so if you want to speak the way you always have, nobody will complain. Well, apart from saying "shit" to random heads of state.' Caroline winked.

'No, it's all right, I know that, I want to do it. Maybe my Debs won't be so ashamed any more. I been starting with the haitches!'

'And it's working.' Caroline realised she was actually

quite excited by this piece of news. 'I noticed it right away!'

'Did you?' Queenie beamed, as someone knocked rather formally on the outer door of the flat. Her eyes widened. 'What do I do? Eugene normally taps quietly then pops his head round the door. No one's knocked like that before. Shall I go and open it?'

'Just say, "Come in," it'll be fine.'

'A hrem. Come. In.' It sounded as though Queenie wished there were some aitches to overaspirate. Eugene opened the door, stood aside and announced, 'Ms Deborah Chandler to see you, ma'am.'

'Ooh, Debs, thank you Eugene, luv! Hhhello, sweetheart! Hhhow are you? Come in and sit down, this is Caroline.'

The woman entered the room and looked around her. She had a coat over her arm, which she handed to Eugene, along with what appeared to be a knockoff Hermès bag. He looked at Queenie, who shrugged. Eugene took the coat and bag and disappeared into the rest of the flat.

'Is this it?' Deborah appeared disappointed. 'All the shenanigans of getting in, security and whatnot, and you're living above the garage.' She sniffed.

Caroline stood and proffered her hand. 'Hello, Deborah.' She smiled the smile she knew didn't reach her eyes; she just couldn't help it sometimes. 'I've been looking forward to meeting you.'

'Be a dear and get me some coffee.' Deborah threw herself into one of the armchairs. 'I've taken a day away from the advertising agency to visit my mother, and I'm sure you can'—her eyes took in the knitting by Caroline's chair—'knit somewhere else.'

'Actually, dearie...' Queenie didn't know where to look.

'It's all right, Queenie, misunderstandings happen.' Caroline returned the unshaken hand to her side and looked the woman up and down. 'We often find that the families of new incumbents are too overwhelmed by their changed circumstances to remember their manners. Ms Chandler, I understand that you are here to collect some knitted items for your husband's...*website*.' She didn't often use that tone of voice that made 'website' sound like 'dog turd', but she had it in her armoury for special occasions and the woman was irking her now. She was used to put-downs—you couldn't get to the top of your chosen discipline as a woman without a few people thinking you made the tea here and there—but Queenie was embarrassed in her new home. That made Caroline cross. 'We are, obviously, in a meeting just now, therefore I hope you won't be holding up proceedings too long. No doubt the advertising agency is in urgent need of your skills.'

'Say a proper hello to Caroline, dear, she's very important, and she's my friend.'

'It doesn't look much like a meeting.' Deborah apparently had the wit to realise she was on the back foot but not the grace to go down without an excuse.

'We both find that knitting helps us think.' Caroline inclined her head to Queenie and decided she had won sufficiently convincingly to act the bigger person without losing control. 'Now, tell me about your work. I have a close friend in advertising, maybe you know her.'

Caroline decided to take lunch in her office. She had one or two calls to make. Crabtree Longfellow Winterbotham, famous as the London ad agency with the most unwieldy name, didn't seem a good fit for the fake-couture, fake-everything character she had just met. It was none of her business really, and she had no wish to bring heartache to anyone's family, but Deborah's attitude clearly upset Queenie. The country would surely be better served by a 'first family' not at war with itself.

She opened the phone directory in her personal smartphone, the one Minnow and co had no idea she owned. The list of guild contacts filled the screen. She tapped one.

'Ali? Hi, how are you?

'Yes, great, thanks, I've got a sneaky new pattern for the next project—

'Uh, huh, Liverpool, that's right. Anyway, I have a question. Are you still with CLW?

'The new Marmite? Whoo, that was you? I love it...

'So, I was wondering, do you have anyone on the staff by the name of Deborah Chandler?'

CHAPTER ELEVEN

Queenie sat in the VIP Gallery overlooking the Commons Chamber, her knitting on her lap. She could see the massive chair she'd sat in last week. *I must have looked a right pillock,* she thought. *Now then, Queenie girl, sort out that language. You might be meetin' a real queen soon. Hai'm shure hay presented hay ridiculous visarge.* She giggled.

Queenie picked up the needles and turned her attention to the goings on downstairs. She could see Gerald down there, in the big chair, telling people when it was their turn to speak. Minnow was sat next to Doug Sideworth with a pile of papers. Caroline was with someone Queenie didn't recognise, pointing at the screen in front of them both.

Queenie had one of those screens too. It was built into the woodwork in front of her, just like the ones downstairs were built into the back of the bench in front. That was except for the front benches; they had to share screens on little sticks like the door seats on a plane.

They'd explained to everyone on the tour that in the

old days the session's work was on bits of paper, and the only technology down there was little loudspeakers in the backs of the benches for people to hear with. They'd put the screens in because it was easier to alter things that way. Now, if something important came up and a new person needed to say something, they just edited it in the computer room and everyone could see it. The little speakers were still in the backs, so you had to lean forward a bit to see who was next, then lean back a bit to hear them. It meant everybody down there was bobbing to and fro like a load of blooming rocking horses. Caroline had said it helped to keep you awake.

This was the first day of everyone meeting together. The reps had had their inductions separately to Queenie and the ministers; their jobs were different, so it made sense to do that, Gerald had told her. Back when it was old democracy, there'd been six hundred and fifty MPs and they all did everything—you could represent a place and be a minister too. But then, how much actual representing did you do when you was busy ministering? Gerald had put some numbers up on a screen and told them that with the money the country saved on elections and party workers and political advisers—and changing everything whenever a new lot got in just so they could say it was changed, never mind if it was good or not—they'd been able to budget for another fifty people. That meant the ones who oversaw the ministries didn't let any constituencies down by being too busy to bother.

The reps came to the House one week a month with the things their local people wanted done. It all got argued about, and the specialists said whether it was possible. The ministers argued about that and made the civil servants do it sometimes. The reps went and told their locals what was happening...and she watched it all. *A ceremonial watching brief*, Gerald had called it. She represented all the normal, ordinary people who could come and listen but normally didn't because they had jobs and lives and stuff.

She looked around the gallery. Quite a lot of journalists. Apparently it was unusual to have an important debate on the first proper working day, and this one was going to be important. She tried again to concentrate.

The Sideworth man was standing up. He looked a bit nervous. Gerald nodded to him and said out loud, 'The Honourable Minister for Employment!' He nodded again. Queenie decided he looked almost human. Was that a tiny tweak of his mouth? Blimey, the man was trying to do an encouraging smile.

Doug cleared his throat and looked at some paper he was holding. 'The issue has, uh, this issue was, has been raised in'—he looked at Minnow, who pointed to something on the paper—'one hundred and forty-three constituencies.' There was some shuffling and whispering on the benches and Gerald put on a fierce face and looked around.

'All the reps whose constituents made significant complaints before the new administration have been advised and should all be here...?' He'd made this bit sound like a question and there was a sprinkle of nods, waves and harrumphings. He went on. 'But it has the potential to affect the whole country, so we want to have overspill in the Lords Chamber listening by'—he consulted his paper again—'closed video link.'

He looked to Gerald, who did the tweak thing again.

'The complaint is that jobs are being lost to

technology.' Doug sounded a bit better now; his voice was louder, less quavery. Queenie wondered if he'd ever had to speak to a lot of people before...well, if any of them had. Maybe some of them were teachers, that might help. But she'd be terrified. It had been bad enough squeaking a few *I will*s out, but having to remember what you needed to say? She felt sorry for the poor man, even if he was a bit rude.

'Companies are saying they can keep prices down by reducing staffing levels, but so many jobs are being lost that local businesses are reporting reduced revenue.' He'd read that bit. He looked up from his paper. 'And people are complaining about not having a human being to interact with. It's not just commercial enterprises with a bottom line to protect.' He'd stopped reading, this was him talking, and he was sort of quoting her! *Good for you, keep going, chummie.*

'Local government and public services are doing it too. You can report a problem with your drains, call the police to an incident, even call an ambulance or book into a hospital casualty department, for goodness' sake, without ever dealing with a person. Even if it makes sound business sense for companies with shareholders, people want human contact in a crisis.'

He stopped again and looked at his papers. A few *hear hears* and *quite rights* and *yesses* wafted up to Queenie's vantage point.

Doug looked up again. 'The discussions we've had in committee have centred on notifications of a union-led general strike ballot.' There were gasps now. And he was reading again. 'Under legislation inherited from old democracy, because it was felt to be in the public interest, strikes are only legal if a postal ballot is taken and a majority of those who vote are in favour. This process is under way within several unions and is likely to take approximately four weeks. We must be prepared for the eventuality that the strike is approved.'

Someone on an opposite bench waved a hand and Gerald looked over.

'The Honourable Representative for Hartlepool?'

'Can we ask questions now or wait till the end?'

'That is a decision for the Honourable Minister for Employment, who may wish to complete his oration at this time.'

'Uh, no, that's okay, go ahead.'

Gerald addressed the House as a whole. 'Please try to remember however, from now on, that you have a button on your screens to press to alert us that you have a question. That way, whomever is speaking knows you are waiting but has the advantage of finishing a thought before deferring.'

A woman in a green trouser suit flapped her hands. 'I'm sorry, I forgot.'

Doug smiled, for the first time. 'We're all learning as we go. If you'd pressed the button I'd have forgotten what it was for anyway and panicked.'

Aw, he's getting nicer. A few people giggled and somebody muttered, 'Hear hear'. Then they all laughed.

Gerald ahem'd. 'Your question, ma'am?'

'Oh, yes, what form would the strike take? I mean the people who are out of jobs can't strike, and the computers do most of it anyway.'

'That's exactly what we've been discussing.' Doug had put his papers down now. 'Most automated systems have a few human troubleshooters, plus several organisations have seen the writing on the wall and want something done before their jobs go. So if it comes off there'll be a financial loss for the companies who still have workers, which might hasten their decision to automate. The systems already in place may not suffer at all. It is possible that the employees left in those posts may merely demonstrate their own redundancy.' Doug looked at the screen in front of him. 'I've got a blinking light, is that a question?'

Gerald nodded. 'The Honourable Representative for Chorley.'

'Does that mean the strike won't do any harm?'

'We don't know at this stage. It depends somewhat whether citizens get behind it or not. If we have streets full of demonstrations in support up and down the country, we'll know that the people have spoken. If, on the other hand, the only thing that happens is that more workers put their jobs on the line, we'll have to consider the automated systems a success and look to other forms of job creation.'

He looked down again. 'The Honourable Representative for Harrow?' His questioning look to Gerald brought forth an actual, real smile. *Blimey.*

'Does that mean that you...we...the ministry...is in support of the strike?'

Doug checked a page. 'The view we came to is that the issue at stake is one which clearly affects a representative portion of the country. So long as we can ensure no emergency or essential services will be put at risk, we should view it as a fact-finding event. We will have a better idea of the will of the people after it than we do now. It will be legal; our task will be to make it safe. We are working with the Home Office and security services to create a committee to plan for public order and, as I understand it, any representative who wishes will be able to audit its proceedings. But the message we wish you to convey to your constituencies is that the government shares their concerns and will be seeing any *legal* industrial action as an information-gathering exercise.'

He looked at Gerald and sat down. *Well done, ducks.* Queenie wondered if she'd be able to listen to the committee.

'Thank you for an admirable maiden speech.' Gerald managed to impersonate a mother hen without twitching a muscle. How could someone built like a poker whose face never moved let you know exactly what he was thinking? 'The Chamber is now open for general discussion. Remember your buttons, honourable ladies and gentlemen...'

Doug sat in the House cafe, his hands round a mug of tea-you-could-stand-a-spoon-in. It contained three sugars. *Sorry, Katie love, I'll cut the sugar back down tomorrow; it's just been a bit of a big day.* His hands had almost stopped shaking.

People he barely recognised had given him thumbs ups and high fives and slaps on the back all the way from the Chamber back to the cafe. It was nice, but he doubted they were actually impressed. Most likely just glad it had been him and not them. Gerald had said he'd made a decent fist of it, though, which was probably as close as he got to effusive.

Now he watched the view from his favourite spot by

the window and wondered what happened next.

A rattle of crockery brought him back into the room as Queenie and Minnow joined him.

'Did you get the real teapot tea?' Queenie settled next to him in conspiratorial mode. 'I've told them to offer it to everyone, but Minnow here still likes his fancy Earl Grey in a tea bag, don't you, dear?'

Minnow stirred his tea methodically. 'I thought you did very well,' he said to the cup in front of him. 'Concise, accurate. You got their agreement for a possibly controversial course of action.'

'Oh yes, well done!' Queenie put her hand over Doug's as it cradled the mug. 'I was really impressed. Have you done lessons for it? You know, public speaking?'

'Yes, I mean, no.' Doug wasn't sure which question to answer first. 'Yes, it's your teapot tea—lovely, reminds me of...of home and family.' He smiled at her hand round his. He'd stopped shaking for real now. 'And no, I've never addressed more than a couple of people in the office before, except a wedding speech once.' He looked down at Queenie. 'Thank you. You're very kind. It was a bit nerve-racking. And Minnow, you're a marvel. Thank you too.' The lad's eyes lifted from his mug. He'd fished out his tea bag and now the lemon slice was balanced on his teaspoon.

'The right information is all you need.'

'Yes, but you gave me the confidence to use it.'

The lad shrugged. 'Maybe. I'm glad you think so.' Doug watched as he placed the lemon slice next to the tea bag on his saucer. *Seems like we've all got our problems, Katie, love. Perhaps mine aren't any bigger than anyone else's.*

'Ooh, Minnow, I've been meanin' to ask you.'

'Yes?'

The lad could look at Queenie, Doug realised. He wondered if everyone trusted her right away.

'Did you ever get to see my little Sammy again?'

Minnow blushed. 'Well, um, sort of. We were both going to a gamers' convention at the weekend so we, you know, kind of, met up. She might come over one night this week. Oh, to compare strategies and stuff.'

Queenie beamed. 'I knew it! You'll be good for each other, you will.'

'We're not...dating, or anything...'

Queenie looked at Doug and winked. For the first time since he'd lost Katie, Doug felt an actual, real smile come to his lips. He looked from face to face. 'I'm not so sure. Somehow, if Queenie's had anything to do with it, I think you might find you probably are.'

CHAPTER TWELVE

Gerald watched Minnow pull the slice of lemon from his Diet Coke and place it on the table. 'Lemon goes in hot things, not cold?' he enquired.

'Food rule,' muttered Minnow, clearly agitated.

'It's a new barman tonight, sorry, I'll remember to specify next time.' Caroline rose to fetch a napkin from the bar. She retrieved the lemon and disposed of it with a quick whisper to the hapless barman. It was the quickest way to move on to matters in hand and Gerald was appreciative, although nothing would, of course, be said.

The bar was filling with excited new reps, all full of their first real day's work. For those who lived too far away to commute on the weeks they were required in Westminster, this would become their watering hole. Until the workload became too great, at least. They were walking distance from Portcullis House, where most of them were billeted, and they could let off a little steam. The after-work alcoholic debrief wasn't exactly encouraged, but it offered a useful opportunity to spot potentially troublesome egos, so it wasn't discouraged either.

The hum of chatter also made it as good an environment for off-the-record chats in the evening as it was at lunchtime. There was so much less chance of being overheard when you hid in plain sight.

'Sideworth ended up in the deep end after all, then?' Caroline voiced what they were all thinking.

'Sod's law,' said Minnow. 'Move him out of the firing line and the game follows him.'

'He produced a solid enough performance.' Gerald sipped his coffee. 'We've seen worse on a first day.'

'Yes, but this could get ugly,' Caroline added. 'He was only convincing because he has no idea what's coming. The last thing we need is a dipso in charge when this thing goes pear-shaped.'

'Well, my dear.' He watched Caroline wince. He knew he'd get away with it, although only just, but then he only goaded her when he thought she was at fault. 'You argued for the move from Treasury to Employment and it's too late now. You will just have to ensure he's up to it.'

She sighed. 'I can leave Queenie to her own devices for a while and shadow him instead, I suppose.'

'How is she doing?'

'Oddly enough, quite well. The husband could be a bit of a liability but she's happy to travel without him. She's lost some of the anxiety, started to take an interest...you know, I think she might be okay.'

'She's started trying to talk posh.' Minnow looked up from his glass. 'It's a bit weird.'

'I've told her to try a bit less hard with that.' Caroline laughed. 'It's a sight worse than the original version, so we're working on just remembering not to swear in front of foreign dignitaries instead.'

'I like her,' added Minnow. 'She's, um, you know, thoughtful.'

'Yes, maybe we got *one* right this time.'

A voice rose above the hubbub at the bar, a music hall Brummie accent. 'I say, I say, I say, when is a biscuit tin like a fountain? When it's a square tin!'

As one, the Cabinet Support Team glanced towards Andy Carswell.

'Square tin, squirtin', geddit?' He jollied his audience along with an invitation to try the accent for themselves. A few people tittered.

Caroline met Gerald's eye. 'Yip, clown.'

'We can work with that.'

'I hope so, it's a bit relentless.'

'Early days.' He turned to Minnow. 'How is the emergency committee coming along?'

'Getting there, I've run a small program to identify the individuals with the widest spread of expertise from Employment, Industry, Home and Defence. They can brief the reps most affected to talk directly with union bosses and the larger companies in their areas, keep everyone on side...the people stuff. The main issue is keeping essential services running. As soon as you ask the brass whether their systems are up to it they tell you it'll be fine because managers can take over.' Minnow took a swig of his Coke. 'It's never fine.' He licked his lips. 'All systems have bugs, and managers aren't systems people.'

'What do you see as a solution?'

'I'd like authority to, um, tap into some of the systems. I know we don't usually do clandestine stuff, answerable to the people and all that, but with a bit of time I could access the emergency services, water, power grids, etcetera, and keep a watching brief, spot any problems.'

'It's a big ask.' Caroline looked from Minnow to Gerald. 'We stopped sneaking into people's computers when we dumped the oligarchies.'

'There are people who would like to see that particular route restored to us, anyway.' Gerald thought aloud. 'Generally we'd need a House discussion, a committee, voting, permission from a majority of reps.'

'But if we publicised that we don't think the emergency service computers are up to the job'—Caroline appeared to continue his thought process—'we're making the unions' case for them.'

'Why can't we do that?' Minnow put his glass to one side and produced a small smartphone from his pocket. He swiped to a page and began typing. 'I can put together a whole list of reasons for—'

'Because we'd be seen to be taking sides.' Gerald sighed. 'We have to stay outside the argument or we risk looking like we're backing public versus private sectors, protecting government jobs.'

'Or vice versa,' Caroline added. 'The people have to have a chance to speak. We can't just tell either sector to dump their computers and re-employ humans without a remit.'

'But we have a remit!' Minnow's frustration was beginning to show in his voice. A few people looked round from the bar. He lowered his voice again. 'Public safety. We know the systems aren't up to it; most of them are just glorified trials. The drive to save money means they always dump jobs without proper testing.'

'We don't override the will of the people any more, Minnow, even if it's for their own good.' Gerald's softened his voice. 'I know you know that, so I don't need to quote chapter and verse of all the administrations that tried it and got overthrown in the end.'

Caroline placed her elbows on the table and leaned forward to put her chin in her hands. 'We have no choice but to run with the Commons line that the strike will be "interesting".' Her voice was low. 'That way we don't take sides. But that doesn't mean we couldn't, *engineer*, some of the outcomes. Minnow, could you do that?'

'What do you mean?'

'If you did, uh, hack...is that the word?' Minnow nodded. 'Into the essential services, purely in the interests of public safety, naturally.'

Gerald and Minnow nodded. 'Naturally,' they muttered, together.

'Would it be possible for one or two messages to maybe go astray? I mean, nobody would die, but perhaps an industry boss wouldn't get his theft report logged? Could a fancy road of mansions have a power cut for half an hour?'

'Oof.' Minnow gave Gerald a questioning look.

'I think we might have to say, right now, that any behaviour of that type would be reprehensible in the extreme.'

'Naturally.' Caroline sat back again. 'I apologise for even having the thought.'

'However,' Gerald continued, 'in the interests of public safety—and because we have, uh, intelligence, that some essential service computers might not be up to the job—I think Minnow's watching brief could be allowable. And of course, in order to keep the nation safe he might need to intervene here and there.'

Caroline's eyes widened. Her surprise was genuine, Gerald knew. He had hired her for her Machiavellian tendencies, twinned with an unerring eye for human behaviour. But he generally refused permission for her wilder ideas.

'How long do you need, Minnow?'

'Could take a while, I should probably start right away.'

'We can't have this sort of activity in government offices.'

'I'd thought of that. I can cloak the server I have at home, should be up to the task.'

'Good man.'

'There's just one more thing.'

'Yes?'

'You've put a rather brilliant programmer into Education, would it be possible to...?'

Caroline grinned. 'Ah yes, young Samantha. This wouldn't all be a ploy to get us to invite her into your boudoir, would it, Minnow?'

'No, uh, well, no, no! It's just, well, she's good. At the stuff we'll need. Honestly. Two of us working on it would be quicker, more accurate, better...'

'Hmm.' Caroline looked at Gerald. 'What do you think?'

'I don't see why not. We can keep her Education workload pretty low without causing suspicion, I think.'

Minnow beamed. 'I'll get started then.'

'Just set the gear up for now. If we are going to plead national interest if this ever comes out, we should wait for the ballots and only deal with the systems of outfits that are striking.'

'Roger that.' Minnow produced a mock salute, knocking the remains of his Coke to the floor. 'Oh, sorry, did I splash you? I'll get a cloth.'

As Minnow leapt from his seat to do just that, Gerald eyed Caroline. 'You might have to watch those two.'

'I won't need to, Queenie's on it already.'

Queenie bundled through the door to the Buck Place flat with an ornate wooden box in her hands and her knitting bag flung over her shoulder.

'Thank you, dearie, it's perfect,' she called over her shoulder to Eugene, who was beaming with pleasure.

'That's okay, ma'am, I'm glad you like it.'

'It's brilliant. Bert!' she yelled as the door closed behind her.

'What?'

'Come here, I've got something to show you.'

'I'm watchin' telly.'

'Oh, for goodness' sake.' She put the knitting down by the chair she had adopted and centred the box on the coffee table. Then she perched on the edge of her chair and regarded the box and its environs.

'Hmm.' She tilted her head to the left, then to the right, then she looked around the rest of the room. *Would it fit on the mantelpiece?* She stood up again and retrieved the box. *Or the windowsill?* She tried the mantel first. It was a bit too deep for the shelf. She moved it to the window and stood back. She walked back to the door and looked at it from there. Then she picked it up and put it back on the coffee table.

'What the...what are you doin'?' Bert appeared in the inner doorway.

'I thought you was watching telly.'

'Ads came on. What's that?' He indicated the box. 'Battered old thing, ain't it?'

'That, I'll have you know, Bertram Mason, is a historic thing and very posh.'

'Prehistoric more like. What is it?'

'It's a despatch box from the Parliament.' Putting on her special voice to say this, Queenie was disappointed to find she'd not used any words with aitches in. 'An old one. Eugene found it for me. They had to replace it back in democracy 'cos one of the prime ministers covered it in pen marks.' She looked more closely at the lid. 'You can sort of see where they tried to scrub it all off but they took the varnish off and then it never looked quite right. That's what Eugene told me anyway, when he gave it to me.'

'So you've got an old box that some idiot drew all over. What's it for?'

'It's for the teapot!' Queenie undid the clasp, opened the lid as reverently as she could and lifted out her teapot. 'Oh, look at you, Bert, shut your mouth.' She laughed her proper laugh. The big one, the one that everyone at Tesco's knew. It wasn't making her cough like it used to. Funny that.

'You've gone stark starin' bonkers, Queenie girl, why do you need a box for the teapot?'

'You'll have to start talking a bit more respectful-like, you know, Bert. I know you think I'm stupid but when we go places people are gonna call me "ma'am".'

'I'll call you late for bleedin' dinner if you don't tell me why you need a bleedin' box for your teapot before the Bond film starts again.'

'And swearin', we have to stop that too.'

'Ho yus, Milady, hov course, Milady, kiss your bleedin' arse, Milady. Maybe I won't come with you when you go out and about and then you won't be ashamed of me, like our Debs is, eh? Will that do?' He turned to go back to his chair and his telly.

'Listen, Bert.' Queenie's voice softened. 'I'm sorry they took me and they didn't take you.' He kept his back to her but she guessed he was listening. 'I don't know why and I haven't had a chance to ask. Maybe we don't want to know. But it's nice here, ain't it? We get to live somewhere posh for three years, you've got your chair and your telly, you can come with me or not as you please, and I'm out of the house all day again like it used to be at Tesco's. You've got it made, me old mucker, you're even gettin' chauffeured to bloomin' darts and doms, so I don't see why you have to yell and swear all the time. That's all I'm sayin'.

'And the Bond film will be on again. Whichever one it is, you've seen it a hundred times. So why don't you come an' sit down an' I'll tell you all about everything that's happening and why I've got the box.'

He turned back to face her. 'Go on, then.' He looked at his watch. 'It's over in a minute anyway, get the talkin' done with.'

'Only if you come and sit down. I'll make us some tea.'

'Don't you 'ave people for that now?' The sarcastic tone had nearly gone, but not quite.

'Only when we're out and about... Listen Bert, how's that cough of yours? Mine's been goin' down the last few days.'

'I 'aven't really thought about it. I suppose maybe it's not so bad.'

That's right, get the man talkin' about his health, works every time. She indicated one of the man-eating comfy chairs and he approached it gingerly. She'd not seen him get eaten by one yet, which made her wonder if he'd been having a bit of a play with the fancy furnishings while she was out.

'I reckon maybe the air's a bit better here. I'm going to ask about it. See if we can't get someone to check what's wrong with the Peabodys—maybe there's damp or mould or something. Have you noticed, everybody coughs there but no one does here?'

'That'll be all the fancy food and private bloomin' doctors they got in this part of town.' Bert's grumbling had taken on a more automatic tone, more...*normal*.

'Now then, you know we all gets our turns. Most of them are just like us.'

'That Eugene isn't, he's as posh as they come.'

'Yes and he works for you and me, how about that?'

'Him and his stupid hair and shiny shoes. I don't like the way he looks at me.'

'Maybe that's because all he hears you do is yell and swear. Try talking to him, he's a nice boy.'

'And as for that stuck-up Caroline cow...'

'There you go again, she's nice too, you won't give anyone a chance who didn't spend their workin' life covered in diesel.'

Bert harrumphed. And pointed to the box. 'Well?'

'It's for when we go places. They can't find another teapot anywhere with the tanning in it. Eugene's got a new one and he's taken it home. He says he's goin' to make tea in it every day and never wash it until I'm happy with it, but for now, this goes with us all over the place. Isn't that sweet of him? Look!' She opened the box and took the teapot out, putting it carefully on the coffee table. 'It's got a waterproof lining, he did that himself, and a little pocket in the lid for a tea cosy.'

Bert looked. Then he laughed. 'You mean to tell me you're goin' to drag that mouldy old thing round the world, demandin' tea from a dirty teapot in all the bleedin' palaces and embassies and goodness knows where else? Other countries are goin' to think we're mad.'

'I don't see why. Eugene told me you can take whatever you want. He said there's a king of some island or other who has his chair taken everywhere…and he reckons the last proper queen we had probaly took her own toilet seat! So there!' She stuck her tongue out at Bert by way of dramatic punctuation.

'Blimey.' He picked up the teapot and clambered out of his chair relatively adeptly. *Caught you.* 'You goin' to stick your tongue out at all them foreign dignitary types instead of swearin'? That's okay, is it? Glad I know. I'll practise while the kettle's on.'

CHAPTER THIRTEEN

'Hello, luv, where's Caroline?' Queenie was surprised to see Gerald's face at the door when Eugene ushered in her morning meeting attendees. And behind him, that bloke with the stupid ties.

'Caroline has another brief for the next few days, and I'm here with the Foreign Minister. Do you remember Andy Carswell?' There was some general nodding. Queenie was getting good at the all-purpose nod. 'We are ready to plan your first overseas visit.'

'Ooh, that's excitin', come and sit down.' She gestured towards the comfy chairs, slightly rearranged to create a focal point at the despatch box. 'I'll get us some tea. Or would you like coffee?'

'I've asked Eugene to organise refreshments, so we can get down to business right away.'

'Oh, sorry.' Queenie put her hand to her mouth. 'It's a *meetin'* not a visit. I'll get used to it soon.'

'I'm sure you will, ma'am.' Gerald was polite enough,

but she couldn't shake the feeling that the ma'am stuff was a teensy bit, you know, sarcastic.

'So, where are we all goin'?' She saw Andy eye the box with curiosity and just stopped herself in time. *This is a meetin, Queenie, old girl—try and concentrate.* 'Oh, before we start, is it okay if I knit? Caroline doesn't mind and it helps me concentrate on what you're saying.'

'Feel free, ma'am, if it helps.'

'Thank you, ducks.' *Was that a slight wince?* 'I mean Gerald, no Chief Secretary, um, what should I call you to be proper?'

'Gerald will be fine, thank you.'

Queenie turned her attention to Andy as Eugene slid noiselessly into the room with a tray of coffee, tea and shortbread biscuits. 'We haven't talked proper yet, have we? But I expect we'll be best friends by the time we get back from wherever we're goin'... Oh, do you like these biscuits? Eugene gets them and they're lovely, I'm goin' to ask him to sneak some in with the teapot when we go abroad.'

The man smiled at her and took one. 'A veritable repast!' he exclaimed, taking a bite. His tie had some sort of puppies on today.

She looked from Andy's face to Gerald's. 'Eh?'

'He means thank you for the biscuit.' Gerald's tone didn't waver, and Queenie wasn't sure if she needed to feel stupid or not.

'A phrase my father used on all comestible occasions.' Andy was brushing shortbread crumbs from his tie now.

Queenie leant over to Gerald and whispered, 'Is he English?'

Gerald offered her a tightening of the lips.

'It's possible, Mr Carswell, that we'd get along a little faster if we were able to speak with you, rather than your estimable parent.'

'Sorry.' Andy was rustling about in the huge briefcase he'd brought with him now. 'He had a maxim for almost every occasion and when you're on the road, meeting different people all the time, persuading them to keep you on the top of the sales leaderboard, well, it becomes a bit of a habit.' He did something weird with his eyebrows and waggled the shortbread biscuit next to his mouth. 'If you've heard this story before, don't stop me, because I'd like to hear it again.'

Queenie and Gerald stared in silence.

'Groucho Marx...?' Andy deflated as the silence deepened.

'You may want to consider avoiding obscure cultural references on your travels.' Gerald brushed a stray shortbread crumb from his trouser leg, where it had settled after its temporary impersonation of a cigar. 'Not everyone shares the British love of, uh, *jokes*.'

'It is a bit scary, isn't it?' Queenie proffered the plate of biscuits. 'I don't know what to say half the time either. Have another bikky.'

'Oh, I'm not scared.' Andy bristled as he retrieved some papers and squared them together by banging the edges on the coffee table. They made an oddly loud *plock plock* sound. 'Just making conversation, breaking the ice, putting people at ease, setting up the positive feedback scenario. When I'm on the road I find that—'

'It's not much of a bleedin' conversation if no one knows what you're on about, dearie...' Queenie began, then had a thought and turned to Gerald. 'Is that why he's doing foreign stuff? Cos nobody here can understand him anyway?'

Gerald coughed politely. 'Not exactly.'

Andy *plocked* a bit more, picked up a pen, glared at Queenie and fell silent.

She picked up her knitting, began a row and said, 'Righty-ho, Gerald, we're listening.'

'Thank you.' He picked up some notes and scanned the first page. 'As you know, you'll be making some overseas visits to accompany trade delegations where we think the presence of our republic's dignitaries'—Queenie looked up and opened her mouth to speak—'important people'—she mouthed *dig-nit-ar-y* and made a mental note to write it down later—'might help ensure profitable trading links.'

'We're not important, though, are we?' Queenie's eyes lifted from her knitting, transfixed by Andy, who had finished playing with his pen and was fiddling with his watch. 'We're just the people doing the job this time round. We're no more important than anyone else, that's the point, isn't it?'

'Indeed, you are correct in that observation.' Gerald's eyes followed the watch-twiddling too. 'And with the nations that have followed our lead into modern sortition, there is little need for such nonsense. We trade with most of them on the basis of mutual gain and cooperation. There are some pockets of democratic oligarchy left in the world, however—as you know—and one or two archaic absolute monarchies. These are mostly smaller nations formed as a result of the breakup of the Middle East, plus a Pacific Island or two. While these countries represent smaller markets, we still choose to trade with them, and it's important to remember that their administrations are far more prone to make decisions based on flattery than on accounting.'

'They like to think we think they're important enough for visits from people they think we think are important!' Queenie grinned. 'Is that it?'

'In a nutshell, ma'am.' Gerald's lip twitched. Was he trying not to smile?

'So, we go along and show them we're not as green as we're cabbage-looking.' Andy's hands were still now. Queenie couldn't help wondering if he'd be less anxious if he was a knitter.

'Try that in English, me old mate, there's a dear, I'm not edumacated enough for the fancy stuff.'

Andy sighed. 'We go along and talk about how advanced we are, tell them they'll be stuck in the Stone Age without us.'

'Not exactly,' Gerald said. 'We do try to portray our system as one that works well, by speaking of our economy as safe and reliable, etcetera, but we also try not to insult our hosts.'

'Fair enough, takes all sorts I suppose, all part of life's rich tapestry and all that.' Andy returned to his pen and papers. Queenie wondered what he was writing. And what else was in the enormous briefcase. Lots more stupid ties, maybe.

'Mostly, you'll be making small talk with minor dignitaries and politicians.' Gerald was addressing her now. 'Generally, there will be one major banquet in the presence of another head of state and several visits to places of interest and potential business partners. The obligatory photo shoot wearing a hard hat at some half-built joint project, an exchange of gifts of some sort and back on the plane home.' He turned to Andy. 'Until you've got used to it, the best idea is to say as little as possible and try not to upset anyone.'

Queenie laughed her new posh laugh. 'You want me to say as little as possible? You got the wrong girl for that job, mate.'

Gerald inclined his head slightly and regarded her as she continued to giggle. 'On the contrary, ma'am, you were chosen for your ability to put people at their ease with small talk.'

'And me?' Andy awaited his compliment like a puppy spying a treat. 'What does a travelling salesman from Solihull bring to the table if you reckon my people skills are so crap?'

'Ah, Mr Carswell, we know that you have people skills. Your job is not easy to succeed at, you meet a lot of people who think they're important and you do break the ice and clearly you make sales. We just have to break you of the habit of needing a script...or props...' Andy stopped rummaging in his briefcase as it fell to the floor. All the contents would have fallen out, if there had been any.

'I'm usually demonstrating something.' He had deflated a little. Queenie strangled the *there there, ducks* before it reached her lips.

'We'll be fine.' She compromised on a soothing tone. 'I'll look after you, we're goin' together, ain't we? Here you go...' She rummaged in her knitting bag for the notebook she'd started carrying around so she could write the long words down. 'Have a scribble on this, it's a bit smaller, it can go in your pocket. Draw me a picture if you like.'

Andy took the notebook with a hand that was shaking. *Is he furious or terrified?* 'And if that don't work for you,' she added, 'we'll just teach you to knit!' No new polite laugh this time, the guffaw was back. Gerald's mouth twitched. 'Now, where are we goin' first?'

'We're starting you both off with an easy visit.'

'Ooh, good, there you go, Andy, duck, it's goin' to be easy.'

Andy began to scribble. Queenie would have placed a bet he'd written *easy*. Maybe she wasn't the stupid one.

'There will be no new contracts to win and a similar political system to ours. As you probably know, Canada embraced modern sortition not long after we did here in Britain. They chose, however, to retain the British head of state. It's a small population; they considered the expense of duplication a waste of taxpayers' money. They were used to having a Governor General, representing the previous monarch, and the Canadian republicans who wanted to break from the UK back then were satisfied with the removal of a hereditary monarch here—'

'We're goin' to Canada?' Queenie was incredulous.

'Yes, ma'am, you are their head of state too.'

'My Deborah went there once on holiday. She sent me an' Bert a postcard of a chipmunk. Oh, will I get to see a chipmunk? I'd love that!'

Andy was still doodling. *What's the bettin' he's just written chipmunk?* 'When do we go?'

'The week after next, it's a standard fixture for new incumbents...' *I hope he's written* in-cum-bent, *another one to look up.* 'So the diary date never varies. By the time you get back we will have some dates for you for further assignments.'

'Bert'll be happy to have the place to himself so soon.' Queenie looked at Andy. 'You an' me, we'll do fine. We just 'ave to stick to talkin' about the weather.' He scowled at her. *Maybe he ain't got a posh phrase about the weather.*

'Your itineraries are here.' Gerald handed them both a plastic sleeve of papers. 'Reception and banquet with the current Governor General at Rideau Hall in Ottawa—he's a new incumbent too—then a photo op at Niagara Falls, open a new clean energy plant in Hamilton, that'll be your hard hat moment.' He referred to the next page. 'Visit a new potash mine in Saskatchewan, admire some green initiatives at the oil sands in Alberta, then finish up with a dragon boat race in Vancouver. Should be fun.'

'I thought Niagara Falls was in America,' Andy said. 'It is in the *Superman* film.'

Gerald looked at his watch. 'I have to go,' he said. 'All the information you need is in your package...*including a map*. Do you have any questions?' He looked at Andy, who had stopped scribbling and started reading.

'No, this all seems pretty clear.'

'Even upside down? Good. Queenie?'

'There's just one thing.'

'I thought there might be. We are arranging to take the teapot. '

'No, it's not that.'

'What then?'

'What's a potash?'

Andy collected a cup of coffee from the counter and looked around at the available seating. Most of the tables were full, since the second House session of the new intake would be starting shortly. He was beginning to get used to the routine: meetings in the mornings, debates in the afternoon. Of course it would all change next week when the reps went back to their constituencies; the place would be a sight quieter for a start. And it would all change again the week after, when he'd be on his first mission. Then he'd feel important. He'd been quite insulted by the way Gerald and Queenie talked down to him. He was good at what he did; he just couldn't measure his performance here by a sales chart. He wasn't quite sure how to succeed without a league table to top and a head full of all the right answers and he felt a bit daft right now, to be honest. He'd almost been shown up by a silly old checkout chick who seemed to be taking it all in her stride. Here he was, a regional top seller three years running, and some of the stuff was going over his head. But the gags always saw him through, so if he relied on them a bit more than normal...well, they'd just have to get used to it.

The table by the window had some space. He recognised the chap who'd spoken yesterday and the good-looking woman who'd shown them round last week. He'd have remembered their names if he'd taken Beth's advice and made notes. He'd write things down today, for sure. Now he came to think of it, he still had the old bat's notebook.

'Hello, hello, hello, evenin' all!' He approached the table and performed a leg bend and small bow. 'Room for a small one?' They looked up and smiled at him.

'Andy? Yes, hello again, we've hardly met since last week, have we?' The woman gestured towards a seat. 'Do you know Doug? Employment. He spoke yesterday.'

'Yes! Fine performance, man, bravo, I'm not looking forward to being in your shoes.' *Doug. Right. Got it.*

The guy seemed pleased. 'Thanks, I'm glad it's over.'

'All part of life's rich tapestry, eh?'

They both gave him a quizzical look. *Ignorant, the lot of them.*

'Andy's our Foreign Minister,' the woman said to Doug. 'Has Gerald been briefing you on the Canada trip?' Andy nodded. 'Normally it would have been me,' she continued, 'but with Doug here in the middle of an early crisis of sorts, I'm spending some time with him over the next few weeks to help him get up to speed.'

Doug grinned at him. 'Lucky me, eh? You might get the foreign jolly while I get the general strike, but at least I have Caroline for company.' *Caroline, that's it.* 'Who's going with you?'

'I'm not sure. Queenie, certainly. '

'Try not to come back knitting, eh?' Doug laughed and winked at Caroline. 'We'll be thinking of you.'

'I'm sure you'll be fine.' Caroline hadn't returned the wink, or had she? 'Canadians are pretty hard to upset.'

'So I gather. I'm looking forward to it.' Andy suddenly realised he wasn't. He'd impress Beth and Sophie—and had already called work to get the glory story started—but more importantly, this Doug bloke had a head start with Caroline and Andy had a bit of an office Lothario image to live up to. He finished his coffee and stood to leave. 'Although, of course, life is never fair.'

He got the feeling none of the three of them actually knew what he meant.

CHAPTER FOURTEEN

Queenie sat in her usual spot, overlooking the reps as they learned the ropes. She'd seen a week of maiden speeches, hiccups and button bloopers and realised everyone was as clueless as she was. Some of the ministers did fine, like the Employment guy. They were nervous, but they treated it like a job and read their notes and looked at their screens and told the world what was going on in their little corner of things.

She had quite taken to the Health woman. She'd got up and read some stuff about a trial thing in the last administration that made it easier for people who were dying to stay at home. Some mobile clinic arrangement. It had saved money too. She wanted the reps to take information about it back to their constituencies and see if hospitals and doctors and hospices and the like would be interested.

Queenie had never thought about it before but she supposed when Bert's time came—not that she wished him any harm—he'd want to die in his ratty old chair, not in some nice, clean hospital bed. Perhaps the mobile team could install a bar and the darts and doms league too. She chuckled. She was glad she liked the Health woman. Caroline had said there was no reason why she couldn't mention that cough every resident of the Peabody Buildings had got, and see about getting the estate checked for damp and mould and stuff.

'You're a constituent too,' she'd said. 'You have a right to bring issues that concern you to the House.' Caroline had suggested, though, that she chat with her own rep for Tower Hamlets as well, and get them to find out if other people thought it mattered. 'It has a better chance of getting committee time that way,' she'd said. Queenie wasn't sure she wanted to do that, really. She'd seen her local rep in the cafe and it was Big Doris from the launderette. Queenie reckoned the system might have fallen down a bit there, despite Minnow's best efforts. She'd never heard Big Doris say anything helpful to anyone, and didn't see how a quick tour of Westminster could turn a nasty gossip into a pillar of the community, but there you went, eh? Thankfully she'd not heard her ask a question in the House yet. She supposed there wasn't much call for 'she never folds her bedding, you know' hereabouts, and she'd not heard Doris say much else.

Queenie planned to ask Big Doris about it that afternoon, then go spend a bit of time with the Health Ministry the following week when the reps went home and all the committees started up again. She picked up her knitting as one of the Treasury blokes started droning again. He'd been told off by Gerald once already for Having Opinions. There was even a button on the computer screens for it. Gerald had pressed it earlier on and then stopped the bloke in mid flow to tell everyone what it was. He'd said he hoped to hardly ever have to use it again, that just because you'd been chosen by ballot to do a job for three years didn't make you anything special, and what you thought about this economist's ideas over that one didn't amount to a hill of beans. The bloke'd had the decency to blush. Now he was talking about the figures they'd inherited from the last lot and where savings needed to be made if taxes weren't going to go up.

Queenie was glad she wasn't a rep. She'd have to learn this stuff in case anyone asked about it next week. As it was, all she had to do was listen to a few committees, open a new computerised control centre for a sewage works, and get ready for her first trip abroad.

A northerner had asked a question now. Something about ringfencing local money? She had no idea what that meant but there were loads of lights going off on the screens, and everyone wanted a say. Caroline had told her about that. She said she divided the reps into two groups: the ones who wanted to go back to their local offices next week able to say, 'Oh yes, I've already asked a question in the House,' and the ones who didn't care.

Queenie had asked her which ones were better. She'd grinned. And said, 'It depends what we want them to do.' Which had left her none the wiser.

She wondered which one Doris would be? She couldn't imagine any circumstances in which anyone at the launderette would be asking about budgets and taxes and that, but Caroline said it was about things going to people's heads. Would things go to Big Doris's head? Had things already gone to Queenie's head? Did this whole thing, governing stuff, really turn people nasty? She wondered about her new friends. Little Sammy seemed quite changed for the better, although that might have more to do with the lad, Minnow, than the system that called her here. The rest of the people she'd met seemed ordinary enough, except for that bloke who was coming to Canada with her. She wasn't sure if he was very clever or very stupid, but either way he was firmly in Queenie's *bit of an arse* pigeonhole.

The only person she could think of who'd had stuff go to her head so far was Deborah! But that was okay, she reckoned she'd be seeing more of her daughter now than she ever had at the Peabodys. Maybe she'd invite her and Colin round for tea at the weekend. They could have a proper chinwag. But first, she had to plan her chinwag with Doris. Should she invite her to Buck Place? Maybe not. She didn't want it getting back to the neighbours that things had gone to *her* head. Maybe send a text on the new phone thingy about catching up over a cuppa in the cafe?

Or just find her office and go in? Yes, businesslike and formal, but not swanky. That would do.

'Hello, luvvie, how are you? And you, hi, how's it goin'? Looking forward to gettin' home, are we?' Queenie greeted each of the reps occupying a desk in the cavernous London Constituencies office. She waved at the ones out of earshot while those she addressed directly muttered a chorus of yeses, hellos, you bets and other pleasantries. She perched on the edge of a desk that had an array of photos of children on. 'Oh, look at the little darlin's, yours?' The woman nodded and beamed. 'You gettin' home to them at nights or stayin' here?' Queenie knew most of the London reps were commuting to Westminster on their weeks in the House but wanted to look interested.

'Yes, I'm getting back to them. They're fascinated by Mummy's new job,' the woman said. 'They've been talking about it at news time on the carpet!'

'Oh, news time on the carpet, do they still do that?' Queenie thought back a lot of years. 'My Deborah used to love it, she'd tell all these mad lies about how posh we was and how we'd 'ad a new swimmin' pool built at the weekend. My Bert would yell and tell her not to tell lies so then one week she told them all about him fallin' into the laundry basket on his way in at night after darts and doms!' She let a proper guffaw go and most of the surrounding reps joined in.

'Anyway, I'm looking for Big Dor…um…I'm looking for the Hhonourable Rep for Whitechapel. No, that's not it, is it?' She pulled a folder from her knitting bag and consulted it. 'Tower Hamlets, that's the one.'

The woman with the photos moved one aside and picked up a folder. She looked inside at a little office plan. 'Over there, by the window, third desk from the left.' She pointed across the room.

'Thank you, dearie.' Queenie heaved herself off the desk and began to toddle away. 'You must bring those kiddies of yours to come and see Buck Place. Do they like horses? We can get some carrots maybe and ask if we can feed them, they're just downstairs.'

'That would be lovely. Thank you!'

'Got to keep those carpet stories coming along, eh? I'll, what's the word, *text* you over the weekend.'

For some reason everyone she passed was grinning.

That was weird.

She approached Doris's desk and looked for signs of life.

'Is this Doris from Tower Hamlets?' she asked the chap next door.

He nodded. 'I think she's just in the loo.'

'Thanks darlin'. Oh, there you are, hello Doris! I've come to see how you're gettin' on.'

Doris looked her up and down. Was that a scowl?

'Bit rum this, eh? Look at us from the Peabodys all done up like dogs' dinners and bein' important.'

Doris said nothing.

'How's the launderette? Did they help you find someone to run it while you're here? They told me that's what they do.'

'The launderette is fine. My Sandra is taking good care of it, thank you very much.'

'Oh good, I'm pleased.'

'Why would it matter to you?'

'Well, because we need it, don't we?'

'You don't any more, do you? Landed on your feet all right, haven't you, Queenie Mason? What are you doing here, eh? Come to gloat? Look at you, three years of fancy living and waving at people while some of us have to leave our jobs, work even harder and risk having nothing to go back to.'

'Don't you want to be here, Doris? I'm sure there's a hardship thing you can apply to.'

'Hardship! How dare you, what, you think my Sandra's useless or something?'

'No, it's just—'

'I'll tell you what it's just, it's just stupid, that's what it's just. I don't want to run the bloody country.'

'Well, we all—'

'We all have to do our bit, I know.' Doris sat down hard in the chair behind her desk and folded her arms. 'I can't see what was wrong before. Anyway, what do you want? I'm going home in a minute, then next week I've got to get used to another bleeding office and listen to all the locals whingein'. Like I didn't do that anyway at the launderette.'

'At least now you can do something about it.' Queenie tried a tentative upbeat note.

'Like I care. The last rep did nothing for me.'

'What did you ask him to do?' Queenie was surprised now. She'd not had Big Doris down as a complaining-to-your-rep type at all.

'Nothing, why would I bother? Nobody does anything for the likes of us.'

'They won't if you don't ask, will they?' Queenie decided it was now or never. 'Anyway, I've got a thing we might be able to do for the likes of us. You and me and your Sandra and the kids, everybody…and you can help…'

They'd got in touch, the Provos. Took a few days but there it was. Justin purged his browsing history right away; he'd been an idiot to check his iSawYou inbox at work. In fact, being a bit new at the whole subterfuge thing, he realised he'd probably been an idiot to check it at home as well. Yeah, Pillocks"R"Us HQ just moved to his flat and he would have to move it right out again. Internet cafes from now on.

Except there didn't really need to be a now on, did there? He'd told them where he worked, they'd said thanks, and they'd let him know if he could ever be of service. But if he didn't want to be of service he just needn't check his inbox and then he'd never know. Forget the whole thing. He liked his job.

'How's your cough, Bert?' Queenie poured a cuppa for herself and a beer for him. She even tipped the glass at a forty-five-degree angle to get the head just right, like she'd learned to do as a slip of a girl, moonlighting behind various bars. She'd pretended to have forgotten for years, just to wind him up, but she was in a forgiving mood. For all his faults, maybe Bert was taking to the changes better than some.

'On the up, Queenie lass, on the up.' He folded himself into one of the fancy chairs, regarded the despatch box on the coffee table and picked up his pint glass. 'Came back a bit at darts and doms, but that might have been all the talkin'. The lads took the piss something rotten.'

'I bet they did. Was it nasty?'

'The cough?'

'No, the piss-taking. Do they hate you for moving?'

'Nah, bit jealous like, maybe, but that's all. They're too busy bein' pleased they kept their star player in the league to get too snarky. Mostly they think it's hilarious they took you and turned me down.'

'Charming, I'm sure.'

'Was you expectin' them to be nasty then?'

'Not really. It's just...I went and saw Big Doris today.

Not as, you know, me, well, yes, as me but not this me.' Bert gave her one of his 'stupid cow' eyerolls. 'No, I mean, I didn't go see her as the state thing, I went as a resident of the Peabodys with a cough. *Has hay constit-u-ent.*' She performed a little bow. 'I told her you and me had realised our coughs was better since we moved and maybe there was damp or something that we could get sorted out. I said she could complain to the Health people on behalf of all of us and get something done. Wanted her to ask around a bit when she got back next week.'

'Why can't you do that? You goes to all the committees anyway.'

'That's what she said too but Caroline said it, um, "carries more weight" if it comes from a rep who's heard from constituents than if it's from me because I'm just one person. But since I am also a constituent too, I can ask her to ask them.'

'Can't do any harm, eh? What did she say?' He wiped his third foam moustache away with his sleeve.

'I think she hates me.' Queenie played idly with her almost empty teacup. 'She certainly hates bein' a rep. She said might not have time.' Over went the cup. Queenie gazed at the leaves. 'Sandra's kids got that cough too, you'd think she'd be glad to do something.'

'Sandra's bloke is mixed up with that election rabble, isn't he? Goes to all the demos and protests and that. Didn't they all get that D shaved onto their bonces last year?'

'Oh yeah, I'd forgotten that. But that was just about bein' troublemakers, wasn't it? Any excuse for a ruckus. I don't reckon any of them could tell you what elections was or wasn't good for any more than I could.'

'There's always people who think it was better back then, Queenie lass, whatever they was doin' at the time.'

'Blimey, Bert, movin' here has made you quite the thinker.'

'You reckon? Pour us another beer then, it's good for the brain.'

CHAPTER FIFTEEN

Caroline examined the coffee table. The despatch box sat centre stage, with the bit part players scattered to left and right, along with folders, forms, notes. The knitting bag had been upstaged completely, huddled in a corner.

'Hello, luvvie, I'm nearly ready to go. You comin' with me? That's nice.'

Caroline turned at the sound of Queenie's voice and produced an involuntary little whistle. 'Goodness, you look splendid!'

'Thank you, dearie.' Queenie made a spirited attempt to twirl around given the joint restrictions of thick carpet and unaccustomed heels. 'My Deborah took me shoppin' over the weekend, to the place she gets her *business wear*.' Queenie tossed her head from side to side as she said this, in what, Caroline decided, was a remarkably accurate imitation of her daughter. 'I remembered what you said about plain pastels and matching bags and that.'

'Yes, the old royals knew a thing or two about being photographed.' Caroline smiled. 'And you will do just fine. Did Deborah enjoy the trip?'

'I think so.' Queenie perched on the edge of a chair and picked up a folder from the table as she spoke. 'She wanted to get one of those fascinator things to go with, but I told her you said no hats.'

'That's right, our head of state always goes bareheaded, to make the point that they're not royalty.'

'Yes, I remembered that bit too, told her all about it and she was quite interested. Normally she joins the chorus of "Shut up, stupid, you're going on and bein' stupid again."' Queenie looked up and out of the window at the sound of the horses clattering about below. 'Oh, that reminds me...'

'Yes?'

'Is there any rules about goin' to see the horses? I thought some of the kids what's had to move here with their reps and that, they might like to come and see them on a weekend.'

'What a nice idea. Nobody's asked that before; I'm sure it could be arranged.'

Queenie beamed. 'It's been hard enough for my Bert to get used to movin', I'm sure the kiddies must be a bit, you know, dislocated.'

Caroline smiled. A real one. 'I know what you mean, I'll find out for you. Now, have you had a chance to look over your speech?'

'Yes, I've got it here.' Queenie waved the folder, as if fanning herself. 'I didn't have to learn it by heart, did I?'

'No, it'll be printed on your lectern.' She saw the question brewing in Queenie's eyes. 'The thing you stand in front of, like a pulpit in a church, it's a sort of desk for reading at when you're standing up.'

'Oh, good! Will I be able to hold onto it and keep my balance on these bloomin' heels?' Queenie cast an unhappy glance over her new footwear—primrose yellow to match the suit.

'Yes.' Caroline affected a conspiratorial whisper. 'That's partly the point of them.' They both giggled, then she added, 'We'll get you something a bit more comfortable before you go to Canada, then you won't be looking for lecterns to hang on to all the time.' She winked. 'Anyway, are there any parts of the speech you want to practise before we go?' She sat herself on the edge of another chair and opened her notebook. 'It's going to be pretty straightforward. The car takes us to the new plant. Then there's a small party of managers and engineers who'll greet you and take you on a tour of the new biogas installation. They'll explain it all to you, and you can chat with the workers as you go round if you want. Then back to the main building, where there'll be an audience of staff and the press. You'll make your speech from the lectern, pull a cord and a curtain will draw back, exposing the plaque that says you've opened the facility.'

'Then we get a cup of tea?'

'Almost. There'll be a few photo ops, you with each of the bigwigs by the plaque, then some refreshments for everyone. Then, that's it.'

'Can we take the teapot?'

Caroline's eyes lifted from her notes and she raised an index finger in triumph. 'No need! Eugene got on the phone and said you wanted real tea for all the workers and did they have anyone on the staff with a traditionally dirty teapot at home. You'll never guess—six people came forward, so there will be enough teapots in the kitchen for real tea all round.'

'Ooh, can I do a special thank you to all the teapot people? I'd like that.'

'I don't see why not. Anyway, did you want one more practice before we go?'

'I'm okay with most of it, but there's a couple of bits I don't want to say wrong.' Queenie handed Caroline the paper she'd been retrieving; some of the words had been underlined.

'Ah yes, this one is "anaerobic" and this one's "liquefied biomethane". Do you want to have a go at that sentence?' She handed the speech back to Queenie.

'Might as well, don't want to make a prawn of meself, do I?' Queenie chortled. 'My Bert said if they can make power out of poo we should have one at the Peabodys. Keep all the lights on after everyone's got bladdered on Guinness on payday.' She stood and tottered to the mantelpiece. 'I'm goin' to pretend this is my *lectern.*' She stood up a little straighter, placed her left hand on the mantel, raised the printed speech in front of her and moved it to and fro, searching for the perfect placement. She executed a half turn towards Caroline and shook her chins for a moment.

'With the opening of this state-of-the-art anaerobic digestion plant, Thames Water will treble the amount of liquefied biomethane available for transport fuel, thus creating the most cost-effective and environmentally friendly sewage treatment system in our nation.' She regarded Caroline over the top of her paper. 'How was that?'

'Perfect!'

'Hhand hhay big thank you to everyone who brought in a teapot!'

'How much farther is it?'

'Half an hour or so. We'll turn off the M40 in a minute.'

'I hope they've got a loo when we get there. I shouldn't have had that last cuppa.'

'I'm sure they'll provide facilities for you to freshen up when you get there.'

'Is it true the last queen used to have a special toilet seat sent ahead of her all the time? I'm sure I read that somewhere. I asked Eugene but he wasn't sure.'

'I don't think so, but some places had special royal toilets set aside, places that have royal boxes, like the Albert Hall and the National Theatre.'

'Ooh, what fun, are they really fancy?'

'I don't think so, just privately accessed.'

'Oh, guess what? I'll be okay here today, won't I? If I get caught short I can just nip to the sludge thing and add a bit of *biogas*...oh, oh no.' She clutched at her belly, wobbling with glee. 'I shouldn't have made meself laugh, I want to go even more now.'

'Best stick to the conventional Ladies', eh?' Caroline couldn't help herself. 'We don't want you overbalancing and getting covered in sludge.'

'Oh no, you've started me off again, I'm cryin' now! Have you got a tissue?'

The pair giggled as they wiped their eyes.

'How come you're with me today, anyway?' Queenie

had finally gained control of her errant chins. 'I thought you was with the employment man now.'

'Doug? Yes, mostly,' Caroline said. 'He's got a rough time coming up, we think, but I'm with you today so we can iron out anything you're not sure of before the Canadian trip. Protocol, etcetera. Once today is out of the way we're sure you'll feel a bit more confident, able to do the trip without any handholding.'

'I certainly hope so.' Queenie's tone darkened a shade. 'I'm not sure I like that Andy bloke, he talks in riddles all the time.'

'That's probably because he's scared, just like you when you're nervous and you chatter on and on.'

'Do I?'

'Um, yes, sorry, that could have come out better.'

'It's okay. Bert says I prattle on all the time too.'

'No, that's just it, you don't, not all the time.'

'He says it's why he tolerates the knitting. He reckons I talk less when I'm knitting and the sound of the needles ain't so irritating as—'

'You talk when nobody's listening properly.'

'Eh?'

'When you expect people to tell you to shut up and not be stupid, you keep going.'

'Well, people—'

'But when people ask you what you think and listen to your answer, you articulate a thought and then stop.'

'Bless you, ducks, I've never articled a thought in me life. You ask Ber—'

'I'm not going to ask Bert. I don't need to. I've heard you do it. When nobody's telling you you're stupid, you're not stupid. You have good ideas.'

'Oh yeah? When did I last have a good idea?'

'Apart from your emergency toileting plans for this afternoon?'

Queenie produced a small bow and a dismissive wave of the hand. 'Hwell, naturally, apart from that.'

'This morning!'

'What? When?'

'When you asked about getting the new intake's children to come and see the horses. Nobody's thought of that before and it's a great idea.'

'Yeah, but that's not bein' clever, that's bein' nice. It's not about numbers and long words and understandin' stuff.'

'There's a difference between lack of intelligence and lack of education, you know. Just because you didn't do a lot of schooling doesn't make you stupid.'

'Doesn't it?'

'No, of course not. Your idea was about understanding people, and that's a clever thing.'

'Well I never did. Who'd have thought?'

'There's even a posh name for it... Oh, look, what's that?'

The car was slowing, and Caroline could see a line of people blocking the road a few hundred yards ahead. She pressed a button in the door and the glass partition between her and Queenie and the driver in front slid noiselessly down.

'Looks like we have a situation up ahead, ma'am,' said the driver.

'Can we take a detour?' Caroline asked.

'That's why I've slowed with plenty of room between us and them, but putting a roadblock into the satnav is producing nothing. We'd have to turn round, back to the M40 and off the next junction.'

'And no knowing if any other roads are affected.' Caroline added. 'Do we know what it is? There was nothing on the news or through the advisers for today.'

'I can call the plant and ask, but we have to either stop or keep going right now. We'll be in amongst it before I get a reply.' The driver punched a button on his hand-free phone on the dash.

'Take it as slow as you can. I'm not happy about stopping but maybe we'll find out what it is when we get a bit closer.'

Just then Caroline's phone rang. She retrieved it from her handbag and answered, 'Yes. What? Now you tell me...Yes, we're approaching it now... What do you mean, not policed? We can't very well turn around... No, I'll ask... Hold on...'

She held the phone away from her ear, looked at Queenie and sighed. 'It looks like this might not be as straightforward as we expected.'

Queenie was leaning over in her seat, trying to see past the driver and out of the windscreen. 'What's happening? Who are all those people? What are they waving?'

Caroline put her hand over Queenie's. 'Can we pull over and stop just for a minute, please, Ron?' The driver nodded and drew the bulletproof limousine to a gentle halt. 'Wildcat strikes.' Caroline's eyeroll was involuntary. 'The union ballots aren't in yet, but everyone's expecting a strike vote, so some places are starting to strike for half a day at a time to get the ball rolling. Half-day strikes aren't illegal, and they don't do a lot of harm, but once the idea takes hold the domino effect can devastate an industry.'

'But why here? What are they upset about? It's a new thingy to make us all greener, isn't it?' Queenie's face was ashen. She peered out of the windscreen again. 'There's a lot of them, what do they want with me? I'm only goin' to cut a bleedin' ribbon.' Her lips quivered.

Caroline fished in her bag for more tissues. 'It'll be for maximum impact,' she said. 'Doing it now. So they get on the news. It's not about you, not personally, just about the cameras and the company wanting to look good.'

Queenie sniffed into a handful of tissues and dabbed her nose. 'What do I do?'

'Nothing, Queenie, dear. They've promised to be non-violent, apparently, according to the police.'

'Police! Oh no.'

'It's okay, you can stay in the car. We're going to tell them that when we get to the roadblock they can give the driver a leaflet and you promise to read it. That should get us through.'

'Is that it?' All this fuss for a leaflet?'

'Whatever it takes, really. They just want their message out there.'

'But what do they really want? What's wrong with the place?'

'Apparently the expansion has led to some layoffs…'

'They've made it bigger and sacked people? How can that be?'

'New computers, I expect.'

'That's terrible.'

'Be that as it may, shall I let the on-site security staff know that you'll read anything they want to give you, in return for getting through the roadblock?'

'Oh yes, and tell them…tell them I'll talk about them in

my speech!'

'There's no need to go that far... Just a moment.' Caroline picked up the mobile again. 'Right, we're primed, let them know.' To the driver she added, 'We'll approach slowly. Any sign of trouble and we'll back off again, okay?'

'Right you are, ma'am.' The driver slipped a button and all the doors of the limo locked. He slid the car into gear and crept towards the mass of people.

Caroline looked at Queenie. She hadn't gained any colour back in her face but her lip was firm. 'It'll be all right. They know it's nothing to do with you.' Queenie nodded. She was sitting bolt upright now, staring straight ahead. As the shouting started to filter through the bulletproof glass she winced. Once. Then she turned back to stone.

They could see the placards now: *Jobs not Machines, People Aren't Sludge, Green but Jobless*. And the shouting got louder. The limo slowed to a crawl as the crowd clustered around it, waving and yelling.

'I'm not happy opening the window with them this close,' the driver said, stopping the vehicle as it began to shake. Some of the crowd were pushing them from side to side. 'Where are the police?'

'Not here,' Caroline muttered. 'They don't want to be replaced by machines either.'

'What do you want me to do, ma'am? We're sitting ducks stopped like this but I don't want to hurt anyone.'

'Let me out,' Queenie demanded.

'No, ma'am, it's not sa—'

'You can't—'

Caroline and the driver spoke at once.

'I can and I will. Let me out.'

'There's no security...' Caroline could already hear Gerald: *You let her do what?*

'I don't need no security. I'm one of them. I lost my job to a computer too. I know why they're angry. I'm angry. I'm goin' to tell them. Let. Me. Out!'

'I'm not auth—' the driver began.

'So what, then? We sit here 'til they turn the bleedin' limo over? Ain't we got a sewage plant to open?'

'Just a moment, I'll see if we can get the local security guard.' Caroline made a call. 'Shit! I'm on hold.'

'Might as well get it over with then, luvvie—open them doors, driver.'

Caroline caught the driver's eye in the rear-view mirror. She nodded. What Gerald would have to say couldn't get much worse now.

The locks clicked open. Queenie pulled the latch on the door on her side. It opened slightly. She pushed gently until she was able to peer out of the gap. She caught the eye of a middle-aged man with one hand on the roof of the limo and the other on a placard that said *People aren't sewage*.

'Oi,' she yelled to him. 'I can't get out and talk to you in this scrum.'

He began to yell too, turning this way and that and gesturing at the people behind him. Slowly, gradually, the crowd dropped away from the door. The shouting dropped a decibel. Queenie opened the door as wide as it would go and clambered out. Caroline heard a localised hush begin to descend as everyone tried to see the diminutive figure in primrose yellow.

'Blimey,' she began, 'ain't you all tall? Give us that box, mate.' A young chap with full sleeve tattoos and a bullhorn stepped down off the milk crate he'd been standing on to lead the chanting and put it by the open limo door. Queenie grabbed his arm as she clambered up. She could see over the top of the car now and used her vantage point to look around the crowd, making eye contact here and there. Then she glared at the bullhorn until he handed it over. Queenie lifted it to her lips.

'Oi, you lot. Have a listen, because I've got something to say.' She recoiled at the loudness of it and nearly toppled off the box. A few wolf whistles rent the air, and the lads on the far side of the car looked up, laughed and carried on trying to rock it over, while she grabbed hold of the tattooed arm again and pulled one heel out of a hole in the milk crate.

She looked at the lad whose arm she was now gripping so tightly she'd have drawn blood if she had decent fingernails. 'I thought they wanted to talk? There's not much else I can bleedin' do, is there?'

He thought for a moment, then reached for the bullhorn and sent his voice over the heads of the crowd. Queenie flinched.

'Shut up, where's your manners? And you, mate. You lot, stop that. Least we can do is listen.' He rounded on the gang pushing at the car. 'Behave, you've got what you wanted, now show a bit of respect.'

Gradually the whistling and laughing died away, and Queenie tried again.

'I only started this thing last week.' Now that she had a sense of how loud and garbly her voice was through the horn thing, she spoke a bit more carefully. 'So there's no point takin' it out on me. I got made redundant by a bleedin' machine too.' She looked around, met a few eyes;

at least it wasn't getting worse. She took another breath. 'We all got a job to do and mine, just now, is to open this thing.'

A few placards waved and somebody yelled, 'We're not sewage!' A few others joined the chant.

'I know that,' Queenie shouted. 'Nobody is. Let me do my bloomin' job and I'll see about it, all right?'

Caroline watched through the windscreen, incredulous, as the crowd thinned to the sides of the road. She could hear the chanting die down in a wave rippling out from the car, as people nearer the back worked out that something had happened.

Queenie turned back to the kid whose arm she was still trying to snap off. 'Oof, I think I'm stuck up here, give me a hand down, would you, ducks?' He took the bullhorn from her, handed it to the man next to him and braced his arm for one last assault. She leant on it heavily and half-jumped, half-fell back to the ground. 'Thank you!' She offered him a beaming smile and he grinned self-consciously.

'No probs,' he said. 'Um...ma'am?'

'Get on with you, call me Queenie.' She busied herself with climbing back into the limo. Just before she closed the door she scanned the faces for the placard man, the one who'd first let her out. 'Thank you too, you're a gentleman.' He blushed. 'Tell them I'm on their side, eh?' she whispered as she began to close the door. He nodded. She waved. He waved.

As the door closed, Caroline placed her hand over her heart and made the rapid tapping gesture of one who wishes to get a head start on their heart attack.

'Please, Queenie, never do that to me again, eh?'

'It worked, didn't it? Look, we're off.'

The car was indeed now cruising, unimpeded, along the lane towards the Thames Water Sewage Works, Didcot, Oxfordshire.

'Mind you, I'll need that loo when we get there even faster now.'

CHAPTER SIXTEEN

Doug had seen the news. Everybody had seen the news. The strikes were under way. He was going to have to do a press conference; tell everyone to wait for the ballot, not to jeopardise the economy unless the people wished it, etcetera. The speech was being written for him right now by some wonk in the specialists' office.

He'd seen the old dear on the news, reckoned she'd done okay. He asked himself how he'd have felt in a car surrounded by angry protesters and decided he'd probably not have coped that well. Maybe being a soppy old thing had its advantages.

He opened the door to his ministry boardroom and looked around; everyone from Trade and Industry was there, a few from the Home Office, and a phalanx of civil service specialists. Queenie was there too, knitting. She'd stopped doing that for a while, he recalled. Ah well, today held bigger problems than clicking needles.

Caroline had warned him to expect trouble. She'd

called round last night to advise him it was time to chair a meeting. She'd briefed him on all the practical implications of the upcoming strike and explained, with hand-drawn diagrams, who would be responsible for what. She'd listed the possible responses the specialists had come up with.

The wildcat strikes were a catalyst, she'd said. They'd have to bring their plans forward; no four-week window while they waited for the formal results. This may not necessarily be a bad thing—she didn't say for whom.

He'd nearly had a Scotch last night. Just the one, to deal with the stress. Help him sleep. But he'd been careful to make sure there was none available in the flat so that, if tempted, he'd balk at having to go out, or order some in. He could see it on the news—'Employment Secretary solves strikes with Scotch!'—and had opted for coffee instead. He'd not slept well.

Caroline was there, sitting with Queenie. He nodded a hello to them and to everyone else round the table and took his position near the screen, currently displaying the bare bones of an agenda in bullet points.

One more chair remained to be filled. Gerald. Doug looked at his watch: two minutes to ten. He breathed a sigh of something approaching relief; at least nobody was late.

The double doors to the conference room flew open. One of them clipped the chair of a specialist seated nearby. Gerald brandished a copy of *The Sun*, striding towards Queenie as though he might bop her on the head with it.

'"Tell them I'm on their side?" What were you thinking, woman?' He turned to Caroline. 'And why on earth did you let her out?'

Doug watched as Caroline and Queenie both opened

their mouths to speak, appeared to think better of it, and closed them again. All faces round the table managed to find something interesting to look at in the files before them. Doug tapped his water glass gently with his pen, and the glances swivelled in his direction. Even Gerald's.

'Excuse me, Mr Lambert, I realise we have some problems today, but Ms Grant advised that I would be chairing this meeting. If that's not so, perhaps you could take your seat here?'

Gerald regarded Doug for a moment longer than was strictly necessary before speaking again. The man was simmering with fury. Doug wondered whether he would be on the next train back to Manchester and decided, for what it was worth, that that would be fine. Gerald's demeanour returned to its usual icy calm, however—a calmness which began at the hands holding the newspaper, and sort of...*spread.*

'I apologise unreservedly.' Gerald spoke with careful deliberation now. 'This is your meeting to control as you see fit.' He sat in the last vacant chair, placed the newspaper on the table in front of him and silently addressed his attention to the agenda on the screen.

'I'm going to suggest'—Doug was treading cautiously now—'that we bring discussion of yesterday's incident to the top of the agenda. It appears to be a matter on which some of us have strong opinions.' A buzz of muttered agreement filled the room. 'Do we need a vote? Or shall we just get on with it?' The buzz started to nod, the room looking like a field of wheat at the mercy of thirty or so little individual zephyrs.

Doug's gaze homed in on Gerald. The man had the audacity to make eye contact.

'I believe the Chief Secretary to the Cabinet may wish to start this discussion.'

'Thank you, Mr Sideworth. I'll begin by reading the headlines from our most influential newspapers.'

Doug glanced over at Caroline, who was whispering something to Queenie. She inclined her head as Doug's gaze registered. Was that a tiny smile? *Did they just cook that up to test me? What the hell are these people for?* He interrupted Gerald's lengthy thesis on the inadvisability of heads of state having opinions.

'Excuse me, but I think we're losing sight of something important here.'

'Indeed? Do tell.' Gerald gave way as though someone had pressed a question button in the House.

'I thought she did well. I mean, it was a nasty situation and she got them out of it.' Doug looked at Queenie, whose face was now a picture of misery. The knitting had stopped and her lips were wobbling. As were her chins. Doug didn't want her to cry. 'And she's meant to be on the side of the people, that's all she said.' A few throaty, almost inaudible *hear hears* wafted about.

'We are all on the side of the people, ladies and gentlemen. However, at this stage in the proceedings we are not able to say which side of this particular divide the people are on. Thus the advance articulation of a position...'

'What did you expect her to do?' A deep bass rumbled across the floor and up everybody's legs to get to their ears. 'Your people, and my people, messed up. Nobody anticipated wildcat action? Call yourselves specialists? It affected my department too; suddenly we had police refusing to take action and no contingency plans.'

Doug leafed quietly through his papers to the mugshot reminders at the back. He found himself unexpectedly grateful for the random melting pot that Minnow's system had come up with. He didn't usually pigeonhole people by colour, but scanning the spectrum for black faces made his search faster, and unlike say, hair colour or a moustache, it wouldn't change if he forgot the bloke's name down the line.

He found him. *Clayton Brown: Chief Minister Home Office (maths teacher).* The huge man continued. 'You put her in the line of fire. You let her down. All this snivelling about *advance articulations,* we can be pretty damned clear what the people want after this. For the record'—Clayton got to his feet, all six-foot-three of him, and addressed himself to Queenie—'I think you did a bloody marvellous job.'

The applause began slowly. People looked around them and began to join in. Clayton stayed on his feet. Doug joined him. As did the remainder of the room.

Gerald allowed the standing ovation to run for a minute before lifting his hand. The room fell silent. *Yup, he's still in control.* 'Mr Chairman, I wonder if we could establish a general precedent for not predetermining the will of the people, and move on to item two on the agenda?'

'Certainly.' Doug scanned the room, allowing the moment or two it took for everyone to stop clapping and regain their seats. He lingered a moment on Queenie's face. Yeah, she was crying now. Decent old biddy—tough, he decided. Mostly. 'Our multi-agency team has been working on some arrangements for a vote to strike, but we'd been waiting for the ballot results before implementation. Obviously we must bring those plans forward, especially if it looks like the police will be taking part.'

'Why is that?' A voice from the far side of the table, someone from Industry, Doug thought. 'They're obliged to take care of public safety, so why weren't they there yesterday? It's disgusting. There should be some sort of disciplinary action. They need to be forced to control these illegal mobs.'

'Unfortunately.' There it was again, the voice working its way up from your feet. 'The strikes are legal so long as they don't last more than half a day.' Clayton shuffled some papers around in his folder and found the one he wanted to read from. 'In the administration before last, the Home Office came to the view that some small disputes with individual employers might be settled in this way. The right to withdraw labour being a human right that the administration had no wish to restrict, while demanding proper balloting for anything more comprehensive to protect the interests of commerce.'

'So it was a legal rabble? I still don't see why the police wouldn't intervene.'

'They weren't breaking any laws.'

'Oh, come on, of course they were—obstructing the highway, threatening behaviour...' Doug checked his cheat sheet: *Alan Winstanley: Industry Secretary (CEO URC Services, Inc)*. He'd heard of this company. Call Centres? He'd look it up. *Probably bricking it that the strikes will affect his dividends; still, he's got a point.*

'The demonstration concerned took place on Thames Water private land.' Clayton was still checking his notes. He turned a sheet. 'And they gave an undertaking to the local police that there would be no lawbreaking. There were no actual threats, I understand?' He looked over at Queenie and Caroline, who shook their heads.

'But there might have been!' The flush swamping Winstanley's face made Doug wonder when he'd last had his blood pressure checked. 'What on earth excuse could the police—your responsibility, man—give for not maintaining public order?'

'As I understand it, the reply our office received from Thames Valley police was, "We'll see if we can send a computer."'

A gasp or two joined some intakes of breath. The Home Office minister continued, 'If this incident is anything to go by, we are likely to be facing a strike by emergency and essential workers as well. If the police, ambulance and fire services come out, along with power, water, gas, etcetera, we could have a national emergency on our hands.' He looked at Winstanley. 'Instead of a few rich blokes losing a bit of profit.'

Doug took the reins back. 'This means we have two immediate focuses.' Somebody muttered, 'foci,' but he wasn't sure who. *Whom? Get a grip, man.* 'Firstly, dissemination of our intent to *let the people speak* through the vote via the reps. We're getting an action plan out to every constituency: the reps will visit union leaders within their bailiwick and assure them the government will respect the vote, either way.' He glanced at Queenie, who was mouthing 'bailiwick?' to Caroline. He attempted eye contact with Winstanley, but the man was having none of it.

'We hope that will buy us some time. And secondly, preparation for public safety if the strike goes ahead and includes emergency and essential staff. The joint committee, working with Employment, Industry, Home, Defence and Health, will bring forward its proposals at the next House session with a statement, an emergency plan for each ministry, and guidance for reps. In the meantime, we'd like every ministry to appoint a specialist and a minister to take responsibility for implementing the plan once devised. I'd like those names emailed to me by the end of tomorrow, please.'

Heads nodded, notes were made.

'Are there any questions, or can we move on?'

Queenie looked up from the knitting she'd picked up again after the ovation and all the drying of eyes. 'Can I say something?'

'Certainly, go ahead.'

'Those people yesterday. They're being chucked on the scrapheap. They had a sign: *People aren't sewage*. I got shown about everywhere, made a fuss of, they made tea and scones and gave me a bloomin' great safety hat so I could admire everything, and I made a speech and they clapped and all...and I'm not sayin' it's not great. The gas from poo thing. It's all green and that, well, not the...' She looked up and grinned at the few people giggling. 'I'm ramblin', I know. And I was goin' to say that poo isn't green, because I'm stupid.' Caroline appeared to dig her in the ribs. 'Ow, oh yes, I'm not supposed to say that, but you probably will. I don't care now. Because I know a thing that you don't know.' She raised her chins and pointed them at Winstanley. 'What I know is that when they replace you with a computer, you feel like *sewage*. And that matters as much as progress and saving the bloomin' planet.'

One or two heads turned uncertainly to Gerald before nodding, very slightly. Doug thought he saw Caroline squeeze Queenie's hand.

'Thank you.' Doug realised he meant it. 'Any more questions, ladies and gentlemen?' Doug checked in with Gerald, who appeared to be inspecting his fingernails for signs of having deteriorated within the last half an hour or so.

'In that case, I'll close the meeting now. I have a press conference to attend. We'll reconvene to complete the agenda after lunch.'

'Blimey, Gerald, that was a bit OTT, even for you.' Caroline approached their usual lunchtime table. The Red Lion was quieter this week; the reps were out of town and the ministries were buzzing with activity. A lot of people were frantically trying to learn their own emergency procedures.

'Do you think? He handled it well, though.'

'I know I told you he seemed up to snuff, but there was no need to go ballistic in public.'

'You seem to have strayed into the land of cliché, my dear. Is everything all right?'

'All right? No it isn't. The people I've been carefully grooming to cope are being shafted one by one.' She saw—and enjoyed—the wince. 'I've been blindsided by a total lack of foresight by the Employment and Home Office wonks, railroaded into a breach of protocol by a little old lady, told to hold the hand of a dipso who now appears to have the safety of the nation in his hands, and just when I've got both of them calm enough to function you cut me off at the knees with a performance worthy of

Machiavelli himself. In case you hadn't noticed, I'm having a rough week. I will cliché if I wish.' She pulled a bag from the floor to her lap and opened it. 'And, if it's all the same to you, I will knit. Queenie is right about some things, and the calming effect of wool around needle might just prevent me from covering you from head to toe with your lunch.'

Gerald eyed the remainder of his bowl of chilli.

'Knit away, I'm getting used to it. Is Minnow on his way?'

'Yes, he had a few calls to make, he'll be along later.'

'He did handle it well, you know.' Gerald never apologised but occasionally his tone softened, which was about as close to the S-word as he ever came.

'Yes, but Queenie's in bits again.'

'She'll perk up. Anyway, Sideworth is going to have to hold himself together with press, unions, demos, the works. He needs to know he's up to it.'

'So long as you don't drive him back to the bottle first. You might at least have warned me so I could prepare Queenie.'

'She wouldn't have reacted properly.'

'You really are a bastard.'

'Thank you, ma'am.' Gerald acknowledged the compliment with an incline of the head.

'What's next? Apart from public statements and reps' campaigns, can we keep the lid on?'

'Wrong question, I think.' Gerald pushed his bowl of chilli to one side, away from Caroline, and steepled his fingers under his chin. 'Do we want to keep the lid on? Or would it serve our purposes better to let it boil over?

CHAPTER SEVENTEEN

Caroline smirked slightly as she slid the knitting onto her knees. If ever there was a day to reintroduce the idea that she could knit in meetings too, it was today, while Gerald knew she was cross with him. The passive-aggressive glee had been so liberating in the pub she thought she'd try it in his office and see how it felt. A lifelong knitter—she remembered the lectures at uni—nobody had minded then; it just made her a bit of an oddball. When had she started leaving it at home? It rendered you invisible in a way—there but not there. Who knew if you were paying attention?

Gerald eyed the growing work. 'God preserve us, what is that? It's vaguely familiar.'

'The pattern? Carswell's tie. Thought it would work well for a...project.'

'Foreign Minister?' Caroline nodded, furrowing her brow with the concentration of counting the number of stitches in that bit of a crescent moon. 'What is that thing anyway? It's a bit small for a bloody scarf, and if it's a sweater it's got no bally arms.'

Caroline opened her mouth to reply as Minnow slipped through the door, loaded with half a dozen laptop cases. She lifted her head to smile at him, grateful for the interruption. She made a mental note to bring something she could explain more easily the next time she used woolly crafts as a weapon of psychological warfare.

'Sorry I'm late.' Minnow placed the laptops on a table by the window, lining them up neatly one by one. 'I've been touring the departments that will need dedicated systems for the strike, identifying the lead specialist and setting them up with one of these.'

'Good man.' Gerald appeared to be counting the cases. 'How many left to do?'

'Just a few on the periphery now. Industry have an old hand taking charge, Employment have Deidre Posner, new but really quite tech savvy. Home Office will bear the brunt of the emergency planning, but their senior was around for the riots so he knows what to expect.'

'Their chief minister seems to be bedding in okay. I thought he cut a calm figure this morning.' Gerald glanced at Caroline, who murmured an agreement.

'They're diaried to meet with Defence this afternoon,' she added. 'Brown seems as collaborative as we'd hoped; we just need to make sure neither he nor...who's the Defence chap again?'

Gerald executed a few swift swipes on the screen on his desk. 'Gordon Morrow, ex-sapper.'

'We worked that one out well then.' She grinned at Minnow. 'The system does it again. Nothing like a sapper to understand keeping the essentials moving.'

'The system aims to please,' Minnow replied with a mock bow.

'Be that as it may, neither of them is likely to realise their ministry is in the firing line until the time comes, especially if we keep promoting this as an Employment issue. They'll need to be watched.'

'Indeed.' Gerald allowed his gaze to leave the flying needles and drift to the window. 'As far as the public is concerned, this has to stay about jobs, not national security.'

'Defence are gearing up to take over if necessary,' Minnow said. 'I've just come from there. They have figures and locations for the usual standbys: Green Goddesses, ambulances, power line repairs, etcetera, and, um, crowd control.'

'Let's hope it doesn't come to that.' Caroline shuddered. 'Nothing like the army on the streets to get the old democracy bullies started.'

'Speaking of which, do we know if we have any sleepers in this intake?' Gerald's attention snapped to his computer screen. 'Any rumours yet?'

Caroline placed her knitting on the desk in order to retrieve her notebook from her briefcase. Gerald regarded it as though it might leap up and choke him if he didn't stare it down. She flipped a few pages and began to read. 'Small incident reported by a listener in the reps' office, one of them had a bit of a barney with Queenie, apparently. We don't think she's bright enough to be a sleeper, but apparently there's some old-democracy support in the family.'

Gerald turned to Minnow. 'Was that not flagged by the system? Why is she here?'

Minnow shrugged. 'Always a close call. You never know if having bringing them in will settle them down, get them to see we're not evil manipulators...'

'Even when we are?' Caroline laughed as she retrieved her knitted stars and moons.

'Ah yes, but we manipulate for the good of the nation; sometimes people get it.'

'And sometimes they don't. We might regret a dissenting voice on the inside if this turns ugly.' Gerald produced an immaculate white silk handkerchief from his breast pocket and brushed away some imaginary fluff from where the knitted threat had lurked on his desk. 'Anyway, it's too late to worry about that now. How is our, uh, *other* little project coming along?'

Minnow looked around the office before speaking. 'It's okay,' Gerald added. 'I've had the mics removed for "overhauling" on the pretext that we can't have anything go wrong with the records with a crisis looming. After today we'll have to discuss this elsewhere, but you can speak freely for now.'

Caroline's mind wandered as Minnow retrieved one of the laptops and fired up some program or other. The recursive nature of the mic system never quite satisfied her. It was part of the system, of course, a sop to those who thought the civil servants were taking over. Theoretically, everything that took place out of sight of a member of the public was recorded, like those phone calls to call centres, or more frequently these days to computer voice recognition systems. *For quality assurance purposes.* So long as the recordings existed, nothing underhand could go on, could it? Except for meeting in the pub. Still, it kept the public happy. Mostly.

'I've set up some meetings with the systems bods of the services we need to watch.' Minnow was swiping the screen on his laptop now. 'Actually, the Thames Water debacle helped a lot; I could say we were offering support for if a picket prevents managers or whoever from overseeing operations. That way I don't have to say I think they're lying.'

Gerald nodded his approval. 'Go on.'

'All I need is physical access to each main server—police, fire, ambulance, the main grids for each utility—and I can install a USB dongle. That should give me remote access from home.'

'You'll need unsupervised access, presumably?' Gerald asked.

'It might be possible to divert attention for long enough; it depends a bit how "official" the visit is.' Minnow made air quotes before continuing. 'And how much they trust us. I can probably take one or two of the savvier geeks into my confid—'

'No.' Gerald chopped at the desk with his right hand, karate-like. 'Line in the sand. If we're going to stick with this *trust the people* bollocks, we can't risk it getting out that we don't.'

'How, then?' Caroline asked.

'How long will you need with each server?' Gerald addressed his question to Minnow.

'Um, five minutes should do it.'

'Right. We'll herald your arrival with a memo, asking for a private tour from the lead geek. We'll send both of you. Caroline can polish up her prettiest heels and undo a button or two.'

Caroline's eyes rolled. 'Not again, I hate that.'

'Flutter your eyes and think of England, my dear, unless you can think of a better way.'

'I'll get back to you on that,' she muttered through gritted teeth. And upped the volume on the needle-clatter.

'That's settled then. We'll get the memos out now, and you can do the rounds next week.'

'I might have a couple of friends who could help.' Minnow offered Caroline a look of sympathy. 'Save you some time and, uh, trouble.'

'That would be nice. My team are going to have plenty else to do without losing me for a whistle-stop tour of the country on cleavage duty.'

Minnow blushed and switched his attention back to Gerald. 'Do we trust the FBI, by the way?'

'Do we have to? Why do you ask?'

'I've just heard an old mentor of mine is in the country. We go way back. In fact, he's the reason I'm here and not still hacking bank accounts…we could use him too. Plus, the Yanks might appreciate a heads-up?'

'Hmm. I suppose it could prevent misunderstandings if the trouble spreads.'

Minnow nodded. He fished a smartphone from his pocket, swiped a screen or two and began to type.

Caroline looked up from her work and met Gerald's eye. 'What about the Canada trip? Who's going along?'

'Can't spare anyone.' Gerald shook his head slowly. 'But you've done excellent work with Queenie. She'll cope.'

'Yes, but nobody's spent any time with Carswell.'

'He's a salesman, he'll do fine. Just find someone to root out the worst of those ties and leave them to it. It's only Canada; they never get upset.'

Sally Farnham was getting used to chairing meetings. Her *senior* had taken charge of the first few, while she settled in, but now she'd had a few goes with the laser pointer she felt more confident. She'd taken note of the way Pam used the agenda and the right of everyone to be heard to shut Dr Wilmslow down when he started on about knowing more than anyone else, and she was starting to enjoy herself.

The trick was to take all the specialists' reports on each item first, then ask for 'observations' from the ministers when time was running out. She'd worked out that Rav, the herbalist, had insights and angles nobody had thought of, so asking the doc to speak last, on the basis that he was best placed to 'sum up', had been a masterstroke. He felt important, although the decisions were all but made and everybody was ready for a coffee break.

She felt a bit guilty, but hey, they were all equal here and she reckoned he'd get it eventually. Doctors ought to have a bit more training in listening instead of spouting. She intended to pop that on the agenda at some point, get reps to ask around in their local hospitals and see if putting listening skills on the syllabus of a few more medical schools could be a thing she could achieve. That would be satisfying.

To be fair, this doc *did* know stuff she didn't. Her residual fury was with the others; flashbacks to screaming at the white coats to talk as though she and her children were in the room weren't this chap's fault. She did know their early clashes had been more about baggage than good governance, so she planned to allow him a bit more 'summing up time' today.

There was only one thing on the agenda this afternoon. All her plans for positive change were going to have to wait. Queenie had wanted to come and talk about something with them too, but that was on hold as well. It sounded like the strike vote would affect medical staff; the geeks were coming to talk about systems and contingency plans.

'Thank you, ladies and gentlemen.' Sally addressed the group from her position at the screen on the wall of the committee room. She held her laser pointer as though it were a talisman, a lucky charm. She'd always hated 'the person with the pointer' at work—*who do you think you are? Pointing at things isn't clever*—but now, well, it made her feel safe. In charge. Entitled to speak. Like the conch shell in whatever that book was. She wondered how many more pet hates would crumble to ashes before her three years were out. She was working at the pace of one a week so far.

'Today's meeting has been turned over to contingency planning for the upcoming strike. Instead of a topic agenda, we have here'—she pointed to the word *Agenda* on the screen—'a list of speakers.'

'You don't say,' wafted towards her, almost inaudible. She'd almost moved Wilmslow up from the bottom, but now she was glad she hadn't. The arrogant arse was going to have to earn his promotion in *her* ministry.

'Firstly, Pam is going to brief us on the information we have to date—which regions are likely to withdraw labour, which hospitals we expect to be affected, whether medical staff will join ancillary workers, etcetera. Then Mr, uh, Minnow?' Minnow winced and nodded. 'Mr, yes, he will explain the stand-alone control system he is providing for the ministry, where all details can be input from multiple sources.' She used her pointer to pick out the laptop on the desk in front of Minnow and somebody giggled.

'Then we have reports from each specialist on their role. If anyone has any questions, please raise them as we go along. I'll park them here.' She indicated a spot below the list of names on the screen, it was headed *PARKING*. 'We can address them at the end. Finally, I'll be asking Mr Banerjee and Dr Wilmslow for their observations.' She nodded at Rav and then the doc. She'd been tempted to pick them out with the pointer, but that giggle had put her off a bit. And it might look a bit like they were about to get taken out by a sniper.

She considered pointing at Pam's notes to get things started, thought better of it, and put her pointer down on the desk as she sat. 'Thank you. Pam, perhaps you could get us up to speed?'

CHAPTER EIGHTEEN

Andy Carswell settled into his seat in the first class section of the Air British Republic plane with a sigh. It would be good to get away for a while, even if he did have to spend five days with the world's most annoying head of state.

He knew it didn't really matter who did these jobs; it could just as easily have been his Beth or even, God forbid, his Sophie in a few years. Although he hoped she'd have learned some sense before she turned twenty-one and became eligible for parliamentary service. But away from the other random selections he did feel kinda important.

Not only that, he was getting earache from the womenfolk about never being at home. Even though all they did was nag at him when he was. He'd presented the option of moving to London and had it turned down flat. Beth didn't want to leave her daft little job...and Sophie, well she'd pointed out in no uncertain terms, punctuated with words he'd never have used when he was her age, that her schooling was 'too important to interrupt at this stage of my development.' Observing that her schooling appeared to be less important than visiting nail bars with Francesca had just caused another door-slamming session.

'I don't know why I bother to come home at weekends,' he said to Beth. 'Nobody seems very pleased to see me.'

'Perhaps you could try bringing less laundry, and actually caring what our week's been like, instead of talking non-stop about how stupid the government is. Oh, and how the people you are supposed to oversee seem to look down their noses at you,' she snapped back. 'If I hear *all fur coat and no knickers, not as green as I'm cabbage-looking,* or *what goes around, comes around* one more time I think I'll scream.'

'It's not every day you get to be Foreign bloody Minister, you know. They must have seen more potential than my family ever gives me credit for.'

Beth turned to the washing machine and bent to unload the clean load as she muttered, 'Maybe they just want you and your infuriating sayings out of the country.'

He pretended not to hear.

'I'll be away anyway, next week,' he added, attempting a hurt tone. 'Five days in Canada. I thought Sophie might have been interested.'

Beth produced a short, mirthless laugh. 'I'd not mention it right now, if I were you.'

'Honestly, Beth, you should come to London. The flats they put the families in are perfectly nice, and I don't want to lose any more influence over Sophie. I know I've been a bit wrapped up in it all, but I'm running the country, for goodness' sake. Things could change if you were there too, if you could see it all...'

She rolled her eyes.

'So we have to move to be able to understand what's going on in your life, while you consistently refuse to care what's going on in mine and Sophie's, even while living under the same roof? No thanks, Andy. Your laundry will be dry in an hour, pack carefully. Enjoy Canada.'

She'd turned her back and left the kitchen.

He was trying to enjoy his new life—it made a change from the office where, to be honest, some people seemed to resent his stellar sales record. But a miserable loneliness seemed to overtake him every time he made the short walk through the tunnel, from his office in the bowels of the Houses of Parliament to the nice little flat they'd given him in Portcullis House. He'd not managed to find anyone to go drinking with after work. He'd tried some of his best gags on the more likely looking women but hardly got as far as the punchlines, let alone, 'How about a reviving snifter and mayhap a veritable repast!'

He'd spent one evening trying to look at the briefings they'd given him, but the words just danced around like they always did, so he put the telly on instead. He missed Beth; if he left documentation lying around long enough, she'd read it and then yell at him for not bothering with things. She tended to include the important points in the lecture, so he never needed to do the grunt work himself. He was a people person, not a pen pusher. He'd have to get by on his wits like he always had.

He turned at the sound of more people stepping into the plane. He'd been first to arrive in the front bit, where the ample leather seats swivelled and tipped to make beds, or loungers, or places at a central conference table. First, that is, except for a silent security guard. A young chap emerged through the door, carrying something that looked like one of the boxes from the House. He had that blasted knitting bag over his shoulder too. He put the bag and the box down on the central table and turned to help Queenie over the little step into the plane.

'Thank you, Eugene, you're a sweetheart, ooh those stairs, my legs ain't gettin' any younger.' Andy heard her before he saw her, and then, the vision in turquoise tottered into the compartment.

'Ooh, look, ain't this swish?' She gazed around, her mouth forming an O of wonder until her eyes landed on Andy, his chair slung halfway back and his legs raised at the angle of the American La-Z-Boy chairs he'd seen on the telly.

'Hello, Andy, luv, made yourself at home, have you? Isn't this something? I've never been in the front bit of a plane before, have you? Well'—she didn't give him a chance to reply—'me an' Bert went to Majorca once and they opened the curtain to let a little boy through to visit the pilot and we saw the big seats an' that, but I never thought I'd get to sit in one.'

She plopped herself down in the seat next to him and began fingering the buttons in the arm. 'Have you worked it all out, what they do? How do you put the feet up like that...oof.' The seat swung around away from Andy and righted itself at the table. 'Blimey, it's like the bleedin' funfair.'

Eugene grinned and leant over the arm of her chair. 'Let me, ma'am. What do you want it to do?'

'I want it all recliney, like he's got his, but facing that way, so's Andy and I can talk.'

Andy groaned inwardly.

Eugene tapped a few buttons and the chair began to behave. Queenie's turquoise shoes levitated towards Andy and, as she swivelled back around so she could see him, she waved.

'Ain't this fun?'

He nodded a combination greeting-stroke-agreement.

'Is that table for meetin's and such?' She addressed Eugene, who appeared to be the only other person accompanying them on the flight. Somehow Andy had expected more of an entourage.

'Yes, ma'am.' Eugene seemed quite fond of the old bat, Andy thought. 'Normally someone from the Service would come with you.'

'Like Caroline?' Andy's stomach gave an odd flutter; was he hungry?

'Yes, in fact she was planning to come with you.' He nodded at Andy, all friendly-like. 'But with things getting a bit hairy at home, they decided Doug Sideworth needed more support than you did.'

'The one what made that speech after I got on the news?'

'That's him, yes.'

Andy wondered if he was more anxious that he'd realised about the flight. He didn't usually suffer from travel sickness but his pulse was racing now. He made a mental note to ask the young chap about whether they'd brought any medications, when he could get a word in edgeways.

'So,' Eugene continued with a grin that wouldn't have shamed the Cheshire Cat, 'you've just got me, and Charlie here.' He indicated the silent, motionless goon. 'He's here to stop anyone trying to hurt you and I'm here to...well...be around, help out...and carry the teapot!'

'Good God, is that what's in there?' Andy couldn't help himself. The lad had pointed at the despatch box. 'What on earth are we taking a teapot to Canada for? Surely they have tea?'

'Ah now, you see...' Queenie began, and Andy realised his mistake. It was going to be a long flight.

Sammy rearranged her scarf and tucked it back into her duffel coat as she waited on the steps outside Minnow's block of flats in Hackney. She'd pressed the bell for number 42 once. The wind was chilly as she stood trying to decide how much longer to give it before pressing again. She looked around her; the arrangement of tower blocks seemed to be creating a wind tunnel right where she needed to be. *Honestly, planning people, how hard is it to do a little maths?* She wondered whether wind tunnels could be employed in the game she was working on, but then decided the civil engineers in fictional worlds were probably more competent than the real thing.

'Uh, hello?' Minnow's voice sounded through the intercom.

'It's me? Sammy?' Her voice let her down a little. *Oh no, he'll think he's got a frog on the doorstep.*

'Hi, come on up, it's the fourth floor.' The buzz that told her the door was open started, and then stopped. She pushed the door. *Shit.* She pressed the bell again.

'Did I just expect you to leap to the door in a single bound? I'm always doing that, I'll hold it a bit longer.'

'Just so long as I can use the stairs instead of flying we'll get there in the end.' She heard Minnow laugh through the intercom as the buzzer went off again.

She pushed the outer door, gaining entry this time, and found herself in a dingy hallway, just like every other sixties tower block. The 'problem families' had been moved out decades ago, to make way for singles who didn't mind having no access to green spaces, but somehow the smell of cabbage persisted. Sammy pondered the scent—*could maybe write it into a game—cabbage-smell debuff? Hmm, would it affect health or accuracy?*—as she climbed the stairs to the fourth floor.

Minnow was waiting for her at his door, which she thought was kinda sweet. In fact, everything about him was kinda sweet, but that sort of nonsense wasn't why she was here; they had work to do.

'I, uh, rearranged some stuff to make room for both of us to work,' Minnow said, as she regarded the room she had just stepped into. It resembled a cross between a school classroom and a computer shop: one long plywood 'desk' ran along the length of the room on the window side, and another spanned the opposite wall. The window desk held a line of six computer monitors; the other, a range of laptops and tablets. The floor was a mass of cables.

'I guess you didn't get the Health and Safety guys in yet?' she said as she placed her laptop case on the end of the 'laptop desk'.

Minnow grimaced. 'Oh, I didn't...'

'Kidding.' She realised she'd have to go carefully with the gags. She also realised it had been several years since a gag had come to mind. 'I can just about manoeuvre round all that lot.' She indicated the tangle at a particularly overloaded extension lead. 'And if all else fails, I'll bring some Day-Glo safety tape next time I'm here.'

'Still kidding, right?' Minnow had a little furrow above his left eye; Sammy thought it was probably an anxiety thing. She fought an impulse to smooth it away.

'Still kidding.' She looked around what appeared to be the only living room in the flat. 'Where do you sit? I mean when you're not at the computers, when you want to relax?'

'I don't really, I suppose. I just work and go to bed. I relax lying down...oh, not that, I didn't mean...'

Sammy laughed. 'I know you didn't. We're here to work. But...it wasn't an insult.'

'Wasn't it?' There went that furrow again.

'No. Anyway, since we are here to work, I've left the health inspectors outside. They're waiting in the lift to help me out of the building. Show me the set-up. Where do we start?'

Minnow seemed to calm down as he turned his attention to the hardware. *You're making him nervous,* Sammy thought. *Poor bloke, he's probably not used to girls in his space being all...what? Sassy? Is that a thing I do? Where the hell did it come from?*

She perched on a stool that looked like it had been purloined from a school chemistry lab and removed her laptop from its case. 'Okay if I take notes while you talk?'

'Um, yes, if it helps, but you might want to do it on one of these.' He indicated the tablets. 'I can't let anything out of here.'

'Oh, right.' She put the laptop away again and stashed the bag by the door. 'Any one of these?' She picked up the nearest tablet.

'Yeah, it's loaded with everything you need. Easier to, uh, dispose of if anything goes wrong.'

Sammy leaned to the left as far as she dared without toppling off the stool and turned her face up until she intercepted Minnow's gaze and made eye contact. 'I thought we were the white hats?'

Minnow's eyes only held for a moment. 'Uh, it's possible our hats might get a bit, um, *grubby*.'

'How grubby?'

'Oh, you know, grey...ish...but it's important. In the nation's interests...' He was mumbling again.

'Why do you sound as though you don't believe the Service's bullshit?'

'Uh, I actually do, I'm...just not normally having to defend it. Other people do that.'

She smiled. 'I'm giving you a hard time.'

'Yeah, but if I were you, I'd give me a hard time too. Just to be sure.'

'I wish I knew what I was trying to be sure of.'

'We just need to watch, that's all. Unless things go wrong.'

'And we are watching...?'

'All the systems. Emergency, essential, so if anything goes down during the strike...'

'We can put it back up. I get that bit. What I don't get is why it's secret.'

'The Service doesn't want it getting out that we know total automation is bollocks. The party line is, it's safe to let the geeks strike because the systems are robust enough to cope.'

'But they aren't?'

'No.'

'But surely...' Sammy put the tablet down again and started to count the points on her fingers. 'If the systems need the people, and the people need the jobs, then, what's wrong with the truth?'

'We can't just *say* the systems aren't ready for full automation; we'd be shot down by the developers. But we can demonstrate it, maybe, so long as nobody dies.'

Sammy smacked her fourth finger a little too hard and bent it back. 'Ow. So it's possible we might, as well as watching to make sure nobody dies...?'

'You won't be involved in that bit...not that it necessarily *is* a bit.'

'I know no-thing.' Her impression of Manuel merely produced a look of incomprehension. 'You don't watch old comedies?'

'Not really.'

Sammy gave the tablet's power button a brief push and looked out the window. The lights of East London spread as far as she could see. She wondered what you'd be able to see in the daytime; which way did the window face? South-west? Maybe you could see the London Eye on a clear day. She shook the idea of being here in the morning from her mind.

'So, moving on, how are you getting in?'

'Ah, well.' Minnow sat on a stool at the other desk and fired up a screen. 'At first we'd planned to just get access to each of the top-level servers and sneak a dongle into place.'

'Giving you remote access?'

'Yes.' Minnow nodded. 'But on further consideration we realised there were too many systems to keep tabs on unless we had a sense of where the weak points were.'

'You're looking at a lot of differently stacked VPNs. You'd need a department, not just you and me,' Sammy mused out loud.

'Precisely, and we weren't happy with the way we'd planned to gain physical access anyway…well, one of us wasn't… You really don't want to know that bit,' he added, as Sammy opened her mouth to ask. 'So, I called in a few favours from old, um, colleagues, and now we've sent a memo round to all the services we need to watch, telling them that we trust them to run just fine but, belt'n braces, we're sending a government-approved penetration-testing consultant to double-check.'

'Nice. And the consultant pops your dongle in place while alerting you to the weak spots to watch on these babies here.' She indicated the line of screens.

'That's it.'

'So, what do I do with this lot for now?' She indicated the desks full of new toys.

'Each penetration assessment will come in on one of these laptops. I'm going to need help interpreting the information and setting parameters into the computer dedicated to monitoring that system.'

Sammy nodded. 'How long have we got?'

'Just under three weeks until the vote's in. Could be any time after that, but we're working to then as a deadline.'

'Better get started then. Are any of your assessments in yet?'

'Just this one, I thought if we went through it together…'

'I'll know what you need when the rush starts?'

'Yes.'

'And if, mayhap, a particularly juicy but non-fatal gap crops up?'

'You know no-thing.' Minnow attempted the accent and failed.

'We really should watch some old telly sometime.' Sammy grinned. 'It's okay, I have chairs at my place.'

'I think I'd like that,' said Minnow.

CHAPTER NINETEEN

Minnow met his team of hastily cobbled together hacktivists in the greasy spoon on Waterloo Road, opposite the London Ambulance Service headquarters. He'd chosen the LAS computer system to work on first for a few reasons. Mostly because it was likely to be the best defended, but partly because he'd always wanted to see where one of the seminal events of automation had occurred.

He'd not been born back then—last century—but it had worked its way into the academic texts. Every IT guy had had to learn about autumn 1992. A lot of uni departments had that infamous quote from the government inquiry over a door somewhere.

The computer system itself did not fail in a technical sense.
Response times did on occasions become unacceptable,
but overall the system did what it had been designed to do.
However, much of the design had fatal flaws that would, and did,
cumulatively lead to all of the symptoms of systems failure.

All systems merely did what they were designed to do, but there was nothing like twenty-six grieving families to give designers a kick up the backside back then and make sure the next design was foolproof. The lecturers were quick to point out, so as not to be sued by anyone even this many years later, that coroners had been unable to attribute a single one of those twenty-six deaths to the delayed arrival of an ambulance...but it wasn't their job to prove a 'what-if', and the accusations lingered.

Minnow knew that, back then, automation wasn't even an issue; people mostly saw it as a grand thing, improving on the human brain. It still was, in a way. Computers didn't get tired or stupid, and automation had made everything cheaper and faster, but every system needed oversight. Somebody had to check for servers failing, validate backups and check system failovers, for, well, failing. Commercially it was merely annoying and occasionally expensive; people grumbled if their shopping didn't arrive at the allotted time, or if their phone line went down, or the power was out for twenty minutes, but it mattered a darn sight more if somebody's house was on fire or a kid had fallen into a paddling pool.

He had his priorities sorted for the penetration team. LAS first. The other ambulance servers next. Fire, then police, then utilities. He was in the happy position of having access to Home and Defence Ministry systems without subterfuge, so he'd made a start on those. Sammy had picked up the finer points of troubleshooting pretty fast. With the brain on that chick, he'd not need anyone else on watch in his makeshift laboratory. Minnow found himself smiling as the guys who were about to form HackPro Enterprises bundled through the door, falling over each other to get in out of the drizzle. He waved them over to his table and recommended the sausage and onion rolls with extra mustard. He'd heard from someone they were good. Not that Minnow was able to eat or drink anything in such a chaotic environment.

Once the newcomers had been set up with breakfast and cups of that muddy liquid with a film on top that could be tea or coffee, depending what you were expecting, they made introductions. HackPro wasn't a real consultancy, of course. Penetration testing agencies existed, and made good money from repeatedly checking the security of private sector systems, but none of them were working for their own redundancy, so people shopped around. No one would notice a new, deniable entity of Minnow's old muckers, a few other black-hat-turned-white guys. They'd all cut their teeth as teenagers trying to hack systems for kicks. Shrimp and Tiddler—their given names lost forever in the joint conceit that the more harmless your moniker, the more dangerous you could be. Plus, the Yank who'd shown him how to go straight.

Minnow actually shook Chad's hand, as affectionate as he ever got, and sat staring at his fingers as Chad retold their history for Shrimp and Tiddler's benefit. He expounded his own journey from juvie—after being discovered in his parents' basement at the age of fifteen, transferring money from their online bank accounts to his—to government wonk, persuaded to use his mind on behalf of the US of A, instead of more time inside. He'd joined the FBI while Minnow was still black hatting. He'd been the fall guy for a harmless stunt and a spot of friendly rivalry had kicked in. Chad had been first with the suggestion that Minnow turn good guy to stay out of jail.

'Bit of luck finally came our way,' Minnow added. 'Chad's here on holiday, going to Comic-Con, sightseeing a bit first.'

Chad nodded. 'First time in London, heard you guys had a bit of a crisis on, always happy to help. Besides, our national security could be affected if this trouble spreads. Americans are losing jobs too, and anything that hits the news creates copycats. I'd value the chance to be in on the work, but I'm on vacation so no one my end needs to know, unless—'

'Unless it all goes horribly wrong?' Tiddler sat back and twirled his thumbs.

'Yeah.'

Caroline and Doug occupied Doug's favourite table by the window. The cafe was quiet. Caroline mused that the serious work of meeting and talking, hidden away in committee rooms and offices, had taken over faster than usual. Emergency briefings everywhere: it was well nigh impossible to cover them all with her small staff.

She planned to cut Doug loose this afternoon and spend a bit of time watching the newcomers wend their way in and out for coffees and teas, on the lookout for signs of stress.

Doug had done reasonably well so far. He'd picked up some confidence after the whole Gerald thing and made a decent fist of the press conference. He'd said the stuff they'd written for him about how heads of state were always on the side of the people, because they were the people, as was the government. He'd made his plea for calm and for workers to await the result of the ballot. He'd acknowledged that the loss of jobs was an issue the government took seriously and that he viewed the upcoming ballot as vital information that would absolutely inform policy. In short, he'd bought them some time.

'I'm going to leave you to your own devices for the next few days,' she said.

'Really? Are you sure that's wise? I thought I had to have my hand held round the clock in case I hit the bottle again.' He glanced at her and looked away.

'How did you—?'

'I'm not stupid.' He met her eye. 'Or as that idiot Carswell is always saying, I'm not as green as I'm cabbage-looking.' Caroline stifled a snigger and stirred her coffee as he continued. 'There are people here with far more to cope with than me. I'm just the front man. I go on the telly and read platitudes. Look, see those two...' He indicated Morrow and Brown, who had just joined the small queue for coffee. Laden with bags of stuff, they must have just come from a joint Home-stroke-Defence ministry powwow. 'They've got a shit load more stuff on their plates than I have if this thing goes tits-up, but I guess they don't have a big red fucking stamp across their files that says ALCOHOLIC.'

'Fair enough.' Caroline placed her spoon in her saucer; everyone seemed to get one now, whether they asked for it or not. 'I was actually planning to spend a bit of time with those two next. We did have some concerns about you, it's true. But not the booze, just the figurehead stuff. It can be stressful taking the flak when the ability to screw up is in someone else's hands.' She took her turn to direct a thousand-yard stare out of the window and along the Thames. 'Believe me, I've been there.'

'Really?' Doug scanned her face. 'I find that hard to believe.'

She returned her mind to the room and smiled at him. 'If it helps you at all, the official line is currently, "Sideworth is a safe pair of hands."'

She beckoned to the two ministers now scanning the room, cups and saucers in hands, looking for somewhere to sit. Doug watched as they both drew, like a couple of magnetised iron filings, towards her.

'Come and join us. How's it going?' She addressed each of them as they pulled chairs away from the table, put their computer bags, folders and tablet cases here and there, and settled down. She was momentarily glad Minnow was elsewhere; he'd have needed to tidy up.

Queenie sat amid tapestried and carefully draped splendour with her feet up on a pouffe big enough to sleep on. It was striped red and white, but then everything was striped red and white. Rideau Hall seemed to be one big inside-out circus tent, but with comfy chairs, a lot of pictures and no animal smells.

She was sewing in the ends of the tea cosy she intended to present to the Governor General at tonight's banquet. Exchanges of gifts were a tradition that dated back to the old days, apparently, and it was still important to give something relatively pointless. Nothing to eat or drink, nothing that wasn't allowed in the country, nothing too expensive. They'd said a tea cosy would do fine, although

Queenie was a bit miffed they thought it was pointless.

Eugene would be along shortly, bringing some local bloke to tell her about who they were meeting. She'd do her best to remember but that was Andy's job really. Especially since he seemed to think she was stupid. She planned to treat them all like she'd treated Bert's cronies all these years. They could do the talking while she knitted. They thought it annoyed them, but it stopped them wondering what she was thinking, which most times was just as well.

There was a thing about the French, she knew that. Most of Canada had gone the way of sortition when Britain went republican, but Quebec had opted not to. So they still had elections and politics and that. The Governor General, whose house she was in, was just like her—picked at random, but the Quebec prime minister was an old-style politician, and he'd be at the dinner. He was one of the ones in office because he'd spent all his money—and a lot of other people's, probably—trying to prove he was more popular than some other poor schmuck who thought they'd like a go at being important.

There'd been riots recently in Montreal, she knew that too. After several decades of separation, the French had twigged they spent a load of tax money on elections and the other Canadians didn't, so there were people who wanted to rejoin and ditch the electing. She reckoned Andy'd be on top of it all. She just had to be nice and not upset anyone.

There was a knock on the adjoining door to the next room in her suite. Eugene popped his head in and asked, 'Nearly done?'

'Yes, luvvie, come in.' He slipped into the room as he

always did, too silently for a lad who looked like some sort of basketball player, and perched on one of the couches with fancy twiddly backs.

'I'll take it down to where they do the photo call for the gift exchange when you're done,' he said. 'They've got a cuddly chipmunk dressed up as a Mountie for you.'

'Aw.' Queenie wrinkled her nose. 'Maybe I'll give it to one of the kiddies comin' to see the horses next weekend. Do a raffle or a competition or something. What do you reckon?'

Eugene returned the nose thing. 'Nice idea. We could maybe do something like that every time you get back from one of these jollies. Oh, by the way, I've taken the teapot to the kitchens,' he added. 'They're going to make your tea in it after dinner, and I've begged them to return it to us dirty.'

Queenie chortled. 'How did they take it?'

'Hmm, difficult to say. They have one old hand down there who looks about sixty.' Queenie shot him a look that was designed to say *watch it mate*, and it appeared to work. 'Sorry, ma'am, you know, someone who was around *before*.'

She let him off the hook. He was a good lad really.

'Yes?'

'Yes, and she remembered all the weird demands when royalty used to visit, she said not washing a teapot was really quite tame.' He offered her a grin and a wink. 'But then Canadians are so nice, it's pretty difficult to annoy them.'

CHAPTER TWENTY

'Move over, Jojo, let a girl sit down.'

Caroline collapsed into the sofa, put her feet up on the coffee table, sipped at her glass of wine—Merlot this evening—and sighed.

It had been a long day. It had been a long week...few weeks. They usually had a gentler handover; time to let the new intake bed in a bit. Not much changed from administration to administration in the general order of things. Once the sort of politicking you needed to do to get elected was out of the equation, running the country was pretty much like running anything else. The art of the possible. Steady hands on tillers, an adjustment here, a tweak there. Interest rates went up and down slightly, depending on exchange rates and trade balances. Taxes shifted a little if a popular idea had to be funded. The absence of stupid manifesto promises that any first year civil servant could tell you would never work made for a peaceful time of it, mostly. Reps came up with ideas. They got discussed in the House. If something developed legs, it went to a ministry committee. Specialists told the ministers why it wouldn't work, and that was the end of that. Unless it could work, in which case it went to a Cabinet vote.

The ship of state resembled a mighty liner crossing the Atlantic these days; the merest of intelligent adjustments to the tiller kept her on course. While the few states that still clung to the insanity of old democracy were more like the Merlin Rocket sailing dinghies she'd crewed around the Welsh Harp reservoir in her teenage years. Tacking into the wind, and permanently unstable. She grinned at the cat, who offered a stony glare in reply. Not a bad metaphor; pity she could only use it on people who sailed.

She'd spent the day with Brown and Morrow. The two ministries were meeting to collaborate on plans each day now, and she was relatively content with their performances. Her staff, or *spies*, as most of the new intake would come to call them by the time they realised what she was really there for, had been spot on with their observations as usual.

Morrow: practical, orderly, with a mind that filed away the expertise of others until it could be useful. He appeared to be capable of sifting the must-knows from the good-to-knows, as each specialist ran through the stand-by procedures for their purview. His biggest asset was his awareness that the brass needed wires laid and provisions shifted before they could do anything fancy. So, although he'd probably never heard of critical path project planning, he recognised it when he saw it.

Brown was a different kind of okay. Used to collecting thoughts and suggestions from a class full of dumb kids and then telling them the right answer, without demolishing anyone, he was a good listener...albeit a little at sea when the right answer was ambiguous.

He seemed aware that his ministry would take the blame if anyone got hurt, despite having no control of how relations with the police unions had deteriorated under the previous administration. Nobody had noticed trouble brewing; that was one of the downsides to sortition. With no opposition candidates poking sticks at things to find stuff to criticise the government over, complacency could allow problems to fester for too long. Replacing 999 calls to human beings with the automated text system had begun as a way to create access for the hard of hearing, which had been a grand thing. Then it had been cheaper than people. Several reps in the last administration had brought complaints from the public about wanting human contact, but they'd been soothed into compliance by figures on speed, accuracy and efficiency.

Who knew the emergency services were at boiling point? Well, everyone did now.

She picked up her knitting bag. The stars and moons were done. She pondered her next make. She was tempted to do a whole series based on Carswell's ties, but the guild's work sometimes made the TV news. Would anyone notice? Probably not, she decided. She riffled about in the bag until she found some squared paper and a pencil. He'd worn one with Snoopy all over it this week; that would work. She'd had someone check his luggage for mad ties before they let him on the plane, of course. It probably wouldn't have mattered to the Canadians, but she wanted him trained into a somewhat blander appearance before they sent him anywhere sensitive.

She wondered how they were getting on. They'd be

back on Friday. She was quite looking forward to hearing about it from Queenie but she had something she wanted to check up on first.

Setting aside the squared paper for a moment, she roused herself to cross the room and pick up her telephone handset. Yeah, landlines, so last century, but she liked them. Having a landline at home helped maintain the illusion that when she was out, she was *out of contact*. 'Hi, Gerald, just a quick message. I have an errand to run tomorrow lunchtime, if that's okay. Minnow won't be around either, I don't think, so if you want a meeting, next time I'll be available is, um, Friday morning at Buck Place for the debrief.'

She clicked off that call and punched another number in. 'Ali? Hi, how are you?'

'Listen, are you free for lunch tomorrow?'

'How about if I come to the office?'

Big Doris stood for a moment, looking through the window of the Mile End Road Launderama. It looked familiar, inviting. She could just make out Sandra through the steamed-up glass, fighting to fold a fitted sheet. If she'd shown the daft ha'p'orth once she'd shown her a dozen times how to tuck the corners into each other first. She sighed. People had been on at her all day in the Tower Hamlets Rep's office. She was a sitting duck. Everybody was up in arms about the strike. This one wanted to know if his bins would still be collected, that one wanted to know if Tesco's would still be open, people whingeing about losing their jobs, it was nothing but moaning.

People moaned in the launderette too, but they didn't expect her to sort it out for them, they just wanted her to moan back at them. That response wasn't going down as well with the *constituents*—she stuck her tongue out at them—as it had with her regulars.

The only good thing Doris could think of to come of the strike was that she'd been too busy answering questions about it to bother with that thing Queenie wanted. Who did the stuck-up cow think she was? Why should Doris traipse around the Peabodys asking people if they had a cough?

Doris pushed the door hard; it stuck a bit with the damp, and the little bell someone had brought her back from a holiday in Majorca jangled. Sandra looked up from her sheet folding.

'Blimey, look what the cat dragged in. How are you, Lady Muck?'

'I'm all right, girlie, came to make sure you wasn't runnin' my business into the ground.' Doris looked around her. 'Nobody in, I see you insult them all into goin' elsewhere?'

'Don't be daft, it's getting late. I've got a bloke coming for this lot.' She nodded to the bedding, which appeared to be climbing out of the laundry basket in a defiant attempt to deny having been folded. 'Then I'm closing up till tomorrow.'

'We stay open till nine, Sandra, you know that.'

'I'm closing early, just for tonight. Got a meeting.'

'Ooh listen to it, "got a meeting." Who with, your bleedin' stockbroker?'

'No. And I can't tell you. Not now you're one of them.'

'Bleedin' sauce. You're not too old to go over my knee,

girly.' Doris wagged a forefinger in her daughter's face. Sandra regarded the index finger with disdain. Then she grinned and snapped her mouth at it. Doris whipped it away just in time and scowled. 'You can't close my business early and not tell me why, we're losin' *revenue*.'

'Hark at her! "Revenue", is it? Whatever. My Bob says I can't tell you because you'll tell them, so there.'

'Don't be so daft, I'm doin' it because I've got to. If your Bobby's up to something, I want to know. I don't want to come bailing you out of another police station.'

'Oh, all right, keep your hair on. They're thinking of joining the demos, that's all.'

'What, the strikes?'

'Yeah.' Sandra sighed and sat down on the wooden bench opposite the dryers. She put her elbows on her knees and her chin in her hands.

'He says they reckon it's a golden opportunity to "get democracy back on the agenda."' She lifted her chin to make the air quotes, then it sank back down.

Doris sat next to her. 'But this is about jobs and that. I've been hearing about it all piggin' week.' Doris's tone softened a little. Sandra was loyal to Bobby, but she got frustrated with his dafter exploits too.

'Look, I really shouldn't be tellin' you.'

'Look at me, girly.' Doris turned and gently guided Sandra's chin with her hand, until they were eye to eye. 'I'm your mum. I might be a poncey government thing right now, but that'll stop and I'll still be your mum, right? What's goin' on?'

Sandra turned away, seemingly fascinated by the falling clothes in the dryer in front of her.

'Bob says...' She took a deep breath and tried again.

'Bob says...the marches and demos are supposed to be peaceful because it's just normal people supporting the workers and that. But his guys want to infiltrate the demos with placards and stuff about democracy and cause a bit of aggro, so it'll show on the news all over the world as pro-democracy riots.'

'But normal people won't turn out for that.'

'No, but he says there's ways to make it look that way. Plant little bunches of two and three here and there in the crowd, then all start yelling at once and it sounds like the whole demo is agreeing with you. He says the older guys remember how to do it. You'd get a bunch of nice people coming out to protest about, oh you know, some tax or other, then the socialist workers would start yelling and before you knew it Russian telly had pictures of Britain turning communist overnight.'

'No violence, though?'

'He says it makes no difference either way—the police ain't showin' up. Someone gets mouthy with them, they'll have to shut them up, won't they?'

'I don't like the sound of it. You ain't goin' along? Please don't.'

'I told him I'd stay here, ready to board up the winders if it turns ugly and there's lootin'. We can't do it the day before, see, or it would look like we knew somethin' was up.'

Doris shook her head. She had no idea what to say.

'What, Mum? You don't like the way it is now, do you? You keep sayin' it's daft. You turned the air blue about "fucking Queenie and her bloody airs and graces" only last week.'

'Yes, but that's because...just that...I don't want to do it.

No, not even that, I don't know if I can do it. It don't mean I think it's wrong. Not when someone else is doin' it.'

'You won't tell them, will you? Bob'd kill me if he thought I'd ratted them out.'

Doris looked from the tumble dryers to the steamy, finger-marked windows and beyond to the metal shutters pulled down over the shop fronts on the opposite side of the street.

'About time we dragged this place into the twenty-first century,' she muttered. 'Maybe I'll see about some shutters like they've got at the pawnshop.'

'Only me!' Sammy sang into the intercom, ready to make a dash for the door the second she heard the buzz.

She trotted past the cabbage smell, up the stairs and rat-tatted on Minnow's door.

He opened the door two inches and stood in the gap, staring at her as though she had green hair and a purple nose.

'How did you get up here?' he asked.

'Uh, through the door and up the stairs, you buzzed me in, remember.'

'Yeah, but I did the really quick buzz thing. So after that I waited for you to buzz again…to say to buzz again.'

'Ah, but I remembered the challenging buzz thing and did the single bound thing.'

'Oh, right.'

'Yeah, thought I'd channel Superwoman today. Shall I wear the costume next time?'

'Um, I'm not sure.' Poor guy looked flustered; was that a blush?

'Joke! Can I come in?' She gestured towards the tiny gap through which Minnow was still regarding her. This was harder work than she had anticipated. She thought maybe they'd made friends, that knowing they'd be spending their evenings poring over ways of hacking into insanely important computer systems would give them an easiness, a joint-geekiness. Now it looked like Minnow would need the same level of effort every day. But then, who was she to complain? She'd only just been rescued from the black pit herself; she'd not have been much fun a year ago. And Minnow had no idea he was part of her personal rescue team. She imagined him scampering through snowy peaks on all fours with a barrel of brandy round his neck and grinned.

'Who are we hacking tonight, Boss?'

'Shhhh! Don't talk like that out here.' Minnow looked up and down the grim hallway.

'Bloody well let me in then.'

'Okay, okay, but don't do that again, right?'

'Right.'

The hallway light was still on. That was odd. Normally when Justin came home from work the timer on the pushbutton light popped off just before he reached his door. Maybe a short circuit; he'd call the caretaker when he got settled. Just for now, though, he was quite grateful to be able to see that his door stood slightly ajar. Burglars? He had nothing worth stealing.

He pushed the door open another inch with his foot and looked in. The place was in darkness. Anyone ransacking the place would need light, wouldn't they? A torch, at least. Still wary, he pushed the door a bit farther open and reached around for the light switch.

Next thing he knew, the arm not attempting to switch on the light was expertly twisted behind his back. It didn't exactly hurt, but felt like it might if he moved.

'What do you want?' Justin was more surprised than frightened. For a moment.

'Let's shut the door and sit down, shall we?'

'I haven't got anything worth stealing.' It began to hurt.

'In, you stupid bastard.'

Justin couldn't help agreeing with the 'stupid' bit—why hadn't he just called the police from the hall?

'What part of "in" didn't you understand?'

'I'm trying...' Justin managed get the light on without too much discomfort from his—now he thought about it—expertly controlled other arm. His assailant kicked the door shut and released his arm while he locked it.

'What do you want?' He could see the chap now, at least. Well, he could mostly see the balaclava. And the knife. He considered screaming. But he could be dead before anyone bothered to come and see what was wrong.

'That's better.' His assailant settled into Justin's favourite armchair and indicated the sofa. 'Sit down.'

Justin sat.

'I have a message for you. From your new colleagues.'

'What colleagues? I...'

'You haven't been checking your inbox, my friend.'

CHAPTER TWENTY-ONE

Deborah Chandler checked the novelty clock above her desk for the umpteenth time. Rarely had she found it more infuriating than she did today. One of the copywriters had brought it back from a holiday in America, telling everyone she'd found it in a *darling* craft-stroke-souvenir shop in Savannah, Georgia. Which is apparently all pretty much *darling*. Deborah had absorbed every detail of her description of the town, ready for the day when she'd tell her mother about the side visit she'd made from one of Colin's trans-Atlantic sales trips. Which would never happen. The clock was made of tile with all the numbers hand-painted, dropping higgledy-piggledy in the bottom right corner. There was a caption that read, *Whatever.* And hands that pointed to empty space. It was supposed to represent *the non-linear timescale of creativity* and was also supposed to be a source of inspiration for the agency's high flyers. The ones who persuaded the nation to spend their money with whimsical brilliance.

The 'creatives' loved it, but Deborah spent a lot of time reassuring clients that it absolutely didn't mean their deadlines weren't important to the agency. Today it was driving her nuts. She had to find a way to get Annie to cover her at the reception desk while she went to the loo at exactly five to one.

'I've got a guest meeting me here for lunch, Debs,' Ali had said, popping her head round the frosted glass door to the creative suite. The door Deborah was tasked with guarding. She'd made the reception area her own, with flowers and sweeties and artfully arranged magazines, but she'd never made it through the door either.

'Can you let me know when she arrives and make her comfy?'

Deborah had undertaken to do that unchallenging task to the very best of her ability, naturally, but then Ali had added, 'You'll have plenty to talk about, she knows your mum! Maybe you've heard the name: Caroline Grant?'

Deborah had felt the colour drain from her face and busied herself with the buttons on her switchboard in order to look away.

'Hmm, not sure,' she'd managed to say.

She had to find a way to leave her desk. She'd started at the ad agency twenty-five years ago as a school leaver with a decent typing speed and a certificate that said she could use one of the newfangled digital switchboards. Her lofty ambitions to rise to the status of creative existed only in the tales she'd told the family over the years, but she had no intention of letting that snooty bitch in on the truth. She checked the clock again. Ten to one. Annie would be back from her lunch break in a couple of minutes, so she'd just check a couple of emails and then give her a buzz.

Deborah opened the email from the Independent and Un-Aligned Workers' Union. She'd not told anyone at work she'd joined up; they would have pooh-poohed the idea that she had anything to worry about, but she could see the level of automation creeping upwards every time they gave her a 'fabulous new machine, darling, it'll save you so much work.' She knew it was just a matter of time before receptionists would be redundant too.

She scanned the figures. Voter turnout: 85 per cent. Votes in favour of industrial action: 67 per cent of those cast. Conclusion: the IUAWY strike would be legal. The email continued with details of meeting points in each city, etc. She just had to decide what to tell the agency. Maybe she'd tell them she needed the day off because of potential transport disruption. But then she wouldn't be on strike, would she? Although she supposed she could be at the demo as a concerned citizen supporter. She could tell Mum she was taking a bigger interest in current affairs these days—the silly old woman would be all pleased about that, think she had something to do with it.

'Hello, Deborah, how nice to see you again. How are you?'

Deborah looked up from her screen in horror.

'I can see you're, uh, *filling in* for the receptionist just now. Would you mind letting Ali know I'm here?' Caroline unleashed a smug, self-satisfied, infuriatingly friendly smile that seemed to say, *I'm being nicer than necessary, don't push it.*

Deborah took the hint. 'Ah yes, she's uh, just a moment. Please, take a seat.' She waved a hand towards the little corner arrangement of chairs, replete with coffee machine and sweetie bowl. Then she pressed the button for Ali's desk and spoke into her headset. 'Ali, your guest is here.'

'Thank you so much.' Caroline oozed the sort of charm you can afford when you know you've won.

'Welcome,' Deborah muttered as she buzzed another desk. 'Annie, can you cover my lunch break please? Yes, right now if you don't mind, I have something, uh, urgent...'

Deborah closed her emails and busied herself with appearing to press buttons until she was finally able to dash to the Ladies' and burst into tears.

Ali was giving Caroline one of her quizzical looks as they settled at a corner table in the Maida Vale Wetherspoon with their BLT ciabattas.

'What's going on with you and Debs?'

'Oh, nothing much.' Caroline sat back and crossed her feet at the ankle. She spotted a patch of dried mud on one taupe French heel and bent to brush it away. 'She's been telling the family she's a creative, lots of airs and graces about her flair for advertising.'

'Oh dear.' Ali giggled. 'She's been on reception since before I joined. I think they keep her because she's cheap. Did you call her on it?'

'No need.' Caroline popped her feet back under the table, satisfied with their cleanliness, and turned her attention to her napkin. 'She knows I know. It's enough.'

'And she knows that you know that she knows that you know?' enquired Ali with the mischievous smirk Caroline remembered from university days.

'Pretty much.'

'Will you tell Queenie?' Ali pulled a bit of bacon from her sandwich and munched it with a level of concentration that reminded Caroline of a particularly fastidious llama chewing the cud. 'What?' Ali asked. 'I like the crispy bits, okay?'

Caroline laughed. 'Yes…and no.'

'Huh?'

'Yes, you like the crispy bits and no, I'm probably not going to let on. It depends. I'm hoping she'll, you know, soften a bit? The whole knowing about knowing thing, which you'—she offered Ali a tiny bow—'articulated so clearly a moment ago.'

'Mmm, hm.' Ali was munching properly now.

'Might just do the trick. Queenie's doing fine but she could do without a family meltdown.' Caroline opened her sandwich, exposed the sliced tomato and dredged it in black pepper. 'Just like she could do without being told she's an embarrassment by a pathological liar,' she added. She reassembled her lunch, cut it in two and began making inroads.

'How are you getting on with the Liverpool project?' Ali asked after a few more moments of bacony communion.

'Okay, I've started taking it to meetings, pisses Gerald off no end.'

Ali laughed. 'I bet. Remember when we'd knit through lectures?'

'Yes, nobody's called me Madame Defarge for years. I'd forgotten what fun it was.'

'I've got three to go and then I'm done my quota,' Ali said. 'But I don't think I'd get much work done if I brought it with me here.'

'That's because you do less listening and more writing than I do.' Caroline agreed. 'I'm on the last one, but next week might get a bit too hairy for pleasant tasks.'

'The strike?' Ali asked. 'It'll be okay, though? Nothing much gets out of hand any more.'

'Oh sure.' Caroline crossed her fingers under the table. 'Just a bit soon for the newbies, is all, keeping me busy.'

'Maybe we should bring the Liverpool thing forward to next week? Give people something else to talk about?'

'Oof, do you think?' Caroline shook her head slowly. 'I'd not be able to help out...'

'We can get the others together, head up there without you. I think it'd be nice.' Ali chased a stray tomato seed round her plate with the last bit of crust.

'Okay, I'll drop what I've got ready over to your place at the weekend.' Caroline looked at her oldest friend. 'But Ali?'

'Yes?'

'Don't get mixed up with any demos, eh? Please. Just in case?'

'It's official.' Clayton Brown held his hands relatively steady as he addressed the emergency cabinet meeting. 'All the major unions have voted for action, and I'm told by the specials who analysed these figures—you've all got a copy in front of you—' He nodded at the conference table, around which a sea of relatively unfamiliar faces were seated. 'I'm told by the analysts that every ballot is legal. Ladies and gentlemen, we have a general strike on our hands.'

Clayton scanned the faces. A mix of excitement, anxiety, furrowed brows and nervous tics. It looked like a class of Year Sixes staring down a spot test on algebra.

'Do we know when?' asked someone at the back of the room.

Clayton looked over; not someone he recognised. 'Not yet, Mr...?'

'Bradley,' the face advised. 'Defence. Taking charge of essential services under Mr Morrow.'

'Ah, yes, thank you.' Clayton acknowledged the chap with a thin-lipped smile. 'It looks as though we will find out when the nation does.' He gestured to the wall screen behind him. 'The joint unions have called a press conference for three thirty today, we've called this meeting so that all the ministries, plus anyone else who needs to know, can watch it together.'

The roomful of people began that mad fidgety dance that heralds a crowd all trying to check the time at once. Some were lifting their hands to look at wristwatches; others were digging in pockets to retrieve mobile phones. By the time all the necessary ribs had been dug by all the dancing elbows and everyone had said 'ow' and 'sorry' to everyone else, the screen was live and showing BBC 24.

Clayton scanned the room one more time. It had filled up as news of the meeting had spread around Westminster. The seats at the table had been taken up first, with the ministers and specialists who would be finalising the emergency plan for the rest of the day, but now the largest conference room in the House looked like it had back on day one, as everyone who was anyone—and a good few people who were no one—slipped in at the back and jostled for space perched on the windowsills. He spotted

Gerald and Caroline, almost the last to arrive. He caught Caroline's eye. Or did she catch his?

He beckoned a question with his head. Did she and Gerald want to make their way to the sharp end of the room? He was rather hoping they'd demand to be let through to become everyone's point of focus. He'd prefer to be facing a class of recalcitrant algebra rebels any day, but no, she'd smiled and shaken her head. They were there to watch. To watch the TV, and presumably, to watch him.

Here goes...

He unmuted the screen and took his seat to find out just how much of a nightmare his—and everybody else's—future was likely to be.

Silence.

Clayton realised he'd not heard absolutely nothing from a packed room ever before. He wished, now he'd muted the TV again, that Queenie's knitting needle clatter was around to ease the atmosphere. He shot a pleading look to Caroline and Gerald. He had no idea what to do next.

'Thank you, ladies and gentlemen.' Gerald came to his rescue, and everyone turned at the sound to locate the speaker by the door. Clayton took the opportunity to wipe a droplet of sweat from his eyebrow. 'This emergency meeting will revert to cabinet only, plus those specialists involved in immediate planning, in five minutes. The cabinet and I thank you for your public-spirited interest in *upcoming events* and will keep you all informed by memo of any decisions taken this afternoon that affect you or your work. In the mean time, the Home Office Chief Minister'—he nodded politely at Clayton—'and I would appreciate it if you'd return to your usual sphere of operation. We still have a country to run.'

He and Caroline stepped aside from their spot in the doorway to allow the flow of people past them and out into the hallways and corridors beyond.

Clayton gathered his wits and turned to the specialist at his side. He proffered the remote.

'How do I switch the screen over from TV to the agenda?'

The youngster smiled and took the remote. He pressed this and that and handed it back. 'You'll be fine, you know,' he whispered. 'You just need to remember the next thing, that's all it takes.'

'Thanks, I think I'll put that on the wall by my desk. It might help get me through next week.' Clayton was genuinely grateful to this kid whose name he hadn't even bothered to look up, let alone memorise. 'Just remember the next thing!'

The kid grinned and turned to his computer.

Gerald and Caroline made their way to a couple of recently vacated chairs at the far end of the conference table. It looked like Clayton's reprieve might continue, but Gerald began to speak again.

'I notice the Home Office Chief Minister has displayed this afternoon's agenda for you.' Clayton shot the pair of them a desperate look. Caroline merely nodded her approval. *Bastards*. They were going to leave him to it. 'So, ladies and gentlemen, let's allow him to take the chair.'

Clayton stood by the screen once more. 'Thank you, Chief Secretary. Well, uh, now we know what and where, we um, well, we have some decisions to make.' He surveyed the faces again. Most had lost a little colour. 'A full walk-out of all staff, including the emergency services on Monday, doesn't leave us much time, but I'm sure if we work point by point down the list that's been prepared for us we can cover all the issues.

'I know everybody has a prototype emergency plan for their remit, prepared by their department and based on previous incidents, and we'll examine each of them one by one.' He indicated the list of ministry functions on the screen. 'But the first decision we need to make is whether to recall the reps. They're supposed to be in the field until the week after next...'

CHAPTER TWENTY-TWO

Queenie analysed the Buck Place reception room for available souvenir display spots. The mantelpiece seemed favourite—the little Mountie chipmunk could sit leaning against that horrible clock, apparently a gift from the Swiss to the *in-cum-bent* before her. She wondered where the gifts nobody wanted ended up. Was there a storeroom somewhere in the belly of the palace, full of stuff that had been graciously accepted by generations of heads of state? She knew most of the artworks and stuff the actual monarchy had looted from here and there round the world had been handed back as part of various peace and cooperation treaties over the years. That left...what? Paperweights and cuddly toys? She could ask Caroline. Once the shouting was over. She was relieved this morning's debrief was going to have to be short; it would leave less time for recriminations. There was a big fuss on about the strike and everyone was busy. Except Queenie. She had no idea what she was supposed to do next, except be yelled at, obviously.

A tentative knock on the door announced the next arrival. Andy Carswell popped his head around it. 'Is it okay if I come in? I can't seem to find Eugene.'

'Oh blimey, ducks, come in, sit down with me. Don't stand on ceremony, we've both had enough of that, eh? Dunno where Eugene's got to, probably still unpacking.'

Carswell plodded over to the seat Queenie pointed out for him.

'Do you get the feeling we're in trouble?'

'Eugene reckons they're not happy.' Queenie changed her mind about the cuddly toy. She picked it back up from its leaning post and brought it with her to the chairs surrounding the coffee table. She lifted the lid of the teapot-despatch box and dropped it inside. 'Hide in there for now.' She addressed the stuffed animal with a tinge of regret as she replaced the lid.

She sat and looked at Andy. Plain blue tie and no gags. Somehow she missed the bumptiousness. They both jumped, startled, at Eugene's more confident knock at the door. He opened it with a hint more formality than usual and announced, 'Mr Lambert and Ms Grant to see you, ma'am.'

That was worrying. Queenie and Andy stood instinctively, but Caroline waved them back into their seats. She took a seat herself, in silence. Gerald strode to the window and looked out, into the Mews below. He took a deep breath and turned.

'Do you have any idea'—he ground the words out through gritted teeth—'how difficult it is to upset a Canadian?' He looked from Queenie to Andy and back. 'Let alone precipitate an international incident over a simple dinner?'

The silence between his words managed to deepen. Queenie decided not to break it. She looked at Andy. He regarded the despatch box with such undivided attention she thought maybe he was expecting the chipmunk to lift the lid and escape if he turned away.

'What happened, Queenie dear?' Caroline tried to catch her eye, but Queenie opted to join the "watching for escaping chipmunks" game. 'Andy? Can you explain? All we know is that the TV news had reports of demonstrations outside the British Embassy in Quebec because the delegation had insulted French-Canadian food.'

'It wasn't me and the teapot, if that's what you're thinking.' Queenie's voice, when it emerged, sounded just like that whiny, defensive tone Deborah used to use when she'd been caught out telling lies at school. 'Eugene made friends with everyone in the kitchen and they was all interested in the tanning and everything...'

'Yes, we know that.' Gerald's tone hadn't softened.

'It was him.' Queenie nodded at the crumpled figure with the conventional tie, who was now trying to bore holes in the despatch box with his eyes. 'He said that thing, what he always says...you know, when there's food...'

Gerald and Caroline both turned questioning gazes to Carswell.

'It's a compliment,' he muttered to the box. 'It was Eugene who got it wrong.'

Gerald and Caroline exchanged a look. Caroline eased herself up from her chair and crossed to the internal door to the rest of the flat. She knocked quietly and then opened it an inch or two. 'Eugene, dear, are you busy?

Could you come and chat to us for a minute?'

'Do we stand a chance of hearing a straight answer, do you think?' Gerald's ramrod-straight military pose turned itself slightly towards Eugene as he entered the room.

'Sit down, dear.' Caroline gestured to a seat. 'And you too, Gerald, you're just making everyone nervous looming over them like that.'

Gerald allowed a couple of beats to pass, just like Bert did, Queenie thought, when he was going to do as he was told but wanted to look like it was his idea. Then he picked up a dining chair and brought it over to join them.

'Can you tell us what happened at the dinner?' Caroline asked Eugene.

'It was all fine, really,' Eugene said. 'Except when it was over I sent a text to the kitchen to say thank you and tell them what people had said about the food.'

'Yes...?' prompted Gerald.

'And Queenie had said it was the best food she'd ever tasted, even though she didn't know what some of the things were.' Eugene was counting points on his fingers now. 'Then the Governor General said he'd ask the kitchen to give her the recipes.'

'Yes...?'

'And then Andy here said it was a veritable repast.'

'Go on.'

'But the chef was a francophone from Montreal, and so I put the text through Google Translate.

'I think I know where this is going.' Caroline put her head in her hands.

'And that bit came out as *very mealy* instead of—'

'Jesus Christ on a bicycle!' Gerald threw his hands in the air and stood again. He began to pace the room. 'I've got a general strike looming, a new intake to coach, no time to plan, and you shower go and screw up the simplest state visit the world has to offer.'

'We told them we were very sorry, and it wasn't what we meant and—' Andy spoke for the first time.

'We went and saw the chef and shook his hand and everything, and it was all fine,' added Queenie.

'But one of the kitchen staff had tweeted it by then.' Now that Andy had started to speak the words all came tumbling out, faster and faster. 'And the TV news got hold of it and it started trending and people went out and you know how fast a thing becomes a thing.' His eyes glistened as he looked up at Caroline. 'We tried so hard to get it all right.'

Queenie nodded. 'They liked the tea cosy.'

'Never mind the fucking tea cosy.'

'Gerald, please!' Queenie hadn't seen Caroline snap at him like that before, but she was grateful. 'It's done now. I'll get the Governor General on the phone, see if we can't sort out a video apology for the evening news. We'll smooth it over and know for another time.' She looked at Eugene, who was wringing his hands, as crestfallen as the others. 'No more Google Translate, eh?'

'I know, I didn't think.'

'It's not usually your responsibility, is it?'

Eugene shook his head. 'I wanted to get it all right.'

'We all did,' added Queenie.

Gerald studied each face in turn.

'I had planned to get you two back out of the country again next week,' he said. 'State visit to the US, so that you could spin any, uh, misrepresentation of events here in a positive way during the strike.' He shook his head slowly.

Queenie wasn't sure if he was saying no to something or exercising his neck. 'Now I'm not so sure.'

'I still think it's a good idea,' said Caroline. 'We can give them a bit more scripting.'

Andy glanced at her with a shred of hope in his eyes.

'Hmm.' Gerald was still easing what appeared to be a very stiff neck. 'We can't spare any more babysitters.'

'It'll be fine.' Caroline consulted her notebook. 'There's a celebratory performance of that play at the White House next week, the one they put on at each inauguration to honour the troops. We can send them to that; then they won't have to do much talking. If anything from here hits the headlines while they're there we can text a scripted response. You can manage that, can't you?' She nodded at each of them in turn. They nodded back.

'Maybe they can,' said Gerald as he watched the nodding faces. 'We'll just have to make sure none of the chefs are bloody Spanish.'

'How's it going?' Caroline asked Minnow as they settled in their usual spot for 'lunchtime talks' at the Red Lion. The usual drinks on the table, the usual arrangement of slices of citrus fruit in the right glasses. It could be an ordinary POETS Day, except for It. And Its timetable.

Minnow pulled a tablet from his bag and swiped the screen a couple of times. 'Slow,' he replied. 'We don't have time for a full pen test of every system, although the guys have been working round the clock since I got them started.'

Caroline and Gerald watched his fingers pull screens

about. He was the only person either of them knew who could talk and work at the same time. In fact, Minnow was at his most eloquent when manipulating some computer at the same time. He seemed to forget the stress of interaction.

'Fortunately, a lot of the services are networked together round the country,' he continued. 'So access to one server can give us access to the others with a bit of, uh, configuring. We don't have time to pinpoint vulnerabilities in individual systems, but we'll have sufficient access to everything that matters to spot a system outage and fire a backup. I've mailed a few USB switchblades out to places we won't get to in time.'

'Do we want to know what those are?' Caroline had to ask, although she knew the answer.

'Probably not.'

'How's the kid from Education working out? Will you need anyone else with you on the day?' Gerald had a tablet in his hands now. He began making a few notes with a stylus.

'Don't think so, she's pretty quick on the uptake. I've had her working on a bit of code to alert us when anything goes down, so we should be able to monitor all the activity okay. We're just unlikely to be able to mess with anything ourselves. We'd need more time than we've got to test various exploits and—'

'That's all right.' Gerald looked up from his screen. 'Probably just as well, come to think of it, although it was a pretty idea. Just so long as anyone who makes a 999 call gets answered—'

'What's that answer going to be?' Caroline didn't usually interrupt Gerald, but this needed asking. 'Now that we know the police, fire and ambulance crews are out as well, are we sending the army to everything?'

'Theoretically that's the easy bit.' Minnow looked up briefly. 'All calls can get routed to a single automated reply system. Everyone will get the response that their emergency is being routed to civil defence but please reconsider whether they really need a bunch of squaddies today.'

'And will all calls generate a turnout?' Gerald looked up from his notes. 'I know Home and Defence have plans for as many standbys as possible, but they can't go to every cat up a tree. Health only have a few managers prepared to man phones and offer triage.'

'And only if they can get in the building,' said Caroline. 'It's all very well being willing to man a phone, but if we set up for it and pickets keep them out?'

'I actually don't see why the front line staff are joining in.' Minnow sat back in his chair and threw his head back to gaze at the ceiling for a moment. 'Computers can't drive to emergencies.'

'Yet.' Caroline finished his sentence for him. 'Driverless transportation isn't far off. If an ambulance or a fire tender can drive itself, the teams get smaller. Onboard computers are already taking care of some of the decision making, and the office jobs have gone, so anyone who gets injured on the front line has no light-duties desk to drive for the rest of their career.'

'But computers can't arrest people, can they? Why the hell are the police coming out?'

'And what do we do about disorder?' Caroline directed her question at Gerald. 'We only need one demo to turn troublesome and we've got the army on the streets against the people. That's hardly very representative, is it?'

'Home Office have been talking with chief constables and the police unions. They want an undertaking that their jobs will be ringfenced, which, obviously, we can't publicly acquiesce to without agreeing to make up fake jobs throughout all sectors and destabilising the private enterprise economy.'

'Which we need the backing of all the people on the streets on Monday to get away with?'

'Precisely.' Gerald laid his tablet on the table and began buffing a fingernail. 'However, our mediation expert—thank you Minnow, inspired positioning—has engineered an unspoken agreement that: should any, uh, *disorder* break out, it will clearly be a sign that computers can't replace sufficient officers on the beat. Their jobs will be deemed to have been agreed to, and any officers nearby will resume work.'

'Nice one.' Minnow nodded.

'Now, we just have to get Sideworth on the TV again, and Queenie and that idiot Carswell on the next plane, and I think we're ready to let events take their course.'

'Citizens of the British Republic. I address you tonight as a fellow citizen. Behind me...' Doug turned from the phalanx of cameras whirring and flashing and the flock of furry microphones swaying about above his head and indicated the assembled cabinet ministers behind him. 'Behind me are the men and women chosen at random to represent us all as your government.' He paused for breath, and double-checked the autocue rolling slowly along on the screen at the far end of the Cabinet Office.

'We have been your cabinet ministers for less than a month,' he continued. 'Before this we were individuals whose livelihoods were as threatened by automation as yours. At the end of this Parliament we will be back in our old lives, and the jobs we left may be no more.

'In short, we understand.' He had a go at the thing Caroline had suggested: look directly into one of the cameras. Apparently it made it feel like you were making eye contact. 'We will be guided by the will of the people. We fully expect there to be some hiccups in non-essential services tomorrow, and we hope you will accept that a temporary inconvenience for some may mean job security for others.

'We know we will see many on the streets tomorrow, and we also know you are angry; however, we make a joint appeal for calm. By all means add your presence and your voice, but there will be no need to shout too loudly, we are already listening.'

Sandra muted the sound on the telly that had been hurriedly fixed to the wall in the Mile End Road Launderama. It was on one of those arm things you could move to and fro. She turned to Bob, who was spreadeagled on the floor with his hand under one of the washing machines. He'd dropped the last nut trying to get the telly mounted in time, and it had rolled as far as it possibly could.

CHAPTER TWENTY-THREE

Deborah had worn her IUAWY badge so she could link up with the others. There were only half a dozen or so, but they'd managed to find each other in the ticket hall of Edgware Road underground station—the Bakerloo Line exit. One of the women had brought along a small placard that read: Independent and Unaligned Workers Align for Jobs! So they could stick together as they joined the throngs marching along the Edgware Road towards Marble Arch.

They'd made rapid introductions. These were strangers whose only connection was that they had no work colleagues, and it looked like this was the entirety of the West London branch, but the woman who'd brought the placard was hoping other people on the march might see it and think about joining. She'd pasted a QR code in the corner, just in case of interest along the route.

Deborah had offered to carry the placard. That way, she'd be surrounded by people without having to make much small talk.

Now, as they made their way slowly under the M40 flyover and south to London's focal point of the day—where there would be speeches from union bosses, and famous singers who had political views—she had a momentary concern that someone might spot her if the TV cameras scanned the crowd. She shook it off, she'd come clean with the agency anyway, and her Mum was in blooming America.

The agency problem had been quite neatly solved for her when Crispin had declared they'd close for the day anyway and 'show some solidarity for the non-creative types, yah?' Everyone had joined in the *yah*-ing and pointed out to each other that the poor people whose jobs could be done by machines were 'really, really worried and rightly so', and 'thank goodness machines can't do what we do.' Deborah had risked piping up then and mentioned she felt a particular affinity with the problem, her switchboards getting cleverer as they were. So she'd joined a union to 'support the others'. There were some lovely, kind reassurances of the 'oh my goodness, we'll always need you' type of thing, but she thought she detected a lack of sincerity. Although it was difficult to tell with ad people. Ali had the decency to be particularly effusive, but that was a worry in itself.

She looked around at the mostly good-natured crowd, converging from every direction into an onward mass, and decided to enjoy the day off and call the new people she'd met her friends. Maybe they'd all have a drink together in a pub afterwards, and she could tell Colin about it. Maybe make plans to meet again and bring partners. She and Colin didn't socialise much.

There were patches of uniforms here and there: A huge Fire Service banner that took several people to carry a few feet in front and some ambulance workers to her left with a big bandaged mannequin and a placard that said, Can a computer patch you up? A group of policemen were being pulled along on some sort of wheeled cart, all singing 'A Policeman's Lot is Not a Happy One', with the requisite knee bends.

Deborah could hear other singing and chanting too. Somewhere behind her a guitar was picking out 'Where Have all the Flowers Gone', and several nearby voices began to join in. As she listened, a new chant started to pick up from several spots in the crowd. She wasn't sure where it had come from but it seemed to spread from point to point of its own volition.

Bring back the vote? Was that it? She listened harder and looked around. A lot of other people looked bewildered too. And now there were new placards. People who'd been carrying stuff about computers and jobs before were in small tussles with more people over their banners. Some of the signs said Democracy Now! They'd not been there before.

'Here we are, dear, new sign for you to carry,' said a voice at her ear.

She turned to face the speaker. 'No,' she began, 'I'm happy with this one.'

The man grabbed her placard and began to pull. 'I don't think you understand,' he muttered through gritted teeth. 'I ain't askin' you. Just give me that one and carry this and no one'll get hurt.'

Deborah held on to the bit of wood her placard was attached to as if it were a baby under threat. 'No, let me go!' she screamed, directing her cry in the direction of the singing policemen.

'They won't help you, luv, they're on strike too.'

Deborah looked about her at the crowd—more and more Democracy Now banners were appearing; the people holding them were mostly looking distressed and were mostly, she now noticed, surrounded by youngish chaps in hoodies who hadn't been there before.

'Just take the sign, there's a good girl.' The man's hand was on her wrist now, twisting slightly. It hurt. The voting chant had got so loud that a few of the singers and dancers had stopped to look around.

Deborah struggled to free her wrist from the man's grip. She knew she was going to have to capitulate eventually, he was too strong for her, but she was damned if she was going down without a fight. Maybe if she made enough fuss people would see what was happening to her. The bloke with the hoodie was walking beside her, pretending to march together, as he twisted her right wrist—the one holding the placard aloft—with his left hand. With his right hand he held the democracy banner he wanted to replace it with. *Clever,* Deborah thought, as time slowed down while she developed a plan. *They've been rolled up until they were needed; nobody saw them before.* She stopped in her tracks, turned to face the thug and, with her left hand, ripped the hood back from his face.

'I can't stop you hurting me,' she yelled, 'but I'm buggered if I'm going to let you hide!' She had no idea where that bit of anger had come from but it was rapidly replaced by surprise. 'Bobby Norris? What the hell do you think you're playing at?'

Bobby released his grip for just long enough. Deborah

sideswiped his ear with the placard handle and down he went.

The singing policemen were off their pull-along cart now. They appeared to have finally noticed something was up and were making their way through the crowd, handcuffing hoodies. 'Thank goodness for that,' Deborah said to the one who approached her. 'Officer, I—'

'Please place your hands behind your back, miss. You're under arrest,' he said.

Minnow and Sammy had been watching computer screens all night. They'd eaten pizza as they worked, with Minnow carefully wiping each keyboard and screen between slices. They'd brought Minnow's little telly into the lounge and popped it on the end of one of the benches. His coffee machine sat at the end of the other. A box of Red Bulls lurked next to a recycle bin under the window bench. Sammy had put her foot down over a bucket to wee in. 'We can go to the loo one at a time,' she'd insisted.

Strictly speaking, the strike had begun at midnight, so they'd been on watch for several hours when the morning news piped up, with the talking heads describing what the marches and demonstrations would probably be like. After hour upon hour of 'we expect good-natured crowds' and old footage of the bands who would be playing at rallies up and down the country, playing at something else, they all agreed something would happen soon.

The bank of screens by the closed blinds showed reassuringly constant code, working its way from top to bottom. There were too many for them to follow, but they'd tested Sammy's little alert system and were satisfied. If any of the networks they were monitoring experienced an unusual event they'd know right away.

'Did you think up something to tell your dad about tonight?' Minnow asked Sammy as they waited for more coffee to brew.

'Yeah, I said we all had to stay in the area today, manning phones and taking enquiries and that.'

'Did he buy it?'

'Yes and no. He has to sneer at something, so he said he couldn't see why *Education* would get any calls.'

'And did you think of a reason?' Minnow poured the coffees. He pondered the oddity. Here he was, someone who only ever drank Earl Grey with lemon and who only ever ate from a white plate in his kitchen, camping out in chaos.

Sammy laughed. 'Yes, I told him university students wouldn't realise the strike meant they couldn't talk to an adviser today.'

'And he bought it because students are stupid?' Minnow grinned at her.

'But of course.'

'What will you do after all this is over?' They had turned their attention back to the screens, coffees in hand, and Minnow picked up the remote to unmute the TV.

'Dunno yet.' Sammy blew across the top of her coffee, and Minnow watched the steam waft away from her lips. 'I know some things I won't do.'

'Oh?'

'Yes. I won't go back home. And I won't go back to university. Maybe something to do with coding. Perhaps I'll finally finish that game and sell it. Whatever it is, I'll stick around in the real world.'

'The real world of fantasy gaming?' Minnow watched her face as he teased her.

'Why not?' She smacked his arm.

'Hey, watch it, that coffee nearly went over.'

'Serves you right.' They were both grinning now. It was kinda comfortable.

He unmuted the TV just as the blonde bimbo said to the suave pundit, 'I think we can go to the outside broadcast team now for a live look at the rally in Marble Arch...'

'Thank you,' replied a windswept woman with a serious expression, as the screen split. 'Here in Marble Arch we were expecting several thousand people, and the organisers will not be disappointed with this turnout!'

The camera panned the crowd, zooming in on the more whimsical dressers and pulling out again to take in the atmosphere.

'The sun is out, the banners are colourful, I can hear singing from the crowd. People are here to party.'

'Thanks for that,' the studio pundit cut in. 'Can you see any signs of trouble at all? We understand that an eleventh hour agreement with the police means that any disorder will be dealt with.'

'All I can see right now are placards demanding job protection and a peaceful crowd, although I do know that trouble makes good TV, and I promise to alert you to anything you can disapprove of back in the studio there.'

'Touché.' The pundit displayed a mouth full of expensive dentition and turned to the bimbo. 'There we have it, a great day out for the family. I understand the government have undertaken to review all aspects of automation if today appears to have majority support in the country.'

She nodded carefully. Her hair stayed put. 'Yes, and it would appear that this is a thing now...'

The outside broadcast camera pulled out from a toddler with 'My dad loves his job' on her T-shirt and swung back to the reporter.

'Ah, it looks like something might be happening here...' The reporter put on an urgent tone. The camera panned the crowd left to right. 'We are starting to see a lot of Democracy Now placards; they're appearing all over the place... As you know, this was billed as a rally for jobs.'

The studio presenters looked at each other. 'Indeed it was,' the pundit opined. 'Are we seeing a groundswell of dissatisfaction in general, do you think?'

'I can't say for certain, but things seem to be turning quite ugly. I'm seeing scuffles...' The camera zoomed in on a couple of young men wearing hoodies grappling a placard out of the hands of a middle-aged man.

'Shit!' yelled Minnow.

'What?' Sammy turned from the TV coverage to the bank of monitors.

Every screen in the room was blank.

'Either we've had a power surge'—Minnow leapt to the floor to check the cables. He followed each to its power bar and pressed the reset button—'or every single fucking server is down.'

'They can't be!' Sammy's face was a picture of disbelief. 'Not all of them, nothing links them together.'

They both stared at the bank of screens as each one blinked back on. The Democracy Now logo flashed back at them from each one.

CHAPTER TWENTY-FOUR

Queenie dabbed her eyes with a tissue as the lights went up. She turned to the US president, seated beside her at the front of a small invited audience in the East Room of the White House.

'That was lovely.'

'Glad you enjoyed it, ma'am. We have it as a small tradition here.'

'I know, I was reading about it.' She waved her programme at Andy, seated on the other side of her. 'Wasn't that lovely? The way it mixed up those soldiers' letters and the love story and the music and that.'

'Indeed,' Andy said, leaning forward to include the president in his reply. 'A glorious rendition of life's rich tapestry.'

'Uh, yeah.' The president gave a nod.

'So, you do this show'—Queenie referred to her programme—'"Letters from the Front", every time the administration changes?'

'Yes, ma'am. The new president invites a representative group of veterans from each segment of the military, and sometimes other heads of state, such as yourself, to a performance of this piece. It has some historical significance for us, you know.'

'Yes, I read that too!' Queenie turned to the first page of her programme and read, '"The World's Most Decorated Play. The first theatrical performance to be produced at the Pentagon." I think it's a lovely thing to do for the soldiers.'

'The administration decided to move it here after the switch from old democracy,' the president said. 'If I remember rightly—and I've not been doing this much longer than you have.' He winked at Queenie and she felt herself blush. 'It's supposed to remind each new intake that war is about people and to remember the reality of the individuals we might send into harm's way.' He flipped open his own programme. 'At least I think that's it. I haven't quite memorised it yet. The speech I'm going to make to the vets in a minute is written down for me.'

'And you didn't know we was coming until the last minute?' Queenie added. 'They decided to send us a bit earlier than—'

'And of course we're delighted to make you welcome at any time.'

'Ooh, you're doing really well at this diplomatic stuff, ain't you? Ain't he the picture of a pukka president, Andy?'

Andy nodded. He seemed to be trying to say as little as possible, which Queenie thought was understandable, but it was starting to feel as though she was doing all the putting of feet into mouths this time. 'Now me, I keep forgetting to be, what's the word, stately? No that's homes.

Anyway, whatever the word is, you've got it and I keep forgettin' how.'

'Not at all, ma'am.' The president took her hand and she tittered. 'There are many ways to be charming, and that is all that is really required of us, I think.' He glanced at Andy for agreement and received a halfhearted nod.

'Now, we should move to the vestibule for the press conference. I have to tell the nation what I'm going to tell the vets at dinner. Plus, make you welcome and answer a few questions. Are you ready for the cameras?'

'I should just check for messages.' Andy found his voice. 'In case there's anything they want us to say.' He retrieved his smartphone from his pocket and switched it on. It bingled an annoying little tune Queenie couldn't place. 'Oh.'

'What's the matter, dear?' Queenie watched the colour drain from his face. 'Your family okay?'

'Yes, I expect so, I don't know.' The man seemed flustered. 'Something's happened at home.' He handed the phone to Queenie and she read: SAY THIS AND NOTHING ELSE!

'What can you tell us about the democracy riots in Britain?'

'Did your administration know democracy was coming back?'

'How do you intend to handle the rioters?'

'Do you have any message for the injured?'

The cacophony of questions and flashing lights took Andy by surprise. He would have had no words to answer each of the questions individually, even if he'd been able to distinguish one from another. He had no idea what they were talking about. They hadn't even seen the news, and now it looked like they *were* the news.

He looked at Queenie. Her eyes were getting wider and wider. She looked at the cameras and the microphones. Then she looked at Andy.

She appeared to make a decision. She walked to the lectern and lifted her chin. The babble in the room subsided slightly.

'Ladies and gentlemen, we can't answer all your questions. Mr President here has things he got to say. But our Foreign Minister, Mr Carswell, is goin' to read a thing on behalf of our government.'

She turned to Andy and whispered, 'All you got to do is read, Andy boy, then it's over and we get some dinner. Go on...'

She stepped back and Andy took her place at the lectern. She was right: he just had to read. He pictured Gerald and Caroline working out every line, considering every nuance, although he knew it might be some random wonk in an office he'd never seen, but it helped to have Gerald in his head. If this went wrong, the shouting and swearing would go the other way. Even so... He smiled at the cameras. His hands stopped shaking. 'I'm going to ask our head of state to read my prepared statement to you all.' He handed his phone to Queenie. She shot him a look filled with venom, took the phone and began to read.

'A peaceful expression of regret that some jobs have become automated took place on the streets of London today. A few democracy rebels attempted to hijack this legal event for purposes of their own but were quickly defeated; not just by police but by the people. Any footage of democracy banners is a mere snapshot of an unfortunate half hour in an otherwise peaceful day. The British Republic is not now, never has been, and never will be, on the verge of a democratic revolution. That is all we have to say at this time. Thank you.' She handed the phone back with an exaggerated flourish.

Andy froze for a moment as the cameras flashed and the questions began again. He guessed Beth would be watching a rabbit caught in headlights on the news at home. And the office too. *Shit*. He felt a touch at his elbow. The president moved to take over the mic.

'Thank you, ladies and gentlemen, the British Foreign Minister will be able to take written questions later. We have a lot to get through today, and I'd like to take some time to speak about our troops...'

'What the hell happened and why weren't we prepared?'

Gerald stood at his office window and gazed at the newly quiet streets. The pandemonium had been total. Parliament Square was still littered with broken and battered placards and banners, the overnight clean-up hampered by strong winds and some disingenuous 'confusion' by council staff over when the strike officially ended.

'I wouldn't say we were completely unprepared.' Clayton Brown looked at Gordon Morrow for support. The Defence Minister nodded. 'We suspected the democracy crew might have something up their sleeves, and we had the police primed to take them down.'

Gerald observed the newly appointed staff and toned

his ire down a notch. 'I do applaud the mobile platform idea.' He tossed a sop to the Home Office Minister. 'It enabled them to spot trouble from a bit of a height.'

'And the army ambulances sorted out most of the injured,' Morrow added.

'The ones they could see on the streets, yes.' Gerald turned to Minnow. 'How many 999 calls didn't go through?'

Minnow swiped a few screens along on the tablet he'd placed on Gerald's desk. 'Uh, thirty-one is all.'

'Thirty-one too many. How long were the systems down for?'

'Only ten minutes, which is interesting. Normally an attack that's about extortion or demands of some sort would have stayed off for days to give us, uh, *motivation* to respond. This was just a bog standard Denial of Service, on then off. A show of strength, I have screenshots of the message.'

Brown and Morrow exchanged a glance. 'Who is this guy, and what does he know about the computer crash? My people could have told you what the screens said; they're the ones who had to try and send vehicles to emergencies with no information.' Morrow sounded incensed. Gerald supposed he had some right.

'We, uh, had a setup to watch the systems...intervene if anything went down.' Gerald considered the office mics. It was a bit late now; they had bigger issues to deal with than whether the government trusted its own computers.

'So this'—Morrow pointed at Minnow—'this *geek* saw it all happen. How exactly did you intervene, if you don't mind a mere minister asking?'

'We, uh, we knew how many systems were down, so we

were able to inform the relevant departments—'

'You think we didn't know?' Morrow was getting louder.

'No, not at all, but sometimes the bigger picture... And we told the TV channels. Their systems were unaffected so that's how we got the word out to people that 999 wasn't working...*and*'—Minnow addressed Morrow directly as he saw him open his mouth—'we'd almost worked out how they got in when the systems came back up.'

Gerald felt for the lad. He knew he'd have wanted a stronger end to that speech, had some idea what it cost him to defend himself with words. But they all knew there was nothing stronger to say.

'At least nobody died.' Brown was playing mediator. Gerald approved.

'No, uh, the BBC put out our information bulletin for anyone who'd called 999 in the previous fifteen minutes to call again, and we—'

'We were lucky.' Morrow remained unplacated. 'Fifteen minutes is a long time if your house is on fire.'

'I know that.' Minnow had returned to his usual mode of speech, muttering into his screens.

'Do we know what they want?' Gerald decided to reclaim the conversation.

'Uh, here...' Brown handed a printed sheet to Gerald. 'This message was emailed to the Home Office after the systems went back up. They want a referendum on bringing back democracy in this administration, otherwise they'll keep shutting us down.'

'Seems a bit lame.' Gerald winced as he heard himself use a spot of the youth parlance he hated so much. 'They know they'd lose, and they know that once the back doors into the systems are closed—'

'What does that mean?' demanded Morrow. 'What back doors?'

'Ah, we um, *obtained access* to the networks with a series of, uh, remote ingresses, we think the hackers managed to—'

'What you mean is, if you hadn't hacked the systems in the first place, the hackers wouldn't have been able to do this? What the hell are you people up to?'

Gerald intervened. 'With hindsight, it is entirely possible that—'

'Don't you start that officialese again.' Morrow's colour was up; Gerald wondered how long it would be before he started spitting.

'Mr Morrow, we all had, have, the nation's interests at heart, and if you wish to direct ire at anyone it should probably be me. However, this debrief should shortly move on to what we have learnt and where we go from here.'

'Where's Sideworth?' Brown looked from person to person. 'He's the front man, isn't he? If we're going to maintain the nonsense that this was about jobs, he needs to be addressing the nation, right now.'

'Indeed.' Gerald decided he had no further need to dominate the discussion from a position of height and returned to his desk to take a seat. 'We have Ms Grant collecting him. He seems to have missed the text about this morning's emergency meeting.'

'Are we going to let on about the computer hacking, then?' Brown appeared to have brought some notes with him. *Good man*, Gerald thought, *moving us on*.

'We think not,' Gerald began, using the finger-steeple

signal that he was offering thoughts now and not orders. 'A ten-minute outage, in which nobody died'—Morrow snorted—'could serve us well. It means a total review of automation is a good idea, despite the fact that we were able rapidly to restore service.'

'But we didn't, did we?' Morrow had subsided somewhat but wasn't quite empty of bile yet. Gerald made a mental note to debrief him one-to-one next time he had a rough day.

'No, Mr Morrow, we didn't. However, we have news footage flying around the world which implies that the democracy movement has taken over the BR. Do you really want to allow the inference that our infrastructure is already under their control?'

'But it is. You might be employed to lie to the people but I don't think we are.' Morrow looked at Brown for agreement. The Home Office Chief Minister found something fascinating to read in his notes.

'I'm pretty sure I know how they got in,' Minnow mumbled. 'It won't happen again.'

'It's not just us, though, is it? People operating the systems will have seen the screen. And the demands.'

'Mostly managers filling in for striking staff; they're scared of losing their jobs too. I'm sure we can get them onside.' Gerald decided the discussion was now over. 'So, we get Sideworth on the lunchtime news,' he added in that brighter tone that meant a decision had been made. 'He thanks the nation for being marvellous, thanks the police and emergency services for sterling service and announces a root and branch review of job losses due to automation. He doesn't mention democracy at all, just observes that disruptions to the people's voice were dealt with quickly and safely. Agreed?'

'Seems fine to me.' Brown looked at Morrow. 'You come out of it a hero, man. Let the rest go, eh?'

'I don't like it. It's not the truth, and it's not right.'

Gerald sighed. He looked Morrow in the eye and stared him down. 'We're not here to do what's right. We're here to do what's feasible. Doing the right thing is for individuals, not nations. We do the possible, the practical...and we do the minimising of unintended consequences. That is why what we do works. Rights and wrongs create wars, famines and economic recessions. We left pious claptrap behind us with democracy. You may not like it but it's now your job.'

Brutal, he knew, but in the end the man would thank him.

Caroline knocked gently on the door of Doug Sideworth's flat in Portcullis House. He'd not been answering calls or texts. She'd considered sending a staffer to find him; having more than enough else to do herself, but had opted to make the time.

She knocked again, more loudly. Nothing. One more knock, urgent and prolonged.

'Doug, Mr Sideworth. Doug, are you okay?' she called through the door. Worried now, she took the lift back to the ground floor and asked the security guard at the door if he'd seen Mr Sideworth leaving the building.

'No, ma'am. Not since he came in yesterday afternoon. It was when the rioting was getting up. I remember because he said to me, "Be careful if you go out there

George, it's getting ugly." And I said I'd not be going out and I called for some more staff at the doors, just in case. I reckoned it was nice of him.'

Caroline smiled her agreement. 'I'm a bit worried about him, George. Do you have a pass key?'

'Yes, I do, but I can't leave here just now, hold on...' He lifted a phone handset from under his little desk arrangement in the corner of the vestibule. 'Can you man the front desk for a few minutes? Thanks.'

He covered the receiver with his hand and spoke to Caroline. 'Won't be a minute, ma'am, just getting some cover.'

It didn't take long for another uniformed guard to take George's place at the desk, and the two of them made their way back to Doug's flat.

George called and knocked, then used his pass key to open the door. Caroline attempted to make sense of what they could see. The floor was littered with a confetti of individually wrapped sticking plasters, the walls were streaked with blood and she was stepping in something sticky. What was that? It didn't smell unpleasant...sort of citrussy?

'What's that smell, do you think?' she asked George.

'Not sure, ma'am,' he replied, equally puzzled. He stepped carefully through the mess into the kitchen. 'I think it's orange juice. Looks like a full carton went over in here.'

'How peculiar...Doug!' Caroline called as she turned the other way from the door and headed for the bedroom. 'Doug, are you here? Are you all right?' She looked around at the chaos, the bedclothes all pulled awry, but saw nobody. She made her way back to the lounge, where

George was shaking his head. 'I don't think he's here.'

At that moment, they both heard it. Their heads turned to the direction of the sound. A thunderous snore. 'I've just checked the bedroom,' Caroline said. 'There was no one—'

'Something's in there.' George led the way. 'Hello there, sir? How did we get down here?' Caroline could still see nothing from the door, so she followed George until she was looking over his shoulder.

Doug was apparently wedged, face down, between the bed and the wall. And apparently unconscious. He was wrapped so tightly in bed linen it looked like he'd been getting ready for some prize-for-the-best-mummy fancy dress party.

'Should I call an ambulance, ma'am? He doesn't look well.'

Caroline counted the empty whisky bottles that had fallen with him. 'Not just yet, let me check something first.' She clambered over the bed and wedged herself between Doug's head and the bedside table. No blood there, so maybe he hadn't hit his head on the way down. There was one way to check: one of the first things Tiny had taught her. She bent to reach his ear, pulled the lobe between her thumb and forefinger and squeezed. Hard.

'Aaaawwahg.' Doug groaned and shook his head away from her grasp. He began to fight the bedding, thrashing this way and that, and then subsided into restless grumbles.

'Doug, can you hear me?' Caroline shook his shoulder and gave the ear another vicious tweak.

'Aaaw. Stop that.'

'Can. You. Hear. Me?' she snapped, a little louder than the bedroom's acoustics could cope with. Her voice echoed. Doug groaned.

'I think he's probably just drunk,' she said to George.

'Should we call someone anyway, to make sure?' George was already keying his radio mic.

'No, not yet! Sorry, George, didn't mean to yell. We can't risk this getting out right now. Let's get him upright and call a doctor to check him over here, eh? No need for blue lights outside.'

'Very well, ma'am, quite understand.' George looked at the prone figure on the floor.

'I think we might be able to use the sheets to turn him.' He put his head to one side, assessing the space they had to work with. 'Then if you can prop his shoulders up, I should be able to lift him onto the side of the bed.'

The two of them pushed, pulled, twisted and grunted until Doug was seated upright on the floor. 'Come on, man, help yourself a bit.' George grunted as his hands found a wet patch in the bedding. 'Ugh, you dirty bastard.' He looked up at Caroline. 'You'll want to wash your hands when we're done, miss.'

'It's okay, George, I think it's only orange juice.'

'What the hell went on here?'

'I wish I knew, but this minister has to address the nation in half an hour.'

George whistled. 'Good luck.'

They unwrapped Doug as best they could and placed his arms round George's shoulders. 'Right, I'll take the weight and lift. Can you swing his bum round onto the bed?'

'I think so, let's try it.'

'On three, then. One. Two. Three.'

With a series of groans from George, puffings from

Caroline and farts from Doug they manoeuvred him into a sitting position. Caroline piled pillows around him to stop him slumping again. 'Thanks, George, I'll take it from here. Would you mind calling a doctor and putting some strong coffee on?'

'Right you are, miss.'

As George took his radio to the kitchen, Doug lifted his head. His eyes almost focused on Caroline's face.

'Hello, Katie, love.' He beamed at Caroline, and vomited into her lap.

CHAPTER TWENTY-FIVE

'Gerald, I've found him.' Caroline was back in her flat for the scant few minutes she hoped it would take to shower, change and get back out the door.

'Yeah, we thought he'd been assassinated when we first got in.' She held the phone to her ear with her shoulder as she kicked off her shoes and began to struggle out of her skirt.

'Turns out he'd had a skinful. Woke up this morning with one hell of a hangover, tried to sort himself out with some vitamin C.' She picked up the skirt with her thumb and forefinger and deposited it in a plastic bin liner. It was probably washable, but she wouldn't be wearing it again.

'Couldn't get the OJ carton open, took a steak knife to it, slashed his hand.' She contemplated the blouse. It wasn't actually sicky in and of itself, but she felt as though it stank. It could go in the wash but... She utilised a second plastic bag for now. That decision could wait.

'Got the shakes trying to do a bit of first aid, gave up

and took a bottle of Scotch back to bed.' She headed for the shower. 'Blood, plasters and OJ everywhere. You should have him in about an hour. The doc gave him an IV to try and perk him up, and George is getting him showered and shaved.' She turned the water on and waited for it to heat up.

'Good man, that, by the way; security at Portcullis? Excellent in a crisis, we should find him something better.' She selected an expensively perfumed shower gel, one she usually kept for special occasions. 'Tell the press he's in a meeting with some security union members, thanking them for their help.' She laughed. 'It's not *not* true. Got to go, I'll see you later. I have to bail someone out of jail.'

Queenie put her cup down and smiled. 'That was a spanking good cuppa.'

'I'll let the kitchen know.' The US president was in shirtsleeves and tieless this morning, and Queenie and Andy were dressed for travelling. It would have been quite cosy in the president's private quarters, except for the huge guards at the doors muttering into their sleeves. Queenie had learned not to offer them cups of tea.

'I'm sorry last night's proposed formal dinner had to go by the board in favour of a working breakfast this morning.'

'Oh, we know, dear, everybody's running round having extra meetings. But to be honest, I prefer a decent drop of tea and a bit of toast and that—it saves wondering what cutlery to use.'

'And it's given me an opportunity to learn the secrets

of English tea making.' The president indicated the Teapot of State, which sat proudly under its red, white and blue woollen cosy on the breakfast table. 'I understand the kitchen has full instructions for making it correctly for your next visit.'

'Yes, Eugene done a little note for them.'

'And they know not to wash it before sending it back with you.'

'Ooh, yes, but I'm amazed you'd be takin' an interest in that sort of stuff!'

'It may surprise you to know, ma'am, that before my call to come and do this, I ran a bed and breakfast.'

'No, really?' Queenie knew in the back of her mind that everyone she'd met in America was just like her and Andy, but she'd been so overwhelmed by the thought of all those films and telly series about American presidents that it was easy to forget.

'And our English guests always complain about the tea.' He adopted a confidential tone. 'Now I know why, and what to do about it. I've already told my partner to go buy a teapot and never wash it!'

'Ooh er, who'd have thought?'

'And that tea cosy'—he indicated the patriotic creation before them—'is coming home with me when my time is done.'

Did Andy just roll his eyes? Queenie wasn't sure; maybe it was indigestion. He'd consumed a lot of waffles. She observed him for a moment longer and saw him look at his watch.

The president noticed too.

'Yes, time's getting on, and we all have more work than expected.' He turned to Andy. 'No doubt you'll be swamped with briefings and debriefings when you get back?'

'All part of life's rich tapestry,' prattled the British Republic's Foreign Minister. Queenie kicked him under the table. 'I mean, we don't really know what's going on—' Queenie kicked him again.

'I don't see why it affects you so much over here.' Queenie decided the best way to keep Andy quiet until he had another script in his hands was to keep talking.

'We do have our own undercurrents of democracy rebels,' the president began.

'Really, who'd have thought? Why? It seems like everything here is so lovely.'

'Not everyone likes the way things are now. As I understand it, and I'll get briefed in more detail later today, some people still think politics should be a career. There's something seductive about the idea of people voting; on the surface it looks perfectly reasonable.'

'We're not as green as we are cabbage-looking these days, though.'

The president eyed Andy over his cup of coffee.

'Quite.' He turned back to Queenie. 'We have a history of civil war in this country, as you will know. The threat never quite goes away. Currently we think democracy sympathisers are being supported and financed from one or two rogue nations, stirring up trouble in the South. The CIA have had their eye on a cell based in Hawaii, probably funded by Tonga.'

'Where's that? I've never heard of it.' Queenie was mildly horrified. She'd been upset enough watching the news, but she'd believed the speech Andy had handed to her. Now it sounded like there was more unpleasantness in the world than she could possibly imagine.

'My daughter did a project about this!' Andy piped up. 'She had to learn a presentation for school, and we all got word perfect testing her on it. Let me think now, "One of the last remaining constitutional monarchies, propped up by an old-fashioned democracy. The king enjoys the support of parliament because the politicians understand the power of mutual protection. Censorship keeps the people off the internet, and the TV runs footage of old elections from the rest of the world all the time."'

'Indeed.' The president appeared as surprised as Queenie was. 'It's so remote that most of the public have no idea the rest of the world has moved on.'

'Oh blimey, those poor people, I had no idea.'

'Although, with worldwide connectivity it's getting harder to keep any populace in the dark indefinitely.' Queenie watched as Andy furrowed his brow and produced a solemn nod, wisely keeping his mouth shut while he was ahead.

'And there's a direct route into the US from the Pacific via Hawaii, which might explain why we've had more trouble with democracy activists than you have. So far,' the president added.

Deborah heard Caroline's voice before she saw her. She'd not really considered who would come for her when she'd demanded to be put through to Buck Place. She'd played the do-you-know-who-I-am? card without thinking it through. 'How dare you! My mother is Queenie Mason, your head of state!' The words had been out of her mouth before she realised how stupid it sounded. She'd been put through to Buck Place after a bit of piss-taking, and some flunkey had taken a message. Colin would have come right away, she told herself. This bitch had presumably left her to spend a night in a cell for the fun of it.

She'd been interviewed, told them what happened, protested self-defence and demanded to be let go because the other guy was the troublemaker. She'd told them his name, said she'd known him at school and he'd always been a thug. They'd said they believed her, but nevertheless he was unconscious and she was charged with assault. She spent a miserable night waiting to be bailed, under the impression that things couldn't get much worse. Now they had.

'Hello, Deborah, how are you?' It was eleven o'clock in the bloody morning and the woman looked as though she'd only just got up. Her hair was still wet.

'How do you think I am? I've been locked up for almost twenty-four hours.'

'Yes, we have been trying to get someone to you but everyone is snowed under.'

'I don't care about snowed under. I'm the daughter of the head of state and they arrested me!'

'As I understand it, you were observed assaulting a member of the public with a placard.'

'Yes, but it was self-defence.'

'No doubt, and I've been told that when this comes to court, there will most likely be no case to answer. However, procedures are—'

'How dare they? They wouldn't have arrested Mum.'

'I think they would have had to, given the same circumstances.'

Deborah took a deep breath and ran her hands through her hair. It was taking all her remaining strength not to burst into tears of fury.

'Shall we sort out the paperwork and get you out of here? I've spoken to your husband. He's worried about you. Maybe a shower and some coffee and we can think about a debrief.'

'Debrief? What the hell for? I'm the victim here.'

'Yes, I know. But we think you may be able to help us. I understand you can identify one of the democracy conspirators...'

Big Doris settled herself in the warmest corner of the launderette. The spot where the dryers went round a corner. She opened up a foil pack of cheese and pickle sandwiches and lifted her eyes to the telly. It needed tweaking round slightly, for the best view. She stood and adjusted the arm that held it on the wall. Bob had done a decent job of installing it, she decided.

She looked at her watch. Sandra had been at the hospital all morning, which was why Doris was at the launderette and not in her stupid rep's office. She wasn't sorry. It would be full of people whingeing again. She'd called for permission and they'd said they understood about her family member being injured in the riots and that, but she'd have to get back to the office as soon as possible. People would want to tell her what they thought. As if anyone cared.

Still, the shutters had worked out well. There was no damage to the launderette, unlike the chippy. She looked at the sandwiches as she sat back down. They'd have to do. She needed something to chew on while she watched the news.

The channel was rerunning some of yesterday's highlights—people complaining they'd had to call 999 twice, and it just went to show that computers were useless; dopey, tarted-up Queenie Mason from the Peabodys standing looking gormless with the greasy salesman and reading from a script in America; shots of a sea of democracy banners. The studio anchors said there was going to be some sort of address to the nation in a minute.

Doris didn't know what she thought. She hated the job. She thought repping was stupid. She'd heard Bob going on about bringing democracy back but she wasn't sure she remembered things being much better. But then, she'd never really thought about it at all before. She just wanted to be left alone to gossip in the launderette. To be fair to the people she'd met so far, they seemed to be decent enough, mostly trying their best. There were some snotty bitches in the civil service trying to tell her what to do all the time, but the reps themselves, they were okay. Sandra had told her something big was going to happen and she'd kept it to herself, but she didn't like it. Not now the Mile End Road was wrecked again, the launderette was empty and Bob was in hospital.

The door opened and Sandra dashed in, flinging her handbag on the nearest washing machine and subsiding onto the bench next to Doris.

'Bloody hell, I'm knackered.'

'Not surprised, luv, you've been there all night. How is he?'

'He came round. They reckon there's no harm done; they're keeping him in another twenty-four hours just to make sure.'

'That's good, then. What happened?'

Sandra sighed. 'He can't remember yet. They said that's common, and he might start rememberin' bit by bit.'

She looked all in. Black bags under her eyes, creases furrowed in her forehead, her daughter was looking...careworn. And not just from a night on a plastic chair at the hospital.

'What about you, girlie? How you doin'?'

'I'm tired, Mum, that's all.'

'Is it? What's going on, Sandra? What's he mixed up in? This is more than just a bit of a demo ain't it?'

'No! Well, yes, sort of. He said there was something else goin' on, more than just the demos. But it's all over now, ain't it?'

'You tell me, girl, is it? 'Cos if your Bob's got himself in deeper than we know—'

'No, it's fine. Honestly, Mum, it's all over. And anyway, now he's got hurt I should be able to stop him doing any more.'

'I bleedin' well hope so. Because you've been looking unhappy and worried for ages, and don't tell me you 'aven't, because I'm your mother and I can see it. If he carries on with this malarkey, it'll be me knocking him unconscious next time, mark my words.'

'Don't you start on me, Mum, I've had enough, I really have.'

'Here.' Doris handed over a sandwich. 'Get some food down you, and then get home to bed. I'll stay here for the rest of the day.'

Sandra stretched her legs and rubbed the back of her neck. She took the sandwich, opened it up and wrinkled her nose. 'Ugh, Branston.'

Doris sighed and rolled her eyes. 'Here, this one's piccalilli.'

Sandra attempted a smile as they swapped sandwiches. 'Thanks, Mum.'

'Now shut up and let's hear what's going on.'

They turned their attention to the telly.

'Blimey.' Sandra giggled. 'He looks like he's had a rougher night than I have!'

'Citizens of the British Republic.' Doug Sideworth's bloodshot eyes filled the close-up shot, and some wise producer dictated a cutaway to a profile camera. 'Your government is taking heed of the extensive show of support for workers whose jobs have been placed at risk by recent advances in computer technology...'

CHAPTER TWENTY-SIX

It was gone three before they met for lunch. The Red Lion was almost empty. Everyone who normally lunched there was back in some office or other, either attending an emergency meeting or holed up in a corner rewatching the news. Caroline had passed a few such huddles on her way to and from her office—old civil service hands explaining what had happened to newcomers who were having trouble reconciling what they thought they'd seen with what they were being advised was the case.

They stared at their drinks in silence.

'Shall I see if they have anything left to put in a sandwich?'

Minnow shook his head. The lad looked more miserable than Caroline had thought possible. His usually placid features, enlivened only when he was talking geekery, had moulded themselves into a passable impression of one of those theatrical masks. And not the smiley one.

Gerald's features, on the other hand, were implacable, unreadable. She was seeing the face he generally saved for people who deserved to be unsettled. He shook his head as well.

'Back in a minute, then. Some of us have had a long morning.'

She headed for the bar, smiled at the staff and asked whether they could rustle something up, anything would do. They undertook to see what the lunchtime cook had left lying about, and she thanked them prettily.

Back at the table Caroline fished about in her glass, squeezing both lemon and lime slices into submission.

'Which of the many and varied disasters would we like to dissect first?' She addressed her question to Gerald.

'Perhaps we could start with listing them in order of magnitude.'

'I'll start some notes.' Minnow jumped at the opportunity to look at the screen on his phone and began swiping, ready to type.

'I was being rhetorical, Minnow. Sarcastic, if you will.'

'Sorry, Gerald.'

'We could maybe start with something that went well?' Caroline attempted a brighter tone.

Gerald regarded her. 'And something did?'

'Well.' She took a sip of her water. 'Queenie did well with the script, and Carswell managed to not add any nonsense about cabbages and repasts.'

'Indeed so. Truly splendid.' Gerald offered an incline of the head by way of celebration.

'And we have the identity of one of the ringleaders.' Caroline decided to push her luck a little. 'And we found

Sideworth!'

'All in all, a triumph of a day?' Gerald blew steam across his coffee and raised the cup to his lips. He put it down again. 'I apologise, Minnow. Perhaps a list wouldn't be such a bad idea.'

'To be fair to all of us,' Minnow muttered as he regained his note-taking screen, 'nobody died.'

Caroline nodded. 'He's right, Gerald. Things could have been worse.'

'What we all seem to be failing to take into account'—Gerald had another go at his coffee and managed to ingest some this time—'is that we lost control. Nobody died because the, uh, infiltrators let us off the hook. We didn't restore service, they did.'

'I wasn't far off, it was a pretty basic buffer overflow exploit, created a temporary denial of service. I was close to getting service back. What's bugging me is who, how and why. Especially why they made it so basic.'

'Is it possible they got in the same way you did?' asked Caroline.

'You mean did one of the guys I'd trust with my life get turned?'

'You have to admit, it's the most obvious explanation. If this was a TV cop show I'd be saying, "Let's eliminate it from our enquiries."'

Minnow sighed. 'Shrimp and Tiddler wouldn't turn me over. We've been watching each other's backs since school. Chad's been a white hat since before I, uh, you know. He's as sound as they come.'

'I think maybe we should have a chat with them anyway. Even if they're as trustworthy as you say maybe someone spoke out of turn, got overheard?'

Gerald finished his coffee and put his cup down. 'Ah, here's your lunch, Caroline. Wonder if they could make another, I think maybe I could eat something after all. Minnow, change of mind on the food front?'

Minnow shook his head and began texting as if his life depended on it.

Caroline winked at the barman who'd brought her a plate of ham, cheese, pickles and freshly sliced crusty bread. 'I'll do up another plate, sir.'

'Perking up, Gerald? All you needed was someone to interrogate, then you're back on the road to control?'

'Hmm, not on the road so much as, ah, in possession of a map.' He offered her the merest flicker of a smile. 'So, once we've spoken with Minnow's hacker chums, we will or possibly won't be any nearer the how. That still leaves the who.'

'Stroke of luck there,' Caroline said. 'I spent the latter part of this morning at Paddington Green nick, bailing out Queenie's daughter.' Gerald and Minnow both looked up from their respective notes and phones with little sparks of curiosity.

'The fragrant Deborah knocked out a democracy thug with her placard.' Caroline realised she was enjoying telling this story, unlike the previous one. 'She recognised him, they were at the same junior school apparently, and the families are passing acquaintances.'

Gerald's smile widened a fraction. 'Useful.'

'Even better,' Caroline continued, 'his mother-in-law is one of our current reps: Tower Hamlets.'

'Didn't we have an eye on her anyway? Some sort of spat with Queenie?' Gerald asked.

'Yup, that's the one.'

'Very useful.'

'The lad's out of danger, so we could bring her in for a debrief any time. Could either do it right away on the pretext of concern for the patient or wait until all the reps are back next week.'

'Hmm.' Gerald's plate of ploughman's leftovers arrived. He thanked the kid from the kitchen who'd brought it over and joined Caroline in thoughtful cheese munching. 'Less chance of it getting out if we do it this week. What was the conclusion your little listener came to?'

Caroline abandoned the cheese and flipped her notebook open. '"Too mouthy to be safe,"' she read. 'So, she mightn't be a sleeper? Just caught up in family strife.'

'In which case she could possibly be turned to our purposes?'

'Risky. Mouthy works both ways.'

'True. Might depend how easily frightened she is.'

'Well, you're on your own tomorrow morning, so bad cop is all you've got. Queenie and Carswell will be home and I want to debrief the family together, felonious daughter and all.'

'Okay, I'll bring the rep in. Will you be free to play good cop with Sideworth in the afternoon? We need Employment coming up with some decent-sounding initiatives pretty fast.'

'Yeah, unless he throws up on me again. But go easy on him, eh? He's got his troubles.'

'Haven't we all?' Gerald eyes appealed to the heavens. 'How about you, Minnow? Spending tomorrow tracking down your pals and talking geekspeak?'

'Uh, yeah, I'm waiting for a text. We're not a hundred

per cent sure where Chad is.'

'That's hardly encouraging. Weren't you guys planning a debrief or something?' Caroline thought she detected a note of concern in Minnow's voice.

'No! We, that is, hackers, I mean, you know, ex-hackers, we don't get together after an exploit. Old habits...oh.'

'What?' Gerald and Caroline spoke together.

'He's, uh, Chad that is, he's left the country. Gone back stateside. Which is weird. He said he was in London for Comic-Con. That's not 'til next weekend. He's on holiday in Hawaii now instead. All right for some.'

'Hawaii?' The colour drained from Gerald's face.

'Shit,' said Caroline.

CHAPTER TWENTY-SEVEN

'How did this one go, Eugene?' Caroline asked, as they stepped along the hallway to Queenie's flat.

'Quite well, considering, miss.' Eugene smiled at the woman who'd decided he was diplomatic enough to be elevated from Buck Place flunkey to international jetsetter: the keeper of the Teapot of State. 'Queenie's getting more confident and if Andy starts off on one of his sayings she kicks him under the table!'

Caroline laughed. 'Good for her, I'd be kicking him too. Oh, by the way, we're expecting the Chandlers shortly. Deborah and Colin?' Eugene turned to nod his filing away of this information as he paused at Queenie's door before knocking.

'Show them in as soon as they arrive?'

'Certainly, miss.'

He gave his quiet you're-expecting-this-person knock and pushed open the door as Queenie called, 'Come in, Eugene, sweetheart!'

She was sitting in Bert's chair, Caroline noticed as she entered the room. Someone must have pulled it through from the television room. She had it fully reclined with the footrest up. Bert was perched on the edge of one of the man-eating formal armchairs.

'Goodness, look at you. Do we need to get a second recliner so you can both have one?' Caroline smiled at the elderly pair.

'Just for today.' Queenie puffed out the words. 'I'm a bit, you know'—she lowered her voice to a whisper—'*knackered*. My Bert said I looked like I needed to rest, ain't that right, Bert?'

'It's a disgrace, if you ask me.' Bert looked Caroline in the eye for the first time since she'd met him. 'She's an old woman.'

'Oi, not so much of the old.'

'Come off it. Them transaplantic trips are hard on her. She didn't hardly get time to recover from the first one and you sent her off again. It's inhuman! She's doin' her best and you're tryin' to kill her.'

'I know and I'm sorry.' Caroline sat in the chair next to Bert, levelled her body to match his and meet his eye. 'We asked a lot this week, and we hope it won't happen again. I'm sure you know we had a national emergency on our hands...and I've just been hearing what a splendid job she did of representing us—'

'That's as may be.' Bert sounded slightly mollified, but only slightly. 'But she needs some rest now, not more of your nagging.'

'I'm just here to chat,' Caroline said. 'Find out how it went. And, um, there's a few things that happened while you were away, Queenie dear, that you need to know about.'

Queenie puffed out a laugh. 'I saw most of it on the news, luvvie.'

'I bet you did. There will be a formal debrief sometime next week, when you've had a chance to rest. But today we need to tell you about Deborah.'

'My Debs? Is she all right? What happened?'

'She's fine, now.' Caroline looked at her watch; they should be here by now. She didn't feel right starting the story before they arrived, mainly because she wanted to see the lying bitch's face when the truth came out.

'She just got mixed up in a bit of trouble during the demonstrations, that's all.'

'Ah, Ms Woolton, do come in. Take a seat.' Gerald had chosen the useful taller-than-thou position at his office window. People didn't perceive their disadvantage until he timed his walk back to the desk.

'You wanted to see me? Mr, er...' Doris wedged herself into the chair she'd been directed to, put her handbag in her lap and began picking bits off the strap where it had frayed.

'Call me Gerald.' He opted to begin with some charm.

'Mr, er, Gerald, yes, thank you.'

'We wanted to ask you about your son-in-law, Ms Woolton—may I call you Doris?'

'Oh, yes, Doris, everybody does. What about him, though? I mean I...'

'Mostly we were concerned. We heard he was injured, terrible business all round. How is he doing?' The relief was visible, Gerald noted.

'Oh, he's okay, thanks for asking. Out of hospital tomorrow. Yes, terrible, you're right there, those thugs—'

'Does he remember much of what happened?' Gerald imagined Minnow's American friend referring to this little entrapment as 'shooting fish in a barrel.'

'Not really. They said it's usual and he might start rememberin' as he recovers.'

'Let us hope so. And your daughter? How is she? It must have been a distressing shock for you all.'

'She's bearin' up, although I needed the day off to run the family business.' Doris's hand went to her mouth. 'Is this what it's about? I told the office, they said it was fine.'

'Naturally so, Doris.' Gerald unleashed his most disarming smile. 'Many reps were absent from their constituency offices yesterday, helping out with clean up and ensuring the well-being of their constituents. We are happy to see such devotion to your family and neighbours.'

'Oh, that's all right then, because my Sandra needed help, bein' at the hospital all night.'

'Quite so.' Gerald approached the desk. He considered his body language options and plumped for perching on the corner, above where Doris sat still wringing her handbag strap. Gerald winced at the little patch of bits on the carpet beneath her feet.

'I wonder whether you are curious as to how we know your son-in-law was one of the ringleaders of this dangerous, antisocial and illegal hijacking of an otherwise peaceful event?' The words dripped out like honey. He watched the wheels turning.

'What, our Bobby? Oh no, Mr, uh, Gerald, my family

don't have no truck with any of that—'

'Ah, but they do don't they? Perhaps when *your Bobby* regains some memory, he will recall being recognised by an old school friend while he forced a democracy banner into her hands.'

'Good to know you ain't embarrassed to know your old mum any more, at any rate.' Bert spat the words at Deborah as she sat deflated, defeated, demolished.

Caroline hadn't enjoyed the denouement as much as she'd expected. It had been too easy. And anyway, Queenie wasn't well. Two return trips, two bouts of jet lag. Even Eugene was looking tired, and he was a youngster. Now she had to take in all of this.

'So you do work for the advertising people, you just don't make the ads?' Queenie was struggling a little with all the new information, Caroline thought.

Deborah nodded. A tear found its way down her nose, and she wiped it away with her hand. Caroline would have had her down as a handkerchief person. *Odd how fast we all revert to the inner child.*

'But that's still a brilliant job, eh?' Queenie smiled at her daughter. 'Better than anyone in our family has ever done before, ain't that right, Bert?'

Bert harrumphed.

'I don't understand the fuss. I know you got arrested and that must have been horrible, but it's over now, eh?'

'The fuss is because she's too good to know us until she's a bleedin' disgrace.'

'Oh stop it, Bert, calm down. You'll give yourself a

heart attack. It's our Debs.' Queenie laid her head back in the chair with a happy smile. 'All I've ever wanted is to see a bit more of you...you're my best girl...I know you hated the Peabodys, I'd have got out if I could too, but I didn't have the advantages you did, no education, see.'

Deborah managed a soggy smile.

'But it's all right now, family's family and we'll stand by you 'til it's over. Won't we, Bert?' Her tone sharpened.

'I expect so.' Bert looked at Colin. *For a bit of male solidarity, probably*, Caroline thought. He was out of luck. Colin was looking nowhere but at his fingernails.

'Anyway, Caroline says you're helpin' find them that did it! That's brilliant, ain't it, Bert?'

The old man grinned. It was the first time Caroline had seen this particular arrangement of his face. 'So you put young Bobby Norris in 'ospital, eh? If I had a pound for every time I wanted to slap him upside the face and down the other when you was all kids.'

'I didn't know he'd married Big Doris's Sandra.' Deborah finally spoke. 'I really will have to keep away from the Peabodys now.'

Queenie laughed her old laugh, that guffaw Caroline remembered from—was it only a few weeks ago? The one that finished in a bout of coughing. Caroline made a mental note to get the doctor in.

'Blimey, luvvie, I'll deal with Big Doris, don't you worry about that.'

'And Bob will be helping the police with their enquiries for quite a while,' Caroline added.

'Worst way, we'll find a new launderette when we goes back. Anyway, how about a nice cup of tea? And we can watch the telly and see what's been goin' on.'

'Good idea,' Caroline said. 'I'll ask Eugene to put the kettle on.'

'Come on, then.' Queenie worked the handle that lowered the footrest on Bert's recliner and sat herself up. 'Now then, Deborah, does your fancy up-west mansion flat have a special telly room? 'Cos we got one now, come and look.' She led the way, puffing a little less now.

Caroline heard the news begin as she made her way to the kitchen.

'And in other news, the Guerrilla Knitters Guild have struck again with their trademark colourful street art. The streets of Liverpool now boast woollen wraps for trees, lampposts and post boxes. A note to the BBC from the anonymous group states that they hope the installation will cheer people up as they go about restoring the damage left by rioters.'

'Aw, ain't that lovely,' wafted through the hallway. 'Oh blimey, look. I've seen that one before!'

Caroline smiled. Time to get Queenie on board.

'So you knew the Democracy Now group had something planned, but not exactly what it was?' Gerald was sitting behind his desk now. Doris required no further bullying.

'My Sandra said something might—'

'And you opted not to pass this information on to the authorities?'

Doris lifted her head and pointed at the neat piles of folders and files on Gerald's desk. 'You see all this?' she said. Gerald surveyed the paperwork at her behest. 'I assumed you knew. You people make out you know all about everything anyway.'

'In which case, mightn't it have been wise to advise your, uh, *relative,* to refrain from involvement?'

'He wouldn't take any notice of me, he never has. Anyway, he told my Sandra the placard stuff was just a diversion, something bigger was going on and they, you, us...would never notice.'

'Indeed?'

'Yes, so we didn't think it would—'

'And do you know what the *something bigger* is?'

'No, honestly, I'd tell you if I did. My Sandra's Bobby, he's only a mug, not one of the big boys. He runs messages is all. But he spouts stuff, like how it was better before.'

'And do you think it was better before, Ms Woolton?'

'No. Maybe. I don't know. I never took much interest 'til I got called in here, and I got to say it's not really my thing.'

'What particular aspect of allowing the people a real voice isn't your thing?'

'You see, when you put it like that it sounds fine, but it ain't about big stuff, is it? What we, you, do, it's not about making laws and changing the system. It's people moaning about litter in the street and damp in their flats.'

'And if those are the things that matter to people the most, that's not important?'

'I don't know. I don't really care. I don't want to have to think about it any more.'

'Ah, and there we have it.' Gerald offered Doris his most disarming smile. He had concluded she knew nothing much. And anyone who was prepared to admit to finding thinking annoying was unlikely to be a democracy hardliner. The diversion, though, that was interesting. The riots as a cover for the computers going down? But that had been pretty damned noticeable. He would run it past the team.

Doris looked at him expectantly. 'Have what?'

'The problem with democracy, ma'am. Giving votes to people who don't want to think.'

'I don't know what you mean.'

'Of course you don't.'

CHAPTER TWENTY-EIGHT

Doug Sideworth knocked back a tot from his hip flask and replaced it in his laptop bag. Then he knocked on the door of the office he'd been summoned to. Caroline usually chatted with him in the cafe, or his flat, or just accompanied him to meetings. He'd not been called to the third floor before and he thought he knew what was coming. Could you sack a minister? Maybe they had reserves waiting for the inevitable failures. Did he want to go back to Lancashire? It would be nice to have no more responsibility, but he'd also have no job, would he? Not after being fired from something any idiot with a teapot and a knitting bag could do.

'Come in.' Sounded like Gerald. He'd been hoping to hear the bad news from Caroline. But then, she probably wanted nothing more to do with him after... He took one more little sip. Just a livener to settle the nerves.

'Ah, Mr Sideworth, do come in, take a seat.' Gerald and Caroline were both there, in a little circle of comfy chairs by the window. He deposited himself in the vacant chair indicated to him and placed his laptop bag on the floor next to him. Did it clink? He wasn't sure. Maybe. Did it matter? Probably not.

'How are you feeling today?' Oh God, they were going to string it out.

'Better, thank you, Mr Lambert. I appreciate your concern.'

'My concern, Mr Sideworth, is for the nation, not for you.'

'I'm sorry, I know, the pressure...'

'And just as you have misinterpreted where concern needs to be directed, I think possibly your apology could find a more suitable recipient?'

'Yes.' He turned to Caroline. 'I am really, really sorry. You've been nothing but kind and supportive and I behaved—'

'Indeed you did,' said Caroline. 'We have had better days, eh, Doug?' Her voice sounded warmer than expected.

'You present us with a conundrum, Mr Sideworth,' Gerald continued. 'We need you in good health. Your department has much to do over the coming weeks.'

'I know, I'm sorry, it's just.'

'What is it just?'

'It's all pretend. You're in control and I'll get the blame.'

'You would prefer more control?'

'No, God, no, I'd have no idea what to do.'

'You consider yourself to be some sort of scapegoat?'

'Not exactly.'

'How long ago did your wife die, Doug?' Caroline

again. He wasn't sure what that had to do with anything but it was an easier question to answer.

'Eighteen months.'

'Have you sought any kind of help at all? Grief therapy, maybe?'

'No, why would I? People die all the time. You get over it.'

'Yes, but getting over it can take more time than you've had before being put under enormous stress, eh?'

'I suppose.'

'The situation is this, Mr Sideworth.' Doug returned his attention to Gerald. 'We are unable to remove you from office, whether we, or you, want to or not. That would be a betrayal of everything this nation believes in. The people can petition for your removal but that, believe me, is an extremely unpleasant process.'

'And you'd rather make a go of it anyway, wouldn't you?' Caroline added.

Doug nodded, unsure where this was going.

'I understand from Caroline that your little, uh, problem with spirits was one you had mastered quite successfully over recent weeks?' Doug offered Caroline a grateful glance and nodded again.

'We therefore propose that you submit to a course of grief counselling in the first instance. Plus attendance at Alcoholics Anonymous for additional support. You are, obviously, free to reject these interventions, in which case we will just have to wait until your *issues* come to the notice of the public.'

'No! I mean, yes, thank you. I never thought of it but maybe...' He looked from one to the other. 'I do want to get it right, you know...maybe this...'

'Thank you, Mr Sideworth. A good decision. Ms Grant will liaise with you regarding the arrangements. Now if you'll excuse us, there is much else to do.'

'Yes, thank you, yeah, thanks again.' Doug extricated himself from the armchair as fast as possible and bolted.

As he reached the door, Gerald added, 'Don't forget your emergency supplies, Mr Sideworth.'

Sally Farnham stood in her favourite spot. She indicated the agenda with her second-best laser. 'We'll be postponing the strike debrief for an hour this afternoon,' she told her ministers and their gaggle of advisers, specialists and secretaries. Everyone had something to say about the crisis. But the chap who was diaried to speak about the computer issues had been held up. It was going to be a long afternoon.

'In the meantime we've compiled a list of items we'd like to present to the reps next week to take back to their communities for consideration.'

'Isn't this a bit premature?' Dr Wilmslow looked around the room, catching the eyes of as many attendees as he could, making sure each was complicit in his eyeroll. 'I mean, we've just had the biggest civil disruption in twenty years on our streets and you want to tinker about with toys in hospitals.'

'People need something new to move on to.' Sally could hear the defensive whine creep into her voice but she battled on. 'And things we can ask them about that are simple to solve might make them feel like they have some control back.'

'I agree.' Sally looked for the quiet voice. *Ah, Rav. Thank you.* She tried to keep the smirk off her face as he continued. 'People feel good when controlling the small things. And feeling good is helpful for health, no?'

'Plus, asking the public for input is part of our remit,' Sally said, determined to take back the initiative.

'What we should be doing'—Wilmslow affected the patient but terse voice of a parent addressing a toddler—'is planning research into the treatment of drug-resistant viruses, not putting the inmates in charge of the asylum.'

Sally heard an intake of breath from several parts of the room at once.

'Unfortunate turn of phrase,' Wilmslow muttered. 'What I mean is, experts are best placed to determine priorities. The nation's health can't be left to a bunch of anecdotal tales about how this toddler or that granny didn't like the colour of a waiting room.'

'And those experts would be doctors?' Rav asked.

'Mostly, yes. Although some nurses know a thing or two, and pharmaceutical companies of course.'

'Are you sure about that?' There was something quite seductive about the little herbalist's gentle tone, Sally decided. She lowered her second-best laser and let him continue. 'Is it possible that patients know how they feel? And that pharmaceutical companies mostly advise on the most productive areas of profit for themselves?'

'Oh, here you go again.' Wilmslow repeated his attempt to catch a few eyes but, Sally noticed, most of the civil service staff were now making notes to fill in the time before something new happened. 'Big Pharma wants us all on unnecessary drugs and your herb teas are the answer to everything from cancer to piles.'

'Those are both disingenuous parodies of that which I would like you to one day come to understand, Dr Wilmslow.' Rav smiled at Sally. 'However, perhaps that debate could wait until another day? I'm sure we have plenty to get through.'

'Thank you.' Sally turned her attention to the agenda on the screen. 'For now, I'd just like to add that these issues were all flagged by the outgoing reps as important to their communities, so our specialists have compiled a list of the suggested solutions, plus the constituencies most suitable for trials. Since we have some time this afternoon, I'd like to get ahead of the game a little by constructing a small working committee for each idea.'

'Never mind how the hell we run hospitals when the Luddites come for the computers with their sledgehammers,' muttered Wilmslow.

Sally was contemplating a withering retort when the door to the committee room opened slightly and Minnow popped his head around it.

'Sorry to interrupt, ma'am,' he began.

'Not at all, are you the computer expert we've been waiting for?'

'Yes, but, well no. I mean, it was me but something has cropped up. I think you have someone here I need to speak to.' Minnow checked the screen on his phone. 'Marjory Alleyne?'

A distinguished-looking black woman looked up from her note-taking. 'That's me.'

'Could I borrow you for a short while?'

The woman looked at Sally, who nodded in bewilderment. Then the chair of the Pandemic Preparedness Committee left the room.

'So we think the street troubles were a deliberate diversion?' Minnow asked as he and Marjory entered Gerald's office.

'Yes,' Gerald said. 'Who's this?'

'I'll explain in a minute.' Minnow wanted to only have to say the next bit once. 'Did you call the others?'

'Yes, Brown and Morrow are on their way, and Carswell, as you requested. What's going on, Minnow?'

'I'm not sure yet.' Minnow retrieved a sheaf of notes from the side pocket of his laptop bag and sat at one of the chairs Gerald had pulled up to his desk. 'I'm still joining the dots...'

Gerald shook hands with Marjory and indicated that she take a seat as well.

'How do you do? I'm sure we've met, but do remind me?'

'Health Ministry, Senior Adviser, Pandemic Prep.' Marjory sat where hidden and opened a notebook. 'And I don't know what's going on either.'

'Are the recorders on?' Minnow scanned the office panelling.

'Yes, is that a problem?'

'No, I think we need this on the record.'

A knock at the door heralded the arrival of the ministers. 'Come in, gentlemen, take seats, I've ordered us some coffee. We apologise for the peremptory call away from your routine meetings, but it is possible that we have a...situation of some sort.'

The coffee arrived. Minnow began to fidget. He knew he had to let everyone settle down, do the small talk about where they were, say hello, offer each other cream and sugar, etcetera. It drove him mad but he had learned that most people only listened after an introductory muddle of trivia. He had once calculated how much extra coding he could get done in a week's worth of pointless social chat. But this needed to get out of his head, and right now.

'Can we start?' He appealed to Gerald as Morrow and Brown began slapping Carswell on the back and telling him how well he'd done on the telly.

'Certainly. We should get these good people back to their regularly scheduled programming as soon as possible. Um, can I have your attention, gentlemen and lady? Our chief technical adviser has something to tell us.'

CHAPTER TWENTY-NINE

'I've called the doctor, Queenie dear. I don't like the sound of that wheezing.' Caroline had returned to Queenie and Bert after seeing Deborah and Colin safely off the premises. She would be organising a well-behaved solicitor for Deborah later in the day. The charge couldn't go away those days had gone, along with the old-style politicians—but she felt sure that self-defence would lead to an acquittal. They might even be able to spin Deborah to the media as a national heroine. Single-handedly taking down the enemy within, yes, they could get a step ahead of the inevitable news machine as soon as the lawyers were on board.

Queenie was back in Bert's chair in the reception room by the time Caroline got back.

'I feel a lot better now,' she said.

'Even so, we should take good care of you. Bert is right, we asked a lot last week.' She smiled at Bert, who was busying himself tucking a rug around Queenie's feet.

It looked like a role he was unused to but, Caroline thought, maybe the old bugger was finally coming round.

'Yeah, well,' he began, somewhat mollified. 'We all know it's got to be done. It's just hard when you're old, that's all.'

'Thank you for looking after Deborah.' Queenie pointed at her knitting bag and Bert lifted it carefully onto her lap.

'You're welcome, but there's no need for thanks, it's what we do.'

'You was good to sort it out.' Bert's voice had turned a little throaty. 'Queenie reckons if I'd answered the phone I'd have gone down there all guns blazin' and made things worse.'

'And Colin would have apologised so much they'd have assumed she done it and thrown away the key!' They all laughed together. This was new.

'I'm sorry you've lost your chair, Bert—the football probably doesn't feel anything like the same.'

'My Queenie deserves it.' The man puffed out his chest. 'I'm bloody proud of her. Did you see her on the telly?'

'I certainly did.' Caroline smiled at them both. 'You were marvellous.'

'And I only 'ad to kick that idiot once!'

Queenie picked up her knitting, looked at the tea cosy in progress and put it back down in her lap. She narrowed her eyes at Caroline.

'What the bloomin' hell is guerilla knitting?'

'I was wondering when you'd ask.'

'If you two is goin' to start talking knittin', I'm off back to the telly.' Bert made for the inner door.

'Thank you, Bertie.'

'What for?'

'Aw, you know, bein' all…nice and that.'

'Stupid mare.'

He slammed the door behind him.

'He doesn't mean it, you know.' Queenie's eyes stayed on the door he'd just gone through.

'He's settling down a bit, I think?'

'He's gettin' used to it. He's just hurtin' because they didn't take him, back when his form came.'

'Oh, I didn't realise that. Do you know why?'

'No, they never said.'

'Would you like me to try and find out?'

'I dunno really, it might be worse to know.'

'Tell you what, if I hear anything I'll let you know, then you can decide that bit. It could stay our secret if you want.'

Queenie smiled at her. 'You're a good kid, ain't you? I was scared of you to start with.'

Caroline checked her watch. 'The doctor will be here soon. Just before I leave you to it, I wanted to ask if you'd like to bring that pattern to the knitting guild?' She indicated the tea cosy in Queenie's lap.

'I still don't get what it is, that mad knitting you do.'

'It's just about fun and colour. It makes people smile.'

'It made me smile seein' the patterns off Andy's tie all over the streets and everywhere!'

'Yes, I should maybe have been a bit subtler about that.'

'But I don't get why it's a big secret.'

'Just because the surprise is part of the fun.'

'Hmm.'

'So let me get this straight.' Gerald did the steepled fingers thing. 'Your reports from the various organisations affected by the hacking include one outlier?'

'Yes, they didn't think anything of it at the time.' Minnow hated having to lead people by the nose to a conclusion but he'd got used to it. And he knew Gerald had got it first time; he was just teasing out the thought process for the others. Probably mostly for Carswell. 'They saw on the news that a lot of computers were down, and their service came back when the rest did, so they didn't go round looking for trouble.'

'But we think the whole outage could just be a cover for this?'

'No other research labs had a problem, just this one.'

'So when we learned that the disorder was a cover for something bigger and assumed the generalised computer outages were the point—'

Minnow finished Gerald's sentence for him. 'The other computer outages look like they might have been a cover for this theft.'

'Which would explain the somewhat ineffective demands.' Gerald continued the thought.

'Porton Down have just reported losing two vials from the RIP lab—'

'And they only just noticed? Good God, man, what were they waiting for? An annual bloody spring clean?'

'I'm sorry to interrupt, but—' Clayton's pen had stopped in mid-air.

Marjory came to his aid. 'Rare and Imported Pathogens.'

'Thank you.' Clayton's pen began again, as did the others'.

'So, whatever was taken has had enough time to leave the country and we are none the wiser as to who or why.'

'That's about it,' Minnow concluded. 'They wouldn't tell me what had gone; my level of security only applies to computer issues.'

'They'll tell me,' Marjory said. 'I'll get over there right away.'

'Thank you.' Gerald offered her an eye crinkle, from which Minnow inferred he'd decided she was good at her job. That would help. 'And I think we need to schedule a full cabinet emergency session to discuss the implications of what Ms Alleyne will be telling us. Needless to say, we have to keep this to ourselves until we have more information. There's no point in panicking people with a threat that may not exist. Especially since we have, at this stage, no demands from anyone.' Gordon Morrow raised a finger to speak. 'Go ahead...'

'If I have this right, we have a potential bioterrorist on the loose? Is secrecy the best option? Surely we need people on the lookout for anything suspicious?'

'Not necessarily.' Gerald sat back from the desk and crossed his legs. 'For all we know, this could just be an accounting error. Cock-up over conspiracy, as the tabloids would put it. Besides, if we ask people to look over their shoulders without telling them what to look for, we'll be swamped with calls from every conspiracy theorist in town.'

'Just because there are conspiracy theorists doesn't mean there aren't conspiracies.'

'Very true, Mr Morrow, and this may well be one of

them. But we are in danger of not seeing the wood for the trees if we let this out. The rise of the conspiracy theorist has correlated almost exactly with the reduction in actual threats to populations. Conspiracy theories feed the need for reasons—a system that has no point other than *being* is existentially terrifying. Therefore governments are assumed to have all manner of nefarious plans whereas, for the most part, we are just here to keep the engine room of state in good repair.'

Minnow tried not to sigh. There was so much to do, and now he had to sit still while Gerald expounded political theory.

'So, we wait?' asked Clayton. 'Doesn't that give who or whatever is out there the upper hand? And we already know it's a democracy thing. We could ask for contacts, take names…do something?'

'Otherwise the bullies win?'

'If you wish to put it like that, Mr Lambert, yes.'

'This is pointless,' said Carswell. 'We're talking round in circles. Why don't we wait for the full meeting?'

Morrow and Clayton eyed him with surprise. 'Blimey.' Morrow grinned. 'It had an original thought.'

'No tapestries,' Clayton added.

'Or cabbages.'

'Gentlemen, please.' The sniggering subsided. 'Ms Alleyne, perhaps you'd be good enough to call us when you've finished your inspection at Porton Down?'

Marjory nodded.

'In the meantime, please return to your scheduled meetings for the day. Keep tomorrow clear of engagements. And keep your pagers handy in case we receive any new information.'

'You mean threats,' Morrow muttered. 'Same old story, hurry up and wait.'

'Most apposite, Mr Morrow. I think that might be a suitable motto for the next few days.' Gerald received a barely disguised sneer by way of reply.

'Minnow, is there anything else you can tell us?'

'Well, I did have a suggestion.'

'Go ahead.'

'The, uh, contact, who left the country? I know the police are planning to talk to him, but I wondered if I might have more success. Shared background and all that?'

'Let's sit with that for a while. That will be all for the rest of you. Thank you for your kind attention.' Gerald dismissed the ministers with a wave of his hand. 'Oh, Ms Alleyne, would you mind waiting here a moment?' Gerald indicated a chair closer to his desk, next to Minnow.

When the door had closed, Gerald spoke again.

'Do you think your hacker is involved in this? We had him down as an accidental leak.'

'Either way, he'd not be able to resist finding out what was going on—that's what I mean, I know how he thinks. If whoever-it-is is logged on a computer anywhere he'll be looking for them. We can't help it...' Somehow he felt the need to turn and apologise to the placid woman sitting next to him. 'It's curiosity got us into the game to start with.'

She smiled. 'Us too.'

'You're proposing to go and find him in Hawaii?'

'If you can spare me, yes.'

'You'll be safe?'

'I don't see why not. If anyone finds out I'm there, it's just a personal spat. I feel let down and embarrassed by the betrayal.' It wasn't *not* true. He did. And responsible and stupid and probably out of a job anyway.

Gerald allowed a small 'hmm' to escape and then turned his attention to Marjory. 'I know you haven't visited Porton Down yet, ma'am, but what are we likely to be facing? What does Minnow need to know?'

'They've been working on drug-resistant viruses recently,' said Marjory. 'So, depending on what's been taken, I can foresee a few possibilities.'

'Go on.'

She counted them off on her fingers. 'One, a pharmaceutical company thinks it can profit from a treatment that's been developed with public money.'

'In which case we're looking at a spot of harmless industrial espionage?'

'Precisely. Alternatively just a screw-up. As you noted, the shutdown could have led to a false reading.'

'In which case we are dealing with nothing. Could it be a prank?'

'Possible, but unlikely.'

'And?'

'Some of the diseases they're working on were originally developed for biological warfare.'

Gerald sighed. 'How can we tell which is more likely?'

'Once I know what's missing. I mean if it's something endemic in this country, a hospital-based supervirus, say, then it's likely about profits.'

'And if it's some awful virus endemic to foreign climes?' Minnow was filling in the gaps to save himself some time.

'Then we could be in trouble.'

'Good to know.' Minnow got to his feet and collected

up his gadgetry. 'Let me know as soon as—'

Marjory rose to leave too. 'Of course.'

'Minnow,' Gerald called as he got to the door.

'Yes, boss?'

'Be careful.'

Minnow surveyed the set-up of computer screens on desks in his living room. He had just under an hour before the taxi arrived. Gerald had pulled a few strings and got him on the next available flight out of Heathrow. Cattle class— no sense alerting anyone who might be watching to government interest in his destination.

He'd managed to locate a headshot of Chad, which now resided in his smartphone. He'd told his family he was taking a few days R & R, after all the stress of the previous week. He'd packed. He just had time to dismantle the 'lab'. If anything did happen to him—if some copper was going to trample mud and crisp crumbs round his flat looking for clues—he didn't want it looking like a hacker's paradise. The least he could do after letting Gerald down so spectacularly would be to erase all evidence of subterfuge.

Should he shred the hard drives? He might need the information again. He considered his options while unplugging wires and placing screens in packing cases. He could store them somewhere, maybe. But not family. He was imagining himself dead at the hand of a democracy thug now. The police would go visit his folks.

He taped up the boxes with a parcel tape dispenser. He didn't know quite why he enjoyed using such a low-tech piece of equipment, but he found great solace in its simple ability to do exactly what was required. He located the receipts for the gear he'd bought in new and taped them to the boxes. It looked just like the stuff had never been opened. He bagged up the pile of extension leads and considered where to dump them.

He contemplated asking Sammy. He didn't want to implicate her either, but nobody knew she'd been part of anything. Not her flat in Westminster, though. How about her parents' place? Would they store a 'box of stuff' for her? It was a lot to ask but if he did ask, it would give him an excuse to call.

'Of course I can do that!' She sounded pleased to hear from him. 'I've been meaning to call and see how, I mean ask what...but I didn't know whether...maybe a game sometime? Or a TV show?'

'Yes.' Minnow didn't process the question; he needed to move the conversation along. 'I'm in a bit of a hurry right now, is the thing, so I need the stuff collected from my place...'

'Are you going somewhere?'

'Uh, yes, um, holiday, need some time off.'

'That is so not true, Minnow. You don't do time off; even when we watch telly you're coding in your head. What's going on?'

Minnow checked his watch. It would be quicker to tell her than to argue. Would she keep it to herself? He guessed so and, anyway, who did she know?

'I'm coming with you!' Sammy said.

'No, you can't, it's not—'

'Not what? Not safe? Don't be stupid, *you're* not safe, you don't know how to talk to anyone...and anyway, you'll look less weird on holiday with me, just a couple checking out the beaches.'

She had a point.

'I'm on my way. We can put the stuff in a cab and send it to my dad's.'

'Won't he ask what it is?'

'I'll tell him it's computer stuff, he'll sigh, put it in the attic and forget all about it.'

'If you're sure.'

'I'm sure. Can your boss cover for me at the ministry for a few days?'

'I don't see why not.'

'Sorted. I'm on my way.'

CHAPTER THIRTY

Things seemed back to normal as Caroline walked into Queenie's reception room on Friday morning. The recliner was still in situ but Queenie was less recliney within it. Her feet were up, but she sat a little straighter, knitting fit to bust.

'Hello, dearie, is it meeting time? Look, I'm working on some samples for your group!'

'So I see. Are you feeling strong enough to come along and meet everyone sometime?'

'Oh, I think so, that doctor gave me some stuff.'

'Ah yes, what did he say?'

'He was quite interesting. He asked all about the cough and when it was bad and that. I told him it got a lot better when we moved here, and he listened to my chest and said he wants to get the Peabodys checked for mould.'

'Really?' Caroline didn't know whether to be relieved or horrified. She'd have to look up the long-term effects before having any idea how Queenie actually was.

'He gave me this puffer thing.' Queenie indicated an inhaler, which had found its way into her knitting bag. 'I have to keep it nearby in case I get wheezy again, but I'm right as rain now.' She directed a happy smile to the inner door. 'Bert says I can keep the chair, until the weekend, anyway. We thought we'd see about another one so he can have this back in front of the telly.'

'That's a nice idea. I'm sure Eugene can help out with that.'

'Oh yes, he's sorting it all out. He's such a nice boy. Thing is…' Queenie put her knitting down in her lap and lowered her voice a little. 'Those shoes you got made for me, the ones with the little heels, you know?'

'Yes?'

'They are lovely and I can stand in them for ages, but then my feet ache a bit after, when we're doin' all that walking around nodding politely at stuff. You don't realise your feet are killing you until you stop.'

Caroline sympathised more than she planned to let on. 'I hear a lot of dancers say that too,' she said.

'Really?'

'Yes, the adrenaline keeps you moving while you have to be on show, and then afterwards you find out what aches.'

'Blimey.' Queenie let out a proper, happy, non-wheezy guffaw. 'I'm a bleedin' dancer now, just wait 'til I tell Bert.'

When the giggle-fest subsided, Caroline returned to matters in hand. 'Did the doctor say what he planned to do about the mould?'

'I told him I'd asked Big Doris to see if anyone else had the cough but she wasn't very keen on the idea, so he's going to get public health round and then do a report to the Health Ministry. He says normally it would be a local council matter but there's loads of Peabodys round the country.'

'I was under the impression the Peabody Estates were a charitable body? I'm surprised they'd let something like this get out of hand.'

'Oh no, not any more. They used to be but the place got sold to a developer a few years back. They had to keep us lifelong tenants on—grandfathered in, they called it. My Bert hated that. Said he'd be a grandfather when our Debs sprogged and not a minute before.' Queenie laughed again. 'But after that, only the smart bits got maintained. We think they want us to get fed up and move out.'

'That's awful!'

'But the doc says once it's a public health thing, they can be forced to sort it out.'

'Let's hope so.'

'I was going to tell Doris all about it. I'm sure her Sandra's kiddies got the cough, but I didn't know, you know, after what happened.'

'I get the feeling Doris might be a bit more amenable these days. Perhaps we could invite her up here for a chat when the reps are back next week? See if we can get a bit of grass-roots support from the tenants?'

'Can you be here? Help with the talking? Just in case she's still got a nasty turn on?'

'Certainly. Let's pencil it in right now. How about Wednesday? I can have the office put it in her diary.'

'That's nice. And can I invite Sandra's kids to the afternoon we're doing for the reps' kiddies?'

'Have you been plotting that some more?'

'Oh, I never told you, what with all the fuss and

trouble. Eugene has put it all together. Some Saturday afternoons we'll have the kiddies over to see the horses and have a ride in the carriages. There's going to be games down in the Mews, and tea, you know, ice cream and jelly and stuff. Maybe a film and popcorn for the older ones. They've all got moved away from their friends and that.'

'That's lovely, Queenie. I had no idea you'd got so far with the planning.'

'And do you know the best thing about it?'

'No, go on...'

'My Deborah and her Colin said they'd come and help!'

'Queenie, you are a marvel. When's the first one planned for?'

'Next weekend. Not tomorrow, 'cos we want to invite the kiddies that come down with their reps who are only here for the week as well.'

'If it goes well and you do another one, maybe we could invite the media to come along...' *and begin Deborah's path to national heroine in time for the hearing...*

'Ooh, yes!' Queenie picked up her needles again. 'You know something, Caroline?'

'What's that?'

'I'm beginning to like bein' able to *do* stuff. I know there's trouble going on, and some of the others are stressed and scared of messing up, but, you know, when you're just stupid Queenie Mason at the checkout and you see something that needs doing, you don't bother because nobody listens.'

'I'm pleased to hear it. People listen because they like you. But, sometimes even we can't make things work how we want—and we think we might have something cropping up that isn't easy to fix. Do you feel well enough to sit in on a cabinet meeting this afternoon?'

Queenie had decided to take her knitting along to the meeting. She knew it annoyed some of the menfolk but it helped her concentrate. And it meant nobody would expect her to say anything.

She wasn't sure what was going on but she assumed it was all about the riots and how to give people their jobs back. Which she was all in favour of, and they knew that.

She looked round the table. Andy was back in a stupid tie. Doug looked a bit green round the gills. Sally, the woman she'd been meaning to chat to from Health, was there and the soldier with the weird little moustache in a tiny horizontal line across his face—she checked the printout of faces in her knitting bag. She knew most of them by sight now, but there were a few she'd not spent any time with. He was Gordon Morrow, Defence. He looked cross. It looked like that nice Clayton Brown was going to run things, although Gerald was there too, in the background for once.

The other different thing was, everyone had been told to put their phones and tablets and suchlike in a box by the door. There was no screen up with a list of things on it, just a few papers in front of each seat at the conference table.

There was a woman Queenie hadn't seen before. She was sitting next to Sally, so probably Health. Queenie sneaked a look at her cheat sheet. And wondered what a pandemic was. Presumably she would find out shortly.

Clayton called the meeting to order and said there was

a potential crisis and everyone had to get ready, just in case. He handed over to the new woman, Marjory.

She mentioned Minnow, and Queenie looked around to give the lad a smile and a thumbs up, but he wasn't there.

As Marjory continued, the room managed to get quieter—even though there had been no noise before. Queenie laid down her needles as a mark of respect because everyone was shocked, even if the finer details had gone over her head.

Someone had stolen something from a lab, and used the riots and the computer crashes to hide it. It was to do with a nasty virus... She looked at the notes she'd been handed. *A virulent form of Marburg fever not generally seen in the BR, endemic to parts of sub-Saharan Africa but modified for biological warfare.* Apparently some democratic government had done that back last century for some war or other that never happened.

The virus sample and some new antidote-thingy were somewhere, with someone, and nobody knew where or who or why.

'While we await a threat, or a demand, or an accidental disaster, we will be requiring all hospitals, clinics and patient transport facilities to improve on existing pandemic protocols,' the woman was saying. 'This will be handled with minimum public panic by instituting a nationwide major incident *rehearsal*. The Health Ministry will take the lead.' She nodded to Sally, who acknowledged the reference. 'However, each ministry will play some part in supporting the project.'

She handed back to Clayton, who outlined how the Home Office would be liaising with Defence and the

Foreign Office over extra health checks at airports, extra security at medical labs, pandemic-control experts seconded to police forces and new, secret isolation units at military bases.

'If and when we hear more, we will call you together again by pager,' Clayton said. 'Nothing you have heard today can leave this room. You have what information we are able to give you in hard copy. Please read it before you leave and hand your papers back before collecting your electronic devices. The notes will be burned. If anyone asks you about this meeting, it was addressed by the Employment Secretary.' He gestured to Doug. 'Before we leave, Mr Sideworth will, indeed, address us, with the portion of this session that may be leaked to the media.'

As he indicated Doug and sat back down, Clayton Brown observed his class. Most were nodding, just like a maths group after a heavy hint about an upcoming exam. He allowed his gaze to rove from eye to eye, on the lookout for *the one*. The clown who always missed the point. There it was. Clayton noted Gerald's focus land in the same spot. *Bloody Carswell.* Presumably they were both thinking, *Please let this be a domestic issue.*

Doug stood as Clayton sat. 'Righty-ho, ladies and gents,' he began. Queenie watched his hands. Were they shaking? He placed them palms down on the table. She made a mental note to pop down to the cafe later, see if he was all right. He said some stuff about what Employment planned to do as a result of the strikes. Meetings with unions, meetings with corporation bosses, a think tank to look at ways companies could move employees into jobs that were about making customers feel good.

He put the screen on and there were some phrases on it. He called them sound bites and asked everyone to try and recall one of them if they spoke to anyone. He said, what with the whole pandemic thing cropping up, the ideas might not get started yet, but it was important to be seen to respond, and his department's 'initiatives' would provide cover for any more emergency meetings about the real trouble until such time as the public had to know.

He asked if anyone had any questions. Silence. He looked at Gerald and inclined his head towards the door. Gerald nodded. He looked at Clayton and did the same. Clayton nodded. Then Sally.

'Actually, I have a question.' Queenie looked round to see whose mouth the words had come out of. Everyone was looking at her. 'When the time comes to tell people what's going on...I mean...if we have to...tell them the truth and that...'

'Yes?'

'Who's going to do it?'

Doug looked at Gerald again, with a slight shrug of the shoulders this time. Gerald got to his feet.

'That will be your prerogative, ma'am.'

CHAPTER THIRTY-ONE

Minnow and Sammy sat on adjacent loungers by the pool. The Honolulu Airport Hotel was a surprising cut above the usual airport dormitory. Minnow had chosen it mostly for the free shuttle and its proximity to the PC Gamerz internet cafe. He'd made the booking when he thought he'd be travelling alone—what better cover than a nerd who can't stop gaming even when on holiday? Now there were two of them, it was even better. The cafe had 'ladies game free' evenings, so Sammy could go and take on the locals while Minnow mooched about, waiting for her to finish. And if anyone happened to recognise the 'old friend' Minnow was hoping to look up while he was there...

'How do you know he's here?' Sammy asked as she sipped a bright orange concoction with leaves in.

'He sent an email.' Minnow eyed Sammy's drink with distaste and started work on removing the lemon from his tea. 'What is that?'

'It's a mai tai. I asked for something really Hawaiian to try, and apparently this is it.'

'Is it nice?'

Sammy wrinkled her nose. 'It'll do. I might just have a martini next time.'

'But you're making the most of our first holiday as a lovey-dovey item?'

'Yes, I told the waiter how special it was for us.'

'Excellent.' Minnow regarded the people round the pool. He sipped his tea. 'You know, jumping in that taxi to come with me was a stroke of genius. We look just like everyone else.'

'As opposed to you sticking out like a nerd who never ventures into sunlight, let alone takes a holiday.'

'Yep.'

'Anyway, the email.'

'Oh yes. He sent a cocky little selfie. Said he'd had to rush back to the US, government business and all, but the IP address traced to here.'

Sammy moved the leaves around until she could sip her drink without them poking up her nose. 'Hmm. Doesn't that strike you as odd?'

'I did wonder why he didn't spoof his IP address, reckoned maybe he hadn't had time to sort it out if he was on the move.'

'If this was an episode of *CSI: Cyber*, he'd have done it deliberately to lead you into a trap.'

Minnow laughed. 'You think? Nah, cock-up over conspiracy every time, as Gerald would say the papers would say. He wanted us to know he was having a ball on some Pacific beach while we were still stuck cleaning up his mess in grimy, wet old London.'

'Are you sure? He must know he's the only possible way in to the systems.'

Minnow shook his head. 'I reckon he realised he's been used. He's taken off somewhere to do a bit of digging to find out what's going on. In fact, come to think of it...'

'Yes? What?'

'If he did make a deliberate slip-up with that IP address, maybe it's because he wants me to follow him, help unmask the real problem.' Minnow sat back on his lounger and crossed his ankles, pleased with his analysis of the options.

Sammy took a deep breath. And removed a mint leaf from her left nostril.

'I hope you're right.'

'I'm always right. I'm a genius.' He lifted his chin to the sun.

'We're all geniuses.' She breathed on her fingernails and buffed them on an imaginary lapel. 'I just wonder if you've been working for the good guys too long.'

'Nah. I tell you, Chad's one of us. He's on the trail of what's going on and he wants our help.'

'So, do we drink up and head straight to every internet cafe in town, or do we rest up a bit first? I'm exhausted.'

'I guess we could head out tomorrow. What would people on holiday do?'

Sammy grinned. 'I was right, you haven't ever been on one, have you?'

'We used to go on awful caravanning trips when I was a kid but I've never seen the point of leaving my computer.'

'Of course you haven't. So, here's what usually happens. People fall off an eighteen-hour flight into their room. They eat and drink, they sleep, they shower and swim and then, when they're rested, they start sightseeing.'

'Oh.' Minnow sat up and stared at her in horror.

'What?'

'I only booked one room!'

Sammy took her turn to lie back, cross her ankles and lift her chin to the sun. 'I rather assumed you would have. I don't mind if you don't.'

'But what about your dad? He'll kill me.'

'Only if one of us tells him.'

'Maybe there'll be a settee or something.'

'Maybe there will...'

Sally handed the laser pointer to Marjory.

'It makes sense for you to take us through the stuff we need to know,' she said.

'Dearie me.' Wilmslow winked at Rav. 'This lady must be important. Is she an expert in children's playrooms?'

'Significant though that issue might be'—Sally adopted what she hoped would come over as a withering tone, but hearing it back it seemed to have come out a bit squeaky again—'Ms Alleyne has some expertise that we are going to need in the coming weeks, and I'd appreciate it if we could put our, uh, professional differences aside.'

'Professional? Since when—'

'Mr Wilmslow, please.' Sally attempted a deeper timbre. Now she sounded like Lady Fucking Bracknell.

'Dr Wilmslow.'

Sally went for the full Maggie Thatcher. '*Doctor* Wilmslow, this specialist is chair of the National Pandemic

Preparedness Committee, and if it's okay with you she is about to tell us how we can prepare the country to face Armageddon.'

He at least had the decency to look surprised, Sally thought. She'd taken most of the morning's cabinet meeting to absorb what was happening; if he took the few minutes that his no doubt superior intellect would require, Marjory might be able to get a few words in.

Wilmslow closed his mouth. He looked at Rav, who shrugged.

'Thank you, Ms Farnham. Now, if we're all ready I'll begin with an overview of the national emergency rehearsal we have planned. We will be telling the press that it's a response to the strikes, to ensure that automated systems have adequate human backup in times of crisis.' Marjory switched on the wall screen to reveal bullet points: *Hospitals, GP Surgeries, Ambulance Stations, Occupational Health Departments, Ports of Entry, Public Buildings, New Isolation Units, Blood and Tissue Transportation, Protective Clothing Manufacture.*

'You will note that in all cases, a civil service specialist has been allotted as liaison officer. Each institution will also come under the jurisdiction of an experienced project manager. If one with sufficient skills cannot be found within the existing staff, my department has a stable of experts we can call on to parachute in.'

Rav raised a finger. 'Yes?' Marjorie turned a polite smile his way.

'It looks as if your plans involve building *new* isolation units—and manufacturing protective clothing?'

Marjory nodded.

'This would seem to me to be an overreaction for a

drill to test the systems.' He spoke slowly, as if thinking the question through as it left his mouth. 'Therefore I think we are entitled to ask, what else is going on?'

Marjory looked at Sally.

'You are, naturally, entitled to ask,' Sally said, picking up the slow delivery and mimicking it back to him. It calmed her down to speak that way. Maybe that was why the little guy did it. It made you listen that bit harder too, being quieter than most. 'And you are entitled to know.' She rubbed her hands together. 'Except, we are not one hundred per cent sure yet what we might be dealing with. As far as the media and everyone outside this room are concerned, we are conducting an exercise.'

'But an actual pandemic is on the cards?' Wilmslow stabbed at the table with his forefinger. 'In which case, all your "project managers" have missed the most important thing.' He managed to make the air quotes look so emphatic Sally half expected them to burst into life and float up to the ceiling to mock her from behind the chandelier. 'I suggest that you place a senior doctor in charge of each section; they at least would know that the first priority is to manufacture and dispense vaccines up and down the country.'

'You are absolutely right, Doctor Wilmslow, they would.' Marjorie took back the reins. Wilmslow sat back with a satisfied smile. 'However, they would neglect everything else that a nation's infrastructure requires to stay functional in a time of crisis—and it has been, uh, decided, that the particular conceit of this exercise will be that no antidote is available.'

Rav lifted a hand to shush Wilmslow's retort.

'What aren't you telling us?'

QUEENIE'S TEAPOT

Queenie found Doug sitting in his usual spot in the cafe. She dumped the knitting bag on the table next to her cup and saucer and sat back in the chair. She eased off her shoes.

'Oof, that's better, feels like I've been on me feet for days.'

Doug turned his thousand-yard stare her way.

'How's it going, then? I see they're sending you round the world with tapestry-features. Is that to keep him in order?'

Queenie laughed. 'Maybe. Apparently I'm supposed to go anyway, but he's doin' all right really.'

'Not what I heard.'

'He just gets nervous without a script, is all.' Queenie took a slurp of tea. 'And anyway, I did hear tell you've needed a bit of keepin' in order as well?'

'Yeah, everyone's heard that. Pity they haven't got something more important to gossip about.'

'This isn't like you, Douggie, what's up, eh?'

'Nothing.' He turned a morose stare back out of the window and up the Thames.

Queenie decided she was getting a bit cross. 'Now just you listen to me for a minute, young man—'

He directed a sneer at a passing pleasure cruiser.

'We're all doin' our best. It ain't no harder for you than anyone else, and you've got it easy compared to some of the other poor buggers. Left their families behind, or uprooted them and their kids are miserable, dumped in the middle of stuff none of us understands.'

'You've got no idea what's hard for me and what isn't.'

He spat the words at her and turned away again.

'So tell me. We can help each other, you know.' She considered the side of his head. 'You know when I was on the tills—and I can see you rollin' your eyes, and I don't care—when I was on the tills awful things happened. My Bert lost 'is job, my Deborah turned against us and was really nasty sometimes, my neighbour lost 'er baby and we was all devastated.'

Doug's mouth set into a line like it had been Araldited together.

'But I went to work and I shoved a bleedin' smile on my boat race because none of that was anyone else's fault. And you know what? It might have been fake to start with but it worked in the end.'

Doug folded his arms.

'So you can tell me to sod off if you want but if you're too much of a baby to tell someone what's wrong and too much of a pig to even try and be civil, then I've got you wrong. I had you down as one of the decent ones. Maybe you're not.'

He turned a look to her of such venom she wondered if she'd gone too far. *Still, no backin' out now, Queenie me luv.*

'I'm an alcoholic.'

'Blimey darlin', we all knew that, ain't hardly a secret.'

'So, they gave me this job because they don't trust me. Brown, Morrow, even fucking Tapestry, they get responsibility. I'm just a ventriloquist's dummy. They put clothes on me, they put bloody makeup on me, they stand me up in front of a camera and tell me what to say.'

'Ain't nothin' wrong with that, that's all I do too. Somebody's got to do it. Would you rather have lives in your hands? I wouldn't.'

'Yes, but you're—'

'I'm what? Stupid?'

'No, I didn't mean—'

'Yes, you did, but I don't care. I know I'm daft, so I'm not too proud to learn. You could do worse than think the same. Just because you're a highfalutin' accountant you think you're too good—'

'No.'

'What do you mean, no?'

'That's not it.'

'What the hell is it then?' Queenie finished her tea and absentmindedly swirled the leaves and overturned her cup into the saucer.

Doug put his elbows on the table and sank his head into his hands. 'I wish I knew. I want to make a success of things, be a good public—whatever-we-are, I want to like everyone. I'm just so...angry. Not at someone, not with anyone, I'm just...'

'Mr Angry?'

He looked up at her face. 'Yeah.'

'There might be people you could talk to about that?'

'I've got to go to counselling.'

'Oh, that's a good idea. Who sorted that out?'

'Gerald and Caroline. They said it was a condition of keeping my job after...what happened.'

'That's good, isn't it? You can tell them all about bein' Mr Angry.'

'Feels like a failure to me.'

'Nah, don't be a pillock all your life, you sound like my Bert. Give it a go. Worst way you can take it all out on them and not on us, eh?'

Doug produced the ghost of a grin.

'When do you start?'

'Tonight. I've got meetings with unions all afternoon, then that this evening, and...'

'And what, luv?'

He turned back to the window and muttered, 'Alcoholics Anonymous tomorrow.'

Queenie laughed. 'Blimey, you ain't goin' to be very bleedin' anonymous, are you? When are you on the telly again?'

Doug shrugged. 'No idea. Whenever they have another pack of lies to spout, I suppose.'

'I reckon what you need is a hobby! Somethin' to do with your hands, apart from liftin' a glass. I should teach you to knit!'

Finally, she'd raised a laugh.

'Why not give it a try, then?'

'Because, Queenie, it's as stupid as everything else you come out with.'

'You could come with me to Caroline's'—she lowered her voice to a whisper—'guerrilla knitting group!'

'What the hell's that?'

'You know, all that knitted stuff that appears on trees and that.'

'Caroline does that?'

'Yes! Come with us. Caroline says loads of men do it. It's got to be better than sittin' all on your own, moping.'

Doug stared at her and shook his head. 'I'd feel daft, and anyway...'

'Anyway what?'

'I might not be around much longer.'

CHAPTER THIRTY-TWO

It had been an awkward breakfast. Sammy had blamed the cocktails and Minnow had blamed the stress. They'd both apologised for something it seemed like they'd both wanted to happen. Minnow knew some people talked about this stuff—he'd seen it on crap American sitcoms—but he had no idea how you started. His history with girls wasn't stellar. Most of them ran a mile when he started talking gaming. He'd got drunk a few times, at parties he'd not wanted to go to, and had woken up occasionally with a woman in his flat. But they tended to bolt out of the door as soon as they were sober enough to focus on all the computers.

Sammy was different; not so much a *woman* as a pal. They got on. He'd not really considered her pulchritude in any specific detail, beyond the cute smile. He'd just been glad of the help. And the company. And the laughs. And the introduction to *Fawlty Towers*. And the tiny corners of chaos she'd introduced into his life that he could tolerate if they were about her. And the dimple.

They were going to have to discuss it. They had an unknown number of nights sharing the same room here, and then, depending what they found out, maybe more joint enterprise when they got back to London. He supposed they could just keep on getting drunk and pretending to be stressed, but he sort of assumed women liked things a bit more...a bit more what? A bit more *talky*.

They had decided to walk the couple of miles to the internet cafe. Why take a cab when you didn't want to leave too much of a trail and it was a glorious day and you were posing as holidaymakers?

The air was full of the scent of some flower or other. Minnow made a mental note to find out what it was; the contrast with the smells of London streets almost brought tears to his eyes. There were flowers everywhere: the trees flowered; even some of the rocks flowered. He could see why all the souvenir shops were full of those flower garlands; people must have to pick a handful of the things just to find somewhere to sit down.

'Oh look, they've got a cafe.' Sammy pointed to the chairs and tables outside Honolulu's allegedly premier gaming and internet establishment.

'And, it would appear, a Vape Lounge, whatever that is.'

Sammy laughed at him. 'You can be so last century, sometimes.'

'I think I'll stick to tea anyway.'

'It'll be a good excuse to stick around. You can have a drink while I ask about the girls-game-free nights.'

They wandered in, past the rows of individuals huddled in worlds of their own, oblivious to everything except the screen in front of them.

'Just like home,' Sammy said, with a grin.

'Except their benches aren't plywood.'

'True.'

They meandered to the reception desk where a young guy who looked as though he'd just stepped off the cover of an Ivy League University prospectus—and not very Hawaiian—was on the phone. 'Yeah, next tourney is on Thursday, room for one more team, twenty bucks a head...let me know soon, all right? Can't hold a spot for long...okay, laters...'

He finished his call and looked up at the newcomers. 'Hi there, can I help you guys?'

'Yes, thanks, we were wondering...' Minnow began with a spark of confidence, but his ability to make words disintegrated in the face of such a dazzling smile.

'What he means is...' Sammy took over, glancing at the name embroidered on the chap's polo shirt. 'Parker? Is that your first name?'

'Parker Rothwell at your service, ma'am.' He twinkled another burst of pricey dentition and made a small bow.

'Yes, hello.' Sammy returned a closed-lip smile. Her dad hadn't been big on the point of orthodontics. 'Anyway, what he means is, we'd like to do a bit of gaming while we're on holiday, and check a few things online as well, so could we buy an hour now and then maybe you could tell us about that thing you do when women can come and game for nothing?'

'Certainly, ma'am, nothing would give me greater pleasure. Here's a leaflet about our gaming nights and tourneys. And we can set you up over there.' He pointed at a free cubicle. 'It's five bucks for the hour, or if you want a bit longer we can do two and a half hours for ten bucks.'

'That'll do fine, won't it?' Sammy tilted her head up to Minnow and he nodded.

'Great.' The preppy smile widened. 'I can't help but notice your accents. You're not looking for Chad by any chance, are you?'

Minnow and Sammy stared at him, open-mouthed.

He riffled about under the counter and produced a sealed brown envelope.

'Some sort of fish name? Yeah, he left this for a guy called Minnow, that you?'

Minnow nodded. Sammy took the proffered envelope and said, 'Thank you very much. This does appear to be for us. We'll, um, we'll get a coffee maybe and log on a bit later?'

'Sure, whatever, let me know.'

Caroline poured a third cup of coffee and addressed the vexing issue of today's agenda. Saturdays were usually for shopping, trying out new recipes, chatting to Lady Jo and catching up with friends. Today, however, she fancied a change. It had been a rough week and she deserved a treat. Maybe she'd call Ali and see about another sneaky lunch out.

'What do I deserve the most, Jojo?' The cat rearranged herself on Caroline's feet. 'Apart from a three-cups-of-coffee morning?' She thought back to the beginning of this intake and asked herself how long ago the last three-cup start to a day had been. She couldn't remember.

'I could be a lunching person.' Lady Josephine took

exception to the conversation and picked herself up to leave the room.

'Or I could sort out a new pattern for the group?' She addressed the tail as it whisked through the door to the kitchen.

'No tuna treats for you, young lady,' Caroline called after her. The cat returned briefly, in order to turn her back a little more flouncily and leave the room again.

Just as Caroline was about to solve her dilemma with the toss of a coin, the phone rang.

'Hello, Queenie? What's the matter, are you all right?'

'Yes, dearie.' Queenie sounded a little agitated. 'I'm sorry to bother you at home and on a Saturday and all.'

'That's okay, what's up?'

'I know this is goin' to sound like a stupid question.'

'Go on...'

'It's...did you or Gerald or anyone tell Doug he was gettin' fired or anythin' like that?'

'No.' Caroline decided to leave *why do you ask* for the time being. Queenie's mind worked in idiosyncratic circles but she'd learnt there was usually a point of some sort to come, eventually. 'We said we couldn't fire him even if we wanted to.'

'I've been turnin' it over and over in my mind...and I'm worried about him.'

'What are you turning over, Queenie dear? Has he said anything to you about being fired?'

'No, that's just it. I was talkin' to him yesterday and he said you'd sorted out some counsellin' and that—'

'Yes, that's right.'

'And, now I know you're going to the think this is daft, but I said he needed a hobby and asked if he wanted to join the knitting thing—'

'Oh, Queenie, you didn't! What must he be thinking?'

'Well, you said men do it and, um, you know his wife died, don't you?'

'Uh huh, yes, we think that might be—'

'I thought he might like some friends and anyway I know it's stupid and it's beside the point, it was what he said after.'

'Yes?' Dear God, it was like pulling teeth.

'He said he wouldn't be around much longer. And I thought he meant goin' back to Lancashire.'

'Oh no.' Caroline groaned.

'So I called him this mornin', you know, just to be nice—see how his counsellin' went and invite him over for a chat, maybe...'

'And?'

'He's not answering the phone.'

'You think he's—'

'I'm scared. His tea leaves didn't look so good.'

'Never mind the sodding tea leaves.'

'I'm sorry, I get daft when—'

'No, *I'm* sorry, Queenie, you are far from daft and I'm glad you called. I'll get over there and check on him right away.'

'Can I come with you?'

'Sure. I'll meet you there.'

Hello Minnow,
If you're reading this, you're the guy I think you are. You knew I'd make a 'mistake' because we all wear white hats now? Of

course I'd drop a spoofed IP on you because, hey, I might be on the tail of the bad guys too.

Now you're in Hawaii and I'm long gone again, but I'm going to make it easy for you and tell you where I am and why. Follow me and you get to be the big investigator who solves the mystery. It's the least I can do.

Naturally, you'll also be the scapegoat if everybody dies, but that depends on your government and can't be helped.

'What the hell?' Sammy was reading upside down from the other side of the cafe table.

'Shh.'

Have you found what went missing yet? I do hope so. I have it with me and here is where it stays. One of the few spots left where democracy is allowed to flourish. I'll not insult you with a location; you'll be able to find it from my activity in the PC Gamerz LAN.

Now I'm sure you're thinking to yourself, "What does he want?" The truth is, Minnow old chap, we will be demanding that power be returned to those who deserve it. It's time to get tough, and pathetic little referendums will no longer do. (I can hear your fancy English accent right now, going tut tut and saying "referenda!")

If the world doesn't listen, the virus will spread soon. As you probably know by now, there is no vaccine and the antidote is in my care. We are isolated enough here to survive and bring democracy back by default when the pandemic works itself out. It'll be obvious then, won't it? People need strong leaders, not random Joes.

Pip pip, old bean.

'Hello, George,'

'Good morning, miss.'

'I think we might have a problem in Mr Sideworth's flat again; would you mind bringing your pass key?'

'I'll just get some cover for the desk.' George picked up his phone as Queenie arrived with Eugene in tow. Caroline raised her eyebrow at Eugene.

'We couldn't spare a security officer to come over with Queenie right away; they're all in an emergency briefing.'

'So Eugene brought me over himself. Ain't he sweet?'

'I'm not sure how much good he'd have been against an armed desperado'—Eugene rolled his eyes—'but you're here now. Thank you, Eugene, another pair of hands might be useful.'

A replacement guard had approached the security desk and George waved his pass key. 'Ready when you are.'

The small troupe headed into the lift in unaccustomed silence. Queenie bit her lip. She took a breath, as though she were about to say something. Then carried on biting.

'What is it?' Caroline asked.

'Nothing. Just. No, nothing.'

'Come on, out with it.'

She sighed and shook her head, as though trying to get a drop of water out of one ear, Caroline thought, although she couldn't visualise Queenie swimming without one of those mad hats that everyone's grandmother used to wear.

'If he's, um, you know. It might be my fault. I shouted at him a bit.'

'Don't go there. He's probably just fallen off the wagon again.'

They exited the lift in a small line: George and Eugene first, Caroline and Queenie bringing up the rear.

George knocked, called and knocked again. He looked at Caroline, who looked at Queenie. 'Why don't you have a go?'

Queenie knocked at the door. 'Doug, Mr Sideworth...Douggie dear, it's me. Are you all right?'

Nothing.

George opened the door and they all stood on the threshold looking in.

'At least there's no mess this time. Maybe he's not here.' Caroline turned to George. 'Did he sign out to go home for the weekend? We should have checked that first.'

'No, miss, not to my knowledge.'

Caroline stepped into the flat and turned left. 'I'll check the bedroom.'

George headed for the kitchen. Queenie and Eugene remained rooted to the spot in the doorway.

'We need an ambulance, George or Eugene, someone!' Caroline called.

Eugene clapped a mobile phone to his ear right away.

Queenie's face appeared over Caroline's shoulder as she attempted to roll Doug onto his side. At least he was still on the bed this time, which gave her a bit more room to work. 'Can I do anything?' Her face was almost as ashen as Doug's.

'You could maybe collect up those pill bottles? The hospital will want to know what he's taken.'

'Oh goodness, will they? I wouldn't have thought of that.' Queenie busied herself with the bottles she could see, creaking down onto her knees to look under the bed.

'Is he—?'

'He's breathing.' Caroline mentally thanked Tiny again. She wished she could tell him just how many of his tricks she'd ended up using on the nation's new Employment Minister.

'Oh, look.' Queenie attempted a reverse out from under the bed, but her hands and knees appeared to be failing her.

'Do you need a hand?' Caroline had Doug in some semblance of a recovery position now; she could afford a spare hand.

'No, it's all right, I just need to...' Queenie leaned over against the wall and swivelled herself until she was sitting on the floor. 'I just needed to be sitting before I could stand, I think. Look here.' She showed Caroline what she'd seen poking out from under the bed. It was a framed photo of a sweet-looking middle-aged woman. She was smiling directly into the camera and waving. 'Do you think that's his wife?'

'Seems likely, doesn't it?'

'Poor man.'

Voices at the door heralded the arrival of the paramedics. Caroline turned her attention to Queenie, still stuck in the little gap by the side of the bed that Doug had fallen into the last time she'd been here. While the uniformed team made quick and efficient work of inserting an airway into the unconscious man and removing him from the bed to a carrying chair and off out of the building, Caroline made increasingly redundant attempts to get Queenie onto her feet.

'Try this arm here...'

'What about that foot there?'

In desperation, Caroline sat down on the floor next to her.

'What are you doin'?'

'I thought if I got down too, I can see which feet I put where to get up again and you can copy me.'

'Trouble is, I should 'ave stayed on me knees I think. Like that joke, the Irish one?'

Caroline shook her head. 'I'm not sure—'

'This bloke asks an Irishman for directions to a place and he says, "Well, if I was you I wouldn't start from here."' Queenie attempted a truly terrible accent. Caroline laughed. 'And now you're down here too, there's no room to move about.'

'Shall I ask Eugene to call us an ambulance?'

The two of them sat with their backs to Doug's bedroom wall and giggled until the tears ran.

'Are you two okay?' George and Eugene appeared in the bedroom doorway. They both peered around the room, their gazes finally coming to rest on the two women on the floor.

'I think we might need a spot of help.' Caroline hiccupped.

'Your first hour is paid for,' Parker told them. 'Chad said you'd probably not need longer, and he put the money back here to cover it.'

'Did he tell you anything else about what we were going to do?' Sammy had a hard time keeping the venom out of her voice.

'Hey, don't take whatever it is out on me, lady, I just

gave you a message, is all.'

'Yes, thank you, we'll take the hour.' Minnow sounded apologetic. Sammy couldn't see for the life of her why they had to be polite towards this baffling set-up. She followed Minnow to the cubicle they'd been shown to.

'These people could be part of it, whatever *it* is,' she hissed as she sat beside him and watched him log on.

'All the more reason to make nice and get out of here as soon as possible.' Minnow's diffident manner had gone now, she noticed. All the man needed was a computer task, even if it was to do with, well, awfulness of some sort, and he was in charge again.

'What are we going to do next?' she whispered.

'Find where he's gone, go home, hand it all over to Gerald. I've no idea how to save the friggin' world, even if I wanted to. This is their stuff. I've done my bit. So have you. When we find him they can send Interpol or the CIA or whoever else is supposed to do dangerous sleuthing.'

'Suppose there's more stuff left for you somewhere?'

'Then some beefy bloke with a gun can swan around calling himself Minnow. I won't be offended.' He turned from the screen and smiled at her. 'I've probably got you into enough trouble already. Your dad would never forgive me if we got tangled up in any more.'

'He probably won't forgive you anyway.' She smirked back.

'That's different.'

Minnow returned his attention to the screen. 'He used one of these machines; this place uses static IPs. We should be able to just go look at whatever he did here. He's making it very easy. I should maybe be insulted.'

'Don't bother, just find him, then we can get out of

here. I'll insult you later if it'll make you feel better.'

'Here's the email he sent us. And he booked a flight. That's all there is.'

'Where did he go?'

'Where the hell is Tonga?'

CHAPTER THIRTY-THREE

Caroline reviewed the new day. Her Saturday had gone to hell in a handbasket, what with hours in casualty and popping back to Queenie's to pass on the news, etcetera. She'd spent at least an hour persuading Queenie that it was okay to have giggled, that people did that in a crisis.

In the end, support had come from the unlikely source of Bert.

'Listen, you mad mare,' he'd started. Caroline's hopes of a quick exit had sunk into her trainers at this point. Trainers that didn't go with the outfit she'd selected for lunch with Ali, but that she'd thrown on as she dashed out the door, not wanting to expose a nice pair of shoes to a possible repeat of the vomit-everywhere scenario.

She still had them on, she'd realised. Wondered if any of the hospital staff were, even at this moment, discussing her strange attire. She supposed they saw stranger things.

She returned her attention to Bert.

'The country is full of people who didn't go dashing off to save the stupid bastard. You did, and he's okay, so stop fretting about a bit of bloody giggling.'

Caroline knew he just wanted some peace and quiet to get back to the football but, to be honest, she couldn't have put it better. She was grateful to have salvaged part of her day after Queenie settled down but, what with a phone call to Gerald to put him in the picture, there hadn't been much of it left.

She wondered whether planning to put her new idea to the guild this afternoon would be tempting fate. She should probably visit Doug. Gerald had arranged with the hospital to keep press coverage to a minimum: *precautionary tests for a digestive complaint* was the party line, as opposed to *frantic stomach pump for an overdose*. But she doubted Gerald had the personal resources to ease Doug back into the human race.

At least they could leave him out of the limelight for a while. The whole 'emergency preparedness exercise', when it finally hit the headlines, could be spun as a result of his department's findings while attention shifted to Sally and Clayton.

She opened her notebook and wrote *check up on Sally Farnham*. She realised she'd not spent any time with the Health Minister and things had spiralled into the poor woman's lap rather suddenly. Somebody should see how she was coping. She also realised she was thinking about work.

'A girl deserves a day off, eh?' She addressed Lady Jo and was rewarded with a whiskery sneer.

She checked the clock and decided she just had time to fit in a visit to the hospital before the guild meeting.

Visiting Doug after the yarny creative escape would keep her mind on work all afternoon.

The phone rang.

Gerald. Probably wanting to see if she was visiting Doug today.

'Hello?'

Caroline turned and settled back on her couch to take the call, putting her feet up on the spot Josie had just vacated to go crunch a couple of treats. The spot was warm; she'd be punished with a look when Jo returned, but she deserved to be comfortable as she took one last work call before her weekend finally began—halfway through Sunday.

'Minnow's on his way back,' she heard Gerald say.

'Oh, what did he find out?' She sighed. It was like turning a battleship, getting her mind back to the big problem. On a guild afternoon.

'He's not saying. Won't email, text or tell me on the phone. All he said is that we need a Red Lion conversation.'

'Bloody hell, does he think he's being bugged?'

'I don't know. And he's not saying.'

'When's he back?'

'They actually.'

'What do you mean, they?'

'The girl we had working with him on the, uh, audit? She went along too.'

'Sammy? Awww. That's clever. And kind of cute. I should tell Queenie.'

'Don't tell anyone anything until we've heard what he has to say.'

'Okay, fair enough.'

'And they're in the air now. Short layover in LA, they should be landing late morning tomorrow. I've arranged a car to bring them straight to the Lion. As soon as we've heard whatever-it-is, I'm sending them home to rest. You and I have an appointment at Scotland Yard mid-afternoon. Full cabinet tomorrow night, press conference first thing Tuesday.'

'Right, just a minute.' Caroline removed her feet from the comfy warm spot, picked up her notebook and pen and began to jot down the arrangements. 'The press conference will be about this? Or Sideworth? Or both?'

'Don't know yet. It depends what we hear. With the reps back in the House we'll find something to chuck at them if necessary.'

'We can't keep the lid on this much longer, you know. All it takes is one of them to decide the public needs the truth. We've got nothing to threaten them with.'

'Unlike the good old days of party loyalty?' Gerald chuckled. 'In a way it's helpful they're all so new. Two years down the line we'd have more trouble with them thinking for themselves.'

'Even so.'

'Yes. Perhaps an announcement in the House that the press conference will cover public reaction to the strike? Invite grass-roots feedback. Then we'll hear what they're all thinking, pinpoint any troublemakers...'

Satisfyingly shod, Caroline followed the hospital security guard into the lift and waited as he used a pass key to authorise access to the seventeenth floor.

'There you go, miss, a colleague will escort you from

the top.'

She smiled her thanks and placed the gift she'd brought for Doug back in her bag. She'd noted with approval the low-key but thorough checks that had necessitated taking the repaired photo frame out for inspection.

Doug was propped up on a pile of pillows, staring out of the window. She tapped a little knock on the door with her fingernails to attract his attention. She could have just walked in—the door to his room was open, with a stoic guard seated outside it, where he had a full view of the patient. It just seemed politer, somehow. He turned at the sound and attempted a smile.

'How are you doing?' She sat in a plastic chair by the bed and put her bag on her lap.

'Okay, I suppose.' His voice was raspy. Caroline supposed the tubes they shoved down your throat might do that. 'Feeling stupid. A nuisance.'

'Oh yes, you're certainly a nuisance.' Caroline smiled at him. 'But you're not stupid. Stupid people don't get quite so upset.'

'It's always you, isn't it?'

'What do you mean?'

'Getting me out of trouble.'

'Oh, well, you know...'

'Yeah, I know, it's your job. You get paid to babysit, otherwise nobody would bother.'

'You think I'm being paid to come and visit you on a Sunday afternoon? What? Did I get overtime for spending all day yesterday picking up after you? You have an odd idea of where taxes go.'

'I'm sorry. Didn't mean it like that.'

'Yes, you did. The pity party in your head told you

nobody cares unless they have to. Just so you know that people care about you when it's not their job, it was Queenie who dashed to the rescue.'

'Really?'

'Yes.'

He took a couple of deep breaths, which seemed to hurt.

She softened her voice. 'I, uh, I brought you this.' She pulled the photo of Katie out of her bag and put it on the bedside locker. 'The frame broke when you dropped it, so we had it fixed. We thought it might help.'

Doug looked at it. A tear began to form in his left eye.

'And the taxpayers didn't find it and worry about you wanting it, Queenie did.'

He sniffed. 'Thank her for me. And thank you.'

'Did you go to the counselling session?'

'Yes.'

'Is that what caused all this?'

'No. Yes. Perhaps. I don't know.'

'What do you need from us, Doug? Do we need to send you home? Would things be better without the stress? We know it's not easy suddenly having to do all this new stuff; not everybody lasts their three years.'

'If I'd been at home...' He turned to the window again.

'Yes?'

'Nobody would have found me.'

'Is that a good or a bad thing?'

'I wish I knew.'

Big Doris shovelled her laundry load out of the washer into a basket and out of the basket into a dryer. She fished in her pocket for a handful of tokens and set it going.

Then she sat back on the wooden bench and turned her attention to the telly. Employment Minister in hospital with a stomach complaint. Extra magistrates' court sittings to accommodate all the ringleaders of the riots. Looked like Bobby had done the decent thing and turned his mates in. She wasn't sure whether that made him a hero or a weasel, but it would certainly make her life a bit easier next week.

Sandra popped her head round the door.

'You still here, Mum?'

'Yeah, just doin' me laundry ready for next week. Back in the madhouse, so I need a bit of decent gear clean. How's Bobby?'

'Pissed off with all the stuff he can't do while he's on bail. Can't go out at night, can't go here, can't see this bloke and that. He's doin' my head in.'

'Has he told them what he knows?'

'Yeah, I think so.'

'About whatever else was goin' on as well?'

'He says he's got no idea. That he'd tell me if he did.'

'Makes sense. If I had something to hide I'd not be blabbing it to your Bobby, not with the mouth on him once he's had a few.'

'It's probably nothing anyway.'

'I don't know about that. Some pretty high-up stuffed shirts want to know what I can tell them.' Doris put her head in her hands. 'Just another three years to go.'

'Makes a change though, eh, Mum? You know what Dad used to say, "Try everything once except folk dancing and incest.'"

'Yeah, well, your dad was an idiot.'

Sandra laughed. 'Get on with you. Hobnobbin' with the great and the good, I'd love a chance at it.'

'I'll tell you who I'm hobnobbin' with: Queenie Bloody Mason, and if I wanted to hobnob with her, which I don't, I could hobnob on me own soddin' doorstep.'

'All right, Mum, have it your way. How long's your drying got to go?'

'Half an hour.'

'Can you cover for me a bit longer, then? Chardonnay's got that wheezy cough back, and I want to get down the chemist for a refill for her inhaler.'

'I thought it was getting better?'

'Nah, she's worse, if anything. Seems to be goin' round the Peabodys. Half the kids in her class have got it.'

'Really? What's the doctor say?'

'He said take her on holiday to the seaside, get her some fresh air. Like we're made of money. Pillock. I told him the freshest air we can get is walking past that bit of Tesco's that blasts the smell of fake baking at you.'

'That's interestin'.'

'What is, the Tesco bakery? I read about it somewhere.'

'No, the other bit.' Doris racked her brains. She knew she'd heard it from someone quite recently. 'You get off, love. Get that inhaler before the chemist closes. I'll wait here.'

Justin tried to give the sensation a name. It usually worked, naming the enemy. If he was a bit shaky during a particularly delicate pipette manoeuvre, he'd sometimes say it out loud. *This is mere anxiety.* His co-workers in the lab were used to it; they all had their quirks. You couldn't mess about with lethal diseases and not occasionally let the potential get to you. He'd named his terror quite easily during the theft. *Terrified. Terrified of. Of being caught; of screwing up; of losing his job; of being prosecuted. Of dying?* Yes, that too. His new friends hadn't left much doubt about the consequences of failure. But it had all gone surprisingly well. He'd been told when the computers would go down. He was the picture of calm—amid such panic—just going to check the secure units. In fact, it had been bloody easy. But now he was waiting.

There was nothing on the news. The world didn't appear to know that a weapon of mass destruction sat in a watertight package in his toilet cistern. Along with a random hard drive that had arrived in the post. And he didn't know how long they had to stay there. Or how, where or to whom he was to hand them over. Someone he'd never meet said someone else would be in touch. Sometime. He had no one to call or email, no one to ask anything. His dad had talked of democracy cells, but this was more diffuse somehow. Random people popping up and then disappearing. The Provos weren't so much an army these days as a game of whack-a-mole. He guessed the internet had made that easier. No one needed to know anything other than their one little detail. If he was ever arrested he'd have nothing to tell. Clever. What was it called when you had no idea what to be frightened of first? Dread. That was it. He didn't say it aloud.

CHAPTER THIRTY-FOUR

Gerald had booked the Red Lion's private upstairs lounge. He and Caroline waited patiently for Minnow and Sammy to arrive. Their invited guest, a gentleman whose casual dress was let down somewhat by his impeccably polished shoes and police regulation haircut, occupied the time by speaking into his sleeve. Caroline pondered the point of this. He'd been invited because he was a bloody copper.

When the pair arrived, Caroline scanned their faces. Exhaustion. Anxiety. And something else? Possibly imagined. But Minnow was carrying Sammy's bag as well as his own. She caught Sammy's eye with an enquiring eyebrow raise. The girl blushed. *Oh, good.* The nation might be about to be brought to its knees, but somebody was happy.

Minnow placed a note in front of Gerald.

'He laid the trail, knew I'd follow. Sammy was right: the IP address wasn't a slip-up.'

Gerald scanned the note, then passed it to shiny-shoes.

'I've invited Dominic to join us. He's from—'

'Scotland Yard?' Sammy looked the undercover officer up and down.

'Yes.' He nodded at the new arrivals, reviewed the note and then handed it on to Caroline.

'Presumably you know where he is?' Caroline asked Minnow.

'Yeah, he made it easy. He took a flight to Tonga.'

'We thought it made more sense to bring you this than to follow him,' Sammy added.

'Quite right,' Gerald said, looking at Dominic for approval. The officer nodded. 'No extradition treaty,' he said.

'More than that,' Caroline added. 'I'll need confirmation on the details, but Tonga is one of the last surviving democracies.'

'It's also the last constitutional monarchy,' added Gerald. 'The king carries his blasted throne round the world much like Queenie's teapot. Come to think of it, seen in that light, the whole teapot thing is relatively sane.'

'What do we do next?' asked Minnow.

'What you two do is go home and get some rest,' Gerald began.

'I'll call Shirley and Brian over from the Foreign Office. Get them started on some up-to-date intel. Maybe bring them with us to Scotland Yard this afternoon?'

Dominic nodded. 'I'll get our guys started on any known democracy cells working from the Pacific Islands and call in a few snouts...'

Sammy snickered, almost succeeding in covering it up with a cough. Caroline caught her eye and winked. 'What about Carswell? If we've got an international incident brewing, he should be in on the planning.'

'Hmm.' Gerald drummed on the table with his fingers for a moment or two. 'Given the lack of experience of our new ministers, I think perhaps we should develop a strategy first. Then maybe let him explain it to the emergency cabinet.'

'Give him a script, you mean?' Caroline pursed her lips. 'I'm going to disagree with you. I think we bring him with us; the more times he hears things explained the better chance we have of him understanding it. Don't forget, if we end up sending a delegation to Tonga, he'll be leading it.'

'Dear God, no.' Gerald put his head in his hands.

Andy Carswell had been drilled and rehearsed. Shirley and Brian had taken him through the procedure time after time. 'We put the order of speakers up on the screen. All you have to do is ask each one to say what they've got to say, then ask if there's any questions, shut anyone up who gets off the point and move on to the next.'

He sort of got it. Chairing a meeting wasn't so hard. You didn't actually have to know anything, or even think up any questions for yourself. And it felt good. The sort of important he'd been looking forward to. He wished Beth could see him now, about to chair his first full cabinet meeting. She'd see how brilliantly he'd taken to international affairs and government business. And he was in charge of a real crisis! Even Sophie would have to admit that was cool. He smoothed his map-of-the-world tie. It seemed appropriate.

He'd been told not to tell anyone what was happening—people had to believe the pandemic exercise was about the computer crash—but he was off to a Pacific island to save the world. He'd save the story for when he got back to work.

He looked around the conference table in the cabinet office. No Sideworth. Maybe this new development didn't concern him, it was all about the Foreign Office now. He could see Caroline at the far end of the table, sitting with the weird computer bloke. She'd be seeing Andy in his element today. He stood a little straighter.

He cleared his throat and tapped on his glass of water with a pen.

'Thank you, ladies and gentlemen, I'd like to call this meeting to order.' The buzz of conversation died down, and he looked at the screen. The mugshots were going to help. 'First up, we have our Chief Technical Officer, who will explain what we know so far. Then Ms Thompson will tell us about the Foreign Office perspective. Mr Lambert will explain what happens next and then we'll hear from Health, the Home Office and Defence. By that time we should all be in the picture and I'll take questions. Then we should know where we all are.' He exhaled through his teeth and gave himself a mental high-five for refraining from adding the words *up shit creek without a paddle*.

The geek took over and Andy sat down. He'd heard most of this earlier on, at Scotland Yard. He'd not understood a huge amount of it, just that some of them were going to see a real, live king and ask for... What were they asking for again? He tried to concentrate.

'We know that the antidote has travelled to Tonga.

What we don't yet know is whether the Tongan government is complicit or whether it is just a handy place to hide. We also have to assume that the virus itself is being held by one of the democracy cells across the globe.'

'Thank you.' Andy stood again as Minnow finished what he had to say. He decided to improvise a little. 'We appear to be at the bottom of the pickle jar without a fork.' Somebody tittered. 'However, my chief secretary is going to tell us what we know about the, uh, about Tonga. We're not as green as we are cabbage-looking, eh, Shirley?'

Shirley Thompson, the specialist who told him stuff about places, gave a thin-lipped almost-smile and got to her feet. They weren't getting on any better since he'd tried his memorised speech of Sophie's about Tonga on her and she'd asked if he wanted a round of applause.

'We're dealing with the last independent nation left using both the constitutional monarchy and old democracy systems. One or two elected democracies do exist elsewhere—Quebec, for example—but they are not propped up by privilege in quite the same way. Tonga's king supports the election system because the government of the day supports keeping the monarchy intact. Everybody wins—except, of course, the people.'

Andy nodded his agreement.

'Our research has identified two possible scenarios for this particular crisis.' Shirley clicked a remote and the screen changed to a map of the Pacific.

'The first possibility is that the Tongan government are involved. You can see the archipelago here, it's is so remote that, with ports and airports closed, the administration could easily survive a pandemic wiping out the populations of larger continents. If worldwide reintroduction of democracy is their goal, they don't need to make demands, just wait.'

'Please tell us the other option is less, uh, Armageddony—' One of the Health ministry specialists interrupted her. Andy looked at the faces. Most had lost a little colour.

'Potentially,' Shirley continued. 'We know the Tongans as peace-loving. The population is tiny, so they tend towards cooperation with other nations, or they have until now. It's possible that the route via Hawaii to Tonga was the easiest way for an American citizen to get to a non-extradition state without attracting attention. The government may have no knowledge of any of this.'

'Has your department managed to speak with the Tongan ambassador yet?' Gerald's question. Andy looked over to where he sat with Caroline, Queenie and the computer guy. Caroline was making notes. Queenie was open-mouthed. At least the old girl wasn't knitting today.

'Yes, Brian visited the embassy this afternoon while we were at Scotland Yard.' Shirley nodded to her undersecretary, who got to his feet.

'The Tongan ambassador found five minutes in his undoubtedly hectic schedule to assure me his government knew nothing of this and that the king had no intention of declaring war on the rest of the world.'

'Did you believe him?' Shirley asked.

'No reason not to. He didn't use any untoward diplomacy-speak. He seemed a little taken aback by the questions, but then he would, wouldn't he?'

'Is he making any plans to leave the country?' Gerald again.

'Not overtly.'

'Perhaps we could ask for some surveillance...Mr Brown'—he turned to the Home Office Minister—'when your department next liaises with Scotland Yard...'

'Noted.' Clayton indicated the specialist next to him, who was nodding.

'Any more questions for the Foreign Office?' Andy took to his feet again. 'Thank you, Ms Thompson. Mr uh, Lambert, would you like to tell us what happens next?'

'Indeed. As you know, Health are already working on extensive pandemic preparations, under the guise of an exercise. I would urge you all to refrain from any comments that would undermine this interpretation until we have more information. To this end, we have once again collected your electronic devices, and all physical notes will be burned at the end of this meeting. I can't stress enough that this secrecy has nothing to do with *bloody civil servants thinking they run the show*.' He directed a look at Morrow.

'The fact that there is currently no antidote available could cause mass panic and a lot of travel. At this stage we would like to be able to spot people leaving for Pacific locations as easily as possible. The Home Office will no doubt update you on efforts in this direction shortly. Scotland Yard are working with the CIA and Interpol to infiltrate known democracy groups and attempt to identify the virus's location, or locations, and possible delivery systems.

'Apart from maximum preparedness at home, we propose two initiatives for the Foreign Office. Mr Wagner'—he nodded to the undersecretary—'will be speaking with his counterparts in Russia, Israel and China, to see whether they have any labs where this strain of

Marburg might still exist and, if so, whether any antidote or vaccine was developed independently.'

'Is that likely?' Sally from Health. Andy smoothed his tie.

'Not very.' Brian shook his head slowly. 'But worth a shot, just in case.'

'Since the threat appears to be worldwide, we are hoping for some cooperation. These governments are all now sortition based, so we fully expect each administration to put safety above any form of misguided patriotism. We just don't expect there to have been any research for so long—'

'Which raises the question...' Morrow, looking irritated. But then, Morrow always looked irritated. Just like Brown always looked smarmy and Sideworth always looked miserable. 'Why did we have this stuff? Who were we planning to declare war on?'

'Nobody, sir.' Morrow's Defence Chief Secretary spoke up. Efficient-looking chap with pebble glasses. 'Just research. Antidote development had to keep up with biological warfare back when democracies threatened each other. The science remains useful.'

'What's the second initiative?' Brown appeared to want to shut Morrow up. Andy mentally thanked him; it saved him the trouble.

'We are sending a delegation to Tonga. It is hoped a face-to-face appeal to the king will, at the very least, determine whether we are dealing with a rogue nation or a deluded individual.'

Brian spoke again. 'I introduced the possibility of a state visit while I was at the embassy. They'll let us know when the king might be able to receive us.'

'Thank you.' Gerald sat back in his seat and nodded to Andy.

'Yes. Um, who's next?' Shirley handed him the remote for the wall screen. He pressed a few buttons. Various lists came and went. He handed it back to her and within a second the list of speakers for the day reappeared.

'Ms Farnham. Could you tell us how the pandemic preparations are coming along...?'

It was late. The cafe was still open, just, and the staff looked tired. Caroline felt bad, but this could be her only chance to check in with Sally Farnham before things got frantic again.

She'd caught up with Sally after the cabinet meeting and asked if she had time for a quick coffee before heading home. The woman seemed happy to talk. Her special had reported she was doing okay, holding her own, give or take some bickering, but that kind of language could hide...what? She was in the firing line now and, pleased though she was that this took a bit of pressure off Doug, Caroline couldn't afford another crack-up.

'I've been meaning to get together for a chat for ages,' Caroline began.

'Don't tell me, did things move a bit fast?' Sally asked with a grin. Caroline decided to like her.

'Something like that.' They both laughed. 'How's it going? You're heading for a bit of time in the limelight...'

'Tell me about it. Bloody Wilmslow has taken it upon himself to tell the specials that he should be making the announcements.'

'Oh? Why would that be?'

'Apparently'—Sally sat up a little straighter, flexed her fingers and mimed putting on an imaginary stethoscope—'the general populace would feel more reassured by hearing from a *doctor*.' She lowered her voice to a confidential boom. 'They have been trained in how to talk soothingly, you see.'

'Oh dear. What have the staff said to him about it?'

'Apparently they said he'd have to take it up with Mr Lambert. He won't—he only bullies women. He tried it with Marjory when she started explaining the pandemic stuff but she just gave him a look and carried on speaking.'

Caroline smiled. 'I can imagine. So, you're not getting on?'

'I expect he's fine in his surgery, but he doesn't seem to like anyone knowing stuff he doesn't. I've got all these ideas I want to implement, but he spends so much time pooh-poohing them we never get anything started.'

'You do know that government isn't about your ideas?'

'Oh yes. It all has to go through the reps, I get that. I want to get them to suggest—'

'No, Sally, that's not quite it.'

'What do you mean?'

'Nothing goes through the reps; it comes from them. Your ideas might be grand, but we don't change anything unless there's a pressing need.'

'But there is a need. I saw it, and I'm a citizen too!'

'Begin with your own local rep, then. Ask them to look into it, just like you would if you weren't here.'

'You're saying Wilmslow's right?'

'Not necessarily. But you're making a rod for your own back by trying to do things backwards. The staff won't like it. Some of them are old enough to remember the yo-yo policy changes of the old party system. Things stay more stable without individual ministers having a load of bright ideas all the time.'

'Well, that sure put me in my place.'

'Not at all, there's nothing wrong with passion for change, or healthy disagreement, for that matter.'

'But we've got bigger things to worry about than my children.'

'Just at the moment, yes, but we've got bigger things to worry about than Wilmslow's ego too. Although that reminds me, how are your children adapting? Twins, isn't it?'

'Yes. They're settled in to school quite well. Having each other helps, but they get a bit bored at the weekends.'

'I can imagine. Have they been invited to the Mews Open Day?'

'Oh yes, this Saturday, isn't it? Sounds like fun, we'll be there.'

'I was looking forward to it myself, but it looks like we might be away by then.' Caroline realised she was slightly disappointed.

'You on the deputation to Tonga?' Caroline nodded.

Sally sat back in her chair and drained her coffee cup. 'I'm going on the telly tomorrow, did you know? Press conference about the pandemic exercise.'

'Yes, that's why I wanted to check in, see how you are.'

'I appreciate it. Even with the bollocking.' The women grinned at each other.

'Has Marjory written the speech for you?'

'Yes. And she's going to be there to take any questions I can't handle.'

'Would you like someone to explain to Wilmslow that you're the patsy? If it all goes pear-shaped, the public can blame you and not him.'

'He'd believe that, wouldn't he?'

'Most likely, yes.' Caroline watched the wheels turn.

'Wait a minute. That's true, isn't it?'

'Yip.' Caroline nodded her head slowly. 'Do you want him to face the press?'

Sally furrowed her brow for a moment. She glanced out of the window, looked at her hands, then returned her gaze to Caroline.

'No. I'll do it. I tell my kids not to chicken out of responsibilities.'

'Okay. And if you like, we could go get something stronger than this when it's over?'

'I'd like that.'

CHAPTER THIRTY-FIVE

Sideworth didn't look good. Gerald was unsurprised but disappointed. He needed the man either functional or gone, which Caroline told him was unreasonable.

He thought back to previous administrations. People occasionally cracked under the pressure but not as often as one would expect, given the tumultuous changes their lives underwent. The ones who made it as far as Westminster were usually either bright enough to adapt and cope or too stupid to process the stress. But random was random. Minnow's program weeded out the potential politicians and Caroline's instincts tried to put pegs in relatively commensurate holes. Her instinct to move Sideworth from the Treasury had been sound enough, or it would have been if not for *events*.

Gerald said the word out loud. Sideworth looked at him. The misery in his eyes gave way to confusion. That was a start. 'Macmillan never actually said that, you know?'

'I didn't know.'

'He should have done. They remain the problem.'

'I'm not sure what you mean.'

'We have all but expunged the most insidious form of population control ever invented. Administering a state should be a relatively humdrum affair. But events remain.'

'I see.'

'I doubt you do but no matter.'

'What do you want from me, Mr Lambert? I've apologised. I've let you down, been an idiot and I know that. Am I here to be yelled at, sacked or patronised?'

'None of those, Mr Sideworth, you are here to be…observed. I'm glad to note a little fire in your eyes. You're fighting back somewhat. According to the manuals, that is a hopeful sign.'

'If hating your supercilious manner is a hopeful sign, then good. Glad to be of service.' Sideworth offered a tight-lipped smile that didn't move any other part of his face.

'Events dictate, Mr Sideworth, that someone carry out your duties. Someone must meet with the unions and have conferences with industry leaders. Someone must stand cheek by jowl with Ms Farnham this very day and face the press.

'We did not place you in this role, the people did. Sortition dictates that when you do these things, you are not you—you are a citizen. Would it be possible for you to get over your undoubtedly deeply felt emotions and do a thing merely because it must be done?'

'You've missed your vocation. You'd have made a great grief counsellor.'

'So I am frequently told.' Gerald allowed a smile to begin around his eyes. Sideworth replied with a short laugh. 'Sympathy and understanding are Ms Grant's bailiwick, Mr Sideworth.'

'You're the bad cop, I know.'

'Indeed. Unfortunately, the current crisis dictates that Ms Grant will be out of the country for a few days, so the bad cop is all you are left with. And, let's face it, the kindly approach seems to have exacerbated matters.'

'I...that grief session...all the other people worse off than me...'

'I am not a counsellor.'

'I know, but if there's an explanation, you're probably owed it.'

'Possibly.'

'I let her down, my wife. I promised her I'd put my life back together, and this seemed like a fresh start, but then I screwed it up.'

'Ah, so you think this is a job that you can do well or badly in?'

'Isn't it?'

'Not at all. You are a placeholder, a cypher. You are everyman. The nation will survive, or not, whatever you do or don't do. If you don't go to the meetings, someone else will. We will have a moment of inconvenience which, to be honest, none of us has time for right now, but doing well or badly is a concept that was made redundant with the end of old democracy. It's not about you, Mr Sideworth. It never was and it never will be.'

'Thanks. I think.'

'Now, we have a press conference to attend. Your speech is written. Shall I call an undersecretary to make it?'

Sideworth took a deep breath, exhaling it through his teeth.

'No. I'll do it, Mr Bad Cop.'

'Should we send a babysitter home with you afterwards?'

'No, thank you. I have a visit to make.'

'Ladies and gentlemen, thank you for your attendance. We have a joint statement from the Ministries of Employment and Health. Following which, we will take some limited questions.'

The cameras flashed. Microphones with those mad furry covers waved about their heads. Sally looked at Doug. Ranged behind them were the other ministers from both departments. She avoided Wilmslow's eye and kept her attention on Doug as he took his place at the lectern. He held on to it to steady himself, and lifted his eyes to the autocue. She knew he'd been in hospital; some digestive complaint. They'd had some early differences, but the man looked rough and she hoped he wasn't back at work too soon. She made a mental note to have a chat, make sure he was okay. If anyone knew what being chucked out of hospital too soon was like, it was her.

'During extensive investigations and consultations arising from the recent withdrawal of work by those who oversee automated systems,' he read, 'a number of issues have been pinpointed as requiring attention. One of the most urgent of those was a partial breakdown of communications within the health service.'

He glanced at Sally. She nodded her agreement and smiled at him.

'While my department and I continue to work with

industry leaders to solve the employment implications of recent...*events*...I have asked my colleagues to put together a robust and comprehensive exercise to test our systems to their limits. Ms Farnworth will take it from here and outline the *exercise* they have devised for this purpose.'

'Thank you, Mr Sideworth. In order to test our public health systems to the greatest extent, we are planning a nationwide pandemic preparedness project. Full details of the project will come to you in the form of a press release later today. However, we would like to take this opportunity to advise your viewers, listeners and readers that this is a comprehensive project to test the interlinking of our health and internal security services and their communication systems...'

Eugene gave his quiet little 'somebody's here' knock. He popped his head round the door. 'Mr Sideworth is here to see you. Can he come in?'

Queenie cocked a head at Caroline, who spread her hands. 'Your home, Queenie, you don't have to ask me.'

Queenie clambered to her feet. 'Come in Douggie, luv.' She toddled towards the door and enveloped the tall man in the closest thing to a bear hug you can achieve with a height difference of over a foot. 'Aw, ain't you a sight for sore eyes? Come and sit down, have some tea.'

He attempted to extricate himself by flapping his arms below where Queenie had them pinned, looking oddly like a penguin, Caroline thought.

'I hope I'm not interrupting, I just came to say, you know, uh...thank you.'

Queenie let him go and stepped back to look up at his face.

'Ms Grant said it was you who—'

'Oh, go on with you, luvvie. No need for that. We're just glad you're all right, ain't we?' She turned to Caroline for agreement. 'Now get yourself in one of these comfy chairs and tell us how you're doing.'

'I'm sorry, were you having a meeting?' He indicated the notebook on Caroline's lap.

'We'd finished, really, just finalising some details for the trip. We've been a bit stop-start anyway this morning, because we broke off to watch the press conference. You did very well.' She smiled at Doug as he settled himself into a chair.

'Nothing like being savaged by Gerald's version of psychotherapy to get you in front of a camera with confidence.'

'Oh dear.' Caroline winced. 'Was it very brutal?'

'I survived.'

'And came out capable of a tiny joke, I notice. Things are definitely looking up.'

Doug managed a smirk. 'Oh, Queenie, these are for you.' He rummaged in the briefcase he'd walked in with and produced a box of continental truffles. 'They were Katie's favourite, I hope you like them.' He turned to Caroline. 'I got some for you too but forgot you'd be here—'

'She can share these for now! Ain't they posh? You're very sweet.'

'There was no need—' Caroline began.

'Every need. I've been a pain in the arse.'

'Well—'

'*Bert!*' Queenie addressed herself to the closed inner door of the flat. She turned to Doug. 'He's got a sweet tooth, it's all right if he shares them, ain't it?'

'Of course.'

Bert opened the door. 'What?'

'Douggie's brought us some chocs! Come and join in.'

Bert observed the newcomer with something approaching concern. 'Blimey, mate, you look rough.'

Doug grimaced at him. 'Thanks.' He held out his hand to Bert. 'I'm here to say thanks.'

'Decent of you.' Bert took the proffered hand and shook it. He joined the group round the coffee table. Eugene emerged with a tray of tea, and Queenie picked up the box of chocolates.

'Hai declare this box of most excellent choccies hofficially hopen!'

'I should have brought a ribbon to cut.'

'Yes, you should, Douggie my lad. Consider yourself told off.'

Even Bert was laughing now.

'So when are you off to Tonga?' Doug asked as the merriment died down.

'Not absolutely sure yet,' Caroline replied. 'We're waiting for the Foreign Office to hear when the king can receive a delegation. But probably before the weekend. It's a long trip, two layovers, and we want to give Queenie a chance to rest when she gets there this time.' She glanced at Bert.

'Bloody right,' he muttered.

'Are you going along too, Bert?'

Queenie laughed. 'Not bloomin likely, he won't miss a dominoes match just because the country's in trouble.'

Bert harrumphed. Doug raised an eyebrow.

'I used to play dominoes, haven't had a game for years.'

Bert looked at him. 'Fives and threes?'

'Yes!'

'Oh, how about that, Bert? You could have a game while I'm away.' She looked at Doug. 'Keep him out of trouble.'

'I'd be delighted, if Bert doesn't mind?'

My work here would be done, Caroline thought, as she watched an unlikely spark of friendship between the two men almost flicker into life. *Except it wasn't me.*

'I suppose it might be okay. Maybe you could come round on Saturday, take my mind off all the screaming kids.'

'Kids?'

'I'm having all the children over to play,' Queenie said. 'The reps and the ministers and that, their kids all moved away from their friends, so we thought we'd have a nice day here, see the horses and stuff.'

'Yeah, she plans it and then buggers off to leave me in charge.'

'You are *not* in charge, Bert. I told you, our Debs and her Colin are coming to help, and Eugene's sorted out some staff too. You won't have to lift a finger.'

'It's a date,' Doug said. 'You can lift a domino instead.'

The House was in uproar. Gerald hadn't seen anything like it in years. Every rep had an opinion; everyone wanted to complain about something. Gerald got it: they'd all been subjected to a barrage of anger and misery since the strike.

They were just passing it on. But some sort of order needed maintaining.

'Citizen Representatives!' He'd had to raise his voice. Most knew his reputation well enough already to take this as a warning. The hubbub died away.

'Your ministers do understand you have had a trying time and that you have many questions and complaints. However, the situation that overtook this new administration is unprecedented in recent years. I must emphasise: the best way to get a question answered is to log it with the relevant ministry for a written reply in the House when that ministry takes questions later in the week. There will be time for you all to be heard but only if we refrain from wasting House time on recriminations that get us nowhere.

'Further to this morning's press conference, this afternoon will be given over to questions to the Health Minister. Please use your screens in an appropriate manner and understand that some questions may require research for a full reply.'

Queenie and Caroline watched from the gallery. They were both knitting.

'I finally feel like Madame Defarge, watching Sally face that lot.'

'Who?'

'Never mind.'

'Is it normally like this?'

'Not usually. Quite often there's a bit of a fuss the first day back in the House; they all think their stuff is more important than anyone else's. But over time that settles down. But this. It's been a tough couple of weeks for all of us, but they're on their own, sitting ducks for everyone's grumbles. I know where I'd rather be.'

'Yeah, Big Doris said something like that.'

'Oh, have you seen her yet?'

'No, was supposed to be tomorrow. But with things the way they are, all the trouble about who took what and where it is, I don't want to say the wrong thing.'

'As long as you do more listening than talking, you'll be fine. And you can act stupid about the pandemic exercise—nobody tells you anything, right?'

'Yeah, she'll believe that, all right.'

'Everything you hear Sally say today'—Caroline nodded down at the Chamber, where the Health Minister was coming to the end of reading the detailed press release to the reps—'is what Doris knows you know. There's no need to try and debrief her, that's someone else's job.'

'Don't mention the virus!'

Caroline giggled. 'I mentioned it once, but I think I got away with it.'

Queenie looked down at Sally, who had put her written press release away and was beginning to take questions.

'I really do have the easiest job, don't I?'

'That depends a little on what happens in Tonga.'

CHAPTER THIRTY-SIX

The seats on the chartered jet were arranged around a central conference table. Queenie knew they'd do all manner of swinging about stuff when it was time to take a snooze, but she had plans to leave all that to someone else this time. She was going to show them she'd learned a thing or two about being a head of state. Unless she got bored, in which case she might just try out a button or two for fun.

At least there were a few more of them this time. The trips with just her, Andy and Eugene—who spent most of his time in the galley with the silent security guard—had made for trying times. If she'd not had her knitting and the telly, the previous flights would have been right boring. Andy seemed to think he was interesting, but all he really talked about was how successful a salesman he was. Plus all the strange sayings. Queenie had asked a bit about his family but he'd been all snarky, so she'd left off trying.

There was quite a crowd this time. Caroline had said

they normally sent the minimum number of people to keep the costs down, but this was different.

'We need to bring Minnow,' she'd said when the plans for the trip were being finalised. 'In case he's the only one who can get through to this Chad chappie.'

'Is Sammy coming too?' Queenie had hoped for a bit of time to chat to her pal, but Caroline had shaken her head.

'We need her back in Education before too many people start asking what her special project was.'

The final line-up was Queenie and Andy as usual, Eugene to bring the teapot and do all the meeting and greeting and sort things out, plus Caroline, Minnow and Shirley from the Foreign Office. She was going to spend the flight telling everyone what to do and what not to say, because she was the expert on that part of the world.

Extra security too. Caroline had said there was no knowing what they were all walking in to. Hence the private plane. 'We might have to leave, uh, precipitously,' she'd said. Queenie had looked that one up afterwards.

'It won't seem odd to the Tongans,' she'd added. 'They are used to a monarch who travels with a retinue.'

'Is that the bloke who brought his own chair to royal weddings?'

'Yes, that's him.'

'Blimey.'

'We're planning to represent Shirley and Minnow as members of your household.'

'What, like maids and butlers and that?'

'Sort of...persons-in-waiting, as it were. We don't want to insult the king by making out we need advisers on how to talk to him.'

'What are they supposed to do? Eugene does all the talking to kitchen staff and that's all I need. I'd do it myself except I'm not allowed.'

'Oh, they can sort out your clothes, see to your diary, liaise with the press, chatter with the king's household. Actually, that can be a good way to find out what's really going on.'

'Did they used to do that for real, back when we had the queen?'

'Oh, yes. And she used to go everywhere with a piper.'

'What sort of piper? To get her on and off boats and planes and things?'

'No, a bagpipes piper, to play in the mornings. And sometimes at dinner.'

Queenie had watched Caroline watch her face; the amusement reached her eyes before Queenie erupted.

'Bloody hell, I could get Bert to bring his mouth organ.'

'Thankfully, we have found over the years that our citizen heads of state arrive in the job fully capable of packing a suitcase and putting their clothes on.'

Queenie had been helpless with laughter by then.

'But smuggling in an adviser or two under the guise of regal uselessness sometimes helps in, uh, ticklish situations.'

Queenie looked over at Caroline now, deep in conversation with Minnow. She transferred her attention to Andy, who was being directed through a sheaf of notes by Shirley. Then she picked up her knitting.

Andy Carswell looked at the pile of paper in astonishment.

'You want me to read all this?'

'We have a long flight ahead of us. Now would be a good time.' Shirley indicated the coloured sticky tabs. 'I've sorted the information into sections for you: history, politics, royal family, politicians, topography, language, etcetera.'

'Yes, but why? We're only there for a few days, we eat a dinner, make small talk, come home. It's only a cover for the geek to do some digging, isn't it?'

Andy had been looking forward to using the time to get to know Caroline a little better.

'We don't know yet.' Shirley looked a bit grim. 'But the more you understand about where we're going, the less likely you are to put your foot in it.'

'What the hell do you mean? I know all about Tonga.'

Shirley sighed. 'Andy, we can't script this for you. You'll be on your own. I can't even be in the room most of the time, since I'm supposed to be some sort of a lady's maid.' She rolled her eyes. 'You have to learn this stuff, I can't sit at the dinner table and work you like a ventriloquist's dummy.'

Andy thought the woman must be under some stress at home; she wasn't usually this rude. He'd ask Caroline about it. That would show her his caring side.

'This is to make your life easier…help you make small talk. Look…' She turned to a page flagged by a yellow sticky that said *family*. 'The youngest son is called George, and he's studying political science at Yale. Once you know that, you can ask how he's getting on at university in the US.'

'I'll ask that, then.'

'No, you need to absorb the information properly, so you can avoid things we don't want you to talk about too—'

'I don't see why I have to read about their language. We've got an interpreter, haven't we?'

'Yes, we have, and the king speaks some academic English—'

'There you are, then.'

'But...' She was getting quite annoyed now, probably got teenaged kids at home. He sympathised. 'Once you understand that the language has three forms of speech—one for ordinary people, one for bosses and betters, and one just for the king or bloody God—you stand a chance of comprehending the sort of people you're dealing with.'

'He thinks he's important, I get it.'

'No, it's more than that.'

Home troubles be damned, he knew how to talk to people. He sold scanners and copiers to all sorts. He was entitled to get a bit irritable himself. 'I'll be fine.'

Shirley sighed again. How rude.

'You do have some idea of what could be at stake here, don't you?'

'I'm not stupid. And I know how to talk to people, I'm a successful salesman.'

'I'm sure you do. It's just that—'

'What?'

'Tongan is primarily a spoken language, there's very little tradition of written literature, which means that some of your, uh, more *whimsical* sayings will have no direct translation.'

'Look, that wasn't my fault, the Canada thing. Eugene caused the trouble, not me. Stupid kid, he should have lost his job.'

'These things do happen, inevitably sometimes, but keeping to clear phraseology can help—'

'And when were you ever Foreign Minister? I was hand-picked for this post because of my people skills, and I'll do it my way, thank you very much.'

He watched her face. She almost replied but gave up. She moved to go and sit with Queenie. Good riddance. He pushed the notes aside, turned his seat away from the conference table and pulled his personal TV screen from the slot in the arm. Teenagers didn't cause that level of venom. Menopause, maybe? He'd speak to Caroline about whether the woman was stable enough to stay in her post.

'Have you found him?' Caroline asked Minnow. They had taken a spot at the far end of the table, partly to be out of the way but also so that Caroline could watch the others. She saw Shirley move away from Andy and take a place next to Queenie. She didn't look happy.

'No, that's the weird thing: he's dropped off the radar.' Minnow looked rested but uncomfortable. Caroline guessed he'd rather be in front of a computer at home than reclined in a huge leather seat on a private jet on its way across the Atlantic. 'No online activity at all; the plane ticket was the last trace. I hope we're not on a wild goose chase. Maybe his idea of a joke is to send us to the middle of the Pacific while he's sitting back in the greasy spoon in Waterloo laughing his head off.'

'It's possible he got arrested walking off the plane,' Caroline told him. 'I got a message from Gerald just before we boarded. Someone flew Honolulu to Tonga last week using one of his FBI undercover alter egos.'

'So he probably did go, then.'

'Yes, but when the FBI contacted the local Tongan police, they said he'd been arrested on landing and refused to say why. Foreign Office checked with the London ambassador and he confirmed the arrest but couldn't, or wouldn't, elaborate.'

'That would explain the lack of computer activity, I guess, but what the hell did he do?'

'Difficult to say, although if he had a bunch of unidentified substances on him, I guess that might do it.'

'But in that case, how the hell would he have been allowed to board in the first place? He'd have had to have got them on and off a plane from Heathrow first.'

'True. Maybe he pulled a few FBI strings?'

'Even so...'

'Security theatre at its finest?'

'Yeah.'

'At least we know where to start. As soon as we're settled in, I'm going to suggest you get out and make a few enquiries. Act daft, your friend got into some trouble coming off the plane and you're here to find him and help.

'In the meantime, I'll get Andy to make some veiled enquiries of their Foreign Minister: we have a small concern that some medical supplies may have got into the wrong hands.'

'And can they help him get it back because he's not as green as he's cabbage-looking?'

'Oh, don't.' Caroline laughed. 'If ever anyone was in the wrong job.'

'I know, we screwed that one up pretty convincingly.'

'He looked fine on paper.' Caroline picked up her knitting bag and rummaged for the work-in-progress. 'No way of knowing how the change will take people. There's usually one who lets it go to his head; it's just not normally this fast.'

'Or this inconvenient?'

'Quite. I'll have a chat with him after he's had a chance to read Shirley's information. If anyone can prepare him for what not to say, it's her; there's nothing she doesn't know about the sensitivities of this part of the world.'

'Just as well. Oh, how's the Employment guy?'

'Doug? Difficult to say. He's going through with the treatment, and George has taken to dropping in of an evening to check on him.'

'That's nice.'

'Yes, he's a diamond. I want to try and find him a better position, but to be honest, he's so good with Doug I'm dragging my feet just now.'

'Makes sense.'

'But the biggest surprise, believe it or not, has been Queenie's Bert.'

'Really?'

'Get this, they both play dominoes for goodness' sake.'

'Dominoes? Is that a thing? It's a kids' game.'

'You'd think, eh? But people play it in pubs. For money! There's this version called fives and threes. They both tried to explain how it was somehow intellectual, but I got a bit lost.'

Minnow laughed. 'I must tell Sammy that dominoes is a thing.'

'But while they were explaining it, Doug seemed to, you know, perk up a bit.'

'Maybe he needs friends more than he needs treatment.'

'Could be. And speaking of friends, how are things going with you and Sammy?'

'Is that a tea cosy you're knitting? Doesn't Queenie produce enough?'

'Yes, no, I've got a bit of a project going on...and don't change the subject.'

Gerald checked his watch. The girl had asked for a meeting, and he'd made five minutes, but Minnow's personal problems were more Caroline's area of expertise than his.

'Come in,' he addressed the timid knock on the door. 'Ms Cho, good afternoon, come and sit down. I only have a few minutes, so perhaps you could let me know quite succinctly what this is about.'

The kid had a laptop bag with her. She placed it on the table and proceeded to unpack a series of pieces of plastic and metal.

'Thank you, Mr Lambert. I know you're busy, it's just, I think this might be important.'

Gerald looked in dismay at the mess on his desk. It appeared to be a disembowelled computer.

'Minnow and I left in a hurry for Hawaii.' He nodded his encouragement to get to the point. 'And before we went he asked me to store the hard drives from the computers we'd used to, um, monitor things, so we packed them up and I sent them to my dad's.'

'Yes...?'

'Then I thought maybe there might be something that could help, so I went over at the weekend and did some digging.'

Gerald's level of interest picked up. This might not be about interpersonal angst after all.

'Indeed, that was very enterprising of you, and this, uh, collection, is the result of your dig?'

'As well as the hard drives from the desktops, we packed up the laptops that Minnow's little *team* had taken with them on their visits.'

'Go on.'

'This is the laptop that Chad returned. Minnow collected them the night before the strike, but we had no time to look at them.'

'And it's in pieces?'

'It wasn't then, but I took it apart and the hard drive has gone.'

'Which means?'

'There's something on it that Chad didn't want us to find.'

'So he has it with him?'

'I can't be sure of that, but Minnow said he'd been arrested and searched in Tonga. If it's not there, then he's left it somewhere, or sent it somewhere…'

Gerald surveyed the chaos before him in a slightly different light.

'If we were able to find it, would you be able to collect the information from it?'

'It's possible, yes. Unless he shredded it, but then he wouldn't have needed to take it away…and there's another thing.'

'Indeed?'

'Yes, Minnow said he was here for Comic-Con. That's this weekend. It starts tonight.'

'I've been meaning to ask someone what that is.' Gerald knew he was a little out of touch, and generally educated himself privately regarding such gaps in his otherwise extensive knowledge, but there hadn't been a lot of spare time recently.

'Oh, uh, geek thing, people who like classic comics, graphic novels, that sort of thing, sometimes we, they, uh, dress up...' She suddenly sounded a lot like Minnow.

'Indeed.'

'I called and asked about his registration, assumed he'd have cancelled, maybe sent his ticket back to resell or something.'

'Yes?' Now he knew it might end up somewhere useful, Gerald was more inclined to let the kid's mind wander where it wanted to.

'They said he's a volunteer and he's *already there*, helping them set up. But if he's in Tonga...'

'Someone has taken his place?'

'And we know where they are.'

Gerald almost smiled at the earnest little scrap sitting in front of him. 'Ms Cho, I am most grateful to you. What are your plans for the rest of the afternoon?'

'I have an Education Ministry meeting. They're looking at the possibility of closing off some of the more isolated university campuses to use as treatment facilities.'

'They can no doubt consider that without you. I think we might formally co-opt you onto the technical support team.'

Sammy's face remained impassive except for a slight release of tension about the eyes. Gerald made a mental note to speak with Caroline about a civil service job when all this was over.

'Thank you, sir.'

'No, Ms Cho, thank you. Would you mind popping that lot back in the bag while I call Scotland Yard?'

CHAPTER THIRTY-SEVEN

Andy heard the polite knock on his hotel room door and waited for a beat before calling, 'Come in.' Caroline's head popped around the door.

'Good morning, Andy, hope you rested well. Did you manage to absorb much of the information Shirley prepared for us?'

'I think I'm up to speed.' Andy had splashed on his best cologne for his morning with Caroline. 'Seems quite straightforward.'

'Goodness, did you manage to get all the names straight? That's always where I struggle. The royal family at least tend to use names that we can get a handle on, but I find the parliamentary committees take a bit more brain power.'

'Uh, yes, I suppose so.' It dawned on Andy there might have been some stuff in that pile of shit he should have looked at. Still, too late now. 'How about a coffee before we go?'

Caroline looked at her watch. 'We've got twenty minutes or so before the car's due, so why not?'

Andy poured some water into the little coffee maker and switched it on. 'I don't see why we have to stay in a poxy hotel.' He gestured to the couch by the window. 'Have a seat. You can see the royal palace from the window, it's insulting. I know they're old-fashioned royalty and that, but they could at least have put us up at the High Commission, like other countries do.'

Caroline glanced out of the window, then took a seat at the table on the other side of the room. 'You haven't read your information pack, have you?'

'What makes you say that?'

'If you had, you'd know there hasn't been a British High Commission here since 2006. The king uses the building for audiences and stuff.' She sighed. 'If we had a bloody ambassador here, we'd probably not have had to come.'

Andy straightened his tie. This private tête-à-tête was not going quite as he'd envisioned.

'Do you even know who we're meeting and why?'

'Yes.' He drew himself up to his full five foot six. 'The Foreign Affairs committee.'

'Foreign Affairs, Defence and Trade.' She opened the dratted pile of papers on the table as he handed her the coffee. 'Thank you. And what are we here to discuss?'

He sat on an adjacent chair and scooted it a bit closer to the table, the notes, and Caroline. 'We're here to ask whether they've got the virus.'

She met his eyes, but not in a good way.

Big Doris breezed into the launderette just as Sandra was pulling a huge purple coat out of the dryer.

'Hello, love, how are you?'

'Mum. Hi.' Sandra began bundling the coat into a sports bag.

'Whoa, don't do that, you'll crease it all up. How many times have I told you to fold stuff straight from the dryer? I hope it's not for a customer.' Doris looked a little more carefully. Something wasn't right. Sandra wasn't meeting her eye.

'It's fine, I'll iron it later,' she muttered.

Doris took charge.

'Come and sit down. Now. Leave that. Look at me. What's going on?'

Sandra fussed with the bag a bit more, kicked it under the seat and lifted her chin in that defiant look she'd had since childhood. It always meant she was lying.

'Don't make me smack it out of you, girlie.'

'It's, uh, a fancy dress thing. Bobby's going to a party.'

'He's on bail! He can't go to parties! He can't go bleedin' anywhere.'

'Yeah, it's a sort of, you know, daytime thing. Get together. Bit of fun. Costumes. You know.'

'No, I don't know. But you're going to tell me. What the hell is going on?'

Sandra took out her phone and flipped to a game. Started swapping multicoloured sweets around. The screen went nuts with stars and stuff.

'It's just a party, okay?'

'Yeah, right, I can just hear it now: "Hey, Bobby, how about an afternoon fancy dress party?" He'd have punched whoever said that in the face, even as a nipper.'

'It's just one last errand.' Sandra's voice couldn't have got any quieter.

'Did you not hear me before? He's on fucking bail. What the hell is he thinking?'

'They said... They said...' Sandra took a deep breath and finally looked her mother in the eye. 'They said they'd find the kids if he didn't.'

Doris knew her mouth was open, but she couldn't process this and move part of her face at the same time. And Sandra filled the silence. As if the faster she said it, the less likely it was she'd actually spoken. 'One last job, just an errand, go to this thing dressed up and collect a package. That's it. No more. He's stopping. They've scared him. And you can't tell anyone, Mum, you really can't. They said they'd hurt him if anything went wrong. They mean it, Mum.'

'But...' She found her voice and spoke as the thoughts formed. 'He's on bail. They know that, right? Did he remind them? The police could be watching him, anyway.'

'They said that's why it has to be him. Because the police would think no one's that stupid.'

'Hah!' Doris couldn't help it. 'They're right about that, aren't they?'

'Minnow, my man, you found me. What took you so long?'

Chad seemed pleased to see him. Minnow attempted to apply a little game theory to the conundrum. If landing up in jail hadn't been part of Chad's plan, then maybe he thought back-pedalling on the whole betrayal of trust thing and greeting a long lost pal with delight would get him a step closer to freedom. If getting arrested was part of some unfathomable master plan, his delight at Minnow turning up might just be hubris. Or he could be bonkers, which was the simplest explanation.

'Taking a while to sort out the whole end-of-the-world-as-we-know-it international incident, Chad.' The man nodded and grinned. 'And I had to grease a few police palms to find you.'

'But here you are; I knew you'd follow.'

'You didn't leave me much choice, man. Is there any chance you'll tell me what the hell's going on?'

'Bail me out first, eh?'

'Me? Why?'

'Because time's running out. The guys holding the virus will release it if they don't hear from me in... What day is it?'

'Friday.' Minnow watched Chad nod his head from side to side as he counted days.

'In less than seventy-two hours, then.'

Minnow laughed. 'This isn't a bloody James Bond film. The CIA and Interpol have infiltrated every democracy cell there is, and nobody knows anything about a virus.'

'My boys are hard to find.'

'Your boys are non-existent, mate. You're stuck in jail in the middle of nowhere, the stuff you tried to bring in to the country is squirrelled away in an evidence locker and nobody in any democracy movement on the face of the planet has heard of you.'

'They're all playing for time. You won't be laughing when the non-democratic world dies out. We'll be fine here. Isolated. With the antidote for security.'

'If it hasn't already been destroyed.'

'They won't do that.' Chad tapped the side of his nose. 'The king will see to that.'

Minnow decided to stick with amusement. 'You've discussed it with him, have you? What, by phone? Or did His Majesty come and visit you here in this crappy cell?' Minnow surveyed their surroundings with as much disgust as he could muster. Although to be honest it was cleaner than he'd expected.

'He believes in preserving democr—'

'By wiping out the rest of humanity? It's not very fucking democratic, is it?'

Chad shrugged.

'Okay, Dr No, explain to me why I should believe any of this bollocks—and what the hell you think you'd get out of it if it was true? And, and...if you get released in time to call them off, what then?'

'What do you mean?'

'You and your "boys" holding the civilised world to ransom...over what? Let's suppose the King of Tonga and his entire government are as mad as you are, what do you want?'

Chad smiled.

'Minnow, my charming, brilliant, English *chum*, I already have what I want. And I don't need to justify myself to you.'

'No, you don't. And I don't need to bail you out. We'll just pick up the samples, take them home and leave you to rot.'

'Actually, I've been stringing you along a little. My bad, couldn't resist it, old bean. There's something you ought to know about the stuff I brought in...'

Toilet cisterns. Justin couldn't help but be amused. His dad had been passionate about two things back in the day. The return of democracy and the saving of water. 'Always put a brick in the cistern, lad, saves gallons in the course of a year.' Or, in this case, a package of contraband. The brick went back in his cistern at home, but the loo he was taping the blasted stuff inside here had had to be drained first, to prevent it overflowing and arousing suspicion. Posh conference centres clearly weren't as parsimonious vis-à-vis water usage as newly recruited terrorists. It had all taken precious time. He'd had to complain of a dodgy kebab the night before to account for the all that time in the toilet.

Still, it was nearly over. The ticket for a bloke called Chad and the Joker costume had arrived in the post. Then he'd had another visit. Not another terrifying ambush, though. No balaclavas this time; maybe they trusted him now. Was that good? He didn't know. The bloke had knocked on the door just like someone normal and chatted up a storm all friendly-like. American accent. Justin had relaxed enough to let his mind wander at one point—did Yanks really think normal teeth were that white?

He'd asked to see the samples, asked a load of semi-literate questions about safe storage temperatures and given him a set of instructions. He had to make up a second pack identical to the samples in his cistern. The guy seemed tickled by the toilet thing. He'd chuckled and said, 'You Brits sure love your restroom humour.'

Justin had to play Chad the volunteer and get both packs in to Comic-Con on set-up day, before security ramped up when the conference opened. A cistern in one of the Gents' stalls would do fine for the real samples, the guy decided. Justin could email its exact location to iSawYou that first night. Then he had to pretend to be this Chad bloke for the entire weekend. Hand over the fake pack to someone else in a Joker suit. He'd protested at that point; it was all too complex. Silly. He was a scientist; he knew the value of simplicity. When it was over, he'd tell them they were too amateurish for him to work with again.

Still, pack one was now in its 'you funny old Brits' hiding place. Pack two was in his swag bag ready for tomorrow, and he was almost free. He had no idea who was collecting either package, or even if he'd be told when the real pickup happened, and he was trying hard not to care. In the meantime, all these bloody people in cheap nylon costumes were getting him down. Everybody smelled of sweat. There were so many Jokers. And it was, well, weird.

CHAPTER THIRTY-EIGHT

It was an unhappy delegation, Queenie realised. She and Eugene made them as welcome as they could in her little hotel suite. They proffered teas and the treats Eugene had found in a nearby market during the morning, but the atmosphere seemed beyond redemption with coconutty, doughnutty things.

Neither Caroline nor Shirley appeared to be speaking to Andy, and Minnow was cocooned in a bubble of misery.

'Now then!' Queenie attempted a bright tone. 'How did it all go yesterday? I had an easy time of it, put a wreath at the war memorial, then went and smiled at some children in a school and they sang and danced and that. I'm sure you worked a lot harder?'

Caroline sniffed. 'Mr Carswell, would you like to brief Queenie on our progress?'

'Look, it wasn't my fault, I didn't know.'

Shirley joined in. 'And why didn't you know? Pray tell us?'

Queenie took pity on the man. 'Okay, ladies, give the poor little sod a break and just tell us what happened, eh? Did somebody mistranslate that tapestry nonsense? Easily done.'

'I did what we came here to do.' Andy responded to Queenie with a touch of defiance. 'We are here to find out if the government is involved with the theft, right? I just asked them outright, instead of pussyfooting around.'

'Yes, but if you'd bothered to read about this country'—Shirley was speaking through gritted teeth—'you'd have known that elected politicians expect and require "pussyfooting."' The air quotes added an extra layer of venom.

'Basically,' Caroline added, 'our Foreign Minister has accused the Tongan government of declaring biological warfare on the rest of the world.'

'Which, even if they are complicit in any of this'—Shirley took back the ball—'would be a bloody dangerous way to go about sorting it out.'

'And they're not.' Minnow spoke for the first time. 'It's not about the Tongans. It's about me.'

They all turned to him in surprise.

'What do you mean, Minnow, dear? How can it be about you?' Caroline was the first to recover her wits.

'Chad says he lured us down here to watch the rest of the world die in agony so we can see the results of him being cleverer than me. I lost him a promotion in the FBI when I was, uh, on the other side.'

'On what other side?' Andy had perked right up now. Presumably sniffing someone else to blame, Queenie thought.

'When I was a kid, I, uh...'

'Hacked the FBI from his bedroom in Cricklewood.' Caroline helped him finish the sentence. 'But honestly, Minnow, I don't think that can be it. Nobody threatens civilisation as we know it over an old grudge. This isn't a Hollywood blockbuster.'

'It's what he said,' Minnow mumbled. 'He said if people still elected police chiefs in America he'd not have been demoted for mere incompetence. That's why he wants democracy back and why he's with the Provisional Democratic Army, who think the democracy cells we know about are too lame to achieve anything, and they'll only release the antidote to countries that agree to have elections. I laughed at him, said we'd get the stuff back from the police now he'd been arrested with it.'

'Quite right.' Caroline nodded. 'Once we sort out this little diplomatic crisis.' She tried hard to refrain from another dirty look in Andy's direction. 'I'm sure the authorities will see sense and hand it over.'

'It's not here.' Minnow raised his eyes to Caroline's. They were red, brimming. 'He brought fake stuff, made sure to get it noticed, all but put it in a bag labelled "swag". He got himself arrested on purpose so we'd come here. He wants me to watch the pandemic on the telly.'

'He's off his rocker.' Queenie put her teacup down with irritable force. She didn't mind Andy having a hard time, but Minnow was her friend and he looked devastated. 'Obviously mad. And I don't believe the Tongans have got anything to do with it, either. They seem very nice, singin' and dancin' and all. This bloke might have brought us all on a wild goose chase for the hell of it, but it'll be because he's nuts.'

'Was it possible to glean anything from the committee

at all?' Shirley asked Caroline.

'Not really, I was only supposed to be there to take notes. They'd not have taken kindly to any questions from me; they have no women in Parliament, as you know. The Foreign Minister just said the government had no knowledge of any biological weapons and no wish to sour trade relationships with *friendly* nations.'

Shirley sighed. 'Presumably your emphasis on the "friendly" means our trade links are done for?'

'I expect so.'

'And we're no nearer any idea whether this supposed plot has support?'

'No.'

'It won't, will it? Not if it's all his fault.' Andy pointed at Minnow.

'We're talking round in circles.' Shirley glared at Andy as though he were something whiffy she'd just found on her shoe. 'We need access to whatever he brought in with him to determine what it is, and that won't happen without the cooperation of a happy, flattered Tongan government.'

'Our best course of action right now will be to appeal directly to the king.' Caroline opened her notebook and started to write. 'The state banquet is tomorrow night. We don't have long to get prepared. In the meantime, we need to tell Gerald that the real samples may have left the country another way. Eugene, could you try and get him on the phone? I've no idea what time it is back home, and it doesn't really matter—get hold of him any way you can.'

'Yes, ma'am.' Eugene left the plates of crumbs where he'd started to pile them up and fished in his pocket for his mobile. 'Presumably you don't want me to use a landline?'

'Goodness no, thank you for thinking of it. Put me on as soon as you're through.' Eugene offered her a grim nod as he left the room, punching numbers. Caroline took absent-minded advantage of the crumbs on the top plate. 'Minnow, is there any chance you could call yourself a private investigator and try and get access to whatever it was they confiscated? Andy, we'll try to schedule an individual drinks do or two with the ministers you pissed off yesterday, so you can apologise. In the meantime, Shirley and I will put together an approach to the king that stands a chance of undoing the damage. Queenie, that will have to be down to you.'

Queenie was trying to keep the little wobble in her bottom lip under control when Eugene's face appeared in the doorway, looking—if it was possible, but she might be imagining it—a tad less grim. She decided that keeping talking might stop her from actually crying. 'Hello, Eugene luv, did you get through? What time is it back home anyway?'

'Not sure, but he was up, trying to call us. He has some news. I'll put him on speaker.'

Doug Sideworth watched the kids rampage around one of Buck Place's smaller state rooms. He guessed it was unlikely to have had quite so much jelly and ice cream trampled into the floor before. It looked to have been a good day, although he'd spent most of it sequestered in Bert and Queenie's flat. News had got out that the adults were playing dominoes, and several reps appeared to see if they could join in. The one called Big Doris, who apparently knew Bert and Queenie from way back, had made an announcement, and then they'd moved the games down here. There was every possibility of a government fives and threes team joining the local league now. That might be fun.

He asked himself how long it had been since the word *fun* had entered his vocabulary.

'Hello there, how are you?'

He turned his attention to the speaker and recognised Sally Farnham. 'Bit of a zoo, isn't it?' She indicated the game of something that looked like tag and winced as someone whipped an expensive-looking vase out of the way of a toddler on a mission.

'Do you think they'll ever get the jelly off the parquet?' Doug asked.

She grimaced. 'Glad I'm not cleaning up.'

'Good fun, though. Do you have kids here?'

'Yes, brought my twins. They loved the horses, had a ride in the open carriage, watched a film. They've had a great day.'

He smiled at her. 'You're Health, aren't you?'

'Yeah.' Her face clouded.

'How's it going? You having a tough time with the planning?'

'Oddly enough, not really, the specials are shit hot'—her hand went to her mouth—'I'm sorry...'

Doug laughed. 'Don't be. You should hear me on a bad day.'

'And you've had a few of those, I understand. How are you doing now? You were in hospital, right?'

He sighed. 'Yup. What did they tell you?'

'Some digestive trouble? Not really my business, but,

you know, it can be tough. We should look out for each other, eh?'

'Yes, I'm beginning to think we should. But I'm fine now, really.'

She looked at him. A real, proper, in-the-eyes look. He could see her decide not to ask any more, but he thought maybe he wouldn't mind if she did.

'You were talking about the plans?'

'Yes. It's mostly going like clockwork; I just have to spout what they write. It's just...'

'What?'

She sighed. 'Bit of a personality clash, that's all. I probably shouldn't tell tales out of school.'

'But you want to or you'll explode?' Doug held her gaze.

She laughed. 'Kinda.'

'Um, well, this might not be the best place, but...if you liked...'

'Yes?'

'We could maybe grab a coffee sometime?'

'I'd like that.'

Parker Rothwell watched it all go down from his vantage point on the conference centre mezzanine. The police were there in force—he could tell from the impossibly polished shoes poking out from various hastily constructed comic character costumes. Presumably they were following the poor schmuck on bail. Stupid and talkative, he was proving a useful stooge. There he went, asking everyone else in a Joker suit if he was Chad. Did he really think that was how this stuff got done? The other one, now, the one with the package—cleverer, but dangerously so. He'd started to think for himself. He'd have to go when it was over.

Looked like they'd found each other. Pair of fucking amateurs, both looking over their shoulders before exchanging swag bags. Parker made eye contact with the security guard watching from the other side of the mezzanine. The guy nodded. Parker made his way towards the Gents as the shots found their targets, two Jokers hit the deck and people started screaming.

As predicted, no one paid him any attention. The sideshow was well under way. He was just another Joker in a sea of the pathetic saddos, and that coat was perfect for popping the package into. By the time he emerged from the restroom, he'd be part of the tide of members of the public being efficiently evacuated from the premises for their own safety.

The hand on his shoulder genuinely surprised him.

CHAPTER THIRTY-NINE

Queenie and Andy gawped at the apparent miles of outstretched food. They'd been welcomed to the banquet by the king and queen and had been formally introduced to an endless procession of community leaders, elders and politicians. Then, in a crocodile of pairs, just like an infant school outing, they'd all made their way along a covered cloth path to the Feasting House. Where they had walked not moments ago, the path was now covered with dishes: roast sucking pigs, coconuts, pineapples, more types of yam than you could shake a stick at and pile upon pile of seafood. It looked like the entire population of the Pacific had come out to join in. The conga line of food gradually collected a conga line of people sitting themselves down on either side.

There was drumming. And more dancing. Queenie decided dancing was a thing more countries should do to each other on fancy visits. It took up the time and gave you something to be nice about afterwards.

She turned to the king, seated between her and Andy at the only actual table in sight. 'This is lovely,' she said. 'A real nice welcome, isn't it, Andy?' Carswell nodded vigorously. He'd been told in no uncertain terms to let Queenie do the talking, and for once he seemed to have listened.

A translator who sat a little back from their chairs muttered to the king, who smiled and nodded his head.

'Yes.' The king spoke for the first time. 'This ceremony has remained unchanged since your queen first visited us in 1954. Although'—he inclined his head towards the item that sat before them between the roast pig and the pile of yams—'she did not bring a teapot.'

Queenie produced the most regal smile she could muster. 'Blimey, Your Majesty, your English is brilliant.'

'That is kind of you; it is at best rudimentary. My translator is here such that possibly you will use words I have not encountered. Such as *blimey*?' The quiet voice interjected.

'Ah, an exclamation of surprise, much favoured in the Cockney vernacular. I see.' He gave a short, throaty laugh. 'Up the apples and pears?'

Queenie clapped her gloved hands. 'Very good!'

'And where do you come from within the delightful English countryside?' The king addressed his question to Andy.

'Uh, I'm from the West Midlands, Birmingham.' Queenie kicked him. 'Your Majesty.'

'Brum!' The king seemed pleased with himself. 'And do you have any quaint and whimsical phrases from this place?'

'Oh, he's got a million of them,' Queenie muttered.

'Tell me a Brum joke!' Queenie was torn between relief that the conversation was going all right so far and concern that she'd not had a chance to bring up topics such as bioterrorism, pandemics and the end of civilisation.

'Well, there is one my father used to tell,' Andy said.

'But it's probably not very funny, really, is it, Mr Carswell?' Queenie tried to catch Andy's eye. And failed.

'No, no, I would like to hear it, and my translator can explain it to me if necessary.'

Queenie felt the panic begin.

'Okay,' said Andy, 'it goes: when is a biscuit tin like a fountain?'

The king looked a little puzzled and turned to the translator. 'Ah, so a biscuit tin is a container for sweetmeats. And a fountain is...a decorative feature that channels water. Do continue...'

'When it's a square tin.'

The king looked at his translator again, who muttered a little more. 'I think I am getting this now, the sweetmeat container is square and this is amusing because—'

'It's only really funny if you recognise the Birmingham accent.' Andy was deflating fast now. 'The way a Brummie says *squirting*, which is what a fountain does, sounds the same...'

The king looked grave. 'I see. So, now I have a funny joke for anyone I meet in England. I can say, "If you are Brummie, why is a sweetmeat box like a fountain? Because it can be square!" Splendid.'

Queenie laughed politely and attempted to change the subject. 'This is a wonderful spread, it must take so long to prepare this much food for so many people.'

'A veritable repast!' Andy added.

The king referred to his translator. Queenie's heart sank into her cute little sunshine-yellow kitten heels. It wasn't worth kicking Andy now. Too late. They both watched the king's face and Queenie realised she was holding her breath.

Suddenly he threw back his head and laughed fit to bust.

'Real food! Yes indeed, it is real food. I have eaten your McDonald's and Kentucky pretend meals. You are right!'

Queenie breathed out and changed the subject again.

'Your Majesty, while we are taking about American imports, I'm wonderin' if I could sort out a bit of misunderstandin'. It was probably a translation that went wrong but...'

CHAPTER FORTY

'What's going to happen to Chad?' Minnow asked Caroline as they settled in to their seats for the long flight home.

'Looks like he's stuck in Tonga for the foreseeable; the US are revoking his passport.'

'Can they do that?'

'There are some antiterrorism statutes still on the books. As far as they're concerned he made the threats, and that's enough.'

'And the Tongans?'

'That depends. Now Queenie's talked them into letting an expert in to test whatever it was he brought in, it'll depend what they find.' Caroline smiled across at Queenie, who appeared to be teaching Shirley to knit. 'If it's yet another decoy, as we suspect, then he's not broken any laws by trying to bring it in.'

'And if it's part of the original sample?'

'I guess they'll throw away the keys.'

'So, how many of us lose our jobs when we get back? Me and Andy for sure.'

Caroline transferred her gaze to the Foreign Minister and sighed.

'If we can keep the lid on enough of this, then everybody stays in post. Sacking people leads to questions. And to be fair to Andy, he did help pull this end of things back together.'

'Only by accident.'

'That's the system. You and I can lose our jobs if things go wrong, but them? They are what they are. Everyone's an everyman. If we trust the people to get it broadly right more often than not, we've got to trust them, eh?'

'So he stays and I go?' Minnow knew what was coming. He wanted to get it over with in time to have his appeal to Sammy ready in his mind before they landed. *I've lost my job and have nowhere to go from here, but we make a good team, so maybe we could design a computer game together...*

'Not necessarily. If it weren't for you we'd have had no leads at all. And if you hadn't brought Sammy on board we'd never have twigged the Comic-Con connection. It's a pity the takedown went a bit pear-shaped. We're still getting to grips with the way the Provos are using the internet. Apparently sleeper cells are old hat; it's all random fanatics getting expendable idiots to do the donkey work these days. Which explains why none of the groups the CIA had infiltrated knew anything about it.'

'A bit pear-shaped? People got shot!'

'Yeah. Gerald's working on a cover story for that bit.'

Minnow's horror finally overcame his misery. 'A cover story? For a sniper taking out two Jokers at a geeks' get-together? What the hell can you say? Someone taking being Batman a tad too seriously? Come on, Caroline, it's got to come out and you and Gerald know it. And it's all my fault. People are dying, for fuck's sake.'

'Not necessarily, it looks like they might pull through. In which case, we'll call it a publicity stunt.'

'Shit.'

'And *it's not your fault*. Gerald thinks Chad just lured us all down here and made it about you to keep our eyes off the real handover. Besides, it gave Queenie a chance to charm the socks off the king. He told her he's sick of rumours about him funding the Provos. Off the record, Andy's gaffe was the last straw in a good way, but don't tell him that. He's planning to root out any sympathisers once and for all. The world is, oddly enough, a tiny bit safer because of Chad's wild goose chase.'

Minnow shook his head. It didn't help the buzzing in his ears, but he thought it might if he did it enough. 'Sammy really worked it out?'

Caroline smiled at him. 'You've got a diamond there, Minnow. Don't let her get away.'

'I don't intend to.'

'Have you spoken to her yet?'

'Only briefly. She said she'd tell me all about it when I got back. Not that she knows much. She and Gerald had just told the Yard about the Comic-Con thing before he rang Eugene.'

'Apparently they put a CCTV camera in the stall, then all the police had to do was watch and wait, after snaffling the hard drive of course.'

'And dodge a few bullets.'

Caroline sighed. 'Democrats used to be a bit cuddlier. Wrong, but non-lethal.'

'I don't get why they would shoot their own guys.'

'Expendable decoys. They assumed the police would be watching our own little democracy mascot, Bobby Norris.'

'Bloody hell. Presumably there'll be an inquiry?'

'Nothing to inquire into, Minnow, my fortunate little friend. The theft never happened.'

'And if it never happened?'

'Nobody gets sacked.'

Minnow shook his head. 'That seems a bit too good to be true.'

'All that happened this week—apart from a little local difficulty among irascible cosplayers—is a successful state visit to Tonga, with the TV full of images of the king enjoying tea from the Teapot of State and laughing uproariously at one of Andy's fabulous jokes.'

Minnow managed a smile. And forced his mind to move on. He looked across the cabin to where Queenie was now affixing a tiny thing made of shells to her lapel.

'Oh, that reminds me, while I think of it, I found out why Bert Mason got rejected. What with all the fuss, I forgot to tell you.'

'Really?' Caroline riffled about in her knitting bag for the notebook. 'Are they going to want to know?'

'That's up to you.' Minnow was grinning now.

'Go on…'

'Committees.'

Caroline put her head in her hands. 'Oh, dear.'

'He wouldn't normally be rejected for a basic membership; sometimes people have no choice, or do it, you know, out of public-spiritedness.'

Caroline snorted her derision.

'But he checked the *yes* box for whether there was a

badge.' He spotted her quizzical look. Was he getting better at faces? 'You only remember if there was a badge or not if you wore the thing, and anyone who needs a badge that says *committee* on it is desperately in need of a very small pond.'

Doug and Sally sat by the lake in St James's Park. They had eschewed a coffee shop for a flask and pad of paper. Doug had shown the twins how to make a variety of paper boats, and they were currently engaged in a scientific project to see which ones floated the best.

'This isn't as easy as you expect, is it?' Doug asked Sally.

'I came here with big plans to make a difference,' she replied.

'And then you discover you're a puppet.'

'Yup.'

'I have no idea what I'm supposed to be doing.'

'But you've done fine. I know you weren't well, but you went on telly and told everybody you're listening to the unions.'

'They write it all. I don't do anything much.'

'But you're working with companies to bring jobs back?'

'Sort of. Bert said I should talk to Tesco, see if I can get Queenie's job back for when we're done, but I don't see the point.'

'I do! I'd love to shop somewhere with real people in, it could be a real money-spinner.'

'Really?' Doug shook his head. 'Odd. Anyway, it'll be

your turn in the spotlight this week, eh? The big pandemic drill will be under way.'

'God, don't remind me. I've got Wilmslow breathing down my neck because doctors know best and I'm just a pleb.'

'We're all just plebs, that's the point. If there's a point at all.'

'Try telling him that. He's permanently insulted because he's not in charge.'

'So, what he needs is something to feel in charge of that would happen anyway.'

'Get devious, you mean?'

Doug smiled. 'My late wife would have called it blokeology.'

'Oh?'

'Katie ran everything. I think it's why I've been a bit at sea. I always thought I was in charge of our lives, but when she wasn't around I realised she just used to give me a simple thing to control.'

Sally laughed. 'I'd forgotten that trick. Maybe I'll give it a go. Thanks.'

Bobby Norris tried to turn over in his hospital bed. Something itched. Something else hurt. His hand wouldn't follow the rest of him. Muzzy-headed, he tried to work it out. He could see a drip stand. He followed the plastic tubing into his arm. That wasn't it. There was a metallic sound. Why was he so groggy? Medicine? Maybe. Where the hell was he?

He wriggled his bum back the way he'd been before

and tried to focus. Something else hurt. But he could see the handcuffs now. He looked around him: small room, no coppers. The bastards had cuffed him to the bed.

He turned his attention to the door as it opened with a tiny squeak. The copper was outside—he could see the back of a uniform—but now someone was talking to him. Done up in operating scrubs. With one of those masks you saw on the telly.

'Hello, Bobby.' The voice was quiet. 'No, don't try and talk, you had an endotracheal breathing tube in for a while there. Makes your throat bloody sore, that does.'

He tried to say *what the hell...who the fuck...go to hell...get these cuffs off me...*

He heard a croak.

'Just listen, Bobby.'

He gave up and listened.

'We kept you alive. No, don't thank me, I didn't make that decision. Your little pal won't be so lucky; I'm off to see him next. Accident with the drip, probably. Apparently someone thinks you might be useful down the line, although I can't see it myself.'

Bobby's head swam. He tried to concentrate.

'Ah yes, this will all feel a bit, what's the current vernacular? Spacey? Trippy? Blame the narcotic analgesics. You won't remember much of this conversation. We'll find a way to remind you we're still around before the police start their interviews.'

CHAPTER FORTY-ONE

Queenie was a little late to the debrief. It was by way of being a full cabinet meeting with extra bits; everybody needed a say in what had gone on. She found it less intimidating these days, even when Gerald was doing the chair stuff. The rules of who said what and when—and who gave way to whom—were a bit clearer. And nobody minded her knitting. She liked it when Caroline knitted too, but the girl was being very tight-lipped about her latest project.

She sat with Sammy and Minnow. Strictly speaking, they weren't part of the meeting, but they both had stories to tell. Queenie had squeezed her first ever Westminster friend's hand really hard as she sat down. There would be tea and tea leaf reading later, she was determined about that.

So much had gone on here while they'd been away, she was flabbergasted. It felt like they were only away a few days, but when you added in time zones and layovers—

hark at me talking all international—it had been over a week.

The news that the antidote had been found in a loo had gone straight to the Health Ministry, and Sally was speaking about that now. She'd not told the other ministers in her department it had been AWOL, she said. They thought it had been a policy wonk decision to run the exercise without it. One of her blokes, the doctor, had been ranting about how it would fail to be a complete exercise without doctors leading education on the storage of mass vaccination supplies.

'I have decided the best way to handle this'—*Did she just wink at Doug Sideworth? Surely not*—'will be to tell him I've considered his point of view, overridden the specials and please would he take charge of delivery and storage of the antidote; and of education regarding the difference between that and a vaccine.'

A few people nodded and chuckled.

'It does look as though we are spending a lot of money over nothing now, but we weren't to know, and it's too late to backtrack from the full exercise.'

'Unless we come clean.' Queenie looked for the speaker, Gordon Morrow. She hadn't had much of a chat with him yet. She took a notebook out of her knitting bag and wrote *Get to know Morrow* in it. Blimey, she was turning into Caroline.

'We're not here to deceive the people.' He thumped the desk with his fist. 'We *are* the people, we're here to stop these bastards'—he indicated Gerald with a pointed finger—'from behaving like petty dictators. If we don't demand the truth, do what's right, what are we here for?'

Gerald put on his frozen face. 'It is not our job to be petty dictators.' He placed his elbows on the desk and steepled his hands, Queenie wondered if Morrow knew yet that this meant trouble. 'It is our job to explain to you the consequences of doing what's right. Once you have defined the concept of "right" for the specific circumstance we find ourselves in. Do go ahead and attempt that.'

Morrow tapped his pen on the conference table.

'Dammit, man, people are in hospital; one of them is dead. Everyone should know what we know. I had enough of "do as you're told" back in the army. We're not at war with the people.'

'We are however, at war with human nature, perhaps?'

'What's that meant to mean?'

'You propose that one of us goes on the evening news and says, "I say, citizenry, we lost a devastating virus and its only known antidote for a few days there and the world was on the brink of disaster, brought about by democracy terrorists who are ruthless enough to kill their own people if necessary. So we decided to put some pandemic infrastructure in place and pretend it was because of the strike. But it's all fine now. Our Foreign Minister nearly blew it in Tonga, but thanks to the intellect of one of our Education ministers, we got it back, so...as you were!"'

'Why not? It's the truth. This makes us no better than the old popularity contest winners.' Morrow looked around the table for support, but most heads were buried in paperwork.

'Does everyone want the truth?' Doug Sideworth asked. 'Genuine question, I'm not grandstanding, I just wonder whether most people prefer not to be bothered with details.'

'When I was in hospital they used to smooth over the

bad bits and tell me I was fine, when all I wanted was a bit of honesty,' Sally said.

'About your personal situation? Or about the state of the nation?' Doug asked.

'What do you mean?'

'You wanted the truth about what affected you directly. Maybe the doctors weren't straight about your prognosis, but would you have wanted them to also bring you a loophole they'd found in the accounts receivable records?'

'Well, no, obviously not.'

'So perhaps there are levels of truth. If we tell the nation we're working to keep it safe it's not *untrue*.'

'It's pretty bloody disingenuous.' Morrow stabbed at the table with his pen.

'Maybe we put it to the vote?' Doug said. 'We are the people, so we can decide? For what it's worth, I think people deserve the truths that directly affect their work and their lives, but that it's our job to carry some stuff that keeps the country on an even keel.'

'Is that so?' Morrow's voice edged towards sarcasm.

'Yes, and that's why I'm going to tell you that I'm struggling with alcoholism and that I was in hospital after an overdose.' Most of the eyes lifted from their notes in surprise. 'I apologise if anyone had to cover my workload and I'm working with some counselling support to get things back on track. That's all I think you need to know. I don't intend to lay out hours of crap, because the rest is irrelevant to you.'

Sally smiled at Doug and nodded. Queenie thought she might have seen a mouthed 'well done'.

Clayton Brown lifted a finger to speak. Gerald acknowledged him with a nod. 'Speaking from a behavioural perspective, people should not be lied to, but sometimes they need information in a way they can process. If I tell a class an exam will be exceedingly difficult and half of them won't pass it—which is the truth—they will give up, or panic, or just do a load of mind-bending substances to take their minds off it.'

'So what do you tell them?' Sammy asked.

'That they will have to work very hard to do well, but the payoffs of the work itself are going to be of value to them for the rest of their lives.'

Morrow tutted. 'So, what are the *consequences* of the truth about this. We still haven't heard any of them.'

Gerald turned to Caroline. 'Would you like to field this one?'

'If you wish.' Gerald handed her the remote for the screen on the wall. She pressed a button and a blank document appeared. She typed into a laptop as she spoke, and bullet points appeared.

1) Panic.

'The press speculate on other items that might have gone missing during the shutdown. Then people start making hoax calls about stuff they've heard about that's on the black market, and we won't stand a chance of sorting the real from the fake if anything else is out there. Which, of course, it might be.'

2) Distrust.

'Anything we try to do as a lesson learned from the strike will be dismissed as a cover for something else. We lose cooperation for genuine improvements.'

3) Fear.

'People start stockpiling supplies in case we're lying and the virus is still in the wrong hands. Attacks on medical storage facilities begin, and we lose control of supply and demand for most essential items. Prices go up.'

4) Recruitment.

'Anyone disaffected or pissed off about anything heads to the nearest democracy cell to support their newest martyr.'

5) International relations.

'Public feeling turns against Tonga, which is likely to lose tourism. In return, we lose trade, credibility and any goodwill that Queenie and Andy managed to salvage last week. Plus, at the very least, the Americans will suffer similar fallout and they will blame us.'

Caroline addressed Morrow directly. 'Is that enough to be going on with?'

He looked like he was chewing a wasp.

Gerald indicated the screen. 'There you have it, ladies and gentlemen. The *policy wonks'* assessment. Shall we move to a vote?'

'Bert!' Queenie yelled as she dashed into the flat. 'You'll never guess what!'

She threw her knitting bag down on the table and went looking for him. He was back in his old chair watching the telly, but the ads were on so she kept talking. 'You won't believe what's happened, no, going to happen, no, in the middle of being done—'

'Slow down, woman. What are you talking about?'

She paced up and down in front of the telly.

'That Doug, the one we was worried about, and then he came and played dominoes while I was away, him?'

'Yes, I remember. Decent bloke. Crap at dominoes.'

'He's been talkin' to Tesco's!'

'Oh yes?' Was that a smirk on Bert's face? *Nah, he never smiles.*

'He told them that, ooh hang on a minute, I got it written down here somewhere... No, it's in the other room, I'll get it, no, Bert, come and see, I've got all the bumf in me bag.'

She dragged the man out of his chair and through to the reception room.

'You could just tell me, instead of readin' it.' He sat down again, trying to be disgruntled.

'No, it's got to be proper.'

She rummaged in the knitting bag for a small document binder. She opened it and cleared her throat.

'He said he'd told them, "The government wants an industry leader to spearhead the reintroduction of public-facing job creation." And then he said he told them, "Public support for the demonstrations shows that it would prove popular enough to be a cost-effective game-changing move for retail."'

She stopped reading to smile at Bert.

'I don't know what the hell any of that means, Queenie, girl.'

'It means, Bert, me old mucker, that Tesco's are changin' that little Metro shop they put in on the Whitechapel Road to a'—she turned a page—'*Tesco Full Serve*! It's a trial of putting people back on the tills! And if it makes money they'll do more of them...and...' She drew herself up to her full height, took a deep breath and did the wave. 'Hai'm goin' along to formally hopen it.' She made a little bow.

'Oh, that.' Bert sniffed. 'I told him to do that.'

'What?'

'When he was here and we was hidin' from the kids. I said it would be good to put people back on tills, and we reckoned it would make money 'cos no one likes them automated things.'

'Oh, Bert.' She bent to hug the bits of him she could reach in the comfy chair and ended up burying his nose in her ample cleavage. 'You are a diamond and I love you.'

'Steady on, Queenie lass, I can't breathe.'

Andy Carswell stood on the path outside his house and watched through the kitchen window. He'd asked for a couple of days at home, pleaded family troubles. Beth and Sophie were pottering about, cleaning up, it looked like. Beth was taking things out of the dishwasher and putting them away, Sophie was putting more things in. He wondered if things were always as routine as that when he wasn't there. He'd thought about calling ahead to let Beth know he was on his way, but he'd decided against it. She couldn't tell him not to bother to come if he was already there.

He wondered if they'd seen him on the news. "New Foreign Minister and Head of State Make Friends on Far Side of Globe," the headlines had run. There were shots of the blasted teapot but also some of the king laughing at what Andy had said. He'd single-handedly saved the mission—he nearly saved the planet, although he wasn't really supposed to talk about that—and he was here to tell them all about it.

He had big plans to take more interest in the home stuff too. He'd done his laundry at the flat and everything. His plan to seduce Caroline might have taken a bit of a tumble in Tonga, but he could see his way in now it looked like Doug had palled up with the Health woman. He reckoned he'd get closer to her as a family man with problems like worrying about his teenaged daughter than he would as a loser who had been chucked out by his wife. So he was going to patch things up.

Naturally, they'd want to know all about Tonga, but he'd admire how clean the kitchen was as well, and ask about their week. That should do it.

Caroline opened a tin of Special Turkey Dinner for Lady Jo. It felt like a celebration, although actually things were merely back to normalish. All her ministers were still alive, an oddly comforting achievement. And the world wasn't facing obliteration, good-oh.

One of the Provo conspirators had died in hospital — which took the shine off things a bit—but it looked like a medical accident, and the world seemed to have swallowed the 'geeks getting overexcited' line. Maybe she was really celebrating a new guerrilla knitting project almost ready for public consumption.

She poured a glass of wine and settled down to count the tea cosies that had been pouring in from knitters round the country. Then she picked up the phone to thank Deborah for agreeing to be the distribution hub.

She put on the TV. Andy Carswell's grin filled the screen. 'How did you enjoy the Tongan hospitality?' a reporter was asking. 'All part of life's rich tapestry,' he replied. The reporter nodded sagely and turned to Queenie.

'I understand the King of Tonga enjoyed his tea?'

'Oh, blimey yes.' Queenie's face beamed at the viewing millions. 'We took the Teapot of State and he said it was the best cuppa he'd ever had.' The camera pulled back to finish with a noddy shot, then panned over to a close-up of the teapot in its despatch box. The sound man almost managed to cut the mics before Andy opened his mouth again. 'He's not as...'

'...green as he's cabbage-looking,' Caroline intoned on his behalf.

'And there we must leave our roundup of the week's foreign news and hand back to the studio.'

Next week it would all be about the pandemic exercise. The week after that, the new Tesco. Then what? The reps would come and go, people would argue about stuff and everything would be just like the last lot. And the next. There might be less vomit and manhandling of unconscious people next week, or maybe not, who knew? Doug seemed to have settled down and made friends at last; she grinned as she caught herself thinking like a boarding school headmistress.

Who would be next to crack? Morrow needed some help with his temper, otherwise he'd be the next hospitalisation. Carswell? Probably too stupid. You needed a modicum of intelligence to get stressed.

She wondered idly how long it would take Minnow to pop the question, and whether Sally was strong enough to cope with Doug's beatification of his dead wife. His problems wouldn't magically go away, she knew that first-hand. She picked up a framed photograph from the coffee table, half hidden under piles of tea cosies.

'I used a lot of the stuff you taught me recently,' she told the smiling lad in the paramedic uniform. 'You'd have laughed at the pickle we got in.'

Sammy stood in Minnow's lounge and stared at the transformation. 'Where did the plywood benches go?'

'Uh, they're in the bedroom. I've stuck them behind the wardrobe for now, just in case we need to set up for saving the universe again sometime.'

'You didn't do this on your own, did you? Nice couches and a telly? The colours go together and everything. Are those new curtains?'

'Caroline helped a bit. I told her I wanted to make it, um, you know, a bit nicer for visitors.'

'And you get a lot of visitors?'

'I think she knew I meant you.' He walked to her side and put a hesitant arm around her shoulder.

Sammy smiled. 'It's just as well I brought some old DVDs of *Fawlty Towers*, then, isn't it? Otherwise we'd have nothing to do on that new sofa of yours.'

'Nothing to do?'

'Hmm, less to do.'

'Yeah, because I ordered pizza too, so we'd be able to eat stuff...'

Sammy smacked his bum. 'Since when did you learn about making jokes?'

'Since I met you, I think.'

'That's a nice thing to say.'

'Is it? It's kinda just true, really.'

'I think we owe it to ourselves to test out the fabulous newness of the seating arrangements before they get covered in pizza. Come here...'

Sammy bounced onto the cushions and pulled Minnow down with her. He pulled away from the kiss she had planned for him.

'Uh, Sammy?'

'Mm-hmm?'

'Is it nice enough here for you to consider, you know, well, we do a lot of gaming and that and it would be kinda useful, no, not useful, you know, like *nice*...'

'Useful and nice? Two things I strive to be!'

'You're making fun of me.'

'Only because I think you're trying to ask me something, but I'm not sure what.' She put a finger to his lips. 'I'll tell you what, we'll make this a case statement.' He wrinkled his brow at her. She loved when he did that. 'I'll iterate three possible cases for what you're trying to say and you can just input the number for your selection.'

'Oh...kay...'

'Case One: you are asking me to come and eat pizza and watch telly a little more often, which I am more than happy to do, although my father might disapprove. He thinks pizza rots people's brains. Case Two: you've had enough of real female personages in your life and you'd like to meet up online only. Safer from a paternal point of view but a bit of a waste of new furnishings. Case Three— which is really a more physically risky subset of Case One—you are asking me to move in, i.e., shack up, which would be lovely, although my father might kill you. This last, if it proves non-fatal, is not in any way a variable upon which Case One might be dependent.'

Minnow tried to open his mouth, but her finger was still there. He settled for nibbling the end of her finger as he deliberated. He lifted three fingers and waggled them at her as the entryphone buzzed.

The Mile End Road Launderama had some balloons outside. Someone had strung some paper chains from the ceiling, those ones you used to stick together at school. A sign said, Welcome Home, Bobby! It was scrawled in felt pen on a piece of cardboard box. Looked like Chardonnay's work, judging by the amount of pink and glitter. Sandra had done a plate of sausage rolls, cut up some pork pies and put bowls of crisps around.

News of free nosh had brought some regulars in, and he'd had a few slaps on the back, on the side without the sling. He kept his mouth shut about the electronic tag. He was, frankly, surprised to be out at all, but the people who told Doris what to do had organised it. All he had to do was keep shtum. He wasn't knocking it.

There were more stories flying around the East End about what happened to him than he could keep track of, but that was the point. He just had to keep saying he couldn't remember. And to be honest, he couldn't. He was trying not to think about it anyway, what with the other poor bastard being dead and all. But one thing he did know: he was done with fucking democracy. Voting was all very well, and he'd never much minded a bit of putting the boot in, but he'd seen enough hospitals. And police cells.

'Oh, Bobby, a card came for you.' Sandra was smiling,

for the first time in, like, forever.

He took it from her and opened the envelope. *Congratulations*, it said. He flipped to the inside to see who it was from. A picture of the kids fell out.

EPILOGUE

Queenie watched in astonishment as the State Landau drew level with them. She'd seen the horses and the carriages and the uniforms before; they were all polished up for the children to see whenever she arranged another Mews Open Day. The kids even sometimes had rides in the carriages, but this— everything all together, shined up and pressed and ready to really go somewhere—this was overwhelming. The horses snickered and waved their plumes about. The footmen sat up high, completely still and terrifying. And now, she and Bert and Doug and Big Doris were going to get in and wave to people all the way to the Whitechapel Road.

Caroline and Eugene had said it was going to be popular. East Londoners had started lining the streets from early morning to get a good view! Doug had been on the telly last night, along with Big Doris. He'd said it was the first step towards hearing the people, and Doris had said she was proud to be the rep for the first constituency to have a full-serve grocery shop restored, like people wanted.

Doris has done all right, Queenie thought. And now her Sandra's Bobby was home and the kiddies' coughs were better because the health people had got the mould dealt with, they were almost, well, not quite friends but, you know, on speaking terms.

There were little steps for her to go up to get in the coach. She was used to Eugene helping with this sort of stuff, but he'd gone on ahead with the teapot. She had George there instead. She liked George. Caroline had got him moved to the palace and he'd told Queenie he really liked his new job the first time she'd seen him and waved hello. He was holding the carriage still now and put out a hand to help her in.

She settled herself down while Bert clambered in next to her. Doris was next, sitting opposite, and then Doug. He and George exchanged a nod of recognition. And then they were off.

As the carriage took off at a walking pace for the horses, Queenie grabbed hold of Bert's arm. 'Oooher, it's a bit bouncier than you expect, eh? Blimey, I hope I don't get seasick.'

'Bet they don't 'ave sick bags in one of these,' said Bert. 'Mind you, you'd look a bit of a pillock waving a bag of vomit at the crowds, wouldn't you?'

'Ugh, Bert, don't be disgustin'.'

'I'm just sayin'.'

'Don't just say. Oh, look!' They were pulling out of the Mews and along the side of Buck Place, towards the mad wedding cake roundabout that was supposed to be Queen Victoria. There were people everywhere. They were waving flags. 'What are they wavin', Bert? I haven't got me glasses.'

'It looks like teapots.' Doug was squinting to see what they were too.

Doris looked out the other side of the carriage, 'Yes, they're bloomin' coloured teapots on sticks.'

They rounded the wedding cake and headed off down Birdcage Walk. More people. 'I guess we oughta be wavin' and that. Doris, you been practisin' that wave I showed you?'

Doris grinned. 'I don't need you to show me how to wave my bleedin' hand, Queenie Mason.'

Queenie humphed. Doris waved. People started cheering.

They saw all the traffic stopped by police cars as they passed Parliament Square and turned on to Embankment. People had got out of their cars to wave and cheer, even the taxi drivers.

'I didn't expect all this, did you?' Queenie turned to Doug, whose face was a picture of incomprehension.

'No,' he said. 'What did we do?'

'I dunno.' Queenie shook her head. 'But whatever it is, people seem to like it.'

'Caroline says there's a bit of a surprise further on, once we get into the East End proper, but she wouldn't say what,' Doug added.

They waved until their arms ached. As they turned up from Embankment, past Tower Hill and up Mansell Street towards the old Tesco, the crowds grew thicker. Everyone seemed to be sporting some sort of multicoloured headgear.

'They've all got woolly hats. Why's that? It's not cold.'

Doug and Doris squinted at the crowds.

'Bloody hell!' Doris yelled. 'They're all wearing tea cosies!'

The cheering crescendoed as they turned into the Whitechapel Road.

'Look!' Bert pointed upwards to the tops of the streetlamps. 'See that bunting? It's all teapots!' And it was. Red, white and blue teapots fluttered from lamppost to lamppost from one end of the Whitechapel Road to the other.

The crush of people outside the new Tesco Full Serve was being held back by two lines of policemen. They had all replaced their helmets with tea cosies for the occasion.

The little raised platform by the entrance, across which was strung a length of teapot-bunting, sported a lectern, a microphone and a line of dignitaries. Every last one of them wearing a tea cosy hat. Queenie attempted a dignified walk from the carriage but gave up halfway to the dais. She hung on to Bert's arm, threw back her head and laughed that throaty guffaw, the one everybody thought Caroline had trained out of her.

THE END

"It is accepted as democratic when public offices are allocated by lot; and as oligarchic when they are filled by election." – Aristotle

THANK YOU

Thank you for taking the time to read *Queenie's Teapot*. If you enjoyed it please consider telling your friends or posting a short review. Word of mouth is an author's best friend and much appreciated.

Sincerely,

Carolyn Steele

COMING SOON

Early beta-readers for *Queenie's Teapot* told Carolyn she was writing a trilogy. Who knew? Book 2, *Floreat Queenio*, is in final edits and should be available in time for Christmas 2017.

To check on its progress and be the first to pre-order copies, follow the happenings at QueeniesTeapot.com.

ABOUT THE AUTHOR

Carolyn has been a psychologist, a paramedic, a proof reader, a patisseur and several other things, not all of them beginning with P. Pre-Queenie, she was a writer of narrative non-fiction: travelogues and the like. She managed to turn an 'ooh, shiny' approach to bonkers pastimes into books, podcasts and blog posts. You can read some of these on her websites TruckingTales.com and CarolynSteele.ca.

Her Armchair Emigration trilogy currently contains books 1 and 3, and book 2 will appear as soon as Queenie obliges by getting out of her head.

Born and bred in London, England, Carolyn now lives in Kitchener, Ontario, with occasional forays back to Blighty when a madcap job-that-could-be-a-book crops up.

Made in the USA
San Bernardino, CA
14 March 2017